The Billionaire Boss's Secretary Bride

HELEN BROOKS

Helen Brooks lives in Northamptonshire and is married with three children. As she is a committed Christian, busy housewife and mother, her spare time is at a premium, but her hobbies include reading, swimming, gardening and walking her old faithful dog. Her long-cherished aspiration to write became a reality when she put pen to paper on reaching the age of forty, and sent the result off to Mills & Boon.

CHAPTER ONE

'I STILL can't believe you're really going, that this is your last day. All along I thought you'd change your mind. I mean, you've been here for ever, Gina.'

Gina Leighton couldn't help but smile at her office junior's plaintive voice. 'Perhaps that's why I'm leaving, Natalie,' she said quietly. 'Because I've been here for ever, as you put it.'

OK, so 'for ever' was actually the last eleven years, since she had left university at the age of twenty-one, but clearly as far as Natalie was concerned Gina was as much a part of Breedon & Son as the bricks and mortar. As far as everyone was concerned, most likely. Especially *him*.

'I know I shan't be able to get on with Susan.' Natalie stared at her mournfully. 'She's not like you.'

'You'll be fine,' Gina said bracingly. She didn't mean it. In the last four weeks since she had been showing Susan Richards—her replacement—the ropes, she had come to realise Susan didn't suffer fools gladly. Not that Natalie was a fool, not at all—but she *was* something of a feather-brain at times, who had to have everything explained at least twice for it to click. Susan had already expressed her impatience with the girl in no uncertain terms, ignoring the fact that Natalie was a hard worker and always willing to go the extra mile.

But this wasn't her problem. In a few hours from now, she would walk out of Breedon & Son for the last time. Not only that but she was leaving the Yorkshire market-town where she had been born and raised along with all her friends and family and moving to London at the weekend. New job, new flat, new lifestyle—new everything.

Her stomach doing a fairly good imitation of a pancake on Shrove Tuesday, Gina waved her hand at the papers on her desk. 'I need to finish some things, Natalie, before the drinks and nibbles.' Her boss was putting on a little farewell party for her for the last couple of hours of the afternoon, and she wanted to tie up any loose ends before she left.

Once Natalie had returned to the outer office, however, Gina sat staring round the large and comfortable room that had been her working domain for the last four years, since she had worked her way up to personal secretary to the founder of the agricultural-machinery firm. She'd been thrilled at first, the prestige and extremely generous salary adding to her sense of self-worth. And Dave Breedon was a good boss, a nice family-man with a sense of humour which matched hers. But then Dave Breedon wasn't the reason she was leaving...

'No eleventh-hour change of heart?'

The deep male voice brought Gina's gaze to the doorway. 'Of course not,' she said with a composure that belied her racing heartbeat. But then she had had plenty of practice in disguising how she felt about Harry Breedon, her boss's only son and right-hand man. She stared into the tanned and ruggedly handsome face, her deep blue eyes revealing nothing beyond cool amusement. 'You didn't seriously think there was any chance of that, surely?'

He shrugged. '"Hoped" is perhaps a better word.'

Ridiculous, because she had long since accepted Harry's flirting meant absolutely nothing, but her breathing quickened in spite of herself. 'Sorry,' she said evenly. 'But my bags are already packed.'

'Dad's devastated, you know.' Harry strolled into her office, perching on the edge of her desk and fixing her with smoky grey eyes. Gina tried very hard not to focus on the way his trousers had pulled tight over lean male thighs. And failed.

'Devastated?' she said briskly. 'Hardly. It's nice he'll be sorry to see me go, but I think that's about it, Harry. And Susan is proving to be very capable, as you know.'

Susan Richards. Blonde, attractive and possessed of the sort of figure any model would be grateful for. Just Harry's type, in fact. Over the last twelve months—since Harry had returned to the United Kingdom following his father's heart attack, and taken on more and more of Dave Breedon's work load—Gina had heard the company gossip about his succession of girlfriends, all allegedly blonde and slender. Whereas she was a redhead—at school she'd been called 'carrot top', but she preferred to label her bright auburn locks Titian. And, although her generous hour-glass shape might have been in fashion in Marilyn Monroe's day, it wasn't now.

So why, knowing all that, had she fallen for him? Gina asked herself silently. Especially as he was the original 'love 'em and leave 'em' male. It was the same question she had mulled over umpteen times in the last year, but she was no nearer to a logical answer. But then love didn't pretend to work on logic. All she knew was that this feeling—which had begun with an earthy lust that had knocked her sideways, and had rapidly grown into a love that was all consuming the more she'd got to know him—was here to stay. Whereas to Harry she was merely the secretary he shared with his father—admittedly someone he liked to chat and laugh and flirt with, but then he'd be the same with any female. End of story.

'I didn't think you liked London when you were at uni there. I remember you saying you couldn't wait to get home.'

Gina frowned. 'I said I was *glad* to come home.' She corrected quietly. 'That didn't mean I didn't like the city.'

He stared at her for a moment before hitching himself off her desk and standing to his feet. 'Well, it's your life,' he said so reasonably Gina wanted to hit him. 'I just hope you don't regret it, that's all. All big cities can be lonely places.'

'The old thing about being surrounded by people but knowing no one?' Gina nodded. 'I've lots of old university friends living in London, so that's not a problem. And I'm sharing a flat with another girl, anyway. I'm not living alone.'

She didn't add she was feeling more than a little trepidation about that. For the last six years she'd had her own place, a small but beautifully positioned top-floor flat in a big house on the edge of town, with views of the river. After living with her parents, she had revelled in having a home of her own, where she was answerable to no one and could please herself at weekends, getting up when she wanted and eating when she felt like it. But renting in London was vastly different from renting in Yorkshire, and although her new job paid very well she couldn't run to her own place.

'Don't forget to leave your new address.' He was already walking to the door. 'I might look you up next time I spend a few days in the capital. Doss down on your sofa for a night.'

Over her dead body. She took a deep breath and let it out evenly. 'Fine,' she said nonchalantly, wishing she could hate him. It would make everything so much easier—she wouldn't be uprooting herself for one thing. Although, no, that wasn't quite fair. Even before she'd fallen for Harry she'd acknowledged she was in a rut and needed to do something with her life. Both her sisters and most of her friends were married with children; going out with them wasn't what it had once been. In the twelve months before Harry had come on the scene, she'd only had the odd date or two, as the only men around had either been boring or convinced they were God's gift to women, or, worse, married and looking for a bit of fun on the side. She'd begun to see herself as a spinster: devoted to her job, her home, and godmother to other people's children.

Her friends thought she was too choosy. She stared at the door Harry had just closed behind him. And maybe she was. Certainly she'd had offers, but she balked at the idea of *trying* to like someone. Either the spark was there or it wasn't. Besides which, she wasn't desperate to settle down. What she *was* desperate for was a life outside work that was interesting and exciting and carried a buzz—nightclubs, the theatre, good restaurants and good company. She was only thirty two, for goodness' sake! So London had beckoned, and she'd embraced the notion.

It was the right decision. She nodded at the thought. Definitely. Without a doubt. Of course, if Harry had shown any interest…But he hadn't. And so roses round the door, cosy log-fires and breakfast in bed for two with the Sunday papers wasn't an option.

Gina swallowed the lump in her throat, telling herself she'd cried enough tears over him. However hard it was going to be to say goodbye, it would have been emotional suicide to stay. That one brief kiss at Christmas had told her that. Merely a friendly peck on her cheek as far as he was concerned, when he'd wished her merry Christmas. But the feel of his lips, the closeness of him, the delicious smell of his aftershave, had sent her into a spin for hours.

Christmas had been a bitter-sweet affair, and it was then she'd decided enough was enough. Self-torture wasn't her style. And it had been added confirmation when on the afternoon of Boxing Day, whilst she'd been walking her parents' dogs in the snowy fields surrounding the town, she'd seen him in the distance with the blonde of the moment. She had hidden behind a tree and prayed they wouldn't see her, but once the danger was over and she'd continued her walk she'd realised merely leaving Breedon & Son wasn't enough. She had to get right away, where there was no chance of running into him.

And now it was the beginning of April. D-Day. Outside spring had come with a vengeance the last few days, croci and daffodils bursting forth, and birds busy nesting—new life sprouting seemingly everywhere. And that was the way she had to look at this, as an opportunity for new life. No point feeling her world had come to an end, no point at all.

Nevertheless, it was with gritted teeth that she joined everyone in the work canteen later that afternoon. She was touched to see most of Breedon & Son's employees—over a hundred in all, counting the folk on the factory floor—had gathered to say goodbye, and even more overcome when she was given a satellite-navigation system for her car to which everyone had contributed.

'So you can find your way back to us now and again,' Bill Dent, the chief accountant, joked as he presented her with the gift. She had a reputation—richly deserved—of having no sense of direction or navigation skills, and over the last weeks had endured a host of teasing about negotiating city streets.

'Thank you all so much.' As she gave a tearful little speech she kept her gaze from focusing on one tall, dark figure standing a little apart from the rest of the throng, but she was still vitally aware of every movement Harry made. She knew exactly when Susan Richards made her way over to him, for instance, and the way the other woman reached up on tiptoe to whisper something in his ear.

All in all, Gina was glad when after an hour or so people began to drift home. Loving someone who didn't love you was bad enough at the best of times, but when you were trying to be bright and cheerful, and keep a lid on a mounting volcano of tears, it didn't help to see the object of your desire receiving the full batting-eyelash treatment from an undeniably attractive blonde.

When there was just a handful of people left, Gina made her way back to her office to pick up the last of her things. She felt like a wet rag. Dropping into her chair, she glanced round the room, feeling unbearably sentimental.

Dave entered a moment later, Harry on his heels. Shaking his head, Dave said, 'Don't look like that. I told you, you shouldn't leave us. Everyone thinks the world of you.'

Not everyone. Forcing a smile, Gina managed to keep her voice light and even as she said, 'The big wide world beckons, and it's now or never. It was always going to be hard to say goodbye.'

'While we're on that subject...' Dave reached into his pocket and brought out a small, oblong gift-wrapped box. 'This is a personal thank-you, lass. I'm not buttering you up when I say you've been the best secretary I've ever had. It's the truth. If London isn't all it's cracked up to be, there'll always be a job somewhere in Breedon & Son for you.'

'Oh, it's beautiful.' After unwrapping the gift, Gina gazed, entranced, at the delicate little gold watch the box held. 'Thank you so much. I didn't expect…' The lump in her throat prevented further speech.

'Harry chose it,' said Dave, looking uncomfortable at the show of emotion. He was all down to earth, blunt Yorkshireman, and prided himself on it. 'I was going to give you a cheque, more practical in my opinion, but he thought you'd like something to remind you of your time here, and he noticed you hadn't been wearing your watch the last few weeks.'

'It broke,' she whispered. *He had noticed.*

'Aye, well, there we are, then.' Dave clearly wanted to end what was to him an embarrassing few moments. 'Don't forget to look us up when you're back visiting your parents. All right, lass? I'll be off now, the missus and I are out for dinner tonight. Lock up the offices, would you, Harry?' he added, turning to his son. 'The factory's already been taken care of.'

'Goodbye, Mr Breedon.' Gina stood up to shake her boss's hand—he was of the old school, and didn't hold with social pleasantries such as kissing or hugging—but then on impulse quickly pressed her lips to the leathery old cheek before she sat down again.

Dave cleared his throat. 'Bye, lass. You look after yourself,' he said gruffly before disappearing out of the door.

Silence reigned for some moments while Gina tidied the last few papers on her desk. Every nerve and muscle was screaming, and the blood was racing through her veins. *Act cool. Keep calm and businesslike. Don't give yourself away. You knew this moment was going to come.*

Yes, she answered the voice in her head. But she hadn't expected they would be alone when she had to say the final goodbye.

'Your car wasn't in its normal spot in the car park this morning.'

Surprised, Gina raised her head, and looked fully at him for the first time since he'd entered the room. He gazed back at her from where he was leaning against the wall, hands in the pockets of his trousers and grey eyes half-closed, their expression inscrutable. She'd noticed this ability to betray nothing of what he was thinking early on. It was probably part and parcel of what had made him so successful in his own right since leaving university and working abroad, first in Germany and Austria, and then in the States. By all accounts he had left an extremely well paid and powerful position in a massive chain of pharmaceutical companies in America when he had returned to help his father, although she had learned this from Dave Breedon. Harry never talked about his past, and when she had asked the odd question his replies had been monosyllabic.

'My car?' She tried to collect her thoughts. It was difficult with him looking so broodingly drop-dead gorgeous. 'I knew I'd be having a drink, so I decided to travel by taxi today.' It was only partly the truth. She hadn't known how she would feel when the knowledge that she would never see him again became reality.

'No need.' He straightened, and her stomach muscles clenched. 'I'll run you home.'

No, no, no. She had seen his car, a sexy sports job that moved like greased lightning, and it was seduction on wheels. 'Thanks, but that's not necessary. It's the wrong direction for you.'

He smiled. She wondered if he knew what a devastating effect it had on the opposite sex. Probably, she thought a trifle maliciously.

'It's a beautiful spring evening, and I'm not doing anything. I've all the time in the world,' he drawled lazily.

'No, really, I'd feel awful putting you to so much trouble.'

'I insist.' He brushed aside the desperate refusal.

'And I insist on travelling by taxi.' She could be just as determined as him. The thought that she might suffer the unthinkable humiliation of giving herself away necessitated it.

'Don't be silly.' He walked over and perched on her desk— a habit of his—lifting her chin and looking into her eyes as he said softly, 'You're all upset at leaving, and no wonder. You've been here since the beginning of time. I can't possibly abandon you to the anonymity of a taxi.'

She didn't like the 'beginning of time' bit. Who did he think she was—Methuselah? And she despised herself for the way her whole insides had tightened at his touch. But they always did, however casual the action. 'You're not abandoning me,' she said stiffly. 'It's my choice.'

'A bad one.' He slid off the desk and walked to the door, opening it before he turned and said, 'And therefore I'm fully justified in overruling it. I'll get my coat.'

'Harry!' she shouted as he went to disappear.

'Yes, Gina?' He popped his head back round the door, grinning.

She gave up. 'This is ridiculous,' she muttered ungraciously. And dangerous. For her.

'Put your coat on and stop grumbling.'

He was back within a minute or so, taking the satellite-navigation system from her as she met him in the outer office. 'You'd better have my keys.' She handed him her office keys, which included those to all the confidential files. 'I meant to give them to Susan earlier.' *But she was so busy making goo-goo eyes at you I never got the chance.*

He pocketed them without comment.

She had slipped the case holding the watch into her handbag, and as they walked towards the lift she said quietly, 'Thank you for thinking of the watch, Harry. It's really beautiful.'

'My pleasure.' Once inside the carpet-lined box, he added, 'Dad really meant what he said, you know, and the watch is from both of us. You were great when he had his heart attack, holding the fort here, and then putting in endless hours once I was having to pick up all the threads. I couldn't have done it without you, Gina.'

This was torture. Exquisite torture, perhaps, but torture nonetheless. 'Anyone would have done the same.'

'No, they wouldn't.' His voice deepened, taking on the smoky quality that was dynamite as he murmured, 'I just wanted to say thank you.'

The lift easily carried twelve people, but suddenly it was much too small. She caught the faintest whiff of his aftershave and breathed it in greedily. Drawing on all her considerable willpower, she said evenly, 'There's no need, I was just doing my job, but it's nice to know I'm appreciated.' She forced a smile as the lift doors opened, stepping into the small reception with a silent sigh of relief. Too cosy. Too intimate. And the car was going to be as bad.

It was worse. Every single nerve in her body registered the impact as, after settling her in the passenger seat and shutting the door, Harry joined her in the car. The interior was all black leather with a state-of-the-art dashboard, but it was the close confines of the car that had Gina swallowing hard. Her voice something of a squeak, she said, 'This is a lovely car.' Understatement of the year. 'Toys for boys?' she added, attempting a wry smile.

He turned his head, smiling. He was so close she could see every little, black hair of his five o'clock stubble in spite of the gathering twilight. 'I had one of these in the States, and I guess I got used to fast cars.'

And fast women, no doubt. Not that any of his girlfriends lasted for more than five minutes. Gina nodded. 'It must have been a wrench to leave America.'

'Yes, it was.' He started the engine before turning to her again. 'How about dinner?'

'What?' She stared at him, utterly taken aback.

'Dinner?' he repeated patiently. 'Unless you've other plans? I thought it might be a nice way to round off your time at Breedon & Son. A small thank-you.'

'You've already thanked me with the watch,' she said, flustered beyond measure, and hoping he wouldn't notice.

'That was a combined thank-you. This is just me.'

Whatever he was, he wasn't 'just' anything. And it would be crazy to say yes. The whole evening would be spent trying to hide her feelings and play at being friendly, when just looking at him made her weak at the knees. But she would never have the chance of another evening of his company, that was for sure. Two more days of tying up all the loose ends, and she was off to London for good. Could she cope with the agony of being with him? It would mess her head up for days.

'My other plans were clearing out cupboards and beginning to spring-clean the flat,' she admitted weakly. 'It can wait.'

'Good. Dinner it is, then. There's a great little Italian place not far from where I live. Do you like Italian food?'

She didn't think she would taste a thing tonight anyway. 'I love it.'

'I'll make sure they've got a table.' He extracted his mobile phone, punching in a number before saying, 'Roberto?' and then speaking in rapid Italian. She hadn't known he could speak the language, but it didn't particularly surprise her. That was Harry all over. 'That's settled.' He smiled at her. 'Eight o'clock. OK with you if we call at my place first? I'd like to put on a fresh shirt before we go.'

His place. She'd see where he lived. She'd be able to picture him there in the weeks and months to follow. Not a good idea, probably, but irresistibly tempting. 'Fine,' she nodded, drawing on the cool aplomb she'd developed over the last twelve months, as the powerful car leapt into life and left the car park far too fast.

She glanced at Harry's hands on the steering wheel. Large, capable, masculine hands. What would it feel like to have them move over every inch of her body, explore her intimate places, along with his mouth and tongue? To savour and taste…

'…parents now and again.'

'Sorry?' Too late she realised he'd spoken, but she had been deep in a shockingly erotic fantasy. Blushing scarlet—an unfortunate attribute which went with the hair and her pale, freckled skin—she lied, 'I was thinking how nice everyone's been today.'

'Of course they've been nice. You're very popular.'

She didn't want to be popular. She wanted to be a slender,

elegant siren with long blonde hair and come-to-bed eyes, the sort of woman who might capture his heart, given half a chance.

'I was just saying we must keep in touch, and perhaps meet up for lunch now and again when you visit your parents,' he continued easily. 'I count you as a friend, Gina. I hope you know that.'

Great. 'As I do you.' She smiled brightly. Once she was in London, he'd forget she'd ever existed within days. Probably by the time he got up tomorrow morning, in fact. Harry wasn't the sort of man who had women *friends*. Just *women*.

The cool spring twilight had almost completely given way to the shadows of night by the time Harry turned the car off the country lane they had been following for some time, and through open wrought-iron gates on to a scrunchy pebble drive. Gina was surprised how far they'd travelled; she hadn't realised his home was so far away from Breedon & Son. She had supposed he'd settled somewhere near his parents' home.

The drive wound briefly between mature evergreens and bushes, which effectively hid all sight of the building from the road, and then suddenly became bordered by a wide expanse of green lawn with the house in front of them. Gina hadn't known what to expect. Probably a no-nonsense modern place or elegant turn-of-the-century manor-type house. In the event the picturesque thatched cottage in front of her was neither of these.

'This is your home?'

She had asked the obvious, but he didn't appear to notice. 'Like it?' he asked casually as the car drew up on the horseshoe-shaped area in front of the cottage.

Did she like it? How could anyone fail to? The two-storey cottage's white walls and traditional mullioned windows were topped by a high thatched roof out of which peeped gothick dormers. The roof overhung to form an encircling veranda, supported on ancient, gnarled tree-trunks on which a table and chairs sat ready for summer evenings. There was even evidence of roses round the door on the trellis bordering the quaint arched door, and red and green ivy covered the walls of the veranda. It was so quintessentially the perfect English country-cottage that Gina was speechless. It was the last place, the *very* last place, she would have expected Harry to buy, and definitely no bachelor pad.

Whether he guessed what she was thinking or her face had given her away Gina wasn't sure, but the next moment he drawled, 'I had a modern stainless-steel and space-age place in the States, overlooking the ocean; I fancied a change.'

'It's wonderful.' He opened the car door as he spoke, and now as he appeared at her side and helped her out of the passenger seat she repeated, 'It's wonderful. A real fairy-tale cottage. I half expect Goldilocks and the three bears to appear any moment.' She liked that. It was light, teasing. She'd got the fleeting impression he hadn't appreciated her amazement at his choice of home, despite his lazy air.

He shrugged. 'It's somewhere to lay my hat for the moment. I'm not into putting down roots.'

She'd been right. He *hadn't* wanted her to assume there was any danger of him becoming a family man in the future. Not that she would. 'Hence your travelling in the past?' she said carefully as they walked to the front door.

'I guess.'

She stared at him. 'Your father's hoping you'll take over the family business at some point, isn't he?'

'That was never on the cards.' He opened the door, standing aside so she preceded him into the wide square hall. The old floorboards had been lovingly restored and varnished, their mellow tones reflected in the honey-coloured walls adorned with the odd print or two. 'I agreed to come and help my father over the next couple of years, partly to ease him into letting go of the strings and making it easier to sell when the time comes, but that's all.'

'I see.' She didn't, but it was none of her business. 'So, you'll go back to the States at some point?'

Again he shrugged. 'The States, Germany, perhaps even Australia. I'm not sure. I invested a good deal of the money I've earned over the last years, played the stock exchange and so on. I don't actually need to work, but I will. I like a challenge.'

It was the most he had ever said about himself, and Gina longed to ask more, but a closed look had come over his face. Changing the subject, she said, 'Everything looks extremely clean and dust free. Do you have a cleaner come in?'

'Are you saying men can't clean for themselves? That's a trifle sexist, isn't it?' He grinned at her, leading the way to what proved to be the sitting room, and he opened the door into a large room dominated by a magnificent open fireplace, the wooden floors scattered with fine rugs, and the sofas and chairs soft and plumpy. 'You're right, though,' he admitted unrepentantly. 'Mrs Rothman comes in three days a week, and does everything from changing the lightbulbs to washing and ironing. She's a treasure.'

'And preparing your meals?' she asked as he waved her to a seat.

'Not at all. I'm a great cook, if I do say so myself, and I prefer to eat what I want when I want to eat it. Glass of wine while you wait?' he added. 'Red or white?'

'Red, please.' She glanced at the fireplace as he disappeared, presumably to the kitchen. There were the remains of a fire in the fireplace, and plenty of logs were stacked in the ample confines of the hearth. She pictured him sitting here in the evenings, sipping a glass of wine maybe, while he stared into the flickering flames. The wrench her heart gave warned her to keep her thoughts in check. And she wasn't going to dwell on the likelihood of the blonde of the moment stretched out on a rug in front of the fire, either, with Harry pampering and pleasing her.

'One glass of wine.'

Gina was brought out of her mental agony as Harry reappeared, an enormous half-full glass of deep-red wine in one hand. She took it with a doubtful smile. There must have been half a bottle in there, and she'd been too het up to eat any of the extensive nibbles earlier, or much lunch, for that matter.

'I won't be long. There's some magazines there—' he gestured towards one of the occasional tables dotted about the room '—and some nuts and olives alongside them. Help yourself.'

'Thank you.' As soon as he'd left again, she scuttled across and made short work of half the bowl of nuts, deciding she'd worry about the calories tomorrow. Tonight she needed to be sober and in full charge of her senses. One slip, one look, and he might guess how she felt about him, and then she'd die. She would, she'd die. Or have to go on living with the knowledge she'd betrayed herself, and that would be worse.

She retrieved her glass of wine and sipped at it as she wandered about the room. Rich, dark and fruity, it was gorgeous. Like Harry. Although he had never been fruity with her, more was the pity.

She glanced at herself in the huge antique mirror over the

fireplace. The mellow lighting in the room made her hair appear more golden than anything else, and blended the pale ginger freckles that covered her creamy skin from head to foot into an overall honey glow. It couldn't do anything for her small snub nose and nondescript features, however. She frowned at her reflection, her blue eyes dark with irritation. This was the reason Harry had never come on to her. She was the epitome of the girl next door, when she longed to be a *femme fatale:* tall, slim, elegant—not busty and hippy. Even her mother had to admit she was 'nicely rounded', which meant—in the terms the rest of the world would use—she was on the plump side.

After staring at herself for a full minute, she walked over to the window and looked out over the grounds at the back of the cottage while she finished her glass of wine. She needed something to give her dutch courage for the evening, considering Harry was accompanying a creature not far removed from the Hunchback of Nôtre Dame.

'You can't see much tonight.'

He must have crept into the room, because she hadn't heard him coming. Gina was glad there was no wine in the glass, because with the jump she gave as he came up behind her it would have been all down her dress. He continued to stand behind her, his hands loosely on her waist, as he said, 'To the left beyond that big chestnut tree there's a swimming pool, but it's too dark to see it, and a tennis court. Are you sporty?'

Sporty? She didn't know what she was with him holding her like this. Dredging up what was left of her thought process, she managed to mumble, 'I swim a bit.' She didn't add that she hadn't played tennis for years, because whatever sports bra she bought it still didn't seem to stop her breasts bobbing about like crazy. Too much information, for sure.

'You'll have to come and have a swim in the summer, if you're up this neck of the woods.'

That *so* wasn't an option. 'That'd be great.'

'If you're ready, we'll make a move.'

When he let go of her, she felt wildly relieved and hopelessly bereft. When she turned to face him it didn't help her shaky equilibrium one bit. He'd obviously had a quick shower along with changing, and his ebony hair was still damp and slightly tousled. Suddenly he appeared vastly different from the immaculately finished product during working hours, and the open-necked black shirt and casual black trousers he was wearing added to the transformation. In the designer suits, shirts and ties he favoured in the office, he was breathtakingly gorgeous. Now he was a walking sex-machine, with enough magnetism to cause a disturbance in the earth's orbit.

Controlling a rush of love so powerful she was amazed it didn't show, Gina handed him her empty glass and walked over to the sofa, where her handbag and jacket were, saying over her shoulder, 'This is very good of you, Harry. There was nothing more exciting than beans on toast waiting for me at the flat.'

'My pleasure.'

No, hers, given the merest encouragement, Gina thought wryly. She had never been tempted to go all the way with any of her boyfriends in the past, and had even begun to wonder if there was something wrong with her. Harry's entrance into her life had put paid to that. She only had to think about him to get embarrassingly aroused. If he ever actually made love to her...

He took her jacket from her, helping her into it with a warm smile. She was everlastingly thankful he couldn't read her mind. Taking a deep breath, she walked briskly out of the room.

CHAPTER TWO

Why had he done this? Why had he invited her out to dinner tonight? He hadn't intended to. He'd meant their goodbye to be friendly, swift and final, and definitely with a third party present.

As Harry slid into the car, he glanced at Gina for a second. He was, by virtue of his genetic background and upbringing, a very rational man. 'Cold' had even been the word used by former girlfriends on occasion, but that had been after he had firmly disabused them of the idea that their relationship had any chance of becoming permanent.

He knew exactly what he wanted out of life. Since Anna. And, because the knowledge had been forged in the furnace, it was not negotiable—Independence. Following his own star, with no tentacles of responsibility to prevent him doing so. Companionship and sex along the way, of course, good times with women who knew the score. But nothing that came with strings and ties and required sacrifices he wasn't willing to make.

He'd left university with a first in business studies, gaining experience in a couple of jobs, before landing the big one in the States where he'd moved to the top of the ladder after acquiring a postgraduate degree, Master of Business Administration. He had enjoyed working for that, although with his job it had meant regular twenty-hour days. But that had been fine. It had happened after Anna, and anything which had enabled him to go to bed too dog-tired to think had been OK by him.

'Is it far?'

The soft voice at the side of him brought his head turning. 'Just a couple of miles,' he said evenly, swinging the car out of the drive onto the quiet tree-lined lane beyond. 'It's only a very small place, by the way, nothing grand, but the food is excellent. Roberto has the knack of turning the most simple dish into something special. The first time I saw a warm-bread salad with roasted red peppers on the menu, I thought it a fairly basic starter. Big mistake. It came with capers and anchovies and fresh basil, and a whole host of other ingredients, that made it out of this world.'

'You're making my mouth water.'

Harry smiled. 'Do I take it you're someone who lives to eat, rather than eats to live?'

His swift glance saw her wrinkle her little nose. 'Can't you tell?' she said a trifle flatly.

His smile vanished. He didn't know what it was about this gentle, ginger-haired woman that had attracted him from day one, but her softly rounded, somewhat voluptuous curves were part of it. 'Your figure's fine,' he said firmly.

'Thank you.'

'I mean it. There are far too many women these days who don't actually *look* like women. Lettuce leaves are great for rabbits, but there's where they should stop. I hate to see a woman nibbling on a stick of celery all evening, and drinking mineral water, while insisting she's full to bursting.'

He'd just pulled up before turning on to the main road, and

in the shadowed confines of the car he caught her glance of disbelief. 'What?' he said, turning to face her.

'You might say that, but I bet the women you date are all stick insects.'

He opened his mouth to deny it before the uncomfortable truth hit. To anyone on the outside looking in, it would appear Gina was spot on-target. He *did* tend to date trim, svelte types. Why? He pulled on to the main road, his very able and intelligent mind dissecting the matter.

Because he'd found by experience that women who were obsessed with their figures, and appearance, and street cred, tended to be on the insular side—especially when they were also career minded, as he made sure all his girlfriends were. Less inclined towards cosy twosomes at home, and more likely to favour a date involving dinner and dancing, or the theatre, where they could see and be seen. Women with their own, forged-in-steel goals who weren't looking for happy-ever-after but good conversation, good company and entertainment, and good sex. He'd made the odd mistake, of course, but mostly he tended to get it right.

In fact, if he thought about it, one criterion for dating a woman more than a couple of times was her level of self-interest. He grimaced mentally. Which made him…what? He decided not to follow that train of thought, but it confirmed he'd been crazy to take Gina out tonight, even on the basis of friendship.

Realising he hadn't given her any reply, he ducked the issue by saying self-righteously, 'Anorexia is becoming an ever-increasing problem these days, and no one in their right mind can say those women, young girls some of them, look attractive.'

'I suppose not.'

They drove in silence for the rest of the short journey. When he finally pulled into Roberto's tiny car-park, he saw Gina looking about her. The restaurant was situated on the edge of a typical Yorkshire market-town, but in the darkness it appeared more secluded than it was. In the muted lighting from the couple of lamps in the car park, her hair gleamed like strands of copper. He wondered what she would say if he asked her to loosen it from the upswept bun she usually favoured for work. He'd seen it down a couple of times, and it was beautiful.

Stupid. He brushed the notion away ruthlessly. This was dinner. Nothing else.

He slid out of the car, walking round the bonnet and then opening Gina's door and helping her out. The air smelt of the burgeoning vegetation, and somewhere close by a blackbird sang two or three flute-like notes—probably disturbed by the car and lights—before falling silent again. He watched as she drew in a lungful of air, her eyes closed. Opening them, she said softly. 'I shall miss this in London.'

'Don't go, then.' He hadn't meant to say it.

'I have to.' Her lashes flickered.

'Why?'

'I start my new job on Monday—I've got a flat, everything. I couldn't let people down.'

He suddenly knew why he had asked her out to dinner. He hadn't believed she would actually leave Breedon & Son when it came to the crunch. He hadn't prepared himself for her disappearing out of his life. There had been so much talk among Natalie and the other employees of Gina changing her mind at the last minute, and he'd found it expedient to believe it. He should have known that once she had committed to something she wouldn't turn back.

'No, I guess you couldn't.' At six feet, he topped her by five or six inches, and as he gazed down at her he caught the scent of her perfume, something warm and silky that reminded him of magnolia flowers. The jump his senses gave provided a warning shot across the bows. 'Let's go in,' he said coolly. 'I'm starving.'

Once Roberto had finished fussing over them, and they were seated at a table for two with menus in front of them and a bottle of wine on order, Harry took himself in hand. This was her last day at Breedon & Son, and it was true that she had been a lifesaver when he'd returned so suddenly to the UK— *that* was why he'd offered to take her out tonight. Nothing else. And of course he'd miss her. You couldn't work closely with someone umpteen hours a day, share the odd coffee break and lunch and learn about her life and so on, without missing her when she was gone. It was as simple as that.

'I think I'm going to try that warm-bread salad you mentioned for starters.' She stared at him, her blue eyes dark in the paleness of her skin. 'And maybe the tagliatelle to follow?'

'Good choice.' He nodded. 'I'll join you.'

Once Roberto had returned with the wine and taken their order, he settled back in his seat and raised his glass in a toast. 'To you and your new life in the great, big city,' he said, purposely injecting a teasing note into his voice. 'May you be protected from all the prowling wolves who might try to gobble you up.'

She laughed. 'I don't somehow think they'll be queueing for the privilege.'

He'd noticed this before, her tendency towards self-deprecation. 'From where I'm sitting, it's a very real possibility,' he said quietly.

Her voice a little uncertain, she said, 'Thank you. You're very gallant.'

'I like to think so, but in this case I am speaking the truth.' He leant forward slightly, not hiding his curiosity as he said, 'You don't rate yourself much, do you, Gina? Why is that—or is that too personal a question?'

He liked it that she could blush. He'd thought it a lost art before he had met her.

She shrugged. 'Legacy of being the ugly duckling of the family, I suppose,' she said quietly. 'My two older sisters inherited the red hair, but theirs is true chestnut, and they don't have freckles. Added to which it was me who had to have the brace on my teeth and see a doctor about acne.'

His eyes wandered over the flawlessly creamy skin, flawless except for the freckles, but he liked those. And her teeth were small, white and even. 'Your dentist and doctor are to be congratulated on their part in assisting the swan to emerge. You're a very lovely woman, even if you don't realise it.'

The blush grew deeper. He watched it with fascination. When she looked ready to explode, he said, 'I seem to remember both your sisters are married, aren't they?' It was more to change the subject and alleviate her distress than because he cared two hoots about them.

She nodded, and her hair reflected a hundred different shades of gold and copper as she moved. 'Bryony has a little boy of three, and Margaret two girls of five and eight, so I'm an aunt three times over. They're all great kids.'

Something in her voice prompted him to say, 'You obviously are very fond of them.'

'Of course.'

There was no 'of course' about it. He knew several women who couldn't seem to stand their own children, let alone anyone else's. 'Do you see yourself settling down and having a family one day?'

A shadow passed over her face. 'Maybe.'

'Maybe?'

She smiled, but he could see it was a little shaky. Her mouth was soft, vulnerable. Muscles knotted in his stomach.

'Settling down and having a family does carry the pre-requisite of meeting the right man,' she said, taking a sip of her wine.

'You're bound to meet someone in London.'

'Why "bound to"?'

Her voice was sharper than he'd heard it before, and his eyes widened momentarily. He'd clearly said the wrong thing, although he couldn't think how.

And then she said quickly, 'Not everyone meets the right one, as I'm sure you'd agree, and personally I'd rather remain single than marry just to be with someone. I'm going to London with a view to furthering my career, and perhaps travelling a little, things like that.'

He stared at her. That wasn't all of it. Had she had a love affair go wrong? Was she moving away because someone had hurt her, broken her heart? But she hadn't said anything to him about a man in her life.

He caught at the feeling of anger, the sense that she had let him down in some way. Drawing on his considerable self-control, he said coolly, 'I hadn't got you down as a career woman, Gina?'

'No?' She glanced up from her wine glass and looked him

full in the face, but he could read nothing from her expression when she said, 'But then you don't really know me, do you?'

He felt as though she had just slapped him round the face, even though her voice had been pleasant and calm. He thought he knew her. She had always been quite free in talking about herself, her family, her friends, although... His eyes narrowed. Come to think of it, she had never discussed her love life at all. He'd just assumed she didn't have one, he supposed.

He felt a dart of self-disgust, and realised how much he had assumed. Trying to justify himself, he argued silently, no, it wasn't altogether that. Because he didn't like to talk about that side of his life, he hadn't pressed her in that direction, that was all.

And the long hours she had put in ever since he had arrived? The devotion to the job, and to him and his father? Her readiness to be prepared to work overtime at the drop of a hat? The way—even when her workload had been huge and she'd been working flat out—she'd spare time to talk him through a procedure he wasn't familiar with? He had taken it all for granted, looking back, in his arrogance having imagined Breedon & Son was all of her life. But why would it be? Looking like Gina did, why wouldn't there have been a man in the background somewhere?

Collecting his racing thoughts, he said, 'So, what's your ultimate goal? Do you intend to stay in the capital for good, now you've made the break?'

She paused to think. He saw her tongue stroke her bottom lip for a moment, and his body responded, stirring to life. 'I'm not sure.' She raised her eyes. 'Possibly. Like I said, I'd like to travel, and perhaps that could be incorporated into a job. That would be perfect.'

This was a new side to her. *Disturbing*. He'd been more than a little taken aback when she had announced her intention to leave shortly after the New Year; it hadn't fitted into his overall picture of her. She was level-headed, reliable, a calm, balanced woman with both feet firmly on the ground. The very last person to suddenly announce they were leaving their home, job and friends to hightail it to the big city, in fact.

'I see.' He tried for nonchalance when he said, 'You're full of surprises, Gina Leighton. I had you down as more of a homebody, I guess. Someone who wouldn't be happy if they were far away from where they were born.'

'London isn't exactly the ends of the earth.'

She lifted her chin as she spoke, and he said quickly, 'Oh, don't get me wrong. That wasn't a criticism.'

'Good.' She sipped at her wine.

'If anyone can understand the urge to travel, I can. It's just that I saw you differently, more...'

'Boring?'

'Boring?' He stared at her in genuine amazement. 'Of course I never thought you were boring. How can you say that? I was going to say contented with what you had, where you were in life.'

'You can be all that and still fancy a change,' she said flatly, just as the waitress came with their warm-bread salads.

Once she'd gone, he reached across the table and touched Gina's hand for one brief moment. 'I didn't mean to offend you,' he said softly. 'And I swear I've never thought of you as boring.' Disconcerting, maybe. Definitely unsettling on occasion, like when he'd stolen a swift kiss at the Christmas party and the scent of her had stayed with him all evening. And, on the couple of instances she'd worn her hair down for work, he'd had to stuff his hands in his pockets all day to avoid the temptation to take a handful of the shining, silky mass and nuzzle his face into it. But boring? Never.

Gina shrugged. 'It doesn't matter one way or the other.'

She had moved her fingers out from under his almost as soon as they had rested on her hand, and it suggested she was still annoyed.

'It does.' Irritated, his voice hardened. 'We're friends, aren't we?'

'We are—we were—work colleagues, first and foremost,' came the dampening answer. 'We were *friendly,* but that's not the same as being friends.'

He stared at her. Her cheeks were flushed and her eyes were bright, and he couldn't read a thing in her closed expression. He couldn't remember the last time he had felt out of his depth when speaking to a woman, but it was happening now. Raking back a lock of hair from his forehead, he leant back in his seat, surveying her broodingly. 'So, what's your definition of friends?'

She ate a morsel of bread and pronounced it delicious, before she said, 'Friends are there for you, right or wrong. You can have fun with them or cry with them. They know plenty about you, but stick in there with you nonetheless. They're part of your life.'

He became aware he was frowning, and straightened his face. He felt monumentally insulted. 'And none of that applies to us, apparently? Is that what you're saying?' he said evenly.

'Well, does it?' she asked matter-of-factly.

'I think so.'

'Harry, we've never met out of work, and know very little about each other.'

He shook his head stubbornly. 'Don't be silly, we know plenty about each other,' he said firmly, his annoyance rising when she narrowed her eyes cynically. He was possessed by the very irrational desire to do or say something remarkable to shock her out of her complacency, something that hadn't happened since he had been a thirteen-year-old schoolboy trying to impress the school beauty. But Delia Sherwood had been a walkover compared to the self-contained, quiet young woman watching him with disbelieving eyes. And this was a crazy conversation. He wasn't even sure how it had come about. Why did Gina's opinion about their relationship matter so much, anyway? 'I know you have two sisters, a best friend called Erica, and that you walk your parents' dog to keep fit, for instance. OK?' Even to himself he sounded petulant.

'Those are head facts. Not *heart* facts.'

'I'm sorry?' he said, his temper rising.

She gave what sounded like a weary sigh and ate another mouthful of food. 'Think about it,' was all she said.

He ate his warm-bread salad without tasting it. There had been undercurrents in their friendship from day one—and it was a friendship, whatever she said—but there she was, as cool as a cucumber, stating they were merely work colleagues. Damn it, he *knew* there was a spark there, even if neither of them had done anything about it. And the reason he'd held his hand had been for *her* sake. An act of consideration on his part.

He speared a piece of pepper with unnecessary violence, feeling extremely hard done by. He had known she wasn't the type of woman to have a meaningless affair, and because he couldn't offer anything permanent he'd kept things light and casual. But that didn't mean there wasn't something real between them.

The waitress appeared as soon as they had finished and whisked their plates away, whereupon Gina immediately stood up, reaching for her handbag as she did so. 'I'm just going to powder my nose,' she said brightly.

He had risen to his feet and now he nodded, sitting down again, watching her make her way to the back of the small restaurant and open the door marked *Ladies*.

He had thought he knew her, but she had proved him wrong. His frown deepened. The woman who had sat there and blatantly told him he could stick their friendship—or as good as—was not the Gina of nine-to-five. In fact, she was a stranger. A beautiful, soft, honey-skinned stranger, admittedly, with eyes that could be uncertain and vulnerable one moment and fiery, to match the hair—the next. But a stranger nonetheless. And he didn't understand it.

Harry finished his glass of wine but resisted pouring himself another as he was driving, instead reaching for the bottle of sparkling mineral-water he'd ordered along with the wine.

He had imagined there was a...buzz between them, and all the time she'd probably been carrying on with someone else. Of course she'd been entitled to; he'd had one or two, maybe three—but very short-lived—relationships in the last twelve months. But it was different for her. And then he grimaced at the hypocrisy, scowling in self-contempt. Damn it, she'd caught him on the raw, and he didn't know which end of him was up. Which only confirmed a million times over he had been absolutely right not to get involved with Gina. She was trouble. In spite of the air of gentle, warm voluptuousness that had a man dreaming he could drown in the depths of her—or perhaps *because* of it—she was trouble.

Swilling back the water, he made himself relax his limbs.

It was ridiculous to get het up like this. She was leaving Yorkshire at the weekend, and that would be that. His mouth tightened. And Susan Richards had made it very plain she was up for a bit of fun with no strings attached. His perfect kind of woman, in fact.

His scowl deepened. When he replaced the empty glass on the table, it was with such force he was fortunate it didn't shatter.

CHAPTER THREE

WHATEVER had possessed her? Why had she challenged him like that? Gina stood, staring at her flushed reflection in the spotted little mirror in the ladies' cloakroom, mentally groaning. He had looked absolutely amazed, and no wonder.

Grabbing her bag, she hunted for her lip gloss and then stood with it in her hand, still staring vacantly. It had been his attitude that had done it. It had brought out the devil in her, and the temper that went with the hair. When she and her two sisters had been growing up, her father had repeatedly warned them about the folly of speaking first and thinking later— often lamenting the fact that he was the only male in a household of four red-haired women, while he'd been about it.

'A homebody.' And, 'you're bound to meet someone in London.' How patronising could you get? And why shouldn't she be a career woman, anyway? It wasn't only scrawny blondes like Susan Richards who had the monopoly on such things.

Suddenly she slumped, her eyes misty. She had behaved badly out there, and if she was being honest with herself it was because the sight of Harry and Susan had acted like salt on a raw wound.

Dabbing her eyes with a tissue, she sniffed loudly and then

repaired her make-up. This was all her own fault—she should never have come out to dinner with him. She had known it was foolish, worse than foolish, but she had done it anyway. Harry couldn't help being Harry. Being so drop-dead gorgeous, he was always going to have women panting after him, but at least after tonight she wouldn't have to watch it any longer.

The lurch her heart gave made her smudge the lip gloss down her chin. She stopped what she was doing and held herself round the middle, swaying back and forth a number of times, until the door opening brought her up straight.

A tall matronly looking woman entered, nodding and smiling at her before entering the one cubicle the tiny room held.

Gina wished she was old, or at least old enough for this to be past history. She wished she didn't love him so much. And more than anything she wished she wasn't so sure that she would never meet anyone who could stir her heart like Harry, which meant she wasn't likely to get the husband and children she'd always imagined herself having. She bit hard on her lip, her eyes cloudy. Harry was right. She *was* a homebody. And because of him she was being forced down a road she had never seen herself walking.

It was all his fault. She glared at her reflection, wiping her streaked chin, and then packing her make-up away. He was so content with his lot, so happy, so completely self-satisfied. The rat.

Taking a deep breath, she told herself to get a grip. He was buying her dinner, hardly a crime. And the watch was beautiful, made even more so by the fact he had noticed she wasn't wearing her old one. It had been kind of him to round off her time at Breedon & Son by taking her out, when all was said and done. So…no more griping. *Get yourself in there and be bright and sparkling, and leave him with a smile when the time comes.*

When Gina walked back into the dining area the sight of him caused her breath to catch in her throat, but then it always did. Which was at best annoying and worst embarrassing— like the time she had been eating a hot sausage-roll in the work canteen and had choked, until Natalie had slapped her on the back so hard she'd thought her spine had snapped in two.

She arrived at the table just as the waitress brought their main course, which was good timing. She could bury herself in the food to some extent, she thought, sliding into her seat and returning his smile. At least he *was* smiling now. He'd looked thoroughly irritated with her when she had left, and she couldn't altogether blame him.

'More wine?' He was refilling her glass as he spoke, and Gina didn't protest. She needed something to help her get through the evening without making a complete fool of herself, and in the absence of anything else alcohol would do. Although, that was flawed thinking, she told herself in the next moment. The wine was more likely to prompt her to do or say something silly.

Warning herself to go steady, she took a small sip and then tried the tagliatelle. It was delicious. The best she had ever tasted. Deciding that she was definitely a girl who would eat for comfort rather than pine away, she tucked in.

By the time the main course was finished, Gina had discovered that you could laugh and really mean it, even if your heart was on the verge of being broken. Harry seemed to put himself out to be the perfect dinner companion after their earlier blip, producing one amusing story after another, and displaying the wicked wit which had bowled her over in the first days of their acquaintance. Back then she had desperately been seeking a way to make him notice her as a woman; now that strain was taken off her shoulders at least. He saw her as a friend, and only as a friend, and she'd long since accepted it.

She chose pistachio meringue with fresh berries for dessert, and it didn't fail to live up to expectations. She didn't think she'd eat for a week after this evening, and she said so as she licked the last morsel of meringue off her spoon.

Harry grinned, his eyes following her pink tongue. 'I'm glad you enjoyed it. If I'd thought I could have introduced you to this place months ago.'

If he had thought. Quite. 'I'm glad you didn't. I'd be two stone heavier by now.'

'You could have taken your parents' dogs for a few extra walks and worked off the pounds,' he said easily.

'There speaks someone who's never had to diet.' Why would he? The man was perfect.

'Do you—have to diet, I mean?'

A bit personal, but she'd brought it on herself. Gina nodded. 'My sisters—wouldn't you just know?—follow after my dad, and he's a tall streak of nothing. My mother on the other hand is like me. We go on a diet every other week, but just as regularly fall by the wayside. My mum blames my dad for her lapses. She says he gives her no incentive because he likes her to be what he calls "cuddly".' She grimaced.

'I'm with your father.'

Gina smiled wryly.

'I mean it.'

Yeah, yeah, yeah. Purposely changing the subject, she said,

'Thank you for a lovely meal, Harry. I've really enjoyed it. It was a nice way to end my time at Breedon & Son.'

He seemed to digest that for a few seconds. 'It'll be odd, coming into work each day and you not being there.'

Be still, my foolish heart. She forced a smile. 'I think you'll find Susan a more than adequate replacement. She's very keen.' In more ways than one.

'I guess so.'

He didn't sound overly impressed, and Gina's heart jumped for joy before she reminded herself it meant nothing. If it wasn't Susan it would be someone else. Her voice even, she said, 'It'll all work out fine. Things always do, given time.' *Except me and you.*

'I think we're both long enough in the tooth to know that's not true,' he said drily. 'It goes hand in hand with accepting there's no Santa Clause.' He cleared his throat, his heavily lashed eyes intent on her face. 'Look, this is none of my business, and tell me to go to blazes if you want, but is this decision to leave Yorkshire anything to do with your personal life?'

She stared at him.

'You know what I mean,' he said after a moment. 'A man. Has a relationship ended unhappily, something like that? Because, if that's the reason, running away won't necessarily improve your state of mind.'

Panic stricken, she opened her mouth to deny it before logic stepped in. He had no idea the man in question was him, and if nothing else confirming his suspicions would work to her advantage. One, he'd have to accept she had a concrete reason for moving away, and two, it would explain her reluctance to visit in the future.

'I'm right, aren't I? Someone has let you down.'

After their earlier conversation, she couldn't bear the idea of Harry thinking she'd been discarded like an old sock. Stiffly, she said, 'It's not like that. *I* made the decision to end the relationship and move away.'

His eyes narrowed. She recognised the look on his face. It was one he adopted when he wouldn't take no for an answer on some business deal or other. It was this formidably tenacious streak in his nature that had seen Breedon & Son go from strength to strength in the last year since he'd come home. And that was great on a business level. Just dandy. It was vastly different when that acutely discerning mind was homed in on her, though. Recognising the wisdom of the old adage that pride went before a fall, she said quickly, 'It wasn't going anywhere, that's all. End of story.'

'What do you mean, not going anywhere? You're obviously upset enough about the finish of it to move away from your family and friends, your whole life,' he finished, somewhat dramatically for him. Then he added suddenly, 'He's not married, is he?'

'*Excuse me?*' It was a relief to hide behind outrage. 'I have never, and *would* never, get involved with someone else's husband.'

'No, of course you wouldn't.' He had the grace to look embarrassed. 'I know that, really I do. But what went wrong, then?'

Gina wondered if she could end this conversation with a few well-chosen words along the lines that he should mind his own business. But this was Harry she was dealing with. He was like one of those predatory fish of the Caribbean she'd read about recently: once it seized hold on something, it couldn't let go even if it wanted to. 'A common scenario,' she said as lightly as she could manage. 'He was content to jog along as we were indefinitely. I wanted more.'

He looked shocked. 'Did he know how much you cared for him?'

That was rich, coming from the man who—if office gossip was to be believed—discarded girlfriends like cherry stones once he'd enjoyed their fruit. Talk about a case of the pot calling the kettle black! Gina shrugged, keeping her voice steady and unemotional when she said, 'That's not really the point. We wanted different things for the future, that's all. I was ready to settle down, and he wasn't. Actually, I don't think he will ever settle down.'

He stared at her, a frown darkening his countenance. 'In other words, he strung you along?'

'No, he didn't string me along,' Gina said severely. 'He was always absolutely straight and above board, if you must know. I suppose I just…hoped for more.' And always had, from the first moment she had laid eyes on him. Always would, for that matter, if she didn't put a good few miles between them.

'You are being too kind. He must have known the sort of girl you are from the start.'

She couldn't do this any more. Her voice low, she said, 'Could we change the subject, please, Harry?'

He opened his mouth to object, but the waitress was at their side with the coffee. He waited until she had bustled off, and then spoke in a very patient tone, which had the effect of making her want to kick him. 'Believe me, Gina,' he said gently, 'I know the type of man he is, and he's not worthy of you.'

That was true at least. 'Really?' she said drily. 'You know this without even having met him?'

'Like I said, I know the type. Now, I'm not saying he's

wrong not to want to settle down, I'm the same way myself. But I wouldn't get involved with someone who had for ever on their mind, and there's the difference. And a man can tell. Always.'

He really was the most arrogant male on the planet. 'How?' 'How?'

'How can you tell if a woman is looking for something permanent or just a roll in the hay?' she asked baldly.

He looked askance at her. 'I hope it's never anything as crude as "just a roll in the hay",' he said stiffly. 'I'm a man, not an animal. I've never yet taken a woman just because she's indicated she's available.'

This self-righteous side of him was new. Gina fixed him with purposely innocent eyes. 'So you have to get to know someone first? Find out if they can provide mental as well as physical stimulation, perhaps? Make sure their slant on life and love is the same as yours?'

He stared at her as though he wasn't sure whether she was mocking him or not. After a moment, his eyes glinting, he said, 'You make it sound very cold-blooded.'

In for a penny, in for a pound. 'Perhaps because it is?' she suggested sweetly.

'I prefer to think of it as honest, and if this man you've been involved with had done the same you wouldn't be in the position you're in now,' he ground out somewhat grimly.

'But attraction, love, desire, doesn't always fit into nicely labelled little packages, does it?' Gina countered, the feeling that she'd hit him on the raw wonderfully satisfying. 'It can be a spontaneous thing, something that hits you wham-bang in the heart and takes you completely by surprise. Something so overpowering and real that everything and everyone else goes out of the window.'

He folded his arms over his chest, settling more comfortably in his seat as he studied her flushed face. 'It can be like that,' he agreed after some moments. 'But, if it is, things inevitably go wrong.'

'Of course they don't—'

'Was it like that for you with this man?' he interjected swiftly. 'A head-over-heels thing?'

She hesitated, and immediately he seized on it. 'You see?' he said coolly.

'What I *see* is that your attitude is a wonderful excuse for playing the field without fear of reprisals.'

'I beg your pardon?'

Refusing to be intimidated by his growl, Gina met his glare without flinching. 'You have the best of all worlds, Harry, you know you do. You can wine, dine and bed a woman as often as you like, and then walk away with a smile and a "I told you what to expect" when you've had enough. I find that…distasteful.'

'Distasteful?'

If the situation had been different, she could have laughed at the sheer outrage on his face. Funnily enough, his mounting temper had the effect of calming her. 'Yes, distasteful,' she said firmly. 'You can't tell me some of your girlfriends haven't fallen for you because, whatever modern thinking tries to promote, sex means more to a woman than a man in the emotional sense. Just the sheer mechanics of it means a woman allows—' She stopped abruptly as he raised a sardonic eyebrow.

'Yes?' he drawled with suspicious blankness.

'It means a woman allows a man into her body,' she said bravely, wondering why she was giving Harry—of all people—a biology lesson. 'Whereas, for a man…'

'It's possession, penetration?'

Ignoring her fiery cheeks, Gina nodded sharply. 'Exactly.'

'You don't think the man feels anything beyond physical satisfaction?'

'I didn't say that.' He knew she hadn't said that. 'But it *is* different.'

'*Vive la différence.*'

Her embarrassment seemed to have restored his equanimity. Drawing on her dignity, Gina said flatly, 'I'm sorry if you find it old-fashioned or amusing, but I happen to think that love should enter the equation however things turn out in the end. And I know there's no guarantee with any relationship; I'm not in cloud cuckoo land.'

He looked at her quietly for a moment. 'I wasn't laughing at you, Gina.'

And pigs fly.

'In fact the time was I might have expressed the same views myself, but—' He paused. 'People change. Life changes them.'

Gina said nothing. In truth she was startled by this last remark. His tone of voice, the look on his face, was different from anything that had gone before.

'I guess I've become self-sufficient, independent. I like my life the way it is, and to share it with another person would be at best inconvenient and worst a nightmare.'

She wished she'd never started this conversation. Breathing shallowly to combat the shaft of pain that had seared her chest, Gina said quietly, 'You missed out cynical.'

'You think I'm cynical?'

She nodded. 'Not just from what you've said tonight, but more over the last twelve months. I wonder, actually, if you really like women much, Harry.'

For a moment he didn't react at all. Then he said softly, 'I assure you, I'm not of the other persuasion.'

'No, I didn't mean—I—I know you're not—'

He cut short her stammerings with a dark smile, his voice self-mocking when he said, 'I know what you meant, Gina. It was my way of prevaricating.'

'Oh.' Sometimes his innate honesty was more than a little disturbing.

'Because you're right. I *am* cynical where the fair sex is concerned.'

Why was being proved right so horribly depressing? Hiding her feelings, Gina nodded slowly. Picking her words carefully, she said, 'Bad experience somewhere in your long-lost youth?' She hoped to defuse what had suddenly become an extremely charged atmosphere with her tone, knowing he wouldn't want to talk about it in any detail. The last year had proved he was a master at deflecting questions about his past.

This time he surprised her. Nodding, he leaned forward, taking one of the mints the waitress had brought with their coffee and unwrapping it before he said, 'Her name was Anna, and it was a wild, hot affair. We were crazy about each other at first, but we were young; I'd just left uni when we met. I thought it would go on for ever, made promises, you know? But after a year or so I found my feelings were beginning to change. I still loved her, cared about her, but I wasn't *in* love with her. That something had gone. Perhaps it had only ever been lust, I don't know.'

'And Anna?'

'She said she loved me with all her heart. Then she got sick. A rare form of cancer. Although, she wasn't. I only found out she'd lied to me after we'd married. One of her friends told me when she was drunk, she thought it was hilarious. I was a joke, apparently.'

'I'm sorry.' She was. His voice was painful to hear.

'So far from Anna only having a few short months to live, months she'd begged me to spend with her as man and wife, she was as healthy as the next person.'

'What did you do?'

'I told her I was leaving. That night she cut her wrists in the bath.'

Unable to believe her ears, Gina could only stare.

'And so it began. Months of manipulation and tears and threats and rages. Two more supposed suicide attempts when I was going to leave. Damn it, I was young, little more than a kid. I was in way over my head, and I was stupid. I really thought she might kill herself. Eventually it came to the point where I began to fear I was going mad. That was the point I walked out. Went abroad.'

'What…what did she do?'

He shrugged. 'Took me for every penny she could get, and made sure my name was mud, then married some other poor sop.'

Appalled, Gina reached out and touched his hand. 'She must have been sick.'

'Sick?' His lips twisted. 'No, I don't think Anna was sick. Manipulative, determined, cruel, hard—all under a cloak of fragile femininity, of course—but sick? I could have forgiven sick, but not the sheer resolve to get her own way no matter whom she trampled underfoot.'

And so he had decided never to get caught like that again. She could understand it. But surely he realised all women weren't like Anna? Quietly, she said, 'I think she was sick,

Harry. I've never met anyone like her. All the women I know would be horrified at what she did.'

He didn't argue the point. Draining his cup of coffee, he shrugged slowly as he replaced the cup on the saucer. 'You're probably right, but it doesn't matter anyway. Like I said, life changes people. She perhaps did me a favour, in the long run. I wouldn't have ended up in the States, maybe, wouldn't have decided what I wanted—and more importantly what I *didn't* want—so early on in life, but for Anna.'

'I'm sorry, but I don't think she did you a favour,' Gina said with more honesty than tact. 'How can living an autonomous life be a favour? You'll miss out on a wife, children—'

'I don't want a wife and children, Gina,' he said calmly and coolly. 'I have what I want, and I consider myself most fortunate.'

She could have believed him one hundred per cent, but for the shadow darkening the smoky-grey eyes. And then he blinked and it was gone. Perhaps she'd imagined it in the first place. Gathering all her courage, she said, 'And what you want is a beautiful empty shell of a house, with no family to make it a home? Not ever? A life of complete independence with no one to grow old with, no one to look back over the years with? No one to cuddle when the night's dark and morning's a long way off?'

For several seconds, seconds that shivered with a curious intimacy, he held her gaze. Then the grey eyes closed against her. When he looked up again, he was smiling, his voice holding an amused note when he said, 'You're a romantic, Gina Leighton.'

How the knowledge that he wasn't smiling inside had come, Gina wasn't sure, but it was there. She didn't smile back, her face sweetly solemn as her eyes searched the sharply defined planes and angles of the hard male features.

'I believe in love,' she said softly. 'I believe in the sort of love between a man and a woman that has the potential to go on for a lifetime, and nothing else can measure up to the contentment and wonder of it. It has the power to sweep away barriers of culture and religion, heal unhealable hurts, and mend broken hearts. It can change the most dyed-in-the-wool cynic for the better and make the world a place worth living in. Yes, I believe all that, and if that fits your definition of a romantic then I hope up my hands and plead guilty, gladly.'

Harry shook his head slowly. 'And all this when the man you wanted to spend the rest of your life with has let you walk away?'

She blinked. That had been below the belt, and it hurt. Lots.

'I'm sorry.' Immediately he reached out and took her hand, holding on to her fingers when she would have pulled away. A thousand nerves responded to the feel of his warm flesh, and as she closed her eyes against the flood of desire his voice came, low and repentant. 'I'm really sorry, Gina. That was unforgivable. I'm the sort of primeval animal that attacks when it's threatened.'

Threatened? Bewildered, she met his gaze. For once his face was open, even vulnerable, and it betrayed something: a need, a longing. For what, she didn't know, but it was there in the smoky depths of the grey eyes. She swallowed hard. 'You objected to my placing you on a par with an animal earlier,' she reminded him, managing a fair attempt at a smile.

'So I did.'

She could read the relief in his face. He hated emotional scenes. She knew the reason for that now. 'Can I have my hand back, please?' she said with the sort of cheerfulness he expected of her. 'I want to drink my coffee.'

'Sure.' He grinned at her, and her heart writhed. She couldn't imagine not seeing him every day. She hadn't tried to, knowing it would weaken her resolve if she did. But now the time was here. In a little while, maybe an hour or two, he would happily drive out of her life without a care in the world. He'd perhaps even sing along to the car radio or one of his CD's on the way home, feeling he'd done his duty to the stalwart secretary who had babysat him in his first weeks at work.

She wondered what he'd do if she succumbed to the sudden temptation to tell him how she felt. To ask him to kiss her, really kiss her, just once. For old times' sake, or whatever he wanted to call it.

He'd be horrified. The answer was there with bells on. Horrified, embarrassed, alarmed. And every time he thought of her from now on—if he ever did, of course—it would be with awkwardness and discomfiture. And she didn't want that. OK, it was probably her pride again, but she would really rather walk through coals of fire than have him mentally squirm if her name came to mind.

'…your address?'

'I'm sorry?' Too late she realised he'd been talking, and she hadn't heard a word.

He shook his head. 'You were thinking of him just now, weren't you?' he accused. 'This guy who's let you down. Are you seeing him again before you leave for London?'

He seemed put out, but she couldn't think why. It was no skin off Harry's nose whether she saw her imaginary lover or not. She shrugged. 'I'm not sure,' she said dismissively. She'd discussed this whole thing enough, besides which she was worried she might trip herself up. Lying didn't come naturally to her, and she knew she was extremely bad at it. 'And he didn't let me down, not like you mean. What did you say before?' she added, before he started to argue the point.

'I said, you'll have to remember to give me your address and telephone number tonight,' he said.

A trifle sullenly, Gina thought. But then Harry never had been able to stand being disagreed with. She nodded. She had no intention of giving Harry her address in London after his comment earlier in the day about dossing down on her sofa if he was in town. She'd make some excuse when he dropped her off, saying she'd post it to him, something like that. And she wasn't going to delay their goodbye, either. She didn't want his last sight of her to be one of her howling her head off.

They finished their coffee and mints, and Harry paid the bill. Gina's heart was beating a tattoo as they walked out to the car, Harry's hand at her elbow. The night was scented with spring and to Gina's heightened emotions, unbearably lovely. She didn't think she had ever felt so miserable in the whole of her life.

Once in the car, Harry didn't start the engine immediately. Instead he twisted in his seat to look at her, frowning slightly. 'I'm worried about you, Gina,' he said quietly.

She became aware her mouth had fallen open, and shut it quickly. If he'd suddenly taken all his clothes off and danced in the moonlight, she couldn't have been more surprised. More thrilled, certainly, but not more surprised. 'I don't follow,' she hedged warily.

'This taking off to London to nurse a broken heart. It's dangerous. You're leaving yourself wide open for the worse sort of guy to take advantage of you. Away from friends and family, all alone in the bit city, you'll be incredibly vulnerable.'

He made her sound like Little Orphan Annie. She stared at him for a moment before she said stiffly, 'I'm thirty-two years old, Harry. Not sweet sixteen.'

'What's that got to do with it?'

'Everything.'

His mouth set in the stubborn pout he did so well. It made her toes curl, but she wasn't about to betray that to this big, hard, sexy man. Just occasionally—like now—she caught a glimpse of what the boy Harry must have looked like, and it was intoxicating. But Harry was no callow youth. He was an experienced and ruthlessly intelligent man who would capitalise on any weakness an opponent revealed. She'd seen him too often in action on the business front to be fooled.

'I don't think you've thought this through,' he said flatly, after a few tense moments had ticked by.

'Excuse me?' She couldn't believe the cheek of it. She hadn't thought it through? She'd done nothing else for months. Months when he'd been busy getting up close and personal with some blonde or other. He clearly didn't only see her as unattractive and sexless, but stupid as well. 'What on earth would you know about it?' she said stonily.

'Don't get on your high horse.' He seemed unaffected by her obvious rage. 'I'm merely pointing out you're on the rebound, because anyone who *is* on the rebound never makes allowance for it.'

Agony aunt as well—there was no limit to his attributes. Gina glared at the man she loved with every fibre of her being. 'So, you've pointed it out,' she said frostily. 'Feel better?'

'If you've taken it on board?'

'Oh, of course I have,' she said sarcastically. *'You* said it, after all.'

'Very funny.' He started the car engine. 'I'm only trying to look out for a friend. What's wrong with that?'

A grey bleakness settled on her. 'Nothing,' she said flatly. 'Thanks.'

'My pleasure.' He swung the car out of the tiny car park and on to the road, the darkness settling round them as only country darkness can.

Gina sat absolutely still, staring out of the windscreen, but without seeing the road in front of them. She felt shattered, emotionally, mentally and physically. The countless sleepless nights she'd endured over the last months as she'd agonised about Harry, the build up to today which she'd been dreading, the surprise invitation to have dinner with him—and not least their conversation throughout—had all served to bring her to a state of exhaustion. And of course all the wine she'd drunk had added to the overall stupor she was feeling, she thought drily, shutting her eyes and relaxing back against the seat.

She didn't know if she had actually dropped off or not when she became aware Harry had brought the car to a halt. She opened her eyes to find they were still deep in country and darkness. 'What is it?' she asked in some alarm as he began to reverse along the narrow lane they'd been travelling down.

'I'm not sure.' He glanced at her. 'Go back to sleep. This isn't a "I've run out of petrol" scenario.'

No, more's the pity. 'I never thought it was,' she said, her voice holding the ring of truth.

He reversed some hundred yards or so before pulling up. 'I saw a car start off from this point, and as we passed I saw a cardboard box by the side of the verge. I just want to look in it.'

'Look in it?'

He nodded, his voice somewhat sheepish as he said, 'I don't know why, but I've got a funny feeling about it. Stay in the car.' He opened the driver's door and climbed out, Gina following a second later. He was already bending over the box, and before he opened it he said, 'I said stay in the car.'

'Don't be silly.' She came round the bonnet. 'What's in it?'

'Hell.' He'd lifted the lid as she had been speaking, and now as she reached him and looked down she saw several tiny shapes moving and squeaking.

'Oh, Harry.' She clutched his sleeve, her eyes wide and horrified. 'Someone's dumped some puppies. Out here, in the middle of nowhere. How could they?'

'Quite easily, it seems,' he said grimly.

'Are they all right?' They were both crouching down by the box now, and could make out four puppies in the moonlight, wriggling about on folded newspaper and smeared with their own excrement. 'Oh, poor little things.' Gina was nearly crying. 'What are we going to do?'

Harry stood up. 'If I put the car blanket over your knee, could you have the box on your lap?'

'Of course. Anything, anything.' She couldn't believe someone had actually been so heartless as to put the puppies in a box, bring them to a deserted spot and just drive off. Not with all the sanctuaries that took unwanted litters these days.

Once they were back in the car again, the box on her lap, Gina peered in. 'They're very small,' she said shakily. 'Do you think there's something the matter with them?'

'Not with the racket they're making,' Harry said drily.

'Where are we going to take them?'

'There must be a vet somewhere around here, but I haven't

got a clue where. Look, my cleaner, Mrs Rothman, has dogs. Do you mind if we retrace our footsteps so to speak, and call on her? If nothing else she might be able to point us in the right direction. It'll mean you're late back, though. We're halfway back to your place.'

She hadn't realised they'd travelled so far. He was right. She *had* been asleep. 'It doesn't matter about being late. I haven't got to get up for work in the morning, remember? It'll be a cleaning and sorting day, so please do go and see your Mrs Rothman.' At least she'd have extra time with him. Not that she would have wished it at the cost of someone dumping the puppies, but still…

The puppies quietened down as the warmth of the car kicked in, but this had the effect of causing Gina to check them every couple of minutes, terrified they'd died. It was a huge relief when eventually they came to the small village, which was a stone's throw from Harry's secluded cottage, and drew up outside a neat terraced house.

Mrs Rothman proved to be a plump, motherly type who drew them into the warmth of her smart little house and insisted on her husband making them all a cup of tea while she oohed and ahhed over the contents of the box. 'Jack Russell crosses, by the look of it,' she announced once she'd inspected the puppies. 'All females. I bet whoever owned the bitch could get rid of the males but not the females. Happens like that sometimes. Or maybe it was just a huge litter.'

After cleaning the four little scraps up, Mrs Rothman lined the box with fresh newspaper while her husband mushed up some of their dog food. The puppies made short if somewhat messy work of it, after which Mrs Rothman popped them back in the box on top of an old towel. All four promptly went to sleep, clearly worn out by their unwelcome adventure.

'How old do you think they are?' Gina asked Mrs Rothman once she and Harry and the older couple were sitting sipping a second cup of tea in front of the blazing coal-fire, the puppies snuggled together in their box to one side of the hearth.

'Hard to tell, but they managed the food fairly well, so I'd say about six weeks or so, maybe seven or eight. They wouldn't have lasted long, left where they were. The nights can still be bitter.' Mrs Rothman turned to Harry. 'I know of a dog sanctuary not far from here. I'll give you the telephone number and address. They'll take them, I'm sure.'

Harry nodded. 'Thanks.'

One of the puppies began to squeak with little piping sounds, and Gina knelt down and lifted the squirming little body out of the box and onto her lap, stroking the silky fur until it went back to sleep again. Harry looked at her. 'I know,' he said. 'What sort of so-and-so could watch them grow to this stage and then leave them to die?'

It was exactly what she had been thinking, and his understanding brought tears to her eyes. That and the fact that she could see he too was deeply affected by the puppies' plight. As another one began to scrabble about, he fetched it out of the box and fussed over it until it settled on his lap.

Mrs Rothman plied them with more tea and a slice of her home-made seed cake, the fire crackled and glowed, the puppies slept, and the big grandfather clock in a corner of the room ticked on. It was cosy and warm, and Gina didn't want the moment ever to end.

And then Harry stood up. 'Right,' he said briskly, depositing his puppy back with her sisters. 'We've bothered you long enough. If you could let me have the address of the sanctuary, and a tin of dog food to tide them over until I drop them off, we'll be on our way.'

The brief interlude was over.

CHAPTER FOUR

HARRY was experiencing a whole host of emotions new to him, and none of them was welcome.

This evening had been a mistake of gigantic proportions from start to finish, he thought grimly as he and Gina made their goodbyes and walked to the car, the box tucked under his arm, and Gina carrying a bag containing several tins of dog food which Mrs Rothman insisted on pressing on them. And finding the puppies had been the icing on the whole damn cake.

Once he'd settled Gina in the car with the box on her lap, he walked round the bonnet to the driver's side.

Gina Leighton was beautiful, sweet, intelligent and heart-wrenchingly vulnerable, and a woman like that definitely didn't feature in his life. No way. With someone like Gina came commitment, responsibilities, ties, problems, and he was done with such things for good. He'd rather jump out of a plane without a parachute than ever consider travelling down that road again in a hundred lifetimes.

Once in the car, the puppies were yelping and mewing and scrabbling about in the box like crazy. 'I think they want their mum,' Gina said as he pulled on his seat belt. 'They must wonder what on earth is happening.'

He knew how they felt. Life had seemed so straightforward this morning. He'd thought that if she followed through on actually leaving—which he'd doubted till the last moment—than a warm goodbye, a little word about the watch and all she'd done for him and how grateful he was, and that would be that. Pleasant departure. Smiles all round. Simple. Clean.

So why had he asked her to have dinner with him? He went to start the car, but one of the puppies made a good attempt at using her sisters as a springboard to catapult on to the rim of the box, causing Gina to squeal before she said quickly, 'Sorry. She made me jump.'

'Nimble little blighters, aren't they?' Harry couldn't help smiling. Abandoned they might be. Quitters they most certainly were not.

'How are you going to travel all the way back from my place without them escaping in the car?' Gina tilted her head at him. 'Wouldn't it be simpler to take them to your house first and settle them somewhere, in the kitchen maybe, before you take me home? Or I could call a taxi. Or, failing that, I'll have them and take them to the sanctuary in the morning.'

He stared at her. None of the women he'd seen over the last few years would have been bothered about him in this situation—or the puppies come to that. Their prime concern would have been their clothes, hair, nails—in that order.

Then he shook himself mentally. He was probably being grossly unfair to the odd one or two. But only the odd one or two. 'It might be a good idea to nip home and put them in the utility room before I take you back,' he admitted. 'The boiler's in there, so it's always warm, and I've got some bits of wood in the garage I can use to pen them in and contain them. It'll give them room to be comfortable.'

She nodded. 'Do that, then.' She gave a weak giggle. 'But quickly. This big one is determined to make a break for it. She's obviously got leadership qualities.'

He smiled back at her. 'There's always one…'

As he started the car, Gina said, 'They're very sweet, aren't they? And that puppy smell. It's gorgeous.'

'It wasn't so gorgeous before Mrs Rothman cleaned them up,' Harry said practically.

She giggled again. He wondered why such a simple, innocent sound should make him so sexually excited. But then, if he was truthful, he'd been fighting the attraction this woman held for him since day one. Her soft, generous curves, the pale, ginger-speckled skin, that mass of silky hair that shone with myriad shades of red and copper when a shaft of sunshine touched it…

He swung the car on to the road, driving automatically, taken up with his thoughts. Sometimes he'd only had to walk into the office and see Gina sitting demurely at her desk to become as hard as a rock. If she knew the sexual fantasies he'd indulged in… The situation had annoyed him, irritated him on occasion, and certainly disturbed him not a little. It had also frightened the dickens out of him, he realised with a little shock of self-awareness.

If she'd been some brassy, hard-boiled piece it would all have been different. They could have enjoyed each other's bodies for as long as it had taken for the attraction to burn itself out. If she *was* attracted to him, that was. He frowned to himself. He'd thought there was a spark between them, but he might be fooling himself here. She'd always been the model of decorum. Damn it, it was an impossible situation. Which was why he had to admit to an initial feeling of relief when she'd said she was leaving.

Did he still feel relief? The car headlights caught a fox crossing the road in front of them, the animal's red fur and thick bushy tail disappearing into the shadows in the next instant.

He wasn't sure what he felt any more. He wanted to take her to bed, no question of that. He did not want a woman in his life permanently, set in concrete. And now she had revealed she was leaving because of a man which, he was forced to acknowledge, had thrown him somewhat. It had been a long time since he'd felt the nasty little gremlin of jealousy jabbing at him, but it had been there tonight. Their whole conversation had made him realise he didn't know Gina as well as he'd thought he did.

She'd said the man wasn't married, and he believed her. Gina wouldn't lie. But selfish he most certainly was. She had clearly been seeing him for a long time, and to let her walk away the way he had... A muscle contracted in his jaw. He'd love five minutes alone with the swine.

Another little squeal from Gina brought his eyes to her as she carefully pushed the biggest puppy down in the box again. 'We're nearly home,' he said, just as he swung the car off the road and on to his drive.

'Not before time.' She glanced at him as he drew up outside the cottage. 'How are you going to get them to the sanctuary in the morning? This box won't be any good.'

'I'll find something else. Failing that, a generous contri-bution to the place might persuade someone to come out and fetch them.'

Once in the cottage, he left Gina in the utility room with the puppies while he went to the garage and sorted out a couple of pieces of wood. When he returned, it was to find her kneeling on the tiles with the puppies scampering about her.

'They're so cute.' She glanced up at him, her eyes alight, and his stomach muscles registered her tousled softness. 'I thought they were all the same at first, but one's bigger than the others, and that one—' she pointed '—is smaller, and the other two are the same size.'

He nodded. 'There are two puddles on the floor,' he said.

She grimaced. 'They can't help that, they're only babies. Aren't you?' she added, lifting the smallest puppy into her arms and stroking the small, downy head. 'You're just little babies without your mum. Take no notice of moany old Harry.'

Harry fought down the urge to take her straight upstairs into his bed, and show her that there was pleasure and enjoyment and life after this rat who had let her down. Instead he positioned the wood so it effectively enclosed a third of the utility room, spreading a wad of newspapers in one corner in the hope further puddles would be kept to one spot. In another corner, he made a bed of towels.

In the meantime Gina had wandered into the kitchen and found a couple of saucers, one of which she filled with water and one with pulped dog-food. The minute she came back and put them down, the puppies were on them.

They stood for a good few minutes, watching them feed and explore their new surroundings, laughing at their antics.

They really were four little clowns, Harry thought as he watched the smallest puppy hanging onto the biggest one's tail by its teeth, before she was bowled over by one of the others. He'd grown up with dogs, but his parents had always chosen ones on the large side—Labradors and German Shepherds. These little mites were quite different, but seemed full of personality.

A stifled yawn at the side of him brought him back to the

realisation it was very late. He glanced at his watch and was amazed to see it was after one o'clock. 'Why don't you stay the night?' he said suddenly.

'What?'

Gina looked as startled as he felt, he told himself with dark humour. Where on earth had that invitation come from?

'Stay the night,' he repeated quietly. 'It's very late, and you're obviously dead beat. It seems sensible to stay here.'

He saw her mouth open and close. Something in the blue eyes made him sure she was going to refuse, and he added quickly, 'Mrs Rothman always keeps the guest-room bed aired and made up.'

He saw her swallow. 'I couldn't.'

'Why?'

'Why?' She appeared lost for words for a moment. 'Because I've loads to do in the morning.'

That wasn't the true story. His mouth dried. He'd bet his bottom dollar she'd arranged to see Lover Boy in the morning. Perhaps before this guy went into work. Damn it, couldn't she see this man was just using her? Perhaps he even expected a *bon-voyage* quickie. Without a shred of remorse for the crudity, he said carefully, 'You'll be home first thing—I've got to go to work, don't forget. Perhaps we could even drop the puppies off at this sanctuary on the way. That'd be a great help to me. In fact, I don't know how I'm going to manage it without you.'

She stared at him, her blue eyes dark with some emotion he couldn't fathom. She was probably weighing up the pain and pleasure of seeing Lover Boy compared to lending him a hand. Feeling he needed to press his cause, he said gently, 'Like you said, they're just little babies without their mum.

I'd hate for things to be more difficult than they need to be in the morning, and handling the four of them might prove a problem.' Deciding the end justified the means, he lied through his teeth as he added, 'You're used to dogs. I'm not.'

He saw her eyes narrow and realised he'd overdone it when she said, 'I thought you once told me your parents have always had dogs?'

They had had too many long chats over coffee breaks. Recovering quickly, he smiled. 'That's true, but I left home well over a decade ago, besides which these little things bear no resemblance to the sort of dogs I grew up with.'

'Mrs Rothman thought they were Jack Russell crossed with fox terriers, something like that. They're not exactly going to be tiny dogs.'

'But they're tiny now. And wriggly.' He wondered how far he could push the helpless-male scenario.

Gina glanced from him to the puppies, who were now quiet again, curled up together and looking pathetically helpless on their bed of towelling. Knowing her soft heart, he murmured, 'I'd hate to drop one of them.'

He saw her shut her eyes for an infinitesimal second. Whether it was with despair at his feebleness, or irritation at her predicament, he wasn't sure.

'All right,' she said ungraciously. 'I'll stay. But I need to be away first thing.'

Definitely expecting a visit from the rat. 'Sure thing. I don't want to be late. Busy day in front of me tomorrow, and Susan's not clued up on things like you are, although she's doing great.'

'Isn't she?' Gina said.

He could tell she was still mad at being trapped here,

because there was an edge to her voice. 'Want a cup of coffee or anything before we turn in?'

'Do you have any cocoa?'

'Cocoa?' he asked in surprise.

She flushed. 'I usually have a mug of milky cocoa in bed,' she said a trifle defensively.

Dampening down a mental image of Gina sitting up in bed stark-naked, her hair about her shoulders while her pink tongue licked at the froth on top of a mug of cocoa, Harry cleared his throat. His voice husky, he said, 'Sorry, no cocoa, but there's plenty of milk. How about a mug of hot milk instead—will that do?'

Gina nodded. He thought she looked very unhappy, and a mixture of anger and resentment slashed through him. Anger at this no-good character she was mixed up with. Resentment that someone he had thought so sensible and discriminating could allow themselves to be treated this way. The sooner she was well away from Yorkshire, the better. And yet he didn't want her to go. How much he didn't want her to go he hadn't realised until just this very moment.

Feeling confused, he led the way into the kitchen. Gina perched on a stool and watched him as he placed two mugs on the breakfast bar, and then poured a pint of milk into a saucepan. 'I'll join you in the milk,' he said obsequiously, aiming to get into her good books.

She nodded but didn't comment.

'And I appreciate you staying and helping with the puppies in the morning.'

His tone had been light, and he saw her rouse herself and stitch a smile on her face. 'I couldn't leave a mere male to cope with four offspring, now, could I?'

'True.' He'd never noticed just how superb her legs were before, but with her sitting on that stool he was probably seeing more of them than usual. Ignoring the stirring in his body, he said cheerfully, 'At least babies of the animal variety don't necessitate the use of nappies.'

'Nappies are no problem these days, even to the most incompetent man. There's no pins or folding them over in a certain way. It's all done for you. You just stick two tabs together, and job's a good 'un.'

'I'll take your word for it,' he said drily.

'Don't tell me—you believe nappy changing and the rest of it is women's work.'

'Actually, I don't,' he said mildly.

'No?' Her lifted eyebrows expressed her disbelief.

'No. If a couple decide to take on the enormous responsibility of bringing a new life into the world, then it's a joint decision all the way, or should be. Taking it as read that certain functions can only be performed by a mother—breast-feeding, for example...I think parenthood should be a fifty-fifty undertaking.' He poured the milk into the mugs.

'Oh.'

'You don't believe me?' he asked, turning to look at her.

'I didn't say that,' she protested quietly.

'You didn't have to. You had a funny look on your face.'

Her face cleared of all expression. 'I can't help my face,' she said with a weak smile. 'So you're a new-age man, then?'

'Ah, now that's a different question. I only said having a child should be a mutual undertaking, not that I'd consider it for myself.'

She nodded. 'No, of course not. You're strictly autonomous. You take what you want when you want, and then move on.'

He'd been in the process of handing a mug of milk to her, and for a moment his body stilled before carrying on. 'Is that how you see me?' he asked very quietly, a surge of emotion warning him he needed to control his temper.

She stared at him, her eyes unreadable. 'That's the picture you've presented to me.'

'I don't think so.'

Shrugging, she said, 'Perhaps you should listen to yourself some time, Harry.'

'I don't need to, damn it. I know what I am and how I think.' Or he had, up till this evening. Glaring at her, he growled, 'I'm not some sort of conscienceless stud, Gina.'

'That's fine, then,' she said flatly, her expression inscrutable.

He didn't know if he wanted to shake her or kiss her, he thought rawly, fighting down an anger he would never have acknowledged had its roots in hurt. 'We've known each other for twelve months, and for most of that time we've met every working day. We've talked and laughed and shared about our lives, and you can honestly say you see me like that?' he asked intensely.

She hesitated, putting down her mug and letting her eyelashes sweep down over her eyes for some moments, before she looked at him again. Her voice soft, she said, 'I don't want to make you angry, Harry, but I think most of the sharing—at least regarding past history—came from me. And that's fine, I wouldn't want to force a confidence from anyone, but you didn't really give anything of yourself. And before you fire off at me, think about it.'

He sat back on his stool, genuinely amazed.

'You're a very private man, and after what you told me about Anna and everything I can understand why you don't want to be involved with anyone. But...' She cleared her throat. 'Sex doesn't equate to much the way you view it. Fact.'

He stated the obvious. 'The women I take to bed know the score.'

'Yes, I know. You've already explained that.'

Silence hung between them like a pulsing entity. He was aware his body was taut with the effort to appear relaxed and unconcerned, and suddenly he threw pretense to one side and said simply, 'I don't like the way you see me, Gina.'

Something in her face changed, and her voice was throaty when she murmured, 'I'm sorry, I shouldn't have said all that. Your life is your own, and I've got no right to criticise one way or the other.'

Was she thinking of this man and the mess she'd made of her own life? So swiftly that it surprised him, his anger was gone, replaced with a desire to comfort her. 'You're probably closer to me than anyone else on earth,' he said quietly. 'So of course you have the right to state your opinion.'

He saw her face contract as though with pain, and felt a growing fury towards the unknown man who had broken her heart, and a surge of protectiveness. 'You're too good for him, you know that, don't you?'

'What?'

Her eyes widened in confusion, and he saw she hadn't followed him. Slightly embarrassed, he said gently, 'You'll meet someone, Gina, and all this will be like a bad dream.'

Her pent-up breath escaped in a little sigh. Shaking her head, she whispered, 'I'm not banking on it. You didn't meet someone else. And anyway, we were talking about you, not me.' She drained the last of her milk and slid off the stool, wisps of hair about her cheeks, and smudges of tiredness staining the pale skin beneath the dark pools of her eyes. 'Could you show me my room?'

A shiver of desire flickered through his blood. He wanted her. More badly than he had wanted any woman. Possibly because he had waited longer for her than anyone else. But, no, it wasn't just that. If it had been just that it would have been easily dealt with. But this was Gina. He not only wanted her but he—His mind came to an abrupt stop, a door slamming shut. He liked her, he finished silently. As a friend. And you didn't take friends to bed.

He stood up, managing a creditable smile. 'Sure.'

When they reached the stairs Harry stood aside for her to precede him, his eyes on her very nicely rounded bottom as he followed her to the landing. By the time they reached her room, he was deep in the grip of an erotic fantasy that was causing problems with a certain part of his anatomy.

'It's lovely.' Gina glanced round the room after he had opened the door and waved her through. She turned, smiling politely. 'Goodnight, then.'

Struggling with his self-induced state of arousal, Harry said thickly, 'Goodnight, Gina. You'll find towels and toiletries and so on in the *en suite;* Mrs Rothman likes to keep everything ready just in case. I'll give you a knock twenty minutes or so before breakfast, OK?'

'Thank you.' She hesitated, and then said in a rush, 'And thank you for offering me a bed for the night. I didn't sound very grateful down there, did I?'

'Why should you? It's you doing me the favour, not the other way round.' Actually he was doing her a massive favour in keeping her from the love rat, but she'd never see it even if he came clean. He watched her rub her small, cute nose, something she did when she was uncertain or wary. He realised there were lots of little things he knew about her.

'Well, thanks anyway,' she repeated.

She was clearly waiting for him to go, so why did he feel glued to the spot? Softly, he said, 'Sleep well, Gina.' And, even knowing it was a mistake, he bent forward and brushed her lips with his.

As kisses went it was fleeting, but the scent of her, the softness of her half-parted lips, produced a reaction that rocked him to his core. Desire, primitive and raw, shot through him and it took all of his control to turn away and walk towards the stairs. He heard the door close as he reached them, and stopped, closing his eyes and resting one hand on the banister as he drew in a hard, shaky breath.

Crazy. Everything about tonight was crazy. Crazy conversations. Crazy feelings. *Crazy situation.*

It would be different in the morning, in the cold, bright light of day. He opened his eyes, his face hardening. It would have to be.

CHAPTER FIVE

GINA didn't know when she became aware that the sound in her dream was actually real. She lay in a state of muzzy half-awareness for a while, unable to come round fully, and then sat up in bed as reality hit. She was in Harry's home, in his bed. Well, not in *his* bed, but in one of his beds.

Switching on the bedside lamp, she reached for her watch which she'd placed on the little cabinet earlier. Half-past three. And she knew she'd still been awake at three o'clock. She'd probably only had twenty minutes of sleep; no wonder she felt so out of it.

It was the puppies. The sound that had woken her was still there, a distant whining and yelping, and now she tiredly brushed the hair out of her eyes and reached for the towelling robe she'd found on the back of the *en suite* door. She'd have to go and see what was the matter. Harry was probably a typical man; once he was asleep nothing short of an earthquake would stir him. Her father could sleep through anything.

She sat on the edge of the bed for a few moments once she'd pulled the robe on, feeling distinctly light-headed. Probably due to the storm of weeping that had ensued once she'd been by herself earlier, she thought dismally. And crying while trying not to make a sound had given her a headache. She'd hunt about for some aspirin while she was downstairs, but first she'd better see what was what in the utility room.

Considering she'd been a stranger to them a few short hours ago, the puppies gave her a rapturous welcome when she padded into the utility room, tumbling over each other in an effort to reach her. Laughing despite her tiredness, she changed the top layer of newspaper, where they'd obligingly done their duties, and then prepared some more food which they polished off in record time.

'You were hungry.' She looked down at them as they moved round the now-empty saucer, small pink tongues still licking for traces of food.

The smallest puppy made her way over to her, beginning to nibble at her toes as the others scrabbled round for attention. 'You want some fuss, is that it?' Curling up on the wad of towelling Harry had put down, Gina allowed the four little warm bodies to make their way on to her lap. 'Missing Mum and home, I suppose,' she murmured as she stroked their furry heads. 'Although, if you did but know it, you're far better off here. Who knows what would have happened to you if Harry hadn't noticed that box?'

'It's ten to four.'

Harry's voice from the doorway brought her head jerking up so fast, she heard her neck crack. He was standing leaning against the wall; she didn't know how long he'd been watching her.

'I know.' Her mouth had gone dry. He was dressed in dark pyjama-bottoms and a black-cotton robe which was hanging loose. His thickly muscled chest was black with body hair, and

his hair was tousled and falling over his brow. He looked...
magnificent. 'It was the puppies,' she mumbled feverishly.
'They were crying. They were hungry.'

'You should have ignored them.'

'I couldn't.' The virile masculinity just feet away reminded
her she was stark naked under her robe. She wanted to tighten
the belt, but with her arms full of puppies she couldn't.
'Anyway, you came down too, I wasn't the only one.'

'True.'

He didn't elaborate as to whether she had disturbed him or
he'd been awake anyway. She was aware he was looking at
her with unconcealed scrutiny, and she wished she'd taken the
time to at least brush her hair. She'd scrubbed at her face
before she had gone to sleep in an effort to remove the last of
the make-up her tears hadn't washed away; she bet her nose
was shining like Rudolph's. When the smallest puppy made
a valiant attempt to bury herself inside the top of her robe,
thereby causing it to gape a little, Gina hastily tipped the four
of them off her lap and pulled the belt tight.

Carefully rising to her feet, she said nervously, 'I'm sorry
if I woke you.'

'You didn't.'

She expected him to move from the doorway as she approached, and when he didn't she stopped a foot or so away,
praying the trembling deep inside wasn't visible.

'You've washed your face,' he said slowly.

'Yes.' She didn't need to be reminded of what she must
look like.

'I can see your freckles better,' he observed, as though that
had been the whole point of the exercise.

She wrinkled her nose. 'Don't remind me.'

'I like freckles, especially with blue eyes and reddish-gold hair.'

'Titian,' she corrected automatically, glad he hadn't said 'ginger'.

'Titian,' he repeated softly. 'But your eyelashes are dark brown. And thick.'

She'd always been glad about that. It was one of the few things about herself she liked. She tried to think of something to say, something witty and light, and failed utterly. It was the look on his face. He was staring at her as though she was a woman. Which she was, of course. It was just that he had never noticed before.

But this was Harry. The warning screamed through her head. Harry, the self-determining. Harry, the mother and father of non-involvement. Harry, who didn't want a woman in his life other than to take care of his sexual needs. And that was what was happening right now, or would happen if she let it. She loved him too much to become just another notch on his bedpost. She wouldn't be able to stand it when he dropped her off later in the morning with a cheery wave and a casual goodbye. Because that's what he'd do.

Lowering her head, she tightened the belt of her robe still more. 'Fancy a cup of tea?' she said, hearing herself with a touch of hysteria. Tea. *Tea?*

There was a brief pause, and then his voice came cool and easy. 'If there's toast to go with it. I'm starving.'

So was she, but not for tea and toast. But she'd had her chance and blown it, she thought with burning regret.

The puppies had settled down again, all but the smallest, who now had her two front paws scrabbling at the wood barrier as she whimpered pitifully. Glad of the diversion, Gina retraced her footsteps and lifted the little scrap into her arms, whereupon the puppy immediately snuggled against her and shut its eyes.

'What?' she challenged as she caught Harry's eyes. 'The poor little thing's due some cuddles after all she's been through.' She was also a welcome third-party if they were going to indulge in tea and toast.

'Will you spoil your children, too?' he murmured smokily, amusement colouring his voice.

'With cuddles, if they're frightened or upset?' she said tartly, ignoring the pang her heart gave. She would never have children because they couldn't be Harry's. 'Absolutely.'

Once in the kitchen with the puppy cradled against her chest, she didn't try to clamber onto a stool, but stood and watched him as he filled the kettle and then placed two slices of bread in the toaster. 'Mind if I go through to the sitting room?' she asked as casually as she could. 'My feet are cold on these tiles.'

'Be my guest. I'll bring the tray through in a minute or two.'

There was a dark stubble on his chin. He was as unlike the perfectly groomed, smooth operator of daylight hours as the man in the moon. And a hundred times more dangerous.

Tingling with something she didn't want to put a name to, Gina made her way to the sitting room and chose a big, plumpy chair to curl up in, carefully positioning her feet under her and making sure the robe was discreetly in place. The puppy stirred briefly and then settled itself again as Gina gently stroked the plump little body. She gazed down at the sleeping animal, a sense of surrealism taking hold.

How on earth had she come to be in this position? Practically naked—apart from one piece of cloth—in Harry's house at four o'clock in the morning, with him equally partially clothed making tea and toast in the kitchen? Worse, with her hair probably resembling a bird's nest, and her face all shiny and devoid of even the tiniest touch of make-up. Even in her wildest dreams—and there had been more than a few where Harry was concerned—she wouldn't have been able to come up with this scenario.

She'd had fantasies, more than she could remember, but they had all featured her perfectly made up and looking ravishing, and Harry suddenly realizing the error of his ways and falling at her feet in adoration before whisking her off to bed. After that, it had been roses round the door and a ring the size of a golf ball.

She sighed. Impossible dreams. Impossible happy-ever-after. Impossible *man*. Still, at least the 'roses round the door' bit was in place. She smiled ruefully. And this was one hundred per cent the sort of house made for a family—babies, children. Harry's babies. She shut her eyes, her heart actually paining her.

Harry had made it clear he would never consider matrimony again, let alone becoming a father. He was now a ruthless bachelor, married to freedom, and only dating women who were happy to embrace their temporary place in his life gracefully. A wife and babies didn't come into the equation anywhere. Perhaps it was a blessing she wasn't his type. If he had fancied her she wouldn't have been able to resist for long, and a brief affair would have left her in a worse emotional mess than she was now.

Hearing his footsteps, she arranged her face into an acceptable expression, even managing a smile as her eyes met his. He was carrying a tray on which reposed two mugs of tea and a large plateful of buttered toast, along with several preserves. 'You have been busy,' she said lightly, thinking how unfair it was that men could look drop-dead gorgeous when they were at their most dishevelled, whereas women merely looked bedraggled. At least, Harry could. She didn't know about other men, never having spent the night with one.

'Dinner seems a long time ago.' He grinned at her, putting the tray down and gesturing towards the puppy in her lap. 'She's adopted you. Sensible puppy.'

Gina grew hot. It was absolutely stupid to be so affected by the soft warmth in his voice, but she couldn't help it, in spite of knowing this was Harry in flirt mode. It didn't mean anything, not to him at least.

Drawing on the iron self-control that had got her through the last months since that Christmas kiss, she said flatly, 'Hardly sensible. I'm leaving at the weekend for good, and a puppy definitely doesn't feature on my agenda.'

He handed her her tea and offered the plate of toast. She took a triangle, not because she really wanted it, but more to give herself something to do. She had never felt so vulnerable and exposed in all her life.

'You're sure you want to go?' he said after a moment or two had ticked by.

Want to go? She had never wanted anything less. 'Absolutely,' she said firmly. To add weight to her words, she looked him straight in the eye, steeling herself to show no emotion as she said, 'And we had this conversation during dinner.'

He nodded. 'I wasn't convinced then either.'

'I thought I'd made it clear, I need to leave Yorkshire.'

'Ah, but *need* isn't necessarily *want*.' There was a significant little silence as he fixed her with a hard, meaningful look. 'You'll be miserable in London,' he declared authoritatively.

'Thanks a bunch. Some friend you are.' Sarcasm was a great hiding place.

'You told me I wasn't a friend.' His eyes mocked her. 'What exactly am I, Gina? How do you see me?'

She didn't like the way this conversation was going. He was playing games, probably just to kill a few minutes as far as he was concerned.

Fighting for composure, she took a deep breath and lifted her head. She smiled thinly. 'You're my boss's son.'

'*Ex*-boss's son,' he returned drily. 'OK, what else?'

'You're very good at what you do—accomplished, experienced.'

'Thank you,' he said gravely. 'What else?'

'Does there have to be more?'

'I should damn well hope so.' He paused and studied her face. 'As a man,' he said quietly. 'A person. Do you like me?'

'You shouldn't have to ask that, we've worked together for just over a year,' she said weakly.

'My point exactly. And I would have termed us as friends. You, on the other hand, would not. So I'm beginning to realise I don't know how your mind works, which means I perhaps don't know the real Gina at all. In fact, I'm sure I don't. I didn't know you had a lover somewhere in the background, for example.'

His eyes were tight on her, questioning. Rallying herself, and aware she was as taut as piano wire, she said coolly, 'Forgive me, Harry, but I don't remember you discussing your personal life, either. Any part of it. Whereas you know about my family, friends—'

'Not all of them, obviously.'

Ignoring that, she continued, 'My childhood, my youth, my time at university— I've discussed all that—whereas you've been…guarded.'

There was an awkward silence. He stared at her, all amusement gone. 'Yes.' His voice sounded odd. 'I have. I was. But for what it's worth I've never told anyone the full story about Anna before. Apart from my parents at the time I left the country, that is. Does that count for anything?'

She looked down at the toast in her hand. Her heart was a tight ball of cotton wool in her throat, choking her. 'I didn't mean I expected you *should* have necessarily talked to me, just that you can hardly take me to task for the same thing.'

The silence stretched longer this time. 'I appreciate that,' he said at last.

It was still quite dark outside the windows; the rest of the world was fast asleep. It added to the curious sense of unreality which had taken over her. The puppy stirred in her sleep, grunting and snuffling, before becoming quiet as Gina began to stroke her again.

'So you can't be persuaded not to go?'

His voice had been husky, and as Gina raised her head she saw his face was dark, brooding. 'Of course not,' she said bleakly. 'It's not feasible. Everything's been arranged. I've got to move out of my flat Saturday morning; I wouldn't even have anywhere to live.'

'You could use my spare room till you find something else.'

There was something in his eyes that made her feel suddenly light-headed and treacherously weak. Painfully, she said, 'I've got a job in London, a flat. I couldn't let people down. Anyway, the reason I wanted to leave in the first place is unchanged.' It was. It *was*. This sudden interest on his part was all about sex, plain and simple. But it wouldn't be simple where she was concerned. It would be horribly complicated.

'I hadn't been to sleep when I heard you come downstairs,' he said suddenly.

Her throat felt dry. She took a sip of the tea before she could say, 'I was worried I'd woken you.' She was prevaricating; she knew it.

It appeared Harry knew it too. 'Don't you want to know why?'

She couldn't answer, and it was a moment before he said softly, 'It was the thought of you just a couple of doors away.'

'I'm sorry.' Inane, but the best she could do.

'I like you, Gina.'

The atmosphere in the room had changed several times in the last minutes, now it was thick with an electricity that quivered in the air.

She couldn't speak, her only movement her hand on the puppy's silky fur as she continued to stroke it, her eyes fixed on the little body.

'I realised tonight I don't want you to leave Yorkshire.'

Taking all her courage into her hands, she raised her face and looked straight at him. She had to kill this stone-dead, right now. The agonies of mind she'd endured over this man had brought her to the inevitable conclusion that she had to walk away from him, and that had not changed. Sooner or later she'd be old news. The only difference was, if she went sooner rather than later, she would still have her self-respect. 'I don't do one-night stands, Harry,' she said flatly, her pain making her stiff.

'I wasn't talking about a one-night stand.'

'Yes, you were.' She moistened dry lips. 'Perhaps a series of them, but essentially that's all an affair would be to you. You told me yourself, that's all you can offer a woman.'

She saw anger flare in the beautiful grey eyes. 'I don't want the full domestic-scene, admittedly, but that doesn't mean I'm quite the heartless so-and-so you're painting. I'd like to show you that you can find fun and happiness after this guy, if nothing else.'

'How noble.' Suddenly she, too, was furiously angry. 'Thanks, but no thanks.'

'You're not listening to me.'

'Oh, I am.' If the puppy hadn't been in her lap, she would have liked to empty her mug of tea straight over his unfeeling head. 'Believe me, I am. Out of the goodness of your heart, you'll take pity on me long enough to take me to bed a few times. About right?'

His face a picture, Harry said, 'I don't know what's got into you.'

'Into *me*?' He took the biscuit, he really did. 'Harry, if all I was looking for was sex, I could get that anywhere. I'm not quite so desperate, OK? I have to engage my heart and my mind as well as my body.'

'I know that.' He glared at her. 'I know that about you. But we get on, we get on really well in my opinion, and I don't think you find me totally repulsive. Do you?' he added a trifle uncertainly.

It was nearly her undoing. Her fingers holding onto the puppy hard enough for it to raise its head and squeak protestingly, Gina said tightly, 'Harry, I'm sure ninety nine out of a hundred women would take you up on your offer, but I'm the hundredth. Can we leave it at that?'

'You're determined to let this man ruin your life? Force you away from your home and friends, everything you're used to? And don't tell me you want to go, because we both know it isn't like that. You're running away, taking the coward's way out.'

'What about you?' she demanded, her blue eyes flashing. 'Isn't this slightly hypocritical? You've let Anna turn you into someone else, someone you were never meant to be. Oh, you can prattle on about life changing and shaping us and all that waffle when it applies to you; that sounds quite lofty. But, where *I* am concerned, it's ruining my life. Well, let me tell you, Harry, I don't intend to let my life be ruined, but I think yours has been. You've become selfish and shallow, without anything of substance to offer a woman beyond the pleasure of your company in bed. And that wouldn't be enough for me, not by a long chalk.'

She stopped, aware she'd said far more than she had intended. The silence seemed to stretch for ever until Harry finally spoke. 'I take it that's a no, then,' he said acidly.

Her eyes snapped up to his, but she could read nothing in his expressionless gaze. His face had become the bland, smooth mask he adopted at times, a mask she hated. It spoke of withdrawal and control, and it was forged in steel. 'I'm sorry, I shouldn't have expressed myself quite that way, but you shouldn't have pushed me.' Her voice was calm now, but a part of her was dying inside. For it to end like this—it couldn't be worse.

'I see. It's all my fault.' He nodded. 'I had no idea your opinion of me was so low.'

She watched him stretch out a hand for another piece of toast, as though the opinion he'd spoken of mattered not a jot. Slowly she took a sip of her tea. It was cold. Like his heart, she thought, a little hysterically. 'It's an opinion formed from the image you project,' she countered shakily.

He seemed to consider this for a moment, his features in shadow as he leant back in his chair. Gina was glad she could tilt her head and let her hair fall in a curtain as she concentrated on the puppy; the angle of her chair cause the light to fall directly on her, and she needed some help in hiding her turbulent emotions.

After a while, when he remained silent, she sighed inwardly. This was awful. So much was going on in this room that the air was crackling. She'd offended and annoyed him, and she couldn't take this deafening silence one more moment.

She opened her mouth to speak, but he was there a second before her. 'The image isn't all of me,' he said gruffly.

She knew that. The man she loved was a hugely complicated human being. Enigmatic and cold, funny and warm. The sort of man who could slaughter an opponent on the telephone with a few well chosen, crisp words, and yet who would stop to rescue four little breathing pieces of flotsam and jetsam the world had abandoned.

The first time she'd accepted her heart was irrevocably his was when she'd discovered he'd delved into his own pocket to pay the rent arrears of a house one of their ex-employees lived in. The man had a drug problem, and had worked one day in five in the couple of months before Harry had sacked him. When the man's wife had come to the works hoping to find him—and it had transpired he'd been even less at home that he'd been at work and she hadn't seen him for weeks—Harry had taken her home to find three young children were also in the equation. He'd paid the rent arrears, found the woman a job at the works, and arranged for nursery care for the children.

She bit her lip and tried to control the tears that were threatening. 'I didn't think it was,' she said. 'But you have to understand where I'm coming from, Harry. In the matter of love, relationships, togetherness—call it what you will—we're aeons apart. I—I don't want to waste any more time on hopeless liaisons.' That was the truth at least. 'I—I want my heart to be my own again, and I'm the sort of woman who couldn't sleep with anyone, even once, without being involved. It…well it wouldn't be a fun thing for me. At least, it being fun wouldn't be enough without love as well.'

She saw him nod. 'I'd like to know his name, just to be able to tell him what a damn fool he is,' he said so softly she could barely hear him.

Gina gulped. 'I'm a fool as well. I knew what I was getting into but I couldn't find the brake. I don't think I ever will. That's why I need to move away. I don't want to become someone I don't like.'

'You love him very much.'

It was a statement, not a question, but Gina answered anyway. 'Yes, I do.'

'Life's not all it's cut out to be at times, is it?'

It was fine until he'd come along. The puppy had never really settled since she'd half-strangled it, and now it began to squirm with definite intent. 'I'll put her back with her sisters.' She stood up, aware of him following her as she walked through to the utility room.

Outside the window, the first pink streaks of dawn were beginning to creep into a charcoal sky, and the dawn chorus was in full song. It was going to be another beautiful spring day.

After depositing her charge with the other sleeping puppies, Gina left the utility room and walked through to the kitchen where Harry was waiting for her. 'We might get in an hour's kip before the alarm goes,' he said, half-smiling. 'Or they wake up.'

She tried to match his easy manner. 'I don't have an alarm.'

'I'll bang on your door, don't worry.'

When they reached the landing, he paused with her outside her room, his voice soft as he said, 'I didn't want to hurt you, Gina.'

'What?' For an awful minute she thought he had guessed.

'By rubbing salt in the wound about this guy.'

Her limbs turning fluid, she managed to say fairly coherently, 'You didn't,' as relief flooded her.

'And you're not a coward. Far from it.'

She had leant against the wall when he'd first spoken, needing its support, and he'd propped one arm over her head, his fingers splayed next to her hair. She was aware of the faint lemony smell of shower gel, the same make as she had found in her *ensuite*, presumably, but mixed with Harry's body chemicals it was altogether more spicy, sexier. Summoning brain power from some deep reserve, she murmured, 'Leaving is more an act of self-survival, Harry.'

He nodded. 'I'm beginning to understand that. And if you need a friend, any time, any place, call me, OK? I'll be there.'

He wasn't a man to offer empty platitudes. Touched and very near to bursting into tears, she didn't dare to attempt to speak. Instead she leaned forward on tiptoe and kissed him swiftly on his cheek.

She heard his quickly indrawn breath, but he remained quite still as she slipped under his arm and opened her bedroom door. It was only when it was shut that she let out her breath, her heart pounding.

She stood frozen inside the room, her ears straining to hear any sound from the landing, but it was absolutely silent. After some minutes she walked over to her bed, the tears streaming down her face, but her mind too weary to struggle with the reason why. With the robe still intact she pulled the duvet over her, shutting her eyes as the tears continued to seep under the lids.

She fell asleep within a minute, her face damp and salty, and her body and mind utterly spent.

CHAPTER SIX

HARRY stood for some time on the landing, shaken to the core. Which was crazy, he told himself vehemently once his racing heart had begun to steady. It had hardly been a kiss, for crying out loud. And Gina had been quite unmoved, sailing into her room and shutting the door as though she hadn't just turned his world upside down.

No. No, it hadn't been.

Yes, it had.

He groaned softly, raking the hair out of his eyes with an unsteady hand and padding to his own room at the far end of the shadowed landing. Once inside he began to pace the floor, his brows drawn together in a ferocious scowl.

What the hell had happened out there? And downstairs; why had he asked her to stay around when he'd promised himself that was the last thing he'd do? What would he have done if she'd agreed to his ridiculous proposal? And it *was* ridiculous, however you looked at it. She was besotted by some bozo who had messed her around for months, if not years, and she was leaving him because she didn't want a no-strings-attached relationship.

So what did he do? Harry asked himself grimly. He offered

her the same sort of deal. No wonder she'd looked at him as if he was mad.

He walked over to the window, looking down at the sleeping garden where the first blackbird was singing its heart out, and then raised his eyes to the pink-streaked sky. The dawn of a new day. In the aftermath of his breakup with Anna, his mother had told him she viewed each dawn as the start of the rest of her life. The past, with all its regrets and mistakes, was gone and unalterable, the present and the future were virgin territory to make of what you would. He'd appreciated she'd been trying to help, but he'd been so full of anger and bitterness he'd dismissed her ideology as coming from one who had never really had anything to contend with. He had been arrogant then. He was still arrogant, perhaps. Gina would say there was no 'perhaps' about it.

Smiling darkly, he turned from the window and looked over the room. When he had bought the house he'd had it redecorated throughout before he had moved in, and his room and *en suite* were a mixture of dark and light coffee-and-cream. No frills, no fuss, but luxurious, from the huge, soft billowy bed to the massive plasma TV and integrated hi-fi system. Everything just the way he liked it. His *life* was the way he liked it.

Harry dragged his hand over his face. Or it had been, up until twelve months ago, when he had walked into his father's office and a blue-eyed, red-haired girl had given him the sweetest smile he'd ever seen. Twelve months. Twelve months of disturbing thoughts and dreams, of dating women he didn't want to date but who would provide a distraction and give his body some relief.

He shook his head, beginning to pace again. Put like that,

it sounded mercenary, even seedy. He'd used those other women, he couldn't deny it. But they'd been happy enough with his conditions, he reasoned in the next breath.

But with Gina there could be no conditions. He caught his breath, stopping dead and groaning softly. He'd known all along she was a till-death-do-us-part woman. What he hadn't allowed for was that he would find it so hard to let her slip out of his life, or that she was desperately in love with another man. His arrogance again. He grimaced sourly. He'd taken her completely for granted, he supposed.

No suppose about it. The retort was so loud in his head, it was as though someone else had spoken it.

He hadn't even considered she was involved with someone. She had always chattered with him so openly he'd felt he knew all about her, from cradle to present day. And all the time there had been another man in the background. Someone she'd laughed and talked and slept with. His stomach muscles clenched.

Was he jealous?

You bet your sweet life he was. And, however he tried to dress it up as anger at this guy who had taken her heart and then carelessly broken it, it was more the picture of them in bed together he couldn't take.

So if—*if*—she'd let him provide a shoulder to cry on, what would that mean? Suppose—*just* suppose—it led to more. It wouldn't be right to assume she could cope with yet further goodbyes. Would it?

No, he knew damn well it wouldn't. His stomach muscles unclenched, but only to turn over in a sick somersault. He'd be taking a darn sight more than he was ready to give. He had been young and idealistic when he'd got involved with Anna;

that was his only excuse for the gigantic mess that had ensued. He only had to shut his eyes to recall the trapped helplessness he'd felt then, the overwhelming panic and despair.

But Gina wasn't Anna. In the twelve months he'd known her, she'd been sweet and funny, serious and determined, honest—painfully so at times, at least where he was concerned—and forthright. But never, *never* manipulative. And 'cruel' wasn't in her vocabulary. She was also as sexy as hell without even knowing it. He'd seen work on the factory floor slow right down when she'd walked through, and some of those guys had had their tongues hanging out.

Using the sort of expletive that would have shocked even the most worldly veteran, Harry thumped his fist into the palm of his hand. He had to get a handle on how he was feeling. Confusion wasn't an option here. Perhaps that was the answer—feeling like this was turning him into someone he didn't recognise, so the obvious, the practical thing to do was to let her walk away and then get on with his life. Out of sight, out of mind. It had worked with all the others since Anna.

Something inside twisted, and he answered the feeling with an irritable growl deep in his throat. Enough. He needed some fresh air to clear his head. You couldn't beat straight-forward logic, and it hadn't let him down in the past. Outside, with no distractions, he could *think*.

He took a deep breath and tried to relax, glancing at his watch. Another couple of hours before he needed to wake her and get going. He had to get himself sorted and back on track in that time.

He pulled on some clothes without bothering to shower first, leaving the room swiftly and making his way downstairs on silent feet. Once in the garden, he paused. His original intention had been to go for a walk, but sitting out here would do as well.

Breathing in the sharp, scented air, he walked to a wooden bench set at an angle to the dry-stone wall that surrounded the grounds. From there he had a perfect view of the house, which slumbered in the early-morning light. Somewhere close by a wood pigeon was cooing, a little rustle at the base of the wall telling him the tiny harvest mice he'd noticed a few times running up and down the old stone were about. No doubt there were myriad nests deep in the crevices, where generations of the enchantingly pretty creatures had been born. This whole place—the house, the garden, the surrounding countryside— spoke of permanence, he realised suddenly. Subconsciously, had that been one of the reasons which had attracted him to the property when he'd first seen it?

He frowned, not liking the idea. It didn't fit into how he saw himself. Like everything else that had happened in the last twenty-four hours, it was acutely disturbing, in fact.

Gradually his revolving thoughts began to slow down as the peace of his surroundings took over. The sky lightened still more, garden birds beginning the job of hunting for breakfast, and the flock of sparrows that had residence in the privet hedge separating the swimming pool and tennis court from the rest of the garden squabbled raucously as they went about their business.

It was cold; he could see his breath fanning in a white cloud in front of him when he breathed out. But still he sat on in the burgeoning morning, his mind clearer than it had been for a long, long time.

He loved her. He'd loved her for months, but had been too damn stubborn to admit it to himself because it was the last thing he'd wanted or needed in his life. And now the laugh was on him, because even if he had declared himself she would have told him—gently and kindly, because that was Gina's way—she was in love with someone else. Height of irony.

It was over an hour later that he rose to his feet, and with measured footsteps went into the house.

CHAPTER SEVEN

WHEN Gina awoke from an extremely decadent and satisfying dream featuring her, Harry and a bowl of whipped-chocolate ice-cream, it was to bright sunlight. She stretched as she opened heavy eyes, and then realised what had woken her as another knock sounded at the bedroom door: Harry's alarm call.

Her voice husky with a mixture of sleep and remembered passion, she called, 'It's OK, I'm awake,' and then squeaked with surprise with the door opened and Harry strode in carrying a tray.

He seemed unaware that she'd hastily dragged the duvet up to her chin, owing to the fact the robe had worked itself open and under her back, smiling as he said, 'I didn't know if you're a tea or coffee girl, so I brought both.'

Her voice higher-pitched than usual, Gina said, 'Either, thanks, but you needn't have bothered.'

'No bother.'

He placed the tray on the bedside cabinet and gazed at her from the advantage of being bright-eyed and bushy-tailed. He was very big and very dark in the pastel-coloured room, and his sheer magnetism detracted from the realisation that he wasn't dressed in his normal suit and tie for a moment or two. When she could get her breath, Gina said carefully, 'Are we taking the puppies and then coming back here?' as she took in his black jeans and casual blue shirt.

He didn't answer this directly. With a smile that turned the grey eyes smoky-warm, he said, 'Drink your "either" and then come downstairs when you're ready. There's no rush.'

She stared at him. Something was different. Or was it just the casual clothes? Still clutching the duvet to her chest with one hand for all the world like a Victorian maiden, she brushed the hair out of her eyes with the other. 'What time is it?'

He glanced at the gold watch on his wrist. 'Eleven o'clock,' he said calmly.

'Eleven o'clock?' She struggled into a sitting position, which wasn't easy with the robe and the need to remain decent hampering her. 'It can't be. What about work?'

'You don't work, or at least not till Monday.'

'I mean *you*.'

'I decided to give work a miss today.'

'You've never given work a miss in all the time I've known you,' she said, astounded.

'Then perhaps it's high time I did.'

'What about your father? And Susan? She's still settling in, and—'

'Will be fine. She's that sort of woman,' he said quietly.

Well, that was true at least. Unable to take in that half the day had gone already, Gina stared up at him. His eyes were dark, unblinking, as they watched her; his slightly uneven mouth curved in a wry smile that told her her bewilderment was plain on her face. She hoped her bout of crying the night before didn't show in pink-rimmed eyes. Gathering her wits, she swallowed hard. 'Are the puppies all right? You haven't taken them already, have you?'

'The puppies are fine,' he said soothingly. 'I had them out on the lawn for half an hour earlier. That was hectic,' he added drily. 'They can shoot off like exocet missiles when they want to.'

She wished she didn't love him so much. Controlling her voice with some difficulty, Gina forced a smile as she said, 'You should have woken me earlier to help.'

'You needed your sleep.'

What did that mean—that the bags under her eyes could carry potatoes, or was he just being thoughtful? Deciding it was probably better she didn't know, Gina wondered how long he was going to continue standing watching her. 'Have you phoned the animal sanctuary?'

'No,' he said calmly.

She waited for him to elaborate and, when he didn't, began to feel acutely uncomfortable. It was all right for him standing there, fully clothed and showered and shaved. She felt like something the cat wouldn't bother to drag in.

His open-necked shirt showed the springy black hair of his chest, and his jeans were tight across the hips. The flagrant masculinity that was such a part of his attraction was even stronger today, and more than a little intimidating. Her mouth dry and her heart racing, she decided to take the bull by the horns. 'I'll see you downstairs in a little while, shall I?' she said pointedly.

'Violet-blue.'

'Sorry?'

'Your eyes are the colour of the wild violets that grow close to the stone wall in my garden,' he said very softly. 'Beautiful little flowers, tiny but exquisite. Much better than the cultivated variety.'

'Oh.' The sudden tightness in her chest made her voice a little husky when she said, 'Thank you.'

'My pleasure.'

He didn't seem in any hurry to go. 'I'll be down shortly and we can take the puppies straight away, if you like. I know you must have things to do, and I need to get home and sort out the last of my things.' Now he *had* to take the hint.

He gave her a long look. 'I'm cooking a bacon flan and baked potatoes for lunch, or perhaps I should say brunch.' His reproachful voice expressed disappointment at her ingratitude.

'Are you?'

He seemed surprised by her astonishment. 'Of course. You didn't think I'd send you home without feeding you, surely?'

He made her sound like a stray dog that had landed on his doorstep—four of which were already occupying his utility room. 'I just thought you'd want the puppies off your hands as soon as possible,' Gina said carefully, wondering when he'd become so touchy.

His frown smoothed to a quizzical ruffle that did the strangest things to her breathing. 'Oh, I see. So you're not in a mad rush to get away, then?'

'Considering it's eleven o'clock in the morning, if I was I've failed miserably, wouldn't you say?' Gina said a little tartly.

He smiled. 'You didn't have anyone calling round first thing, I hope?'

She thought about Janice in the flat below. Until this very moment she had forgotten she'd promised to cook Janice breakfast before she went on her shift at the local hospital, where she worked as a nurse. It was to have been a goodbye-and-we'll-keep-in-touch meal and, because of the shift Janice was on this month, breakfast had been the most appropriate time. Blow and double blow. She hated to let people down. The trouble was when she was in Harry's company the rest of the world faded into the background. 'I did, actually.' She felt awful now. 'But I can put that right later.'

A thick black eyebrow lifted. 'I'm sorry.'

He didn't sound sorry. In fact for some reason he seemed put out, if the look on his face was anything to go by. 'It doesn't matter.' *Just go, go.*

Harry didn't go. His mouth had thinned, accentuating its uneven curve, and his gaze was hard when he said, 'It never pays to let someone walk all over you, you know.'

She stared at him. 'No, I suppose it doesn't,' she agreed bewilderedly.

'And a clean break should be just that—a clean break.'

Had she missed something here? 'I'm sorry, Harry, but I don't follow.'

'It was him, this guy who's effectively told you thanks but no thanks, who was calling round, wasn't it? Hell, can't you see him for what he is, Gina? He knows how you feel about him and why you're leaving, and yet he calls round to...what? Why was he calling round?'

Gina tried not to gape. For a moment her brain whirled, and then she forced her face into an indignant expression. 'A friend of mine who lives in the flat below, a *female* friend, was coming for breakfast,' she said haughtily. 'OK? So, whatever your overactive little mind has come up with, it's wrong.'

It took a second or two for the outrage to be replaced by a sheepish expression that immediately melted Gina's heart— not that she would have revealed it for all the tea in China. 'Sorry,' he said. 'I put two and two together and made—'

'Going on a hundred? Yes, that much was perfectly clear.' She ought to be furious at the assumption she was giving house room—or, perhaps more accurately, bedroom—to her supposed lover. But his concern for her—and she didn't flatter herself it was anything but the *friendly* concern he'd spoken of before—warmed her aching heart. Harry had had lots of women in his life, he didn't try to pretend otherwise, but she doubted if he would have been so genuinely solicitous for the females who flitted in and out of his bed at regular intervals. And he certainly wouldn't have referred to them as friends. Perhaps she ought to be grateful for small mercies? She was distinct and different to the rest, in some small way, at least.

'I jumped to an erroneous conclusion, and I should have known better.'

He could do the gracious-apology thing really well, Gina thought, as she watched a slow smile spread over his handsome face.

'You're not the sort of woman to have second thoughts once you've made up your mind about something, or to say one thing and mean another.'

Oh boy, little did he know. 'Quite,' she said firmly.

'I'll leave you to get dressed,' he said with silky gentleness. 'Brunch will be ready in about twenty minutes.'

When the door closed behind him, Gina continued to lie in complete immobility for another moment or two. Then she flung back the duvet, swinging her legs out of bed and wrapping the robe back round her, before padding to the bathroom. There she scrutinised herself in the mirror and groaned softly. Dark smudges under eyes that definitely bore evidence of the weeping of the night before. And her hair! Why did her hair always decide to party during the night? At uni she'd shared with girls who'd gone to bed sleek and immaculate, and woken up sleep and immaculate. Or, at the most, slightly tousled.

Fifteen minutes later the mirror told her she'd transformed herself into someone who wouldn't frighten little children.

She had washed her hair and rubbed it as dry as she could before bundling it into a high ponytail at the back of her head. The essentials she always took to work in her bag—moisturiser, mascara, eye-shadow and lip gloss—had done their work and made her feel human again. Just.

She'd had the foresight to wash her panties through before going to bed and drape them over the radiator in her room—she did so hope Harry hadn't noticed the skimpy piece of black lace—and, armed with the knowledge she was clean and fresh, she took a deep breath and opened the bedroom door.

Brunch with Harry. The last meal she would ever eat with him, she thought a trifle dramatically, but without making any apology for it. She *felt* dramatic. In fact she felt a whole host of emotions surging in her breast, none of which were uplifting.

Once downstairs she paused in the hall. Sunlight was slanting in through the window on to the ancient floorboards, causing a timelessness that was enchanting. The whole cottage was enchanting. She could imagine what it would be like in the height of summer, with the outside of the house engulfed in roses and honeysuckle and jasmine. Violet dusks, the fragrance of burning leaves drifting in the warm air, dark-velvet skies pierced with stars, and overall a sense of whispering stillness. Did he sit on the verandah on such evenings, a glass of wine in his hand and his eyes wandering over the shadows, sombre and broodingly alone?

The image wrenched her heart and she mentally shook herself. It was far more likely the current blonde would be sitting on his lap or as near to him as she could get, no doubt anticipating the night ahead with some relish, she told herself caustically. And who could blame her?

A slight movement at the end of the hall brought her head swinging to see Harry standing watching her. 'I thought we'd eat in the breakfast room, OK? It's less formal than the dining room, but a bit more comfortable than perching at the breakfast bar in the kitchen.'

Gina nodded, quickly arranging her face into a smile as she walked towards him. 'Can I do anything to help?'

'Carry the salad through? I'll bring the other dishes.'

The breakfast room was situated off the kitchen and was quite small but charming, with wooden shutters at the leaded windows, and an old, gnarled table and chairs in the centre of the room. The only other furniture consisted of an equally old dresser on which brightly blue-and-red-patterned crockery sat, a bowl of flowering hyacinths on the deepset window sill filling the room with their sweet perfume.

After looking in on the puppies, who were all sound asleep, Gina seated herself as Harry said, 'Red or white wine? Or there's sparkling mineral water or orange-and-mango juice, if you'd prefer?'

'Fizzy water, please.'

She watched him as he poured her a glass, and then one for himself, after which he served her a portion of the flan and she helped herself to a baked potato and some salad.

The breakfast room was cosy, too cosy. Gina hadn't reckoned on them sitting so close. There was a small nick on the hard, square jaw where he'd cut himself shaving, and her body registered it with every cell. Clearing her throat, she looked at her plate as she said, 'This—this looks lovely, Harry.'

'Thank you,' he said gravely.

'Did—did you make the flan yourself?' *For goodness' sake, stop stammering. What's the matter with you, girl?* She wanted to close her eyes and sink through the floor.

He nodded lazily, taking a sip of his drink before he said, 'I told you, I like cooking. There are those who've said they haven't lived until they've tasted my chunky borsch.'

She glanced at him to see if he was joking, but he appeared perfectly serious. Taking him at face value, she said primly, 'I'm sorry, but I don't know what that is.'

'No?'

He grinned at her, his eyes warm, and his mouth doing the uneven thing that always turned her insides to melted marshmallow. She was used to banter with Harry, mild flirting and harmless innuendo. It was part of office life, and meant nothing. It was altogether different when sitting at his table in cosy intimacy. 'No,' she said flatly, her voice at odds with the army of butterflies in her stomach.

'Well, I make mine with smoky bacon and red peppers and celery, so it has a sweet-and-sour flavour. You put cabbage, potato, bacon, tomatoes, carrots, onion and a few other things in a pan and simmer for forty minutes or so before adding beetroot, sugar and vinegar and simmering some more. Serve with fresh herbs and soured cream.'

His eyes had focused on her mouth as he had been speaking, and something in their smoky depths brought warm colour to Gina's cheeks. She'd never have dreamt talking cookery could be so sexy.

'It's a nice dish on cold winter evenings, curled up in front of a log fire. You ought to try it some time.'

She swallowed. Curled up on a rug in front of a roaring fire with Harry would be food enough. 'I don't think my new life in London will feature many log fires.'

'Shame. You seem a chunky-borsch-and-log-fire girl to me.

Her eyebrows lifted on a careful inhalation. Play the game, she told herself. Keep it casual and funny. 'I'll just have to make do with caviar and glitzy nightclubs instead,' she said lightly. 'As befits a city girl.'

He regarded her across the table, but she couldn't read what was going on behind the grey eyes. 'Nope, don't see it,' he said at last. 'Sorry.'

'You don't think there'll be men queueing to buy me caviar and champagne and take me to all the best places?' she asked with mock annoyance.

'I didn't say that.'

Suddenly in the space of a heartbeat the atmosphere had tightened and shifted; there was no teasing in his voice or eyes now, but only an intent kind of urgency which took her aback.

He leaned forward, his face close and his eyes glinting. 'There'll be men, Gina. Plenty, I should think. But I don't think they will be what you need.'

She couldn't drag her eyes from his, and the moment hung between them like an unanswered question, but it was a question she'd never ask. It might open up something she would never be able to handle, she told herself frantically. This was just Harry being Harry. She was here, available and perhaps he fancied a change from his usual diet of cool, slender blondes. He didn't have, and would never have, any interest in an ongoing relationship, probably not even in a lengthy fling. He'd made that perfectly clear yesterday, when he'd confided in her about Anna and his disastrous marriage.

Better to have loved and lost than never have loved at all? The little voice in her head was probing, insistent.

Not in this case. If she gave herself to him it would be heart, mind, soul and body, and when he walked away she'd never recover from it. Especially if it ended badly.

Forcing her gaze down to her plate again, she picked up her fork, hoping he wouldn't notice the shakiness in her voice when she said, 'I'll just have to take each day as it comes, I guess.'

There was a pause, as though he was weighing his next words. She waited with a kind of breathless urgency while pretending to enjoy the flan.

When he said, 'Including this one?' she breathed out twice before lifting her eyes.

'Meaning?' she asked quietly, amazed she could sound so cool when there was an inferno inside.

'I need your help.'

'Oh?' She nodded. 'To take the puppies to the sanctuary? I've already said I'll come with you.' The inferno was out, deluged by stark reality. He was a rich, intelligent and hugely gorgeous man. Of course he wasn't interested in her.

'Not exactly.' Another brief pause. 'I've decided to keep them.'

'What?' She genuinely thought she'd misheard him. He couldn't possibly have said what she thought he had said.

'The puppies, I'm going to keep them.' He ate a large chunk of flan with every appearance of enjoyment. 'I already rang Mrs Rothman this morning to tell her she needn't come in today because I was going to be around, and I asked her if she'd be prepared to extend her days from Monday to Friday, essentially to be here from ten to four each day, to take care of them for the large part of the time I'm away.'

'And she said yes?'

'On the proviso she could bring her own dogs any time her husband isn't able to be home.'

'But—'

'What?'

'Well, I hate to coin a phrase, but dogs are for life, not just for Christmas. You talked of travelling some more, moving abroad, no—no responsibilities.' She stared at him, utterly in shock. This wasn't the Harry she knew. 'You can't have them for a while and then dump them at some sanctuary or other in a year or two. That wouldn't be fair. And *four* of them!'

Her voice had risen the more she'd spoken, and now she was aware of Harry settling back in his chair and surveying her over the top of his glass. 'You don't think much of me, do you?' he drawled mildly.

If you only knew, she thought for the second time that morning.

'I don't intend to dump them, as you so graphically put it. Not in a year or two, not ever. The poor little scraps have gone down that road once, and once is enough for any poor mutt. I've decided to take them on, and that means for life. OK?'

Not OK. *So* not OK. Feeling the world had shifted on its axis, Gina tried again. 'Harry, travelling or moving to another country is one thing, but something else entirely with four dogs in tow.'

'I do actually know that.'

She ignored the edge to his voice. 'I don't think you do.'

'I've decided to stay put, Gina.'

'What?' She blinked.

Her astonishment caused his anger to vanish like smoke, and now he grinned. 'Don't know me as well as you think you do, eh?' There was immense satisfaction in his voice. 'It's not just a woman's prerogative to change her mind. I've decided I'd go a long way before I found another house like this one, and it suits me. England suits me.'

'But you said—'

'Excuse me,' he interrupted mildly, 'But wasn't it you who was saying this house was a beautiful empty shell?'

Her eyes met his. *Touché*, she thought with a mixture of irritation and gratification. Irritation that he always had an answer for everything, and gratification that her words had obviously registered. 'I wasn't recommending that you fill it with a pack of dogs.'

'And I probably wouldn't have considered it myself right at this moment in time, but for fate taking a hand,' he admitted. 'But the grounds are extensive, they say dogs are the best burglar deterrent there is, and I rather like the idea of keeping the four of them together after all that's happened. I'll give Mrs Rothman a hefty pay rise for the extra work they'll involve until they're house-trained and so on, and with her ever-increasing brood of grandchildren the money will come in handy.'

Gina bit her lip. This was ridiculous. 'Keep one or perhaps two, if you must,' she said slowly, unable to believe he could have had such a radical change of heart regarding the future and his plans to travel. 'But not all of them.'

'Why not?'

She couldn't very well say she didn't believe him when he'd spoken of staying put. 'Four times the amount of mess and trouble?' she prevaricated.

'Four times the amount of fun and pleasure.'

She frowned. 'Four times the amount of squabbling and barking?'

'Four times the amount of canine love.'

He waited for her to continue, one dark brow raised. Gina mentally conceded defeat. It was true the dogs would have a wonderful life here, with the huge garden and each other—doggy paradise—but... 'Dogs shouldn't be left alone all day.'

'I thought I'd explained, they won't be,' he said with elaborate patience. 'Weekends I'm home, I might even arrange things so I work from home some mornings, and Mrs Rothman will be around for most of the time I'm out.' He seemed amused. 'I thought you'd congratulate me for taking some responsibility after your scathing words yesterday.'

'They weren't scathing.' She averted her gaze to the hyacinths. She supposed they *had* been.

'No? I'd hate to be in the firing line if you really get the bit between your teeth, then.'

She should never have agreed to stay the night, Gina told herself miserably, every nerve in her body as tight as piano wire at the closeness of him. 'Harry, you must do as you please,' she said quietly after a few moments had ticked by. 'This is nothing to do with me.'

'I guess not,' Harry said levelly. 'It's just that I've an appointment with the local vet this afternoon. I want him to look the puppies over and start their inoculations, if he thinks they're old enough. I was going to ask you to stay long enough to help me with them. I thought you might help me choose some bedding, leads, collars, that sort of thing, and of course I need to pick up some food and so on.'

She stared at him, feeling slightly hysterical. Today was supposed to have been spent clearing out the flat of the last bits and pieces, ready to spring-clean it from top to bottom before the new occupants took over on Saturday. She'd arranged to leave work on Wednesday evening so she had two clear days to sort everything out. Now that was already severely curtailed, and he was asking her for more of her time. This was utterly unreasonable and the whole situation was surreal. Harry didn't *do* permanence, dependability and personal responsibility, not where other people—or, rather, females—were concerned. But then these weren't people, they were dogs.

'Eat your food.' His voice came quiet and steady. 'I'll take you home after lunch. I shouldn't have asked.'

No, he shouldn't. And she shouldn't be considering his request for one second. She swallowed, her tongue stumbling over her words as she said, 'Are you absolutely sure you want to keep them? Have you really considered what you're taking on? It'll mean twelve, thirteen years of commitment, maybe longer. Have you really changed your mind so completely from yesterday, Harry? I...I need to know.'

He looked back at her, and she was aware that a tiny detached part of her mind was thinking that the hard angles of his chiselled face and body made him look older than his thirty-three years. But then he had the sort of bone structure that was ageless; at fifty, sixty, he'd still probably give the impression of being in his forties.

He reached across and took her hand as though he had the perfect right to touch her, and she had to remind herself the gesture was an expression of the easy friendship he felt for her as a sharp tingle shot up her arm with the power of an electric shock. 'I can understand your scepticism,' he said softly, 'But I mean every word, Gina. Perhaps there's been a part of me hankering for a more settled existence for some time, I'm not sure, but our conversation yesterday, finding the puppies...' He shrugged. 'Something gelled over the last twenty-four hours. They'll be company.'

She wondered how she could retrieve her hand without it being a big deal, and decided she couldn't. The trouble was, loving Harry as she did, *wanting* him, made any physical contact acutely painful in an exhilarating, pulsing kind of way. Stiffening her spine, she aimed to look at him levelly, face expressionless. 'So you're saying you intend to be around for some good time?' Even more reason for her to get away, then. 'Have you had a change of heart about taking over the firm too, when the time comes? Your father would like that.'

'Whoa, there.' He smiled, leaning back and letting go of her hand. She felt the loss in every pore. 'I didn't say that. To be truthful, I don't see myself in Dad's role, I never have. We're two very different people. I'd like to steer towards business consultancy, something which will enable me to decide where and when I work. That way, if I want a few weeks off at any time, it's no big deal. I pick and choose.'

Gina stared at him doubtfully. 'Could you afford to do that? And would enough people want you?'

His eyes were deep pools of laughter. 'If I had a problem with the size of my ego you'd be the perfect antidote. But, in answer to your question, I have enough contacts to succeed.'

Independent to the last. Nothing had changed, not really. He might have decided to establish some kind of base in his life but he was still a free spirit, not willing to be answerable to anyone, even in his work life.

Smothering her anguish with difficulty, Gina nodded. 'Lucky you,' she said as nonchalantly as she could manage. 'It sounds the perfect scenario.'

'I think so,' he agreed. Taking another large bite of the flan, he chewed and swallowed before saying, 'What do you think of my cooking expertise, then?'

Surmising he'd had enough intense conversation for one day, she tried to match his lightness. 'Marks out of ten?' She tilted her head, as though considering. 'Eight, nine, perhaps.'

'Not the full quota?' he asked in mock disappointment. 'I can see you're a very hard lady to impress.'

'Absolutely.' A shaft of sunlight was touching the ebony hair, slanting across the hard, tanned face and picking out the blue-and-red pattern on the plates. She wondered how you could love someone so much you ached and trembled with it and yet it didn't show. 'But you've won regarding the pooches. I'll help this afternoon. For their sake, though,' she added with what she thought was admirable casualness. 'Not yours.'

She'd expected some laughing words of thanks, or a teasing remark, along the lines that he knew she wouldn't hold out against him *and* the puppies. Instead, his eyes stroking over her face, he said gently, 'Thank you, Gina. You're a very special lady.'

Don't. Don't do tender. She could cope with almost anything else but that. The lump in her throat prevented speech, and she wasn't going to risk her luck by trying to force the words past it. Instead she compromised with a bright smile.

It seemed to satisfy him, if the warmth in his eyes was anything to go by. Feeling as though she was swimming against the tide and liable to drown at any moment, she applied herself to the food on her plate, even though each mouthful could have been sawdust for all the impact it made on her taste buds.

CHAPTER EIGHT

WHEN Gina and Harry left the house a couple of hours later the puppies were contained in a large robust pet-carrier Mrs Rothman had popped round just as they'd been finishing lunch. Snuggled on one of Harry's jumpers on top of a layer of newspapers, they seemed perfectly happy gazing out of the wire front as they travelled to the veterinary surgery, apparently suffering no bad memories of their fateful car trip the day before.

After a thorough examination the vet pronounced them fit and well, but declined to start their inoculation process for another two weeks. He also wryly wished Harry good luck.

Gina and Harry came back armed with a mountain of feeding and drinking bowls, pet beds, rubber toys, puppy collars, leads, brushes, combs and special puppy-feed, and once home the utility room quickly resembled a pet shop. Gina stood, gazing around at all the paraphernalia, unaware her thoughts were mirrored on her face until Harry said drily, 'No, I haven't taken on more than I can handle.'

'I didn't say a word.'

'You didn't have to.' He smiled. 'I'm a big boy, Gina, or hadn't you noticed?'

She'd noticed all right. If anyone had noticed, she had.

'And I'm more than capable of taking care of this little lot. I shall build a temporary pen in the garden for when they're outdoors, like the vet suggested, and put some strategies in place, OK?' He gestured at the book the vet had recommended—*Your Dog from Puppyhood To Old Age*—and which they had bought on the way home. 'And I'll read that from cover to cover tonight.'

His enthusiasm melted her. Realising it was imperative she maintained her cool facade, she nodded. 'Good, you'll have to. And I hope Mrs Rothman's pay rise is going to be a huge one.'

He grinned. 'Massive. Now, what are we going to call them?' he asked cheerfully. 'Any ideas?'

'Call them?' *We?*

'You had as much to do with their rescue as I did. I'd like you to choose their names.'

'I couldn't.' How could something so simple cause such pain? 'They're your dogs, Harry.'

'And I'd like you to name them. Women are so much better at these sorts of things than men. I'm getting into the mental habit of referring to them as One, Two, Three and Four, and that's no good. Don't worry—I shan't turn up in London with them in my arms, demanding you make an honest man out of me for the sake of the babies,' he added, his grin widening. 'You're only naming them.'

Not funny. She laughed obligingly, hating him and loving him in equal measure. He could talk about her being so far away with total unconcern now, apparently. Bully for him. Well, she could show she didn't give a hoot either. 'Well, it's spring,' she said slowly. 'How about flower names? Daisy for the little one, Rosie for the biggest, and perhaps Poppy and Pansy for the middle two.'

Harry eyed her in horror. 'If you think I'm standing in the middle of a field shouting Pansy you've got another think coming,' he said bluntly.

'OK, perhaps not Pansy, then. How about Petunia?'

'I don't think so, for the same reason.'

'Primrose?'

'You've already got Rosie.'

'Iris?'

'The name of my mother's best friend. She might take it personally.'

'Violet?' Gina was getting desperate.

'Mrs Rothman's christian name. I'd rather keep her on side, if you don't mind.'

'Oh, I don't know.' She glared at him. 'I've named three out of the four, the last one you'll have to think of.'

'OK.' He stood leaning against the wall, watching her with unfathomable grey eyes.

His hair had been slightly ruffled by the spring breeze outside, and his black-leather jacket was slung over his shoulder. He looked good enough to eat.

'I'll take you home now, if you're ready,' he said calmly.

It felt like a slap in the face. Somehow, and she wasn't sure from where, Gina found the strength to nod casually and smile.

She said goodbye to the puppies—who were curled up fast asleep in a heap in the corner, worn out by their afternoon excursion—as though her heart wasn't breaking, and then fetched her handbag and jacket. It felt like the end of the world as they walked out to the car, and she was vitally aware of Harry whistling under his breath. Silently calling him every name she could think of, she smiled her thanks and slid gracefully into the car when he opened the passenger door.

The late afternoon was one of bright, crisp sunlight and bird song, but already the shadows of evening were beginning to encroach across the garden. She'd get nothing done today, Gina thought as she watched Harry. Not that that mattered. Nothing mattered. This was the last time she was going to see him, and the swine didn't give a damn. He was whistling. He was actually *whistling*.

Harry didn't say much on the drive back, and for this Gina was thankful. She would have found it terribly difficult to make polite conversation the way she was feeling.

When they drew up outside the house in which her flat was situated, she was out of the car before he had even left his seat, saying, 'No, please don't get out,' when he opened the driver's door. 'You need to get back to the puppies.'

'A minute or two will make no difference.' He walked round the bonnet, handing her the satellite-navigation system the folk had bought her as he said, 'You'll need this, won't you?'

Forcing a smile, she took the box. 'Definitely. Well, I'd better get cracking on cleaning the flat. Goodbye, Harry.'

His eyes narrowed, glittering in the gathering twilight. 'I thought you were going to let me have your new address.'

As if you really care. Hurt causing a constriction in her chest that made it difficult to breathe, Gina nodded. 'Of course,' she lied flatly. 'I'll phone it through tomorrow, if that's all right? I've got your mobile number.'

'Thanks for all you've done over the last twenty-four hours,' he said very softly. 'I appreciate it.'

Of course you do. I fell in with what you asked me to do, like the weak fool I am where you're concerned. What's not to appreciate? 'It was nothing. Glad to help.' *Please go. Go before*

I break down completely or grab hold of you and can't let go.
Something that was becoming more likely with each moment.

He still didn't move. 'I'll let you know how the puppies get on,' he said pleasantly.

'Thank you.'

'You must come and see them when you're next up visiting your parents.'

'Yes.'

'By then I'll have sorted out a name worthy of her sisters for Number Four.'

Gina nodded.

Whether her lack of enthusiasm got through to him she didn't know, but he studied her face for a long moment as she stood perfectly still and tense. 'I must let you go, I've delayed you long enough.'

You could delay me for ever if I thought I had the slightest chance of meaning anything to you. She knew she ought to say something light and casual, something which meant they would part on easy, friendly terms, but words were beyond her. The ache inside overpowering, she made to turn away just as he bent and lowered his mouth to hers.

She froze. His lips were warm and firm, and it was no brief peck but more a caressing exploration that deepened moment by moment. Utterly captivated, she couldn't have moved away if her life had depended on it, but she fought responding to his kiss with every fibre of her being, knowing once she did she would be lost. He thought she was in love with someone else, but if she kissed him back in the way she wanted to it might set that intimidatingly intelligent mind thinking.

Grasping the box in her hands so tight her knuckles were shiny white, she told herself over and over again to remain absolutely impassive, but it was no good. This was Harry and he was kissing her. As her mouth began to open beneath his, she told herself she didn't want to think or reason, she wanted to *feel*. In thirty-six hours she would be gone for good, and this would have to last her a lifetime. What did self-respect and dignity matter compared to that?

It was the box in her hands that saved her, preventing her from throwing her arms round his neck and pressing against him as she wanted to. As it made its presence felt by digging into her chest, he became aware of it too, straightening and smiling a faintly rueful smile as he said, 'Sorry.'

The blood thundering in her ears, she couldn't match his cool aplomb. Hoping the trembling inside wasn't visible to those intent grey eyes, she lowered her flushed face, her voice a murmur as she said, 'I have to go, Harry.'

'I know.' A moment passed, then another. 'Goodbye, Gina.'

'Goodbye.' This time she did turn from him, walking towards the front of the house by instinct rather than sight, her eyes dry but unseeing.

It took enormous self-will to turn after she had opened the front door to the house and wave, but somehow she did it. She was aware of his arm lifting in response, and then she almost fell into the hall, shutting the front door and leaning against it as her heart beat a violent tattoo.

How long she stood there after she heard his car start and then draw away she didn't know, a mixture of crushing regret and sheer undiluted dread at never seeing him again turning her into a frozen statue. He had gone. Nothing she had experienced in her life thus far had prepared her for this moment, for desolation so consuming she could taste it.

Eventually she made her way to her flat on leaden feet, her

head thudding. She felt physically sick. Opening the door, she walked in, carefully placing the box on the small table in the tiny square of hall before continuing into the sitting room. It was all exactly as she had left it the morning before, several cardboard boxes half-filled with this and that standing on the carpet, and the loose cream covers of her two two-seater sofas in a pile on the coffee table waiting to be ironed. The young couple who were renting the flat after her had made her an offer for her furniture, and she had been glad to accept it, the flat in London being already furnished.

Numbly she walked across to the big picture-window and looked out over the river and rolling fields beyond. This view had thrilled her soul when she had first found the place; it still did, normally. This evening she felt as though nothing would ever touch that inner place wherein lay joy and happiness and everything good ever again.

As though in an effort to prove her wrong, the sky slowly began to flood with colour as the twilight deepened. A blaze of deep scarlet and gold turned the evening shadows into vibrant mauve and burnt-orange, all nature conspiring to put on a breathtaking display. All Gina could think of was Harry. She pictured him returning home in the quiet of the scented evening, the peacefulness of the old thatched cottage, the puppies scrambling to meet him when he walked into the utility room.

It was worse now she had seen where he lived, this constant stream of images in her mind. How was she going to escape them? How was she ever going to live the rest of her life with this leaden emptiness weighing her down? And why couldn't she cry? She had expected to cry when the last goodbye was over.

Eventually the sunset was blanketed by darkness, a

crescent moon hanging in the velvety blackness surrounded by tiny, twinkling stars.

Her legs stiff with standing in one position for so long, Gina roused herself to walk through to the kitchen where she made herself a cup of coffee before checking her answer machine. Two somewhat plaintive messages from her mother, reminding her she was due to have dinner with them the next evening, one from Margaret, checking up on how she was on leaving work, and another from Janice, wondering where she'd got to that morning. The last two had also come through as text messages on her mobile, but she hadn't replied to them, partly because it would have been difficult to explain she had gone home from work with Harry and stayed the night. Some things were best said face to face, or at least voice to voice.

She rolled her shoulders, attempting to stretch the tension from her neck. Considering she'd only had a few hours' sleep in the last twenty-four hours, and that the nights before last hadn't been particularly good either as she'd gnawed at the prospect of leaving Yorkshire and Harry until the early hours, she didn't feel particularly tired. Odd, light-headed, numb, but not tired.

One long hot bath, and two aspirin for the headache drumming at her brain later, Gina sat in her pyjamas, staring at a TV programme she had no interest in as she sipped at another cup of coffee. She forced herself to eat two chocolate biscuits, a separate segment of her brain expressing amazement she could quite easily stop at two rather than half a packet, as was normal.

The telephone rang at eleven o'clock, but she made no attempt to answer it, not wanting to talk to anyone. After the answer machine had delivered the perky message she'd thought so funny when she'd first recorded it, Harry's voice said quietly, 'You're probably asleep by now, but I just wanted you to know I've thought of a name for the puppy, and it *is* one I could yell in the middle of a field. Zinnia. What do you think? My gardening book tells me it's a plant of the daisy family with showy rayed flowers of deep red and gold, like your hair. I thought it appropriate.'

There was a pause, and Gina found she wasn't breathing.

'Oh, and the book also said in the language of flowers it means "thoughts of absent friends",' he finished even more softly. 'Goodnight, Gina. Sleep well.'

Sleep well? You've made me a mental and emotional wreck, and you calmly say 'sleep well'? And talking about her hair, and naming the puppy in memory of absent friends! All nice and chatty and 'I don't give a damn', while she was in pieces here. The anger that suddenly consumed her was so strong it was palpable.

He was a heartless so-and-so, that was what he was. She began to pace the room in her rage. Keeping everyone at a distance, pushing them away, not caring how many hearts he broke along the way.

No, that wasn't quite true. She stopped for a moment before beginning to pace again. He had his affairs with women who knew the score; it wasn't his fault she'd fallen in love with him so irrevocably. And one thing was for certain: if he'd had the faintest idea of how she felt, he'd have run a mile. She'd only got the invite to his home because he'd thought she regarded him as a friend. She smiled bitterly. Friend!

After a few minutes she took control of herself and played back the message again. This time there was no anger, but Harry's voice released the dam of tears that had been building all day. She cried until there were no more tears left and her face was a mess, whereupon she walked into the kitchen and made herself another coffee. She stood staring at it, and then very purposefully walked across to the sink and tipped it away.

She needed milky cocoa to help her sleep, she told herself firmly. And perhaps a couple of slices of buttered toast too. Her heart might be in shreds, she might be looking at an empty future devoid of husband and children and all the things she'd thought she'd have one day, but she wasn't going to crumble into tiny pieces now or at any other time. She wouldn't let herself. And she wasn't going to let this sour her either, not if she could help it.

The cocoa and toast helped. As she ate, she felt she was becoming herself again rather than the desperate, partly unhinged creature she'd felt since walking in the door earlier.

After finishing her supper, she washed the mug and plate and put them away. Tomorrow they would be packed with all her other bits and pieces, ready to be transported to her new life.

She didn't want to go. She bit hard on her lip as tears threatened again. But she would. Not for ever; she realised that now. But maybe for a year or two, long enough to come to terms with the fact that Harry would never be hers. She just couldn't do that here. All the time she would be hoping, hoping. It had sapped her strength over the last months, turned her into someone she didn't want to be.

But she would come back home. Not to this flat, or to Breedon & Son, not even to this town where she'd been born and grown up. But somewhere close. She wasn't a city girl and she never would be. The country was in her blood, in her veins and bones: swelling moorlands, wooded valleys where rivers wind over ageless stones and rocks, empty moors with the curlews crying and swooping; that was her. She had been born into a land of wide expanse, of pure summer air heavy with the sweetness of warm grass, and winter winds so cold they could take your breath away. She would never be happy for long hemmed in by buildings and concrete.

Straightening her shoulders, she walked out of the kitchen and into her pretty gold-and-white bathroom. She brushed her teeth thoroughly, refusing to dwell on the reflection of pink-rimmed swollen eyes in the mirror, eyes that held an expression that actually pained her. She didn't want to look like the lost, sad girl in the mirror.

Once in bed Gina lay quietly in the darkness, her arms behind her head. She was doing the right thing. She was doing what she had to do, it was as simple as that.

Within a few minutes she was fast asleep.

CHAPTER NINE

HARRY sat watching the glowing embers in the grate. The fire had burned low, sending flickering shadows across the room, and the puppies had long since gone to sleep, the four of them ignoring their individual beds and all curling up together in one. He smiled as he recalled the plump tangle of paws and tummies and tails, before his face took on the brooding expression it had worn for the last hour or two.

Who was this man who had captivated Gina? And 'captivated' wasn't too strong a word. It couldn't be anyone at work; he'd have noticed. More to the point, so would the die-hard gossips in two minutes flat. Nothing escaped them. No, it was no one at Breedon's, so it had to be someone she'd met elsewhere. A neighbour? Someone she'd perhaps grown up with and then noticed when she'd come back from university? It happened like that sometimes. How long had she been with him?

He stretched his long legs, glancing at his watch, and then reaching for the glass of brandy at the side of him. Taking a swallow, he let the neat alcohol burn a path down his throat into his stomach before replacing the glass on the table by his chair.

She hadn't been living with him. Had that been her decision or his, bearing in mind the man's reluctance to put a ring on her finger? When he thought about it, she'd really told him very little, just the bare facts without the slightest embellishment. Which wasn't like Gina.

Or was it? He blew out a sigh, then scrubbed his hands over his face. He was blowed if he knew any more. He thought he'd got her all taped, but he couldn't have been more wrong. Which proved—if nothing else—that women were a different species. Not that he'd had any doubts about that in the first place.

Gina had said she didn't think he liked women much, and he'd admitted to being cynical. The truth of the matter was that for the last decade he'd been guided by fear, plain and simple. Although it hadn't been plain to him, and it had been anything but simple. But fear was what had controlled him, galling though it was to concede the truth. He had believed falling in love again would strip him naked, and nothing was worth that.

The fire crackled and spat as an ember fell inwards in a shower of sparks, and Harry shivered although the room was warm.

And so for years he'd had his cake and eaten it too—up to a point. But everything had to be paid for. He hadn't realised the sort of man he had become until she had pointed it out in her warm, soft voice. And then the genie had been out of the bottle and there'd been no going back. He had had to face the feelings which had steadily grown and matured over the last twelve months. Gina. Oh, Gina. And all the time there'd been a shadowy figure in the background he hadn't had the slightest idea about.

Needles of jealousy pierced him, and he found himself struggling against the emotional vulnerability. Just as he had always known, love didn't play fair.

The temptation to wallow in his own self-pity was strong, and for a few minutes he indulged himself. Then he raised his head, finishing off the remaining brandy and standing to his feet.

OK, so he had missed the love boat where Gina was concerned. He had to deal with that and get on with life. She liked him; he still believed there was a kind of spark between them, and if her heart hadn't been elsewhere who knew how things would have developed? But since she had told him about this man she had made it very clear she wasn't in the running for anything from him beyond friendship. He could scarcely argue with that. Even in the friendship stakes the ball was in her court. He had asked her for her new address in London more than once. If she wanted to give it, she would. If not…

He placed the fireguard in front of the grate, but after straightening stood gazing, unseeing, into the dying embers. Anna had made a fool of him in more ways than one. Tricking him into marriage, lying to him, laughing about it with her friends, and then the constant threat of taking her own life. And all in the name of love, a love that had taken him for every penny he'd had in the divorce settlement whilst painting him as the worst sort of villain. To cap it all, she'd married again within the year. Some love.

But, if he was honest, once the exhaustion and pain and anger had receded, it was the humiliation that had hurt the most. Shame that he had ever been fooled so completely, that people had been laughing at him behind his back. The degradation had bit deep, and he hadn't known how to handle it except by running away. Not the most noble or impressive episode of his life. His mouth twisted. He'd been confused, shamefaced, scared—all those things a man wasn't supposed to be. And, although time had brought logic and reason to bear, he only had to shut his eyes to recall the panic he'd felt as his life had spiralled out of his control.

What would she make of his phone message when she heard it in the morning? She would know what he was really saying, of course, but at least this way he would save them both the embarrassment of her having to reiterate her love for this man. But it would keep the door open for her to contact him in the future if she came to a point where she put this guy behind her.

Damn it. He moved irritably, shaking his head. He was rusty in the twists and turns of the love game. Taking what he wanted when he wanted it had been so much simpler.

He walked quietly through to the utility room to check on the puppies before he went upstairs. It was still hard to determine which head went with which body in the heap of gently snoring canines. Had he decided to keep them purely to show Gina he was prepared to take on responsibility and commitment—a sprat to catch a mackerel?

No. The answer was a relief, and he realised the question had been at the back of his mind all day. Convincing Gina he'd been talking a load of rubbish before had been part of it, certainly, but he wanted—he *needed*—them for himself. They were the beginning of a new phase of his life, whether Gina played a part in it or not. He was tired of his shallow love-resistant life plan. Sure, it had meant an existence free from pain and emotional doubts and worry, but of late it had left a nasty taste in his mouth.

He was sick of coming home to an immaculate silent house, of autonomy. Maybe the kick start to all this had been the shock of his father's heart attack, when he'd realised for the first time that his parents were mortal, that one day they wouldn't be around. Certainly there had been no question of staying in the States and continuing to do his own thing when his father had needed him so badly. And then he had met Gina.

Maybe the last decade he had been screwed up. Or maybe he had just been working through issues that had had to have their time. Whatever. He shrugged. That time was gone, and he didn't believe in harping back or castigating himself with regrets about a past he couldn't change.

Right now, what would once have been stifling and terrifying had become satisfying, and all the maybes he'd been chewing over boiled down to that. He had been slowly changing the last year without knowing it, and although the realisation had come as a hell of a shock, now he thought about it, it hadn't been a sudden process. Loving Gina hadn't been a sudden process but a quiet, steady growth of something incredible. *She* was incredible. And she was walking out of his life in twenty-four hours, and there wasn't a damn thing he could do about it.

He closed his eyes for an infinitesimal moment and then turned and walked upstairs, wondering which of the gods of fate and destiny were having a good laugh at his expense.

CHAPTER TEN

WHEN Gina emerged from a troubled restless sleep early on Saturday morning, the big black cloud which had hovered over her constantly the day before was still firmly *in situ*.

All Friday she had cleaned and scrubbed and sorted, only stopping to answer the telephone—Bryony and Margaret had called, along with a work colleague and two friends—and make herself some lunch. She'd fed Janice breakfast first thing, thereby fulfilling her obligations of the day before, and then had gone to see her parents for dinner as arranged. She'd been bright and cheerful throughout. It had nearly killed her.

Rolling over onto her back, she stared at the cream-painted ceiling. This was it. D-Day. She was packed and sorted, all she needed to do this morning was to strip the bed and give the bathroom one last, quick clean after she had showered and washed her hair.

Outside her reliable little car was bulging at the seams with her belongings. The young couple who were taking over the flat were due to arrive at eleven o'clock with the letting agent who handled things for the landlord. He'd called by yesterday to inspect the place, and had expressed himself more than satisfied with its décor. So, everything going like clockwork, then.

Gina sat up in bed, brushing a strand of hair out of her eyes. *He hadn't phoned back yesterday.* She looked towards the window where weak sunlight was struggling to break through the soft muslin curtains. But then, why would he?

Swinging her legs out of bed, she stared miserably at the carpet. She didn't doubt for a moment that out of sight meant out of mind with Harry. It had been stupid to imagine—to *hope*—he would call. But then that was it with Harry, she couldn't *help* hoping. Which was exactly why she had to leave. And she would *not* call him, not now, not ever. This had to be a once-and-for-all solution to what had become a gigantic problem, a clean, swift finale.

When the telephone rang she reached out for it automatically. The only person who would ring at this time in the morning was her mother. Her father had been very positive about the move to London, or at least he'd pretended to be, which was all that mattered. On the other hand her mother had been in a state last night, and had cried when she had left their house. Anyone would have thought she was emigrating to Australia, rather than taking up residence in London for a while, she thought wryly, steeling herself for more reasons why it was ridiculous if she left Yorkshire as she said, 'Hello, Mum,' into the receiver.

There was a moment of silence. 'Sorry, this isn't Mum.'

She was glad she was sitting down. Unfortunately she couldn't say a word, though.

'Gina? It's Harry. I know it's early, but I wasn't sure what time you were planning to leave.'

Respond. Say something. Squeak. Anything. 'I—not yet. I mean—' Her throat started to tighten but she pushed past it. 'I'm still in bed.'

'I've woken you. I'm sorry.'

She didn't disabuse him. Let him think her stuttering and stammering was due to being woken up. 'It's all right,' she managed fairly coherently, her heart hammering so hard it actually hurt. 'Is anything the matter?'

'The matter?'

She might sound odd, but he didn't sound much better. A sudden thought struck. 'The puppies, is anything wrong?'

'What? Oh no, they're fine.' She heard him clear his throat. 'Look, I didn't thank you properly for all you did the night we found them, staying like you did and then helping the next day.'

'Of course you did.' She glanced at her wrist where the gold watch gleamed in the dim light. She had slept with it on, needing the link with him. Her throat tightened still more.

'I don't think so. Anyway, I thought it might be nice if we had breakfast together on your last morning in Yorkshire. That's if you haven't other plans?'

He definitely sounded odd. Easing the air past her constricted throat, she closed her eyes. It would be madness to see him this morning. Crazy to invite more pain. And for what? An hour of his company, maybe two if she was lucky. It would knock her sideways again, she knew it. The sensible thing, the *only* thing, was to make an excuse.

The silence seemed to stretch for ever. Then Harry said, 'Gina? Are you there?'

'Yes.' Her voice was calm, but part of her was screaming inside. She was such a fool where this man was concerned. 'And breakfast would be lovely.'

'Good. I know a great café not far from where you live.'

He sounded really pleased; she wished she could see his face. Gathering her wits, she said, 'What time will you be here?'

Another silence. Then he said, 'Actually I'm sitting in my car outside your house. I watched the sun come up.'

Her train of thought crashed. 'Why?' she asked stupidly.

'Couldn't sleep.'

He was here, outside? She fell backwards on the bed, her hair fanning around her on the cream duvet like flames. Her legs dangled off the edge as she stared upwards. 'I shall need to have a shower,' she mumbled helplessly.

'Fine, take as long as you want, there's no rush.'

'I've got to hand over the keys at eleven.'

'You'll be back in plenty of time, don't worry.'

'Do you want to come and wait up here?' she asked reluctantly, wondering if he was forever destined to see her looking as though she'd been dragged through a hedge backwards. Oh, for sleek, manageable hair that didn't require dampening down every morning.

He must have sensed her unwillingness. 'No, I'm fine where I am, listening to the radio. Did you know it's going to be another beautiful day once the morning mist clears? Cold but sunny, the forecast says.'

It was going to be the most beautiful day in the world because she would see him again one last time—and also the worst, because she was going to have to say goodbye all over again. But he had thought enough of her to come. She hugged the fact to her. OK, it might be because he'd had a bad night and couldn't sleep, but it was *her* house he'd ended up at. 'How long do you have before you have to get home and see to the puppies?'

'Mrs Rothman's taking care of them. I've been around the last forty-eight hours, so she agreed to change her days and come over the weekend. Relax, Gina.' His voice held a touch of amusement now. 'I haven't absolved myself of all responsibility so soon.'

'I didn't think you had,' she said, hurt he could think so. 'I'll be down shortly.'

A quick shower later, and with her hair bundled into a high ponytail on top of her head, she dressed in the jeans and top she had laid out the night before. They weren't the best clothes for the last meeting with the man she loved; she'd have preferred to leave him with a picture of something far sexier. But they were certainly appropriate for breakfast in a café.

As she pulled on her light jacket, she stopped suddenly. Her body was zingingly alive and on full alert, her heart pumping like a piston engine. She groaned softly. In every other area of her life she was a grown woman with complete control over her emotions; Harry was her Achilles heel. Just look at her. She'd woken up this morning feeling like the world had ended, and now she was—

What was she? She paused, considering. Daft. Stupid. Utterly crazy. Still, hey, no one was perfect.

He wasn't sitting in his car when she emerged from the house, but was standing leaning against it, gazing out over the river with his back towards her. She felt her breath catch in her throat as she took in the big dark figure clothed in jeans and a black-leather jacket. The rush of love that swamped her was so powerful that for a moment it blinded her. And then her vision cleared and he was still standing there, ebony hair shining in the sunlight, and the faintly brooding quality that was habitual with him more marked in the fresh spring morning.

He turned as she walked towards him, his handsome face breaking into a smile that warmed her aching heart. 'Hi.' The smoky voice caressed her nerve endings. 'You were quicker than I expected.'

'Good. I don't like to be predictable.'

'Predictable?' He shook his head. 'Not you.'

She liked that. It made her feel more in control, even slightly racy. Of course she knew it wasn't true, but that didn't matter. 'Where are we going exactly?' she asked as she reached him.

'Exactly?' His head tilted, teasing her. 'A couple of miles away to a somewhat infamous lorry-driver's café I found by chance one morning months ago. It's slightly off the beaten track, but always full. Apparently the lorry drivers' grape-vine highly recommends it, and that's all the advertising the place needs.'

'Infamous?' she questioned doubtfully.

'Well, perhaps not infamous. Just a little basic, and popu-lated by characters who look more suited to some weird cult-movie half the time, but the food's great and it's clean. OK?' His smile widened. 'It's all right, Gina. You'll be perfectly safe with me. I wouldn't let anything happen to you.'

A light reply hovered on her lips, but it was never voiced. It was the way he was looking at her. She couldn't quite fathom what was in his eyes, but it increased the ache in her heart a hundredfold.

Then he opened the car door for her and the earth began to spin again.

Once he joined her in the car her senses picked up on the faint scent of aftershave on fresh male skin. She shivered.

'Cold?' He'd noticed, immediately starting the engine and turning up the heating. 'You'll soon warm up.'

Oh yes. Her body was always in danger of internally combusting around Harry. 'This is nice,' she said with a casualness she was extremely proud of. 'An impromptu breakfast.'

'I'm glad you think so.' He pulled out of the parking space in front of the house, glancing at her little car as he did so. 'Sure there's enough room for you in there?' he asked mildly. 'I'm not sure it's safe to drive packed to the hilt like that.'

She brindled immediately. 'Of course it is.'

'Gina, you're supposed to be able to see out of the back window.'

'I need to get my stuff to London, don't I?'

'So why don't I take some of it for you and follow you down?' he suggested nonchalantly.

'You?' She stared at the dark profile, utterly taken aback. 'No, no, it's OK.' The last thing she wanted was to start her new life with Harry a step or two behind her. 'Loads of people have offered to help, but I prefer to do this myself.'

'Loads of people?' The odd note in his voice was back.

'My parents, my sisters…'

'Right.' He paused and then said slowly, 'Do you mind if I ask you something on the personal side?'

Her stomach fluttered. 'No,' she said warily. 'Ask away.'

'This guy you've been seeing—is this move to London a definite conclusion to all that? What I mean is—' he paused again, checking both ways before pulling on to the main road '—is there any chance he'll be able to wheedle his way back into your life if he comes begging and pleading?'

'He won't,' she said faintly.

'But if he did?' Harry persisted. 'Look, what I'm really asking is whether you want to move on. Start dating again.'

Gina knew her eyes had widened. She nervously moistened her lips, utterly out of her depth, and every nerve in her body sensitized and pulsing. Why did he always have to have such a *physical* effect on her? It didn't help. Swallowing hard, she said, 'I don't know,' because he was waiting for an answer and she had to say something.

Then she knew what it was to have her heart jump into her throat as he pulled the car off the main thoroughfare and into a minor road where he immediately parked on the grass verge. His eyes were so dark they were almost black as he turned to her, his voice throaty as he said, 'He's not the be all and end all, Gina, whatever you think now. I can prove it to you.'

She was mesmerized as he bent his head and took her lips, one arm sliding round her shoulders and his other hand cupping her chin. It was a deep kiss, long and warm and without reserve, and she was helpless before the flood of desire racing through her. Her hands were resting on his chest, and the warmth and scent of him was engulfing her, the hard, strong beat of his heart beneath her fingers.

His lips left hers, moving over her cheek to her ear, then her temple, the tip of her nose and back to her mouth. Her lips parted to allow him greater access, and he took the vanquished ground with a low growl in his throat, kissing her until there was no past and no present, just the two of them in a world of touch and taste and smell.

When he finally released her and drew back she couldn't move or speak for a moment, every ounce of her will fighting to regain control over her composure. She watched him rake a hand through his hair before he said, 'I'd like us to start seeing each other, Gina. We can take it as slow as you want, but you can't deny there's something between us.'

She drew in a ragged breath. Now he wasn't touching her,

she had to try and *think*. She stared at him, trying to take in what had just happened and—more importantly—what he'd said.

Something between us. What did that mean? Sexual attraction on his part—more than she'd ever dreamt or hoped for, admittedly—but now…not enough. Not loving him as she did. If this encounter had happened when he had first come back to England, then she might have been able to convince herself that with time and patience on her part he could learn to love her. But this wasn't a romantic movie where the guy suddenly realized what he'd wanted all his life was right under his nose with the girl next door.

This was real life. This was Harry. He might have decided to allow four very small dogs into his life, but that was vastly different to changing his mind about happy-ever-after. He avoided entanglements like the plague.

Slowly, she said, 'I'm going to London, Harry. It wouldn't be realistic to think we could date, surely?' She hoped the trembling in her body wasn't reflected in her voice.

'I don't see why not.' He still had one arm resting across the back of her seat, and as he shifted slightly every part of her registered the action. 'It's hardly the end of the world.'

'But—'

'What?' he asked softly.

'Why now?' She knew her cheeks were firing up, but still she ploughed on. 'I mean, we've known each other for over twelve months, and you've never—' She stopped. 'Never asked me out,' she finished awkwardly.

He surveyed her under half-closed lids. 'Perhaps I don't believe in mixing work and pleasure.'

Pleasure. The word trickled along her nerve endings like warm, silky honey. Warning herself not to falter, she said quietly, 'I'm sorry, but I don't buy that. Be truthful. You've never noticed me in that way before. So I ask again, why now?' She studied his face, trying to find a clue in the chiseled features as to how he was really feeling.

He smiled, but this time it didn't reach his eyes. 'You're wrong, Gina. I noticed you in *that* way, as you put it, the first moment of the first morning.'

She couldn't say anything, she was stunned by his admission. A brief thought of all the days and nights of agony she had endured thinking he could never—would never—see her as a desirable woman darkened her eyes, but then he was speaking again.

'As to the reason why I never asked you out, that kiss might have had something to do with it,' he said cryptically.

She stared at him, confused. 'I'm sorry but I don't understand.'

'I knew that if we got together it would mean something.' The keen eyes were tight on her face.

Feeling as though she was wading through treacle, Gina made a huge effort to clear her whirling mind. This was probably the most important conversation she would have in her life, and she had to remain calm and focused. 'And that was bad?'

'Oh yes,' he said with a sardonic twist of the lips. 'Then. I wasn't ready. I needed to work some things through in my head. But now circumstances have changed. *I've* changed. And when you said your relationship with the other guy was over…'

Suddenly, with the force of a blow in the solar plexus, she understood. He thought she was in love with someone else, someone she was leaving Yorkshire to forget. She was moving to London where she'd be finding her feet for a while. He fancied her, but he hadn't wanted any close involvement or complications, and so he'd done nothing about it. *Now it was all different.* He could indulge in a long-distance affair, which would of necessity mean it was much less intense, her being at one end of the country and him at the other. Secure in the knowledge she loved someone else, he could pop down to London now and again for the odd bit of sex—perhaps even convincing himself he was doing her a favour. The poor little country girl all alone in the big city.

Gina took a deep breath. 'Let me get this straight,' she said, with a composure born of silent fury. 'You're suggesting we start dating, even though I'm in London and you're up here. Right?'

He nodded. 'Motorways made short work of distance these days.'

True, but distance could also be a very pliable tool in the hands of someone dedicated to non-commitment as he was. 'And how often would these…dates occur?'

'That would be up to you,' he said quietly. 'Of course, with you wanting to get away from here, I'd be prepared to come to you.'

How magnanimous. That way the ball would always be entirely in his court. If he thought she was getting a little clingy at some time in the future, curtail the visits. In the past she had often wondered if love and hate were equally powerful emotions. Now she knew.

Gina thought of screaming at him that he was the most insensitive, selfish man since the beginning of time. That she would rather die than become his little weekend diversion. That he could take his cold heart and stuff it where the sun didn't shine. But she had come this far—to the last minute of the last hour, metaphorically speaking—without losing her dignity, and without him guessing how she felt about him, and all the pain of the last twelve months had to be worth something. She turned and looked out of her side window while she fought for control. Then, turning back to face him, she arched an eyebrow, keeping her voice pleasant when she said, 'I'm sorry, Harry, but it wouldn't work.'

'I disagree.'

I just bet you do. Trying to ignore the breadth of his shoulders and the way a muscle had clenched in the hard male jaw—always a sign with Harry he wasn't prepared to take no for an answer—she forced a smile, although it nearly killed her. 'I'm sorry,' she said again, 'But for me it wouldn't.'

'Because of this guy?'

Although his eyes were hooded and his face was betraying nothing she sensed there was an awful lot going on behind the expressionless façade. Resentment that she hadn't got down on her knees and thanked him for his so generous offer? Pique at her imaginary lover who had cheated him out of what he'd seen as a very nice, no-strings-attached little set-up? Irritability that she couldn't see the sense of such a logical arrangement?

Inclining her head, Gina said, 'Partly because of him, yes. I'm afraid I'm not the sort of girl to go to bed with one man when I'm thinking about another.'

She had thought the implied insult would be enough to put him off but she should have known his tenacity was stronger. 'I never imagined you were. How far and how swiftly our relationship would develop would be entirely up to you. Contrary to what you obviously think, it *is* in my capacity to wine and dine a woman without insisting on the evening ending in bed.'

Believe me, you wouldn't have to insist. And that was the trouble. She wouldn't be able to resist him on the first date, let alone the second, and then where would she be? Counting the hours till the next time he phoned or came to see her? Driving herself crazy imagining him with someone else when he wasn't with her? Fearing every time he left it would be the last time, that he'd finally got tired of her? The previous year had told her she was in danger of becoming someone she didn't like because of how she felt about him; if she allowed herself to become little more than his clandestine affair tucked out of sight in London, the last of her self-esteem would be gone.

She knew she could be as tenacious as him, especially when emotional suicide was the alternative. She shrugged carefully. 'I guess the bottom line is that I don't want any links to Yorkshire, Harry. It's as simple as that. I want—I *need*—this to be a clean break if it's going to work. And it has to work.' Horrified, she heard the catch of a sob in the last words, and prayed he hadn't heard it too.

He had. His voice husky, he said, 'I didn't want to upset you, Gina.'

Upset me? You've taken my heart and I can never have it back for anyone else. She shook her head blindly. 'You haven't. I'm fine.'

'I could wring his neck.' He lifted a hand and traced the outline of her lips, his eyes stormy with an emotion she couldn't put a name to.

For a moment she didn't grasp what he meant and then she sighed, her skin burning where he had touched. How had all this come about? This time last week she would have thought the events of the last forty-eight hours impossible, and yet they'd happened. She'd seen his home, *slept* in his home, got to know him even better, and now this…breathtakingly fright-ening proposal. Frightening, because every cell in her body was urging her to say yes and to hell with the consequences. Breathtaking, because the thought of making love with him would be all she ever asked of life.

A strange feeling came over her. For a moment it was as though she had stepped out of her skin and was watching the pair of them from outside the car. She could have times like this—of being with him, sharing part of his life—if she agreed to start seeing him. They would be a couple, if only to a point. But she would be in his life. And, when it finished—and it *would* finish—there would be memories to linger over down the years, recollections of shared meals, laughter, *love.* Love on her part, at least. It would be something. Surely it would be something, whereas now she had nothing.

She stared at him, her lips already forming the words that would take her down a path she'd sworn just minutes before she wouldn't walk down, when he said, 'You need to eat. Hell, I need to eat.' And he turned from her, starting the engine in the same movement.

For a second she felt sheer, undiluted panic that she had lost the moment. Her heartbeat in her throat, she felt anger and helplessness and a hundred other emotions besides, but then he was turning the car in a semi-circle and they'd snaked onto the main road again.

After a few moments she glanced at Harry out of the corner of her eye. Tight lines of tension radiated from his grim mouth, and his rugged good looks could have been set in stone. Clenching her hands together in her lap, in a small voice she said, 'I'm sorry, Harry.'

'Three "I'm sorry"s in the space of as many minutes are

two too many between friends.' He glanced at her for one swift moment, but the hard countenance had mellowed. 'Besides which, you have nothing to be sorry for. It's too soon, I should have known that. Damn it, you haven't even left yet.'

She didn't want to leave. Ask me again and I'll stay. Don't be understanding and considerate, not at this late stage.

'We're going to have breakfast, and then I'll take you home so you can see to the last-minute bits and pieces, OK?'

She nodded, sunk in misery.

And then he surprised her, reaching out and taking one of her hands and holding it tight as he said, 'Don't look so tragic; that wasn't the point of the exercise, believe it or not. It might be somewhat ungallant to say it, but I don't usually have such an adverse effect on women.'

He was trying to lighten the moment, but it only increased her pain. That and the feel of his warm flesh holding hers. She wanted him so badly she could taste it. He had offered himself—something of himself anyway—and she had turned him down. What was the matter with her? So what if he couldn't do roses round the door and happy-ever-after, at least he'd been honest about it. How many men sweet-talked a woman into bed with promises of for ever and then did a runner? Hundreds, thousands, every day of every week, worldwide. She would have given everything she possessed to hear him say what he'd just said a few months ago, even as little as a week ago.

But something had changed irrevocably in the last three days. It had started the moment she had walked out of Breedon & Son with him and had continued ever since.

It had to be all or nothing. OK, most women would say she was mad, but there would be at least one who understood. She loved him too much to compromise. In the long run, it really was as simple as that. And it sucked, because she was going to end up with nothing.

She felt as though her mind was a pendulum, swinging from one extreme to the other.

He only held her hand for a moment or two, but the feel of him remained much longer, and when they drew up outside a strange ramshackle building tucked away in a tree-bordered lay-by her body was still burning. She glanced at the sprawling one-storey building, which was mostly of wood, a few tables and chairs scattered haphazardly outside.

'I told you it wasn't lace doilies and china cups,' said Harry, grinning, his mouth lifted in an appealing curve that made her want to kiss the corner of it.

'I think the word you used was infamous.'

'Ah, yes. Well, come and see what you think. We don't have to eat outside, by the way, there's plenty of room in the café.'

Gina felt a little apprehensive as they walked into the café. She saw immediately that, although it appeared spotlessly clean, everything appeared to be on its last legs. The tables and chairs were basic to say the least, and quite a few appeared to have been mended with odd scraps of wood. The wooden floor was horribly scuffed and marked, and there were oil-cloths on the tables rather than linen tablecloths. A small wiry man with an incredibly lined face and shock of grey hair hailed Harry immediately. 'Harry, m'boy! You're in luck the day. Got a nice delivery of black pudding in this morning.'

Guiding her to a table for two in a corner by the window—the glass of which looked as though it was held in by wishful thinking rather than anything else—Harry called back,

'Great, Mick. Could you bring two cups of tea while we look at the menu?'

'Done job.'

Gina sat down and tried not to stare at the assorted diners. There were lots of them, almost every table was full, and although some were what she'd term ordinary folk, there were others who were anything but that. One man was literally covered from head to foot in tattoos, his hooked nose being a hawk's body and with two wings sweeping across his cheeks, and there were a couple of Hell's Angels along with some gothic types in the far corner. More surprisingly still, a man in full evening-dress was sitting with a woman dripping with jewels, and both appeared to be half asleep.

Harry saw where she was looking. 'Mick gets a few Hooray Henrys from time to time,' he murmured. 'I gather this place is the latest rage with the hunt set after a night on the tiles.'

Mick was at their side before Gina could respond, his cheeky face split in a wide grin as he placed two huge, steaming mugs of tea on the table, all the time looking at her. 'Aren't you going to introduce us, Harry?'

'Mick, Gina. Gina, Mick.'

Mick nodded. 'Pleased to meet you, Gina.'

She smiled. There was something immensely likeable about this funny little man. 'Likewise, Mick.'

'Harry going to treat you to one of my big breakfast bonanzas, then?' Mick asked cheerfully. 'Eggs, bacon, sausages, hash browns, baked beans, tomatoes, black pudding and mushrooms, along with a couple of rounds of toast?' He paused, cocking his head as he surveyed her through bright black eyes.

Gina felt as though it was some sort of test. 'Sounds great.'

'I like her.' Mick turned to Harry approvingly. 'And I'm

pleased you've found yourself a good woman at last.' Focusing on Gina again, he added, 'I've been on at him ever since he first set foot over the threshold to find himself a nice lassie.'

She blinked, but the twinkle in Mick's beady eyes was disarming. 'How do you know I'm a nice lassie?' she returned, grinning. 'Perhaps Harry prefers the other sort.'

Mick shook his head. 'No, he's not as daft as he looks. He knows which side his bread's buttered, all right.'

'When you two have quite finished...' Harry's voice was dry in the extreme.

'Two bonanzas coming up.' Mick trotted off happily.

Gina took a sip of her tea and then looked up to see Harry watching her thoughtfully, his dark eyes serious. 'What?' she said nervously.

'Is there anyone or anything you can't handle?' he murmured with warm approval.

Feeling as though she'd just been given a million dollars, Gina wondered what his reaction would be if she admitted the answer to his question was sitting opposite her. 'Of course not,' she said lightly. 'I'm a modern woman, didn't you know? We can handle any problem that comes our way, and do it while juggling a hundred and one other things, incidentally. Unlike the male of the species.'

She had decided a minute ago that the only way she would be able to deal with Harry, Mick and this whole surreal morning was to keep things on a humorous level from now on.

He smiled. Her heart melted.

'The old one about men can only do one thing at a time?' he asked lazily. 'Whereas women are miracle workers.'

'Absolutely.' She couldn't help her heartbeat speeding up just a fraction, or the way her breath caught in her throat. He looked so altogether *sexy* sitting there; the way his smile mellowed the hard, handsome lines of his face was silver-screen material.

And then, because she couldn't resist asking, although she knew she shouldn't, she said, 'What did Mick mean about you finding yourself a woman at last? You've had girlfriends since you've been back in England.'

He shrugged. 'Not ones I'd choose to have breakfast with.' He paused, then added, 'And none I'd take home either.'

Warning herself none of that meant a thing, she murmured, 'The entanglement thing?'

'Self-protection would be a better description.'

He was staring at her, his emotions for once openly displayed in his gaze. Gina swallowed, jerking her eyes away as she warned herself she couldn't trust her sight where Harry was concerned—or the rest of her senses, come to that. She wanted him too much. It was too easy to project what she *wanted* to imagine she was seeing and hearing. And back there in the car he'd made no mention of commitment when he'd proposi-tioned her, no hint that he saw her differently from all the others.

Nevertheless, her eyes on the mug of tea, she said quietly, 'You took *me* to your home.'

'Yes, I did.'

The tiny voice deep inside prompted her to carry on, 'Because we're friends?'

'If you're asking *only* friends, then I think we both know that was never true. I appreciate your friendship, Gina, I have all along, but on my part there was something more and I can't help that. I've wanted you from the first moment I saw you.'

'Physically.' She looked at him squarely, praying her face was as expressionless as she needed it to be.

'There was an immediate physical attraction, yes. I'm a man, I can't help it. Then...' He paused. 'I got to know *you*.'

Gina's movements were slow and deliberate as she picked up her mug and took several sips of the scalding-hot tea. If ever she needed the boost of caffeine it was now. Warning herself to remain outwardly calm, she said, 'I'm confused, Harry. Are you saying the self-protection thing is wearing thin? And, if so, why now?'

Did he know her whole body had stilled as she waited for his answer? she thought in the next heartbeat.

'Because it's time?' he suggested softly.

It was an answer, and yet not an answer. Was he saying in the future he intended to let his girlfriends have more access into his life? Certainly his emotions had been in cold storage for over a decade, by his own admission. Dredging up a smile, she lifted her eyes to his. 'So you started off with four little canines but hope to progress to bigger things?' she asked lightly. 'Something along those lines?'

He smiled back, but only with his mouth. 'I wouldn't put it quite like that.' He leant forward in his chair, his expression suddenly intense. 'The thing is, Gina—'

'Two bonanzas as ordered, and the toast's coming.' Neither of them had noticed Mick's approach, and Gina could have kicked the jovial little man. Instead she forced herself to smile politely as he placed one loaded plate in front of her and the other in front of Harry. How was she going to eat a morsel with her stomach doing cartwheels and her heart threatening palpitations?

As soon as Mick had scurried off, she said, 'You were saying?'

He stared at her for a moment. 'It doesn't matter. It would

be a case of rushing in where angels fear to tread, the way things are.'

She opened her mouth to ask him what he meant just as Mick said, 'Here's the toast. More tea for anyone?'

Go away. 'I'm fine,' she said brightly as Harry shook his head.

Mick obviously wasn't the most sensitive of souls, because the next moment he hooked himself a chair from another table and sat down beside Harry. 'That business plan you advised me to look into?' he said in a low voice. 'I've decided to do it.'

Harry inclined his head. 'Good.'

'I mean, like you said, I'm not necessarily committing to anything, am I? And the way profits are piling up, it's a good time. How do I set the ball rolling?'

Gina sighed inwardly. End of intimate discussion. Now she had to make some attempt at eating this enormous breakfast when all she wanted to do was to burst into tears. She revised her earlier opinion and decided she didn't like Mick at all.

CHAPTER ELEVEN

IT WAS just after half-past ten when they pulled up outside the house in which Gina's flat was situated later that morning.

When Mick had left their table after a few minutes of unashamedly picking Harry's brains, the resulting conversation had been inconsequential and light. Harry had made sure of that, acknowledging Mick's interruption had been timely.

What had he been doing, going in there with all the finesse of a charging bull-elephant? he asked himself now as he glanced at Gina's withdrawn face. It was the one thing he'd promised himself he wouldn't do when he'd suggested breakfast earlier. That had been a bad idea, too. Hell, this whole thing was a bad idea. He should have cut his losses when he'd found out about this other guy. Masochism had never been his scene.

And kissing her. He groaned mentally. Biggest mistake of all. He'd been as hard as a rock ever since. A hot arrow of humiliation zinged through him as the full weight of his vulnerability where Gina was concerned hit home. She could tie him up in knots with one glance from those blue eyes, and that wasn't good. Time to back-pedal.

Cutting the engine, he stretched his legs as far as he could in the close confines of the car, saying easily, 'I'm full. Mick's breakfasts always make me feel I need a visit to the gym in atonement, all that fat and so on. So, handover at eleven, you said?'

She nodded, a wisp of hair that had escaped the ponytail on top of her head skimming her cheek.

He wondered how such a simple thing could cause a further problem with a certain part of his anatomy. Although it wasn't simple. *She* wasn't simple. He'd thought she was accessible, soft and tender—and she was, in a way. But the defencelessness he'd sensed had a thick steel armour over it where the male of the species was concerned, thanks to this jerk who had let her down so badly. Knowing her as he'd imagined he did, seeing her every week-day and working with her so closely, hadn't prepared him for the guarded wariness that clothed her out of the office.

But perhaps she'd always been this way. He'd been so tied up with how *he'd* been feeling, would he have noticed? He had taken her absolutely for granted, and it was galling to admit he didn't know how to handle this new Gina.

'Need any help with anything?' He heard himself make the offer with a sense of shock. He had intended a swift goodbye and then an even swifter exit, the way things had gone.

She shook her head. 'No, I'm fine.'

'I don't think you're fine, Gina.' In spite of himself he leant forward and touched her mouth in the gentlest of kisses, drawing on every scrap of his considerable willpower to draw away in the next instant. 'And I'm sorry things have turned out this way.'

'This way?'

For a moment he was startled by the look on her face. 'You having to leave because of this guy.' He wasn't going to ask for her address again. If she offered it, he would know he had a chance.

She got out of the car. He joined her, his smile the best bit of acting he'd done for a long while as he said, 'Guess this is goodbye, then? Shame; Daisy and crew would have loved to have seen more of you.

'They've got you,' she whispered, without raising her eyes.

She looked very small and unprotected, and his guts were in spasm with the effort it was taking not to gather her into his arms. He wondered how someone so small and cuddly looking could be so formidable. And how he could have been so blind and stupid for so long.

Taking a woman to bed had become a pleasant pastime since Anna, but nothing more. Physically satisfying—even, on occasion, mentally stimulating too—but that was all. But from the day he'd met Gina an unsettled feeling had begun to grow, slowly and insidiously at first. The more he'd tried to ignore it, the more it had nagged at him, but still he'd been too damn stubborn to take notice. He'd wasted months messing about, months when he could have been persuading her this creep she was mixed up with was history. But he'd been scared. Scared of what he felt, scared of being out of control, scared of so many things he couldn't even put a name to some of them.

So was he going to let her walk out of his life because he was too proud to persist where he obviously wasn't wanted? Or was he going to make her want him?

'Yes, Daisy and crew have got me,' he agreed softly, keeping his voice easy and steady. 'But I'm an old-fashioned kind of guy at heart. You know: the man does the discipline and "this is for your own good" routine, and the woman undoes it all and spoils the kids rotten.'

She raised her face, a small smile on her lips, although he

could swear they were trembling. 'All the women I know would call you a male-chauvinist pig for that remark.'

'I never said I was perfect.' He shrugged, smiling. 'But then, you know that.'

'Yes, I know that.'

'And, because I'm a selfish so-and-so, I really don't want to lose touch with the one woman in my life I can *talk* to. I mean that, Gina.' He reached out and took her chin in his hand, enjoying the soft feel of her skin. He noticed a peculiar look in her eyes, and wondered for a moment if she found his touch repellent. But when her mouth had been under his he knew she'd responded to him, he told himself in the next instant. 'I know you want to cut ties with your old life, but face facts. Your parents are here, your sisters, your friends. It won't be as easy as that. They'll all be dropping in to see you now and again, and you'll be visiting them. I insist on being added to the list, OK?'

She took a step backwards and he dropped his hand. 'I've told you, I don't think that's a good idea, Harry.'

'And I've told you I disagree.' He held up his hands. 'OK, so I was a bit out of order suggesting what I did earlier, but there's nothing to stop us remaining friends.'

Her sigh was really more of a shudder. She hooked a strand of silken red hair behind her ear and gave what sounded like a nervous laugh. 'Same old Harry,' she said, shaking her head. 'You're just not very good at taking no for an answer, are you?'

'Terrible,' he agreed. 'Fault since childhood.'

She met his gaze then. He tried to keep his features open and friendly, and nothing more. 'Did it ever occur to you I can be equally as determined?' she asked quietly.

'Oh yes.' He looked down into those beautiful blue eyes that were strangely veiled this morning. An increase in pressure from somewhere inside his chest made it difficult for him to breathe for a long moment. He was aware of birds chirruping in the trees lining the road, of a dog barking somewhere in the distance and the sound of children playing in a garden close by, but the world was narrowed down to two deep, violet orbs. 'But I think you're a pretty sensible woman at heart,' he said as lightly as he could. 'The odd meal together, a visit to the theatre or the cinema, you joining me in taking the dogs for a walk when you're in these parts—what's wrong with that? All gain, no pain.'

The parody of a smile twisted her features. 'A pretty sensible woman,' she echoed, but he heard the tremor in her voice. 'Sensible women don't let themselves be hurt by egotistical, self-centred men, do they?'

Him again. He'd like five minutes in a soundproof room with this guy. By the time he'd finished with him, even his own mother wouldn't have recognised him. Taking a deep pull of air, he shrugged. 'Not habitually, which only bears out what I'm saying. You tried, it didn't work, he didn't appreciate what he'd got, you're leaving. That sounds sensible to me.'

She was quiet for a long moment. In the distance the dog had stopped barking and the children must have been called indoors. Even the birds had stopped their frenzied twittering. Suddenly it was very silent.

He saw her take a long swallow before she said, 'Harry, I can see I have to tell you something.'

His eyes narrowed. Whatever she was going to say, he wasn't going to like it; her body language told him so. There was nothing short of an expression of doom on her face. He shoved his hands into the pockets of his jeans, because it was either that or take her in his arms and force her to acknowledge the physical attraction between them. OK, so it wasn't love like she felt for this bozo, but it was a start. Plenty of people had built something on less. 'Go ahead,' he said flatly. 'I'm all ears.'

'What I told you about my going to London is true…' she began jerkily, only to pause and glance over his shoulder a second before Harry registered someone calling her name. Raising her hand in response, Gina said quickly, 'It's my estate agent with the new owners. I have to go.'

'Wait.' He caught her arm. 'Not yet. What were you going to say?'

'It doesn't matter.' Her withdrawal had been quick and complete.

He stared at her in frustration. However unpalatable it was, he knew it had been important. 'The hell it doesn't,' he said softly. 'Tell me, whatever it is. The estate agent can wait.'

It appeared he couldn't. The next moment the man was at their side, the young couple who were with him standing a few yards away. 'We said eleven o'clock, Gina,' the man said with a toothy—and, to Harry, insincere—smile. 'I trust there's not a problem?'

Harry glanced at his watch pointedly. 'You've ten minutes to go,' he said coolly, his eyes icy. 'And there's no problem, other than that you happen to be interrupting an important conversation.

The man blinked. 'Well, really!'

'You go in, Robert.' Gina was as red as her hair, something which made him even more angry with the estate agent— irrationally, Harry acknowledged. 'I'll be with you in a moment.' The instant the three had disappeared, she rounded on him. 'I can't believe you could be so rude.'

'Having known me for twelve months, I doubt that.'

'This is not funny, Harry.'

'Who's laughing?' He found himself glaring at her, which was the last thing he wanted to do. Warning himself to calm down, he said more reasonably, 'The guy was downright ignorant, Gina, and you know it. His whole attitude was—' He stopped abruptly. 'Hell, what are we wasting time talking about him for? What were you going to say?'

She shook her head helplessly. 'You're unbelievable.' It wasn't laudatory. 'And it would take too long now. Another time.'

Harry had taken the last seconds to put his voice into neutral. 'Fine. I'll wait till you're finished with the suit.'

'No, not now. I—' She shook her head again. 'I'll phone you, all right?'

'Is that in the same context as giving me your address? Because if so I get the impression I'll wait a long time,' he ground out with grim honesty.

She searched his face for a long moment. He tried to keep his features expressionless. Then she said slowly, 'I don't want to have this conversation any more. I've got a long and tiring day in front of me, and you're not helping. Please go.' She turned her head away as though she couldn't bear to look at him.

'Fine.' The rage that swept over him was stronger than anything he'd felt before, even in the worst times with Anna. 'Goodbye, Gina.'

'Goodbye.'

Her voice had changed, the cold note had gone to be replaced with a huskiness. A pain he had not thought possible knifed through his chest and took the capacity for further speech away. He couldn't reach her, he realised painfully.

And he couldn't tolerate any more of this without saying something he'd regret in hindsight.

He would have turned and walked away at that instant, if she hadn't raised her eyes and looked at him. The emptiness and stark desolation were too much. Nothing on earth could have stopped what happened next.

At first she resisted being in his arms, but then as his mouth continued its sensual assault she started to shake; he could feel it. He kissed her as he had wanted to do all morning since that first embrace in the car, his hands moving up and down her back as he moulded her into the hard length of him. The innate softness of her, the tantalising warmth of her perfume on silky skin, her lips open beneath his, all added to the fire that had taken him over, and he made no effort to pull back. Helplessly he devoured her mouth; desire was a flame inside him spreading rapidly. The need was too hot to resist.

She was sweet, potent. The taste, the smell of her, spun in his head and he knew she was with him; the tiny, uncontrolled moans against his mouth told him so. Whatever this other man meant to her, he—Harry Breedon—could make her tremble and sigh. And if sexual desire was all there was at first, he would use it as ruthlessly as he had to.

Using all his considerable experience, he skilfully demanded her submission, his lips moving to her long neck as she quivered in his hold. Her head was back, her eyes closed, her throat laid bare and vulnerable, and he heard himself groan with pleasure as he ran his lips over the honey, freckled skin.

'Gina, Gina.' He breathed her name against the scented flesh, revelling in her closeness. The feel of her firm breasts against the wall of his chest was a compelling aphrodisiac, and for a second he marvelled that she could move him so fiercely when they were both still fully clothed. She must be aware of the powerful attraction their bodies held for each other, the way every nerve and sinew was honed into the other's desire. The pulse in her throat was racing madly, proving she was as aroused as he was.

And then the quiet, sleepy nature of the empty street was shattered as the roar of a motorbike broke the silence. Although he registered the sound at the same moment as she broke the kiss and jerked away, he tried to hold on to her.

'No, Harry.' She pushed against him. 'Please, let me go.'

'Gina—'

'I mean it, I don't want this. *No!*'

When she pushed again he let her go free, his voice husky as he said, 'You see? You see how it could be between us? You can't deny there's something special, Gina. I want you, and I know you want me. Your body tells me so.'

She stared at him, her big blue eyes wide with what he put down to shock at what had transpired between them. The motorbike flashed past them, going much too fast for a lazy Saturday morning. 'There has to be more than sexual satisfaction for me, Harry. It wouldn't be enough, however well our bodies fitted together.'

He raked back his hair, frustration and irritation at her stubbornness vying with the need to make her *see*. 'Was it as good for you with this other guy?' he ground out. 'Could he turn you on with one kiss?'

She continued to look at him, her face white under the sprinkling of freckles. Slowly the sound of the bike receded and the scented quiet of the morning took over again. 'Yes,' she said at last.

'Was it better, just because you think you love him? Can you truthfully tell me that?'

Again she stared at him for long moments, not moving a muscle. He wished he knew what was going on behind the blue gaze. He was barely breathing as he waited for her answer, his chest tight.

'I don't think I love him,' she said so softly he could barely hear her. 'I know I do. I always will. And, however good sex might be with someone else, it couldn't begin to compare with the briefest of kisses from him. I can't change that, Harry. I don't want to change it. And I don't want any other man touching me or kissing me. Only him. That's the way I'm made.'

He felt sick inside, his insides twisting at the ring of truth in her voice. He had pushed it, he told himself, and this was his answer. He only had himself to blame.

Years of training made his face a blank mask. 'I see.' He nodded, a crisp movement, while his eyes remained locked on hers. 'Then I'm sorry for you, because he won't change. Men like him never do.'

'I know that.' There was a wealth of sadness in her smile. 'Goodbye, Harry. I hope you find what you're looking for some day.'

I did. I have. 'Goodbye, Gina.' He couldn't return the smile. 'Good luck.'

Without another word she turned from him and walked towards the house. He stood staring after her, wondering if she would look round and wave when she had opened the door. She didn't. The door closed behind her, and all was still.

He continued to stand where he was for a full minute, feeling as if his feet had been glued to the floor. But it wasn't his feet that were the problem, he told himself grimly once he was seated in his car. It was his heart. And his brain. Somehow he had to get his head round the fact that he was not going to see her again, because if ever a woman had meant what she said, Gina had.

His chest rose and fell as he took in deep breaths, trying to clear his scrambled thoughts and shake off the bitter regret that he had pushed things to their ultimate conclusion. It would have happened anyway, he consoled himself bleakly. Tomorrow, the next day, the next week or month, whenever he had seen her again. *If* he had seen her again. Which he doubted. She had been determined to keep her whereabouts hidden all along, he just hadn't accepted what was under his nose.

So, what now? He started the car, drawing away from the kerb after checking his mirrors and warning himself to concentrate. He couldn't go back to the way he was before he'd met her, more especially before he had acknowledged just what she meant to him. And the peripatetic life held no appeal now. He had promised his father he'd build the business into a good, marketable position in order for it to be sold before he pulled out, calculating that would mean a period of two, three years at the most. And then he'd imagined he'd take off again for pastures new.

Damn it! He drove his fist against the steering wheel, swearing long and loud. It didn't help. Why did she have to be a one-man woman, anyway? He'd spent the last decade around women who had cultivated a cool, philosophical attitude to life and love, women who were rational and logical, who cut their losses when a relationship came to an end and moved on serenely to the next man. Why couldn't Gina be like one of them?

Because then she wouldn't be Gina, and he wouldn't have fallen in love with her. Much good that it had done him.

His heart felt as though it was being squeezed by a giant hand, and he made a deep impatient sound in his throat. He didn't want to feel like this, damn it. He didn't want to be drowning helplessly in his own emotions. This was everything he had fought to avoid since his marriage. Perhaps it was best she was in love with someone else if this was what she did to him. She'd have had him running round in circles.

It was empty comfort. Which matched the future pretty well, he thought bleakly. How he was going to get through the rest of his life, he didn't know.

CHAPTER TWELVE

'GINA, I hate to be so boring as to state the obvious, but it's Friday night and you're in the big city. Moreover, this is the umpteenth time you've refused to come out with the girls. What do I have to do to get you to party?'

Gina smiled at the tall, skinny girl sitting cross-legged on her bed. Candy was an attractive, languid brunette whose somewhat vague, dreamy exterior hid the fact that she was in fact an extremely intelligent and successful career-woman with a responsible position in a merchant bank. She was also genuinely nice, something Gina had learned in the first twenty-four hours of being in London, when she had broken down so completely she hadn't been able to hide she was a total emotional mess.

From keeping her love for Harry hidden from everyone at home, even her mother, she had found herself telling Candy everything that first weekend, getting through a couple of boxes of tissues in the process. And Candy had responded magnificently, offering unlimited concern and sympathy, and calling Harry every name under the sun. Since then she had taken it as her mission in life to initiate Gina into the party scene, even though Gina had resisted to date.

'Look.' Candy leant forward, her big brown eyes earnest. 'You've been in London over two months, and it's a gorgeous June evening, much too nice to be stuck indoors. And don't say you're going to go on one of your endless walks, because that's not the sort of outdoors I mean.'

Gina's smile widened. 'You mean the sort of stuffy-night-club outdoors, I take it?'

Candy rolled her eyes. 'A nightclub full of good-looking guys who are positively *aching* for you to make an entrance.'

'Yeah, right.' She couldn't help laughing. 'I don't think so, somehow, Candy.'

'You'll never know if you don't try it. And there's safety in numbers. Kath and Linda and Nikki are coming, and Lucy and Samantha. Even if one or two of us get lucky, there'll be someone to get a cab home with. It's not *good* for you to stay in moping all the time.'

'I don't, and you know it.' Gina decided a little firmness was in order. 'But the club scene doesn't do it for me.'

'How do you know, if you don't try it?' Candy wailed.

'I don't *want* to meet anyone at the moment.'

'So just come out and have a good time with the girls,' Candy said promptly. 'We're going to eat first, and then go on to Blades or the Edition. You've met everyone, you like them and they like you. Just let your hair down for once. Have a dance and act silly. Flirt. Tease. You know.'

Actually she didn't, but Candy's grin was infectious. 'You aren't going to be satisfied until you see me bleary-eyed and hung over like you on a Saturday morning, are you?' she said resignedly.

'Is that a yes?' Candy whooped her delight. 'Great. We can do the girly thing of deciding what to wear in a minute. I've missed that since Jennie swapped the good life for boring old matrimony.' Jennie, Candy's previous flatmate of some years standing, had decided to opt and get married, much to Candy's disgust. Having been brought up by her mother after her father had run out on his wife and two children when Candy was five, Gina's flatmate was determined never to walk down the aisle.

It was only when Gina began to try on some of the more dressy items in her wardrobe that she realised just how much weight she'd lost in the last few weeks. She'd noticed her work skirts were looser, of course, and buttons she'd struggled with in the past were no longer a problem, but she liked to feel comfortable at work, and the easy fit had been agreeable. It wasn't as though she had dieted or anything, the pounds had simply melted away due to hectic busy days and restless evenings spent walking in the surrounding district until she was tired enough to drop into bed and go straight to sleep.

She had always longed to be slimmer, but now it had actually happened she found she wasn't sure if she liked her new shape or not. Or perhaps it was the small lines of misery which seemed to have taken residence between her brows, and the faint, bruised-looking shadows beneath her eyes she didn't like. Whatever, she discovered her favourite couple of dresses didn't look right at all.

She saw Candy look at her as she stood in front of the mirror in her room. The sleeveless sheer twisted-tulle dress with an attached shift beneath was perfectly suited to an evening such as this, but suddenly it hung on her like a sack. With a quick 'Hang on a sec,' Candy disappeared, returning a moment later with a wide and frighteningly expensive soft leather belt she had bought the weekend before.

'Here.' Candy thrust the belt at her. 'I think this will look fabulous with that dress. I must have been thinking of you when I bought it.'

'You haven't even worn it yet.'

Gina tried to give it back but Candy was having none of it, and when she tried it on she had to admit the cream-coloured belt against the seductive, taupe dress gave her a waist that appeared about eighteen inches wide, emphasising her hour-glass shape in a way that made Candy groan with envy.

'What I'd give for a bust like yours, but after seeing a few horror stories on the TV and in magazines I know I'm not brave enough to go under the knife for it.' Candy grimaced as she adjusted her sparkly top over her 32A cups with a deep sigh. 'I don't care what men say about some of them being a leg man, they all love a girl with plenty up top.'

'Some not enough, though.'

Their eyes met in the mirror, and immediately Candy pulled a face. 'No, none of that, I forbid it. You're not thinking of him tonight, Gina. This evening is strictly a Harry-free zone, OK?'

'OK.' Gina wondered—and not for the first time—how she would have got through the last nine weeks but for her flatmate. The utter desolation she had felt over Harry, the considerable pressure of taking on a new job along with a complete change of environment, had all been difficult to a greater or lesser degree, but Candy had been there for her one hundred and ten per cent.

Comforter, clown, advisor—whatever Gina's need had been, Candy had delivered. Her flatmate was one of those wonderful, irrepressible souls who would fit Gina's father's northern accolade of being 'salt of the earth', not that the highly independent and totally modern Candy would have particularly appreciated that, or any other label.

Gina grinned at her friend now as she said, 'You would actually like Harry if you met him, Candy. He's got the one thing you admire more than anything else: absolute honesty in his dealings with the opposite sex.'

Candy snorted. She had a huge repertoire of snorts, and they were infinitely more expressive than any words. 'He's one in a million, then,' she said darkly.

'Well, I'd agree with that of course, but then you know that. On a serious note—' She hesitated, then went on gently. 'All men aren't like your father, Candy.'

'I know that. There's always the exception to the rule but, believe me, Gina, most of them are motivated by what's in their trousers. And don't look at me like that, it's true. They're a different *species* to us, let alone a different sex. You have to play them at their own game to win. Take what you want when you want it and without getting involved heart-wise. It's the only way to remain your own person.'

'You sound more like Harry than Harry.'

'Perhaps we *would* get on, then.' Candy grinned. 'But you're far too nice for a man like that. Now, what shoes are you going to wear with that dress? Seriously sexy high-heels, I think. What have we got?'

Gina bent down and rifled through the bottom of her wardrobe before straightening and waving a pair of shoes in the same manner as a magician producing a rabbit out of a hat. 'These do?'

'Oh, wow, perfect.' Candy looked at the vertiginous, slinky court-shoes with their ruffled bow in the exact colour of the dress with respect. Gina didn't tell her that both the dress and shoes had been bought on a shopping trip with Bryony when her sister had insisted she buy something fabulous for a friend's wedding. Left to her own devices, she would probably have gone for something a little less eye-catching.

Now, taking the full credit for herself, she said smugly, 'Not bad for a little country yokel, eh?'

'Not bad at all.' Candy eyed her up and down. 'I tell you, girl, when you walk in that club tonight there's going to be more than one man straining at the leash. I'm going to make sure you're introduced to a new world of fun and frolicking, the like you've never dreamt of, or my name isn't Candy Robinson.'

Gina's smile dimmed. She didn't want a world of fun and frolicking unless it included Harry. Fun and frolicking with him would be an entirely different kettle of fish, though.

Proving 'mind reader' could be added to her CV, Candy waved a reproving finger. 'Stop it this minute. I told you, Harry-free zone tonight. I'm going to pour us both an enormous glass of wine while we do our hair in some outrageous style. Feathers I think for tonight, and I've got a sparkly spray in a wonderful shade of pink that'll wash out tomorrow morning.'

Gina stared at her in horror. 'Pink? With my hair? I don't think so, Candy.'

'OK, perhaps not the spray for you, then, but a spiky top-knot with a couple of my feathers would look funky.'

Gina nodded resignedly. 'Whatever you think.'

'Good girl. You know it makes sense.'

Despite her qualms, Gina had to admit that by the time they were ready to leave she looked good, thanks to Candy. She didn't look like herself, she didn't *feel* like herself, but that— Candy insisted firmly—was part of the fun. Certainly, in her bubblegum-pink dress and with streaks of vivid pink in her hair Candy was as different from the neat businesswoman of daylight hours as the man in the moon.

'I just love dressing up,' Candy said happily, finishing the last of her wine and smacking her lips. 'I don't think I've ever grown up, to be honest, which is why I'm the worst person in the world to have kids.'

'Not necessarily,' Gina said rationally. 'Being childlike in certain respects could mean you connect better with children, if anything.'

This time the snort expressed scorn. 'I don't like kids,' Candy stated firmly. 'Too demanding, too time-consuming, too messy. You can't do what you want when the mood takes you if you've got a kid to consider, let alone a husband. And carrying a baby for nine months…gross. My mum was really pretty in the photos she's got before she had us, but now she looks ten years older than what she is.'

'It doesn't have to be that way.'

Candy looked at her as she reached for her light cotton waist-length cardigan. 'You'd really choose to give up your freedom for eighteen, twenty-odd years to bring up some man's children?'

'Not *some man's*, no.'

'Oh, no, he's back, isn't he?'

Gina flushed. 'You asked, so I told you, and to be honest I can't think of anything more wonderful than being with him and having his babies. Sorry, but that's me.'

'So why didn't you take what he offered and then accidentally-on-purpose fall pregnant or something? That would have kept you in his life, if nothing else.'

'I couldn't have done that.' Gina was appalled.

Candy surveyed her for a long moment. 'No, I don't suppose you could,' she said softly. 'And you know what? He's a fool, this Harry of yours.'

This was getting too heavy before a night on the tiles. Gina forced a smile. 'Now, there I *would* agree with you,' she said lightly. She put her half-full glass of wine on the table as she spoke. When Candy had spoken about large glasses she'd meant large glasses—glass buckets would be a better description. If she finished this, she would be in no fit state to walk, let alone go to the nightclub. She was already feeling light-headed. 'Come on, then,' she said, linking her arm through Candy's. 'Let's go and meet the others. I'm starving.'

They clattered down the stairs from their second-floor flat in the tall Victorian terrace, giggling and talking. Candy opened the door into the street, stepping backwards in the next moment right on Gina's toe. Candy's gasp of surprise and Gina's yelp of pain intermingled, before a deep male voice said, 'Sorry. I didn't mean to make you jump. I was just about to ring the bell.'

Gina's lips formed his name, but her locked throat uttered no sound. Candy glanced at her and then back to the tall, dark man standing on the step. Her tone dry, she said coolly, 'I take it you're Harry Breedon?'

Harry's eyes had been intent on Gina. Now there was a flash of surprise apparent as he glanced at Candy for a moment. 'Yes. How did you know?'

'Are you kidding?'

His brow wrinkled, but, his gaze returning to Gina, he said softly, 'How are you?'

'She's fine.' Candy was clearly determined to imitate a pit bull terrier. 'Next question.'

Gina knew she had to say something, had to stop the potential disaster that could occur with Candy in this mood, but the power of speech was beyond her. In fact if it hadn't been for the wall she was leaning against she'd have been on the floor at his feet, her legs having turned to jelly.

She was terrified Candy might say something indiscreet, especially in view of the amount of wine her flatmate had consumed on an empty stomach, and she was bitterly regretting having confided in the other girl. She had just never considered Candy and Harry would ever meet.

Harry's gaze had switched back to Candy, and now there was pure steel in the smoky-grey eyes, his facial muscles having tightened ominously. 'Forgive me,' he said with silky menace, 'But I don't think we've met?'

Physical and mental intimidation had no effect on Candy. She stared back at him as though he was something that had just crawled out from under a stone.

From somewhere Gina found the strength to croak, 'Please, Candy, leave it,' before turning to Harry and saying, 'What are you doing here?'

His eyes had narrowed, but he drew in a deep pull of air before he said, 'I was passing, and I thought I'd drop in and see how you are.'

Candy's flat chest swelled to glamour-model proportions. 'Is that "see how you are" meaning a quickie, or "see how you are" meaning I'm sorry I've screwed you up so badly?' she asked scathingly.

Gina closed her eyes. The silence was profound. Then one exploding *'What?'* reverberated. When she opened her eyes, Harry's face was blazing with fury. 'I'm not sure where you're coming from, lady,' he ground out at Candy, 'But you're way off-beam.'

Candy's hands were on her hips, her body bent slightly forwards, but before she could say anything else Gina intervened. 'That's right, she's got it all wrong,' she said desperately. 'But we have to go. We're late already—'

'No way.' To Gina's horror he literally barred the way. 'Not till I find out what the hell is going on. *You*—' The razor-sharp gaze cut into Candy's indignant face. 'I don't know what you're thinking here, but Gina and I are friends, OK? From back home.'

Candy turned to Gina. Taking in the look on her face, she appeared to suddenly deflate. 'I'm sorry, I didn't mean to—' She stopped abruptly. 'But you ought to say something, you know that at heart. You can't move on till you do, the way you're made.'

'Candy, *please*,' Gina pleaded in anguish.

'Excuse me, but am I missing something here?' Harry said icily. And then, as both women stood, surveying him dumbly, he glanced from one to the other. 'Right, at the risk of making you even later, we're all having a nice little chat. In the street, in a taxi, wherever, but I'm not budging till I get an answer. Along with an apology,' he added grimly, shooting a glance at Candy.

'An *apology*?' Candy was back in fighting mode. 'Over my dead body.'

'Not an unappealing thought,' Harry returned tightly.

'Look, you rat—'

'Stop it.' There was a note in Gina's voice that brought a cessation in hostilities. With two pairs of eyes on her face, she said flatly, 'We'll talk upstairs in the flat, Harry. You go, Candy. Tell the others I'm not coming.'

'I'm not leaving you alone with him.'

'For crying out loud!' Harry looked ready to explode. 'What the hell do you think I'm going to do to her?'

'I'm not going.' Ignoring Harry, Candy pursed her lips at Gina. 'Not till I know you're going to be all right.'

'I'll be fine.'

'I'm still not going.'

She couldn't cope with the pair of them standing there with mulish frowns. Gina fought down the sudden flood of pure irritation filling her chest as she reflected *she* was the one who had every right to be awkward here. *She* was the one who had been telling herself for weeks that people didn't waste away from unrequited love these days, and that she had to keep going, that she wasn't going to allow anyone to ruin her life. *She* had walked herself into the ground every evening so she could sleep at night. *She* was the one who had battled against the devastating truth that she would never marry, never have children, a truth that had threatened to crush her more times than she could remember.

Her voice sharp, she said crisply, 'We'd better go upstairs, then, the three of us.' And she turned before either of them could react. Marching ahead, she wished she'd worn shoes other than ones which required her to sway so provocatively just to balance. She had seen the look in Harry's eyes when he had first taken in her appearance. It had been shock, she knew it. Did he think she had dressed like this purely to get a man tonight? That two months in the city had turned her into a man-eater?

It doesn't matter what he thinks. This thought was so ludicrous she dismissed it in the next moment. It mattered. It mattered so much she felt faint.

Gina opened the flat's front door with fingers that trembled, and walked through to the small sitting-room. She turned to face him. Candy had sidled in and already sat down, but Harry was still standing in the doorway.

'Can I get you a drink?' she asked with rigid self-control,

knowing in the next few minutes she was about to humiliate herself utterly. Because Candy had been right, down there in the hall—she *did* have to tell Harry how she felt about him, if only so he would leave her alone. And he would, oh, he would. He would run a mile once he knew she cared, *really* cared, about him.

Was that why she had not said anything before? Because a tiny part of her—a really weird, tiny part probably—hadn't been able to face the final, no-hope goodbye? Candy had spoken about her moving on, but she didn't *want* to move on into a world in which Harry played no part—even on the distant perimeter. But neither could a situation like the one tonight happen again, she did see that.

'I don't want a drink, Gina,' Harry said with cold control. 'And explanation would be good, though. Since when did my name become synonymous with the Marquis de Sade?'

She took a deep breath. Truth time. And maybe it was better to tell him looking like this—as someone else. Perhaps he would think that, however she felt about him, she was determined to build a full and satisfying life for herself.

'This is not Candy's fault,' she said shakily. 'She is only reacting to what I've told her.'

A muscle in his cheek twitched and the sensual mouth tightened. 'Which is?'

She hesitated. *Coward*, she screamed inside. *Say it. Tell him.*

Harry took a step into the room and then stopped. His lips were white with anger, she noticed with the part of her brain that was still registering facts. 'Hell, woman,' he ground out. 'What do you want from me? I backed off when you made it clear how you felt, I rolled over and played dead. So I turn up tonight, is that a crime?'

'No.' It wasn't. Not really. She couldn't blame him for following through and contacting her, after the way she had responded sexually to him that last morning. And, seeing her tonight, he'd think she was game for anything! 'No, it's not a crime.'

'So what did I do that was so bad as to get the sort of reaction your friend gave me tonight, eh? Now, if it had been that cretin who messed up your head so badly—'

He stopped. Whether it was the movement of Candy behind him, or the look on her face, Gina wasn't sure, but suddenly she saw incredulity in the hard, handsome face. Wishing the floor would open and swallow her, she forced herself to stand straight. There would be time afterwards, all the time in the world, to crumple. For now it was desperately important she faced him with her head held high. Because he knew.

'I didn't want you to know,' she said dully. 'It was better you didn't know, for both of us.'

She could see the highly intelligent brain trying to assimilate the knowledge that had been thrust at it. His eyes were blank, expressionless, as he struggled to come to terms with the fact he was the man who had driven her away.

'I don't believe it.' He moved his head in a rapid movement, signifying a silent apology for his disbelief. 'Why—why didn't you tell me? You're saying I—' He stopped, clearly still unable to believe what he knew she was saying.

Gina knew what it was to die a hundred times before she could bring herself to answer. 'You're the man I love, Harry. There's no one else, there never has been. I guess I'm what is quaintly called a one-man woman. That means for me it's all or nothing.'

He stared at her for an endless moment. And then she watched, unbelieving, as the most beautiful smile lit up his face. He covered the distance between them in a heartbeat, neither of them hearing Candy's 'Whoa,' of protest.

'Why didn't you tell me?' He pulled her into his arms with enough force to make her feathered top-knot bob precariously. 'Why put us both through torment?'

For a moment she thought she hadn't heard right, that the stress of his sudden appearance had addled her brain. Pulling back, she stared up into his face. 'You don't want anyone to— to love you,' she stammered helplessly.

'Not anyone, I want *you*.'

'No. You said you couldn't handle commitment, togetherness. You said that. And the way I feel…' She shook her head, trying to find the words to make him understand. 'It's for ever, Harry. And you said—'

'I said a damn sight too much, and all of it rubbish.'

She was in his arms, and he was looking at her in a way she had dreamt of in a thousand dreams, but still she didn't dare believe it. 'No,' she said again. 'You had girlfriends, you didn't look at me that way until you knew I was moving away, and there'd be no real commitment. But I can't be what you'd want me to be.'

'You *are* what I want you to be.' A soft sigh shuddered through his body and she felt the echo of it in hers. 'I've been going crazy without you, believe me. Stark staring crazy. The day you left I promised myself I wouldn't try to muscle in on you again, not when you'd told me there was no chance, that this guy would always be there. But it was no good. I couldn't eat, couldn't sleep.' He took a deep breath. 'I love you, Gina. And if I'm honest it frightens me to death. But I'm more frightened at the thought of living another day, another minute, without you.'

Neither of them knew Candy had left until they heard the click of the sitting-room door as she closed it behind her. 'Candy, she's gone,' Gina said vacantly, staring up into his face. 'I'm supposed to be going out with her tonight.'

'You're going nowhere unless it's with me.'

'But you didn't say you loved me.' Her voice was almost plaintive. 'You let me leave.'

'I thought you were madly in love with someone else, how could I tell you how I felt? It would only have been adding another reason for you to get away, or that's the way I saw it. But I tried to make you understand you were different—'

'No.' She didn't dare believe this because when he told her he had made a mistake, changed his mind, she would die. 'No, you aren't that sort of man.'

'What sort of man, my love?' he asked softly.

'My love.' Her breath caught at the words she'd never thought to hear from his lips, but still she couldn't let herself hope. 'The for ever kind.'

He gave a choked laugh and buried his face in the soft skin of her neck for a moment. 'I'm eternally for ever where you're concerned,' he said thickly, moulding her against him and holding her as though he would never let her go. 'Till death do us part and beyond. I realised that when you went away. If you don't want me I'm destined to live my life alone, apart from four rapidly growing small dogs, that is, who happen to be spending the weekend with my parents.'

Her arms wound around his neck tightly. If she didn't want him? What was he talking about? Surely he knew by now he was her world, the very air she breathed? 'How—how are the puppies?' she whispered dazedly.

'Missing you.' He lowered his head, crushing her soft lips

under his in a kiss that spoke of his profound hunger. He kissed her deeply, a long, lingering kiss, and when he finally raised his head she was sure her soul had merged with his. 'Marry me soon?' he murmured huskily. 'I mean *real* soon?'

Gina tried to ignore the effect his hand sliding up and down her back was having. It was difficult. Her breathing shallow, she said, 'Harry, are you sure?'

'That it has to be soon? Dead sure.'

'That…that you want to marry me. After what you've been through…' She took a deep breath, wondering if she should go on. 'I mean, after Anna and everything.'

Harry didn't even blink. 'I have never been more sure of anything in my life.' He covered her mouth in another hungry kiss that left her reeling. 'I want you for my wife. I want you as the mother of my children. But more than anything I want to make love to you every day for the rest of our lives.' He brushed a strand of hair from her forehead with infinite tenderness. 'All day, every day, and all night.'

She smiled, a wave of fierce desire washing over her body as she felt the hard ridge of his arousal against her softness. 'Just now and again, then?' she murmured teasingly.

'And again and again and again…'

Suddenly terrified that this was all a dream, she pressed into him, kissing him with an intensity that touched him to the core. Growling softly, he curved over her, the scent and feel of him encompassing her as he savoured the sweetness of her mouth. Her hands moved feverishly under the thin cotton shirt he was wearing, her fingers running over the shifting muscles of his back, then curling round to tangle themselves in the thick black hair of his chest, glorying in the warmth and strength of the hard male body. 'I didn't think I was ever going to see you again,' she half-sobbed against his mouth. 'I thought you wanted me for a brief affair, like all the others.'

'They didn't mean anything, Gina.' He raised his head, looking deep into her eyes. 'Not a thing. Does that disgust you?'

Nothing he had done or would ever do could disgust her. She shook her head.

'Looking back now, I'm not proud of the last ten years of my life, but I can't change them. What I can do is make sure you know every moment of every day from now on that you are the one and only woman for me. I knew twelve months ago, deep inside. I wouldn't admit it, even to myself, but there was something about you that tore at my heart even then.'

She thought of all the nights she'd cried herself to sleep, the heartache, loneliness and despair. Suddenly it didn't matter. It was worth it for this.

'I love you, Gina, with everything I am, every part of me,' he whispered, running his hands up and down her body as her fingers continued to trace the wide musculature of his chest. 'And we're going to do this right. I want our wedding night to be special, can you understand that?'

She nodded, loving him. It had all been so wrong with Anna. This time he wanted it to be different from the outset.

'But I'm only human.' As her hands moved over his body, his breath caught jaggedly. Catching her fingers in his, he breathed deeply before he said, 'I want you so badly it hurts. How much time do you need to get married?'

'No time at all.' She loosened one of her hands, reaching up and stroking the hard, male jaw. 'My sisters both had big weddings with bridesmaids and all the trimmings, and I hated every minute of them. I'd like to slip away somewhere, with just our parents in tow.' She smiled dreamily. 'A white dress for me, a light suit for you, with maybe a carnation in your buttonhole. No fuss and no frills, just the two of us saying our vows before God and man.'

He stared at her. 'You're an amazing woman.'

'It's taken you long enough to find that out.'

They each gave a small laugh before he picked her up and carried her over to the small sofa, sitting down with her on his lap and kissing her once more. She kissed him back with all her heart, and again it was Harry who applied the brake, his mouth leaving hers and trailing a row of nibbling kisses along her jawline.

Gina reached up and trailed her fingers through his crisp dark hair in a way she'd longed to do for more than twelve months. 'How did you find out my address?' she asked breathlessly, enchanted she could touch him like this.

'I lied to your mother.'

'What?' She stared at him, pulling back slightly to look into his face and see if he was serious.

'I phoned her in the capacity of your ex-boss and said there were a couple of things the account department needed to forward to you for your new employers. Fortunately, she didn't ask what they were.' He paused. 'Do I take it you hadn't told her how you felt about me? Because she seemed very friendly. I'd have thought if she knew I'd driven her daughter away she might have been a little less polite.'

'I didn't tell anyone, not till I got here. Then I was in such a state Candy got the full story,' Gina admitted shyly. 'She's very nice, really, you know.'

He raised his eyebrows but didn't comment on that. What he did say was, 'Are you free tomorrow to go hunting for an engagement ring? We'll buy the wedding rings at the same time.'

She had to make sure. In spite of all he had said, the last year or so had taken its toll, and this had happened so quickly her head was still spinning. 'You don't have to do that,' she said slowly, her fingers playing with one of the buttons on his shirt. 'It would perhaps be more sensible to wait and see how you feel in a month or two.'

'In a month or two I'm hoping you might be carrying my child in there,' he said very softly, touching her belly.

Shocked, she raised her eyes to his and saw all the reassurance she'd ever need shining there.

'I love you, Gina. I'll love you for ever. I want to fill our house with love so it spills over onto our children and grandchildren, and their children. I want it all, OK? Cats, dogs, roses round the door, and you in my arms every night.'

She gulped, telling herself she couldn't cry, not when everything was so wonderful, but as a tear caught on her eyelashes she said brokenly, 'I've been so miserable without you.'

'And I without you. When you left the world became grey, you know?'

She nodded, joy, like warm honey, spreading throughout her body and healing all the hurt and pain.

'I'd look at the sunset and all I could think of was you. Were you looking at the same night sky? The knowledge that you were somewhere living, breathing, laughing, sleeping without me, was torture. All around the world was going on the same, and yet I was dying inside.'

She reached up and touched his face. 'I know.'

'Stay with me like this tonight?' he asked softly. 'I can't bear to let you out of my arms.'

She nodded. 'Can I change?' She wanted to wipe off the heavy eye make-up and brush out her hair, to feel herself again.

A smile curved his lips. 'Be quick.'

She was quick, slipping into her silk pyjamas and robe before she came back to him. Her heart jumped as she saw him, his legs stretched out and his head lying against the back of the sofa, eyes shut. He was so big and dark and handsome, so sexy. She couldn't believe he wanted her. But he did. Her heart told her so, even if logic was against it.

In the moment before he opened his eyes and held out his arms, she saw she wasn't the only one who was thinner. There was a raw leanness to the big frame that hadn't been there before. It melted her heart, but then everything about him melted her heart.

They talked and kissed, dozed and embraced the night away, and when Candy returned to the flat at first light she found them wrapped in each other's arms. She stood in the entrance to the sitting room, a big grin on her face as she took in Gina's shining face. 'Congratulations are in order, I take it?' she said drily.

Gina nodded. 'We're looking for an engagement ring today.'

Candy glanced at Harry, her brown eyes slightly mocking. 'You might be a late bloomer, but when you cotton on there's no stopping you, is there?' she drawled.

'You bet.' Harry's eyes had narrowed and his smile was controlled. 'And you'd better start looking for another flat-mate this week, because by this time next Saturday Gina will be Mrs Breedon.'

'No problem.'

'I'll cover her rent and any expenses until you get someone, of course.'

'You don't have to do that.'

'Yes, I do.' His smile took a wry twist. 'Without you, we might have gone on for months with our wires crossed.'

'Only months?' Candy queried, tilting her head.

He shrugged. 'I wouldn't have given up, however long it took.'

Candy surveyed him for a long moment. 'No, I don't think you would,' she said thoughtfully. 'From a bad start, I think I might get to like you after all, Gina's Harry.'

'Likewise.'

They were married by special licence within ten days, a quiet wedding with just immediate family in attendance. Harry had promised all their friends a big party when they were back from honeymoon.

Gina looked beautiful in her white dress, a silk crêpe frock which fell gracefully to the hips before flaring out in a plethora of Monroe-esque sunray pleats. And Harry looked very dashing in a grey suit with a white-and-gold waistcoat and white shirt and tie.

Everyone had a magical day, thoroughly enjoying the magnificent wedding lunch Mrs Rothman and one of her friends had had waiting for them when they returned to the cottage after the service. Gina didn't think she had ever been so happy.

Harry's parents were taking care of the dogs until Gina and Harry were back from their honeymoon in Italy, and so once everyone had left later that evening Gina and Harry were alone in their own home. Gina had expressly wanted it that way, refusing to go to a hotel or straight on honeymoon. Since Harry had proposed, she'd dreamt of waking up in his arms after a night of making love in their thatched cottage, the sun streaming through the windows, and wood pigeons cooing in the trees in the garden. Which was exactly what happened.

When she opened her eyes the room was bathed in sunlight,

the curtains moving gently in the warm breeze from the open window. Harry was still asleep, one hairy arm lying possessively over her stomach, and his long eyelashes resting on the tanned skin of his face. She lay, drinking in every curve and hollow of his face, before her eyes moved over the strong tanned throat and muscled chest.

This was her *husband*. She lifted her left hand and looked at the exquisite diamond engagement-ring and white-gold band nestling beside it. She had the right to lie beside him every night in this huge bed, to wake up next to him, to touch and caress him. It was more than she had ever hoped for. *He* was more than she had dared to hope for.

And their wedding night... She closed her eyes for a moment, a delicious thrill trickling over her whole body.

She had been embarrassed to admit she hadn't slept with a man before him, but she needn't have been. He had taken it as a gift, a precious gift—he'd told her so. And then he had set out to initiate her into all she had been missing.

She had expected the first time to be... She shook her head. She didn't know, not really, but certainly not the night of passion that had ensued. He had spent hours showing her how much he loved her, and he had been so tender and patient, touching and tasting her, bringing her to the brink of fulfillment time and time again, before he had finally taken her. And even then he had restrained his own need and desire until she'd been as ready as him, prolonging the exquisite pleasure his possession had caused, until there'd been no room for anything but the delicious quest for the next peak of delectation.

Her body felt sensuously alive, the core of her throbbing with a pleasurable ache, and every part of her tingling with the knowledge she was loved. Whatever happened now, whatever life threw at them, they would weather it together. There were no promises the sky would always be blue as it was today, how could there be? Life was a series of milestones, it was that way for everyone. But not everyone had love as the anchor of their soul.

She was lucky. She was so, *so* lucky.

'Good morning, Mrs Breedon.'

His deep smoky voice brought her out of her thoughts, and she focused on his face. He was smiling. She smiled back, turning into the curve of him as she whispered, 'Good morning, Mr Breedon.'

'Every day for the rest of our lives we can say that.' His voice reflected the wonder in her own heart.

'I know.' Her eyes brimming with love, she murmured huskily, 'And every night we can lie in each other's arms and make love.'

'Well, actually…' He ran his hands over her body, bringing her hips into his where she felt his body's response of her nakedness. 'We can do that in the morning too.'

She giggled, moving her hips in a sinuous and blatant invitation as she whispered, 'Are you sure it's allowed?'

'Oh yes,' he said, his breath catching in his throat on a groan. 'In fact, it's written into the marriage document. Didn't you know?'

She shook her head, sliding her hands down and caressing his erection so he nearly shot out of his skin. 'But I approve,' she whispered against his mouth. 'We'll have to make sure we adhere to that, if it's official.'

And they did.

The Secretary's Secret

MICHELLE
CELMER

Michelle Celmer lives in a southeastern Michigan zoo. Well, okay, it's really a house, but with three kids (two of them teenagers and all three musicians), three dogs ranging from seventy to ninety pounds each, three cats (two longhaired) and a fifty-gallon tank full of various marine life, sometimes it feels like a zoo. It's rarely quiet, seldom clean, and between after-school jobs, various extra-curricular activities and band practice, getting everyone home at the same time to share a meal is next to impossible.

You can often find Michelle locked in her office, writing her heart out and loving the fact that she doesn't have to leave the house to go to work, or even change out of her pyjamas.

Michelle *loves* to hear from her readers. Drop her a line at: PO Box 300, Clawson, MI 48017, or visit her website at: www.michellecelmer.com

This book is in honour of the dedicated
volunteers at Regap of Michigan (Retired Grey-
hounds as Pets), www.rescuedgreyhound.org
It has been a pleasure and a privilege to be
a part of something so special.

One

Nick Bateman lay in bed in the honeymoon suite of the hotel, pretending to be asleep, wondering what the hell he'd just done.

Instead of spending his wedding night with the woman who was supposed to be his new wife—the one he'd left at the altar halfway through their vows—he'd slept with Zoë, his office manager.

He would have liked to blame the champagne for what had happened, but two shared bottles wasn't exactly enough to get him rip roaring drunk. He'd been too intoxicated to drive, no question, but sober enough to know it was a really bad idea to sleep with an employee.

And even worse, he considered Zoë one of his best friends.

He rubbed a hand across the opposite side of the mattress and could feel lingering traces of heat. The scent of sex and pheromones and her spicy perfume clung to his skin and the sheets.

He heard a thump and a softly muttered curse from somewhere across the room. She had been slinking through the darkness for several minutes now, probably looking for her clothes.

His only excuse for what he'd let happen, even if it was a lame one, was that on the night of his failed wedding he'd been discouraged and depressed and obviously not thinking straight.

Instead of saying *I do*, he'd said *I don't* and skipped out on his fiancée. His second, in fact. Could he help it if it had only occurred to him just then the terrible mistake he was making? That his desire for a wife and family was clouding his judgment? That after a month of courtship he barely knew the woman standing beside him, and she was in fact—as his friends had tried to warn him—only after his money.

What a nightmare.

He would never forget the look of stunned indignation on Lynn's face when, halfway through their vows, he had turned to her and said, "I'm sorry, I can't do this." He could still feel the sting of her fist where it had connected solidly with his jaw.

He'd deserved it. Despite being a lying, blood-sucking vampire, she didn't deserve to be humiliated that way. Why was it that he couldn't seem to find the right woman? It had been five years since he decided he was ready to settle down. He'd figured by now he would be happily married with at least one baby and another on the way.

Nothing in his life was going the way it was supposed to. The way he'd planned.

After the abrupt end of the service, Zoë had driven him to the hotel where the honeymoon suite awaited and the champagne was already chilling. He'd been in no mood to drink alone, so he'd invited her in. She'd ordered room service—even though he hadn't been particularly hungry—and made him an ice pack for his jaw.

She always took care of him. And damn, had she taken care of him last night.

He wasn't even sure how it started. One minute they were sitting there talking, then she gave him this look, and the next thing he knew his tongue was in her mouth and they were tearing each other's clothes off.

Her mouth had been so hot and sweet, her body soft and warm and responsive. And the sex? It had been freaking fantastic. He'd never been with a woman quite so…*vocal* in bed. He'd never once had to guess what she wanted because she wasn't shy about asking.

God, he'd really slept with Zoë.

It's not that he'd never looked at her in a sexual way. He'd always been attracted to her. She wasn't the kind of woman who hypnotized a man with her dazzling good looks—not that she wasn't pretty— but Zoë's beauty was subtle. It came from the inside, from her quirky personality and strength.

But there were some lines you just didn't cross. The quickest way for a man to ruin a friendship with a woman was to have sex with her.

He knew this from experience.

Thankfully, he hadn't done irrevocable damage. As much as he wanted a family, Zoë wanted to stay single and childless just as badly. Unlike other female employees he'd made the mistake of sleeping with—back when he was still young, arrogant and monumentally stupid—she wouldn't expect or want a commitment.

Which was a *good* thing, right?

There was another thump, and what sounded like a gasp of pain, right beside the bed this time. He had two choices, he could continue to pretend he was asleep and let her stumble around in the dark, or he could face what they had done.

He reached over and switched on the lamp, squinting against the sudden bright light, both surprised and pleased to find a completely bare, shapely rear end not twelve inches from his face.

Zoë Simmons let out a shriek and swung around, blinking against the harsh light, clutching her crumpled dress to her bare breasts. This was like the dream she frequently had where she was walking through the grocery store naked. Only this was worse, because she was awake.

And honestly, right now, she would rather be caught naked in a room full of strangers than with Nick.

"You scared me," she admonished. So much for sneaking out before he woke up. Call her a chicken, but she hadn't been ready to face what they'd done. How many times they had done it.

How many different positions they had done it in...

The bed was in shambles and there were discarded condom wrappers on the bedside table and floor. She winced when she thought of the way they'd touched each other, the places they had touched. How incredibly, shockingly, mind-meltingly *fantastic* it had been.

And how it could never, *ever* happen again.

"Going somewhere?" he asked.

"'Fraid so."

He looked over at the digital clock beside the bed. "It's the middle of the night."

Exactly.

"I thought it would be best if I leave." But God help her, he wasn't making it easy. He sat there naked from the waist up, looking like a Greek god, a picture of bulging muscle and golden skin, and all she wanted to do was climb back into bed with him.

No. *Bad* Zoë.

This had to end, and it had to end *now*.

She edged toward the bathroom, snagging her purse from the floor. "I'm going to go get dressed, then we'll...talk."

She backed into the bathroom, his eyes never

leaving her face. She shut and locked the door, then switched on the light, saw her reflection and let out a sound that ranked somewhere between a horrified gasp and a gurgle of surprise.

Just when she thought this night couldn't get any worse.

Her hair was smashed flat on one side of her head and sticking up on the other, last night's eyeliner was smeared under her red, puffy eyes, and she had pillow indentations all over her left cheek. Unlike Nick who woke up looking like a Playgirl centerfold. It's a miracle he hadn't run screaming from the room when he saw her.

Had there been a window in the bathroom, she would have climbed through it.

She splashed water on her face, used a tissue to wipe away the smudges under her eyes, then dug through her purse for a hair band. Finger combing her hair with damp hands, she pulled it taut and fastened it into a ponytail. She had no clue where her bra and panties had disappeared to, and there was no way in hell she was going to go hunting for them. She would just have to go commando until she got home.

She tugged on her battered dress, smoothing out the wrinkles as best she could. In his haste to undress her, Nick had torn one of the spaghetti straps loose. One side of the bodice hung dangerously low. The form-fitting silk skirt was still a little damp and stained from the glass of champagne she'd spilled on herself.

It was the dress she'd worn to both of Nick's weddings. It looked as if maybe it was time to retire it.

Or incinerate it.

Zoë studied her reflection, hiking the bodice up over her half exposed breast. Not great, but passable. Maybe everyone wouldn't look at her and automatically think, *tramp*, as she traipsed through the five-star hotel lobby. Not that she would run into too many people at three-thirty in the morning.

She heard movement from the other room, and fearing she would catch him as naked and exposed as he had caught her—she cringed at the thought of her big rear end in his face when he turned the light on—she called, "I'm coming out now!"

When he didn't respond, she unlocked the door and edged it open, peeking out. He sat on the bed wearing only the slacks from last night, his chest bare.

And boy what a chest it was. It's not as if she'd never seen it before. But after touching it…and oh my, was that a bite mark on his left shoulder? She also seemed to recall giving him a hickey somewhere south of his belt, not to mention the other things she'd done with her mouth…

Shame seared her inside and out. What had they done?

As she stepped toward him, she noticed the gaping hole in the front of his pants. She was about to point out that the barn door was open, then remembered that in her haste to get his slacks off last night, she'd broken the zipper. They'd torn at each other's clothes, unable to get naked fast enough, as if they'd been working up to that moment for ten long years and couldn't bear to wait a second longer. She would never forget the way he'd plunged inside her, hard and fast and deep. The way she'd wrapped her legs around his hips and ground herself against him, how she'd moaned and begged for more…

Oh God, what had they done?

She clutched her purse to her chest, searching the floor for her shoes. She needed to get out of there pronto, before she did something even stupider, like whip her dress off and jump him.

"I think these belong to you." Nick was holding up her black lace bra and matching thong. "I found them under the covers."

Swell.

"Thanks." She snatched them from him and stuffed both in her tiny purse.

"Should we talk about this?" he asked.

"If it's all the same to you, I'd rather leave and pretend it never happened."

He raked a hand through his short blue-black hair. Thick dark stubble shadowed his jaw, which explained the chafing on her inner thighs.

"That is one way to handle it," he said, sounding almost disappointed.

He had to know as well as she did that this was a fluke. It never should have happened. And it sure as hell would never, *ever* happen again.

Not that he was a bad guy. Nick was rich,

gorgeous and genuinely nice—and okay, a touch stubborn and overbearing at times. And there were occasional moments when she wanted to smack him upside the head. But he was sweet when he wanted to be and generous to a fault.

How he hadn't found the right woman yet, she would never understand. Maybe he was just trying too hard. Either that or he had really bad luck. When it came to finding the wrong woman, he was like a magnet.

Personally, she liked her life just the way it was. No commitments. No accountability to anyone but herself and Dexter, her cat. She'd already done the mommy-caregiver gig back home. While both her parents worked full time jobs she'd been responsible for her eight younger brothers and sisters. All Nick had talked about during the past five years was marrying Susie homemaker and having a brood of children. The closest she was going to get to a diaper was in the grocery store, and that was only because it was across the aisle from the cat food.

The day Zoë turned eighteen she'd run like hell, clear across Michigan, from Petoskey to Detroit. And if it hadn't been for Nick, she wouldn't have lasted a month on her own. Despite having just started his construction company, or maybe because of it, he hadn't fired her when he found out she'd lied on her application about having office experience.

The truth was, she couldn't even type and her phone skills were questionable. Instead of kicking her out the door, which she admittedly deserved, his alpha male gene had gone into overdrive and he'd set out to save her. He'd helped put her through college, trained her in the business—in life. She'd been more than a tad sheltered and naïve.

To this day Zoë didn't know why he'd been so good to her, why he'd taken her under his wing. When they met, something just clicked.

And, in turn, Zoë had been Nick's only family. The only person he could depend on. He never seemed to expect or want more than that.

No way she would throw it all away on one stupid lapse in judgment, because the truth of the matter was, in a relationship, they wouldn't last. They were too different.

They would kill each other the first week.

"We've obviously made a big mistake," she said. She spotted her brand new Jimmy Choo pumps peeking out from under the bed. She used her big toe to drag them out and shoved her feet in. "We've known each other a long time. I'd hate to see our friendship, our working relationship, screwed up because of this."

"That would suck," he agreed. He sure was taking this well. Not that she'd expected him to be upset. But he didn't have to be so…*agreeable*. He could at least pretend he was sorry it wouldn't happen again.

She hooked a thumb over her shoulder. "I'm going to go now."

He pulled himself to his feet. She was wearing three-inch heels and he was still a head taller. "I'll drive you home."

She held up a hand to stop him. "No, no. That's not necessary. I'll call a cab."

He looked down at the clock. "It's after three."

All the more reason not to let him drive her home. In the middle of the night she felt less...accountable. What if, when they got there, she invited him in? She didn't want him getting the wrong idea, and she wasn't sure if she could trust herself.

Astonishing what a night of incredible sex could do to cloud a girl's judgment. "I'd really rather you didn't. I'll be fine, honest."

"Then take my truck," he said, taking her hand and pressing his keys into it. "I'll catch a cab in the morning."

"You're sure?"

"I'm sure."

He gestured toward the bedroom door and followed her into the dark sitting room. When they got to the door she turned to face him. The light from the bedroom illuminated the right side of his face. The side with the dimple.

But he wasn't smiling. He looked almost sad.

Well, duh, he'd just split up with his fiancée. Of course he was sad.

"I'm really sorry about what happened with Lynn. You'll meet someone else, I promise." Someone unlike fiancée number one, who informed him on their wedding day that she'd decided to put off having kids for ten years so she could focus on her career. Or fiancée number two who'd been a real prize. Lynn had obviously been after Nick's money, but he'd been so desperate to satisfy his driving need to procreate, he'd been blind to what he was getting himself into. Thank goodness he'd come to his senses, let himself see her for what she was.

"I know I will," he said.

"This probably goes without saying, but it would be best if we kept what happened to ourselves. Things could get weird around the office if anyone found out."

"Okay," he agreed. "Not a word."

Huh. That was easy.

Almost *too* easy.

"Well, I should go." She hooked her purse over her shoulder and reached for the doorknob. "I guess I'll see you at work Monday."

He leaned forward and propped a hand above her head on the door, so she couldn't pull it open. "Since this isn't going to happen again, how about one last kiss?"

Oh no, *bad* idea. Nick's kiss is what had gotten them into this mess in the first place. The man could work miracles with his mouth. Had he been a lousy kisser, she never would have slept with him. "I don't think that would be a good idea."

He was giving her that look again, that heavy-lidded hungry look he'd had just before they had attacked each other the first time. And suddenly he seemed to be standing a lot closer. And he smelled so good, *looked* so good in the pale light that her head felt a little swimmy.

"Come on," he coaxed, "one little kiss."

Like a magnet she felt drawn to him. She could feel herself leaning forward even as she told him, "That would be a bad idea."

"Probably," he agreed, easing in to meet her halfway. He caressed her cheek with the tips of his fingers, combed them gently through her hair. The hair band pulled loose and a riot of blond curls sprang free, hanging in damp ringlets around her face.

"Nick, don't," she said. But she didn't do anything to stop him. "We agreed this wouldn't happen again."

"Did we?" His hand slipped down to her shoulder. She felt a tug, and heard the snap of her other spaghetti strap being torn. Her dress was now officially strapless. And in another second it would be lying on the floor.

Oh God, here we go again.

Nick pushed the strap of her purse off the opposite shoulder and it landed with a soft thump on the floor at their feet and his truck keys landed beside it. "We're already here, the damage has been done. Is one more time really going to make that much of a difference?"

It was hard to argue with logic like that, especially when he was nibbling her ear. And he was right. The damage had already been done.

What difference could one more time possibly make?

"Just a quick one," she said, reaching for the fastener on his slacks. She tugged it free and shoved them down his hips. "As long as we agree that what goes on in this room stays in this room."

His lips brushed her shoulder and her knees went weak. "Agreed."

Then he kissed her and she melted.

One more time, she promised herself as he bunched the skirt of her dress up around her waist and lifted her off the floor.

"One more time," she murmured as she locked her legs around his hips and he pinned her body to the wall, entered her with one deep, penetrating thrust.

One more time and they would forget this ever happened...

Two

What difference could one more time *possibly* make? Apparently, more than either she or Nick had anticipated.

Zoë glanced up at the clock above her desk, then down to the bottom drawer of the file cabinet where she'd stashed the bag from the pharmacy behind the employment records. The bag that had been sitting there for four days now because she conveniently kept forgetting to bring it home every night after work. Mostly because she'd been trying to convince herself that she was probably overreacting. She was most likely suffering some funky virus that would clear up on its own. A virus that just happened to zap all of her energy, made her queasy every morning when she rolled out of bed and made her breasts swollen and sore.

And, oh yeah, made her period late.

She was sure there had to be a virus like that, because there was no chance in hell this condition was actually something that would require 2 a.m. feedings and diapers.

She would have a much easier time explaining this away if she wasn't ninety-nine percent sure Nick hadn't been wearing a condom that last time up against the hotel room wall.

It's not as if she could come right out and ask him. Not without him freaking out and things getting really complicated. It had taken several weeks to get past the post-coital weirdness. At first, it had been hard to look him in the eye, knowing he'd seen her naked, had touched her intimately.

Every time she looked at his hands, she remembered the way they felt against her skin. Rough and calloused, but oh so tender. And so big they seemed to swallow up every part of her that he touched.

His slim hips reminded her of the way she'd locked her legs around him as he'd pinned her to the wall. The way he'd entered her, swift and deep. How she'd come apart in his arms.

And his mouth. That wonderfully sinful mouth that melted her like butter in a hot skillet…

No. No. *No.*

Bad Zoë.

She shook away the lingering memory of his lean,

muscular body, of his weight sinking her into the mattress, her body shuddering with pleasure. She'd promised herself at least a hundred times a day that she wasn't going to think about that anymore. Finally things seemed to be getting back to normal. She and Nick could have a conversation without that undertone of awkwardness.

Zoë didn't want to risk rocking the boat.

She hadn't even told her sister Faith, and they told each other almost everything. Although, after their last phone conversation Zoë was under the distinct impression Faith knew something was up. It wouldn't be unlike her sister to drop everything and show up unannounced if she thought there was something that Zoë wasn't telling her.

She took a deep, fortifying breath. She was being ridiculous. She should just take the damned test and get it over with. She'd spent the ten bucks, after all. She might as well get her money's worth. Waiting yet another week wouldn't change the final outcome. Either she was or she wasn't. It would be good to know now, so she could decide what to do.

And decide what she would tell Nick.

As she was reaching for the bottom drawer handle, Shannon from accounting appeared in the doorway and Zoë breathed a sigh of relief.

"Hey, hon, you up for lunch with the girls? We're heading over to Shooters."

Despite being a nervous wreck, she was starving. Though she normally ate a salad for lunch, she would sell her soul for a burger and fries and a gigantic milkshake. And for dessert, a double chocolate sundae. Hold the pickles.

"Lunch sounds wonderful."

She grabbed her purse and jacket and gave the file cabinet one last glance before she followed Shannon into the hall.

As soon as she got back from lunch, she promised herself. She would put the test in her purse so she wouldn't forget it, and tonight when she got home she would get to the bottom of this.

Nick walked down the hall to Zoë's office and popped his head inside, finding it empty and feeling a screwy mix of relief and disappointment. He'd come to her office now, knowing she would probably be on her lunch break. Though they'd promised to pretend it hadn't happened, he couldn't seem to make himself forget every erotic detail of their night together. He'd been doing his best to pretend nothing had changed, but something was still a little...*off*.

Something about Zoë—a thing he couldn't quite put his finger on—seemed different.

He couldn't stop himself from wondering, *what if*? What if he'd told her he didn't want to pretend like it hadn't happened?

He just wasn't sure if that's what he really wanted. Were he and Zoë too different for that kind of relationship?

She was a cat person and he had a dog. He was

faded Levi's and worn leather and she was so prim and...*girly*. His music preferences ranged from classic rock to rich, earthy blues with a little jazz piano thrown in for flavor. Zoë seemed to sway toward eighties pop and any female singer, and she had the annoying habit of blaring Christmas music in July.

He was a meat and potatoes man, and as far as he could tell, Zoë existed on salads and bottled mineral water. He watched reality television and ESPN and she preferred crime dramas and chick flicks.

In fact, he couldn't think of a single thing they had in common. Besides the sex, which frankly they did pretty damned well.

Even if they could get past all of their differences, there was the problem of them wanting completely different things from life. In all the years he'd known her, she'd never once expressed a desire to have children. Not that he could blame her given her family history. But he'd grown up an only child raised by an aunt and uncle who'd had no use for the eight-year-old bastard dumped in their care. He'd spent his childhood in boarding schools and camps.

He wanted a family—at least three kids, maybe more. He just had to find a woman who wanted that, too. One who wasn't more interested in climbing the corporate ladder than having a family. And definitely one who wouldn't insist on a two week European honeymoon followed by mansion hunting in one of Detroit's most exclusive communities.

Material things didn't mean much to him. He was

content with his modest condo and modest vehicle. His modest life. All the money in the world didn't buy happiness. Thousands of dollars in gifts from his aunt and uncle had never made up for a lack of love and affection. His children would always know they were loved. They would never be made to feel like an inconvenience. And he sure as hell would never abandon them.

It had taken him years to realize there wasn't anything wrong with him. That he didn't drive people away. With a long history of mental illness, his mother could barely take care of herself much less a child, and his aunt and uncle simply had no interest in being parents. It would have been easy for them to hand him back over to social services when his mom lost custody. At least they'd taken responsibility for him.

If not for the lack of affection, one might even say he'd been spoiled as a kid. If he wanted or needed something all it took was a phone call to his uncle and it was his.

A convertible sports car the day he got his driver's license? No problem.

An all-expenses-paid trip to Cancún for graduation? It's yours.

The best education money can buy at a first-rate East Coast school? Absolutely.

But no one had handed him his education. He'd worked his tail off to make the dean's list every semester, to graduate at the top of his class. To make his aunt and uncle proud, even if they didn't know how to show it. And when he'd asked his uncle to loan him the money to start his company, the entire astronomical sum had been wired to his account within twenty-four hours.

They wouldn't win any awards for parents of the year, but his aunt and uncle had done the best they could.

He would do better.

There had to be a Ms. Right out there just waiting for him to sweep her off her feet. A woman who wanted the same things he did. And hopefully he would find her before he was too old to play ball with his son, to teach his daughter to Rollerblade.

He stepped into Zoë's office, trying to remember where in the file cabinet she kept the personnel files. Seeing as how she wasn't exactly organized, they could be pretty much anywhere.

Despite the disarray, she somehow managed to keep the office running like a finely tuned watch. She'd become indispensable. He would be lost without her.

He started at the top and worked his way down, finding them, of course, in the bottom drawer. He located the file of a new employee, Mark O'Connell, to see if there was some reason why the guy would be missing so much work. Not to mention showing up late. Nick was particular when he hired new employees. He didn't understand how someone with such impeccable references could be so unpredictable on the job.

He grabbed the file and was about to shut the

drawer when he saw the edge of a brown paper bag poking up from the back.

Huh. What could that be? He didn't remember seeing that the last time he looked in here.

He grabbed the bag and pulled it out. He was about to peek inside, when behind him he heard a gasp.

"What are you doing?"

Nick turned, the pharmacy bag in his hand, and Zoë stood in the office doorway, back from lunch, frozen. If he opened that bag, things were going to get really complicated really fast.

"I found this in the file cabinet," he said.

When she finally found her voice, she did her best to keep it calm and rational. Freaking out would only make things worse. "I don't appreciate you going through my things."

He gave her an annoyed look. "How was I supposed to know it's yours? It was in the file cabinet with the personnel files. The files I need to have access to, to run my company."

He was right. She should have kept it in her car, or her purse. Of course, then what excuse would she have had for not using it? She walked toward him and held out a hand. "You're right, I apologize. Can I have it back please?"

He looked at her, then at the bag. "What is it?"

"Something personal."

She took another step toward him, hand outstretched, and he took a step back.

A devious grin curled his lips, showing off the dent in his right cheek. "How much is it worth to you?"

He hadn't teased her in weeks. Now was not the time to start acting like his pain-in-the-behind old self. "That isn't funny, Nick. Give it to me."

He held the bag behind his back. "Make me."

How could a grown man act so damned juvenile? He didn't have kids, so what, he'd act like one?

She stepped toward him, her temper flaring, and held out her hand. "*Please.*"

He sidestepped out of her way, around her desk, thoroughly enjoying himself if his goofy grin was any indication.

She felt like punching him.

Couldn't he see that she was fuming mad? Didn't he care that he was upsetting her?

Heat climbed up her throat and into her cheeks. "You're acting like an ass, Nick. Give it back to me *now.*"

The angrier she became, the more amused he looked. "Must be something pretty important to get your panties in such a twist," he teased, clasping the bag with two fingers and swinging it just out of her reach. Why did he have to be so darned tall? "If you want it so badly, come and get it."

She slung her hands up in defeat. "Fine, look if you have to. If you find tampons so thoroughly interesting."

Tampons. Didn't she wish.

He raised a brow at her, as if he wasn't sure he should believe her or not. As he lowered the bag, uncurling the edge to take a peek, she lunged for him. Her fingers skimmed the bag and he jerked his arm back, inadvertently flinging the test box out. In slow motion it spiraled across the room, hit the wall with a smack and landed label side up on the carpet.

Uh-oh.

For several long seconds time seemed to stand still, then it surged forward with a force that nearly gave her whiplash.

Nick looked at the box, then at her, then back at the box and all the amusement evaporated from his face. "What the hell is this?"

She closed her eyes. Damn, damn, damn.

"*Zoë?*"

She opened her eyes and glared at him. "What, you can't read?"

She grabbed the bag from his slack fingers then marched over and snatched the box from the floor.

"Zoë, do you think you're—"

"Of course not!" More like, God, she hoped not.

"Are you late?"

She gave him a *duh* look.

"Of course you are, or you wouldn't need the test." He raked a hand through his hair. "How late are you exactly?"

"I'm just a little late. I'm sure it's nothing."

"We slept together over a month ago. How late is a *little* late?"

She shrugged. "Two weeks, maybe three."

"Which is it, two or three?"

Oh, hell. She slumped into her desk chair. "Probably closer to three."

He took a long deep breath and blew it out. She could tell he was fighting to stay calm. "And why am I just hearing about this now?"

"I thought maybe it was a virus or an infection or something," she said, and he gave her an incredulous look. "I was in *denial,* okay?"

"Missed periods can happen for lots of reasons, right? Like stress?"

She flicked her thumbnail nervously back and forth, fraying the edge of the box. Stressed? Who me? "Sure, I guess."

"Besides, we used protection."

"Did we?"

He shot back an indignant, "You know we did."

She felt a glimmer of hope. Condoms could fail, but the odds were slim. Maybe she really wasn't pregnant. Maybe this was all in her head. "Even the last time?"

There was a pause, then he asked, "The last time?"

Suddenly he didn't sound so confident. Suddenly he had an, *Oh-damn-what-have-I-done?* look on his face.

Her stomach began to slither down from her abdomen. "You know, against the wall, by the door. We used a condom then too, right?" she asked hopefully, as if wishing it were true would actually make it true.

He scratched the coarse stubble on his chin. The guy could shave ten times a day but he was so dark he almost always had a five o'clock shadow. "Honestly, I can't remember."

Oh, this was not good. She could feel her control slipping, panic squeezing the air from her lungs. "You can't *remember?*"

He sat on the corner of her desk. "Apparently, you can't either."

He was right. That wasn't fair. This was in no way his fault. "I'm sorry. I'm just...edgy."

"If I had to guess, I would say that since I have no memory of using one, and my wallet was in the other room, we probably didn't."

At least he was being honest. Obviously they had both been too swept away by passion to think about contraceptives. But that had been what, their fourth time? Didn't a man's body take a certain amount of time to...*reinforce the troops*. Were there even any little swimmers left by then?

Leave it to her to have unprotected sex with a guy who had super sperm.

"I guess there's only one way to find out for sure," he said. "Taking the test here would probably be a bad idea, seeing as how anyone could walk into the bathroom. So would you be more comfortable taking it at your place or mine?"

This was really happening. With *Nick* of all people.

When she didn't answer right away he asked, "Or is this something you need to be alone for?"

Being alone was the last thing she wanted. They were in this together. She didn't doubt for an instant that he would be there for her, whatever the outcome. "We'll do it at my house."

He rose to his feet. "Okay, let's go."

Her eyes went wide. "You want to go *now?* It's the middle of the workday."

"It's not like we're going to get fired. I own the company. Besides, you know what they say."

She thought about it for a second then said, "Curiosity killed the cat?"

He grinned. "There's no time like the present."

Three

Nick drove them the ten minutes to Zoë's house in Birmingham. They didn't say much. What could they say? Zoë spent the majority of her time praying, Please, God, let it be negative.

How had she gotten herself into this mess?

Her devout Catholic parents still believed that at the age of twenty-eight she was as pure as the driven snow. If the test was positive, what would she tell them? Well, Mom and Dad, I was snow-white, but I drifted.

They were going to kill her. Or disown her.

Or both.

And this would surely be enough to send her fragile, ailing grandmother hurtling through death's door. She would instantly be labeled the family black sheep.

It didn't matter that her parents had been nagging her to settle down for years.

When are you going to find a nice man? When are you going to have babies?

How about never?

And if the man she settled down with was Nick they would be ecstatic. Despite the fact that he wasn't Catholic, they adored him. Since the first time she'd brought him home for Thanksgiving dinner they'd adopted him into the fold. And Nick had been swept up into the total chaos and craziness that was her family. He loved it almost as much as it drove her nuts.

So, if she were to call home and tell them she and Nick were getting hitched, she'd be daughter of the year. But the premarital sex thing would still be a major issue. In her parents' eyes, what they had done was a sin.

She let her head fall back against the seat and closed her eyes. Maybe this was just a bad dream. Maybe all she needed to do was pinch herself real hard and she would wake up.

She caught a hunk of skin between her thumb and forefinger, the fleshy part under her upper arm that the self-defense people claim is the most sensitive, and gave it a good hard squeeze.

"Ow!"

"What's wrong?"

She opened her eyes and looked around. Still in Nick's monster truck, rumbling down the street, and he was shooting her a concerned look.

She sighed. So much for her dream theory.

"Nothing. I'm just swell," she said, turning to look out the window, barely seeing the houses of her street whizzing past.

"Don't get upset until we know for sure," he said, but she was pretty sure he, like her, already knew what the result would be. They'd had unprotected sex and her period was late. The test was going to be positive.

She was going to have Nick's baby.

When they got to her house, he took her keys from her and opened the door. He'd been inside her house a thousand times, but today it felt so...*surreal*. As if she'd stepped onto the set of film.

A horror film.

She and Nick were the stars, and any second some lunatic was going to pop out of the kitchen wielding a knife and hack them to pieces.

She slipped her jacket off and tossed it over the back of the couch while Nick took in her cluttered living room.

Last night's dinner dishes still sat on the coffee table, the plate covered with little kitty lick marks from Dexter her cat. Newspapers from the past two weeks lay in a messy pile at one end of the couch.

She looked down at the rug, at the tufts of white cat fur poking out from the Berber and realized it had been too long since she'd last vacuumed. Her entire house—entire life—was more than a little chaotic right now. As if acting irresponsibly would somehow prove what a lousy parent she would be.

Nick looked around and made a face. "You really need to hire a maid."

She tossed her purse down on the cluttered coffee table. "I am *so* not in the mood for a lecture on my domestic shortcomings."

He had the decency to look apologetic.

"Sorry." He reached inside his leather bomber jacket and pulled out the test kit. "I guess we should just get this over with, huh?"

"We?" Like he had to go in the bathroom and pee on a stick. Like he had to endure months of torture if it was positive. A guy like him wouldn't last a week on the nest. He may have been tough, may have been able to bench press a compact car, but five minutes of hard labor and he would be toast.

Her mother had done home births for Zoë's three youngest siblings and Zoë had had the misfortune of being stuck in the room with her for the last one. She had witnessed the horror. Going through it once seemed like torture enough, but understandable since most women probably didn't realize what they were getting themselves into. But *nine* times. That was just crazy.

"I'm afraid to go in there," she said.

Nick reached up and dropped one big, work-roughened hand on her shoulder, giving it a gentle squeeze. "We're in this together, Zoë. Whatever the outcome. We'll get through it."

It amazed her at times, how such a big, burly guy who oozed testosterone could be so damned tender and sweet. Not that the stubborn, overbearing alpha male gene had passed him by. He could be a major pain in the behind, too. But he'd never let her down in a time of need and she didn't believe for a second that he would now.

"Okay, here goes." She took the test kit from him and walked to the bathroom, closing and locking the door behind her, her stomach tangled in knots. She opened the box and with a trembling hand spilled the contents out onto the vanity.

"Please, God," she whispered, "let it be negative."

She read the instructions three times, just to be sure she was doing it right, then followed them word for word. It was amazingly quick and simple for such a life-altering procedure. *Too simple.*

Less than five minutes later, after rereading the instructions one more time just to be sure, she had her answer.

Nick paced the living room rug, his eye on the bathroom door, wondering what in the heck was taking Zoë so long. She'd been in there almost twenty minutes now and he hadn't heard a peep out of her. No curdling screams, no thud to indicate she'd hit the floor in a dead faint. And no whoops of joy.

It was ironic that not five minutes before she stepped into her office he'd been thinking about having children. Just not with her, and not quite so soon. Ideally he would like to be married, but life had a way of throwing a curve ball.

At least, his life did.

He let out a thundering sneeze and glanced with disdain at the fluffy white ball of fur sunbathing on the front windowsill. It stared back at him with scornful green eyes.

He was so not a cat person.

He sat on the couch, propped his elbows on his knees and rested his chin on his fisted hands.

So what if she was pregnant?

The truth was, this was all happening so fast, he wasn't sure how he felt about it. What he did know is that if she didn't come out of the damned bathroom soon, he was going to pound the door down. It couldn't possibly take this long. He remembered the box specifically stating something about results in only minutes.

As if conjuring her through sheer will, the bathroom door swung open and Zoë stepped out. Nick shot to his feet. He didn't have to ask what the results were, he could see it in her waxy, pasty-white pallor. Her wide, glassy-eyed disbelief.

"Oh boy," he breathed. Zoë was pregnant.

He was going to be a father. They were going to be parents.

Together.

She looked about two seconds from passing out cold, so he walked over to where she stood and pulled her into his arms. She collapsed against him, her entire body trembling.

She rested her forehead on his chest, wrapped her

arms around him, and he buried his nose in her hair. She smelled spicy and sweet, like cinnamon and apples. He realized, he'd missed this. Since that night in the hotel, he'd been itching to get his arms around her again.

He'd almost forgotten just how good it felt to be close to her, how perfectly she fit in his arms. Something had definitely changed between them that night in the hotel. Something that he doubted would ever change back.

For a while they only held each other, until she'd stopped shaking and she wasn't breathing so hard. Until she had gone from cold and rigid to warm and relaxed in his arms.

He cupped her chin and tilted her face up. "It's going to be okay."

"What are we going to do?" she asked.

"Well, I guess we're going to have a baby," he said, and felt the corners of his mouth begin to tip up.

Zoë gaped at him, her look going from bewilderment to abject horror. She broke from his grasp and took a step back. "Oh my God."

"What?"

"You're smiling. You're *happy* about this."

Was he?

The smile spread to encompass his entire face. He tried to stop it, then realized it was impossible. He really *was* happy. For five years now he'd felt it was time to settle down and start a family. True, this wasn't exactly how he planned it, and he sure as hell hadn't planned on doing it with Zoë, but that didn't mean it wouldn't work. That didn't mean they shouldn't at least give it a shot.

He gave her a shrug. "Yeah, I guess I am. Would you feel better if I was angry?"

"Of course not. But do you have even the slightest clue what we're getting into? What *I'll* have to go through?"

She made it sound as though he was making her remove an appendage. "You're having a baby, Zoë. It's not as if it's never been done before."

"Of course it has, but have you ever actually witnessed a baby being born?"

No, but he definitely wanted to be in the delivery room. He wouldn't miss that for anything. "I'm sure it will be fascinating."

"*Fascinating*? I was there when my mom had Jonah, my youngest brother."

"And?"

"Have you ever seen the movie, *The Thing?*" she asked, and he nodded. "You remember the scene where the alien bursts out of the guy and there is this huge spray of blood and guts? Well, it's kinda' like that. Only it goes on for *hours*. And hurts twice as much.

"And that's only the beginning," she went on, in full rant. "After it's born there are sleepless nights to look forward to and endless dirty diapers. Never having a second to yourself…a *moment's* silence. They cry and whine and demand and smother. Not to mention that they cost a fortune. Then they get older and there's school and homework and rebellion. It never ends. They're yours to worry about and pull your hair out over until the day you *die*."

Wow. He knew she was jaded by her past, but he'd never expected her to be this traumatized.

"Zoë, you were just a kid when you had to take care of your brothers and sisters. It wasn't fair for your parents to burden you with that much responsibility." He rubbed a hand down her arm, trying to get her to relax and see things rationally. "Right now you're still in shock. I know that when you take some time to digest it, you'll be happy."

She closed her eyes and shook her head. "I'm not ready for this. I don't know if I'll *ever* be ready for it."

A startling, disturbing thought occurred to him. What if she didn't want to have the baby? What if she was thinking about terminating the pregnancy? It was her body so, of course, the choice was up to her, but he'd do whatever he could to talk her out of it, to rationalize with her.

"Are you saying you don't want to have the baby?" he asked.

She looked up at him, confused. "It's not like I have a choice."

"Every woman has a choice, Zoë."

She gave him another one of those horrified looks and folded a hand protectively over her stomach. He didn't think she even realized she was doing it. "I'm not going to get rid of it if that's what you mean. What kind of person do you think I am?"

Thankfully, not that kind. "I've never considered raising a baby on my own, but I will if that's what you want."

"Of course that's not what I want! I could never give a baby up. Once you have it, it's yours. My brothers and sisters may have driven me crazy but I love them to death. I wouldn't trade them in for anything."

He rubbed a hand across the stubble on his jaw. "You're confusing the hell out of me."

"I'm keeping the baby," she said firmly. "I'm just…I guess I'm still in shock. This was not a part of my master plan. And you're the last man on earth I saw myself doing it with. No offense."

"None taken." How could he be offended when he'd been thinking the same thing earlier. Although maybe not the *last on earth* part.

She walked over to the couch and crumpled onto the cushions. "My parents are going to kill me. They think I'm still a good Catholic girl. A twenty-eight-year-old, snow-white virgin who goes to church twice a week. What am I going to tell them?"

Nick sat down beside her. He slipped an arm around her shoulder and she leaned into him, soft and warm.

Yeah, this was nice. It felt…right.

And just like that he knew exactly what he needed to do.

"I guess you only have one choice," he said.

"Live the rest of my life in shame?"

Her pessimism made him grin. "No. I think you should marry me."

* * *

Zoë pulled out of Nick's arms and stared up at him. "Marry you? Are you *crazy?*"

Dumb question, Zoë. Of course he was crazy.

Rather than being angry with her, he smiled, as if he'd been expecting her to question his sanity. "What's so crazy about it?"

If he couldn't figure that out himself, he really was nuts.

"If we get married right away, your parents don't have to know you were already pregnant. Problem solved."

And he thought marrying someone he didn't love *wouldn't* be a problem? Not that kind of love anyway. She didn't doubt that he loved her as a friend, and she him, but that wasn't enough.

"We're both feeling emotional and confused," she said. He more than her, obviously. "Maybe we should take a day or two to process this before we make any kind of life altering decisions."

"We're having a baby together, Zoë. You don't get much more life altering than that."

"My point exactly. We have a lot to consider."

"Look, I know you're not crazy about the idea of getting married to anyone—"

"And you're *too* crazy about it. Did you even stop to think that you would be marrying me for all the wrong reasons? You want Susie homemaker. Someone to squeeze out your babies, keep your house clean and have dinner waiting in the oven when you get home from work. Well, take a look around you, Nick. My life is in shambles. My house is a disaster and if I can't microwave myself a meal in five minutes or less, I don't buy it."

He didn't look hurt by her refusal, which made her that much more certain marrying him would be a bad idea. She could never be the cardboard cutout wife he was looking for. She wouldn't be any kind of a wife at all.

And even if they could get past all of that, it still wouldn't work. He was such a good guy. Perfect in so many ways. Except the one that counted the most.

He didn't love her.

She took his hand between her two. It was rough and slightly calloused from years of working construction with his employees. He may have owned the company, may have had more money than God, but he liked getting his hands dirty. He liked to feel the sun on his back and fresh air in his lungs. One day cooped up in the office and he was climbing the walls.

She didn't doubt that he would put just as much of himself into his marriage. He was going to make some lucky woman one hell of a good husband.

Just not her.

"It was a noble gesture. But I think we both need to take some time and decide what it is we really want."

"How much time?" he asked.

"I'm going to have to make a doctor's appointment. Let's get through that first then we'll worry about the other stuff."

Who knows, maybe she got a false positive from the pregnancy test. Maybe she would get a blood test at the doctor's office and find out they had done all this worrying for nothing.

Four

"Congratulations! Your test was positive! If you haven't yet made a follow-up appointment with Doctor Gordon, please dial one. If you need to speak to a nurse, dial two—"

Zoë hung up the phone in her office, cutting short the obnoxiously perky prerecorded message she'd gotten when she phoned the doctor's office for her blood test results.

It was official. Not that it hadn't been official before. The blood test had just been a formality. She was definitely, without a doubt, having Nick's baby.

Oh boy.

Or girl, she supposed.

She would walk down to his office and tell him,

but he'd been in her office every ten minutes wondering if she'd made the call.

She looked down at her watch. Why get up when he was due back in another six minutes?

"Well?"

She looked up to find him standing in her doorway watching her expectantly. "You're early."

"Early?" His brow knit into a frown. "Did you call yet?"

"I called."

He stepped into her office and shut the door. "And?"

She sighed. "As my mother used to say, 'I'm in the family way.'"

"Wow." He took deep breath and blew it out. "Are you okay?"

She nodded. She really was. She'd had a few days to think about it, and she was definitely warming to the idea. Not that it wouldn't complicate things. But it wasn't the end of the world either. She would have one kid. She could handle that. "I'm okay."

He walked over to her desk and sat on the edge, facing her. She could see that he was happy, even though he was trying to hide it. And why should he? What normal woman wouldn't want the father of her baby to be excited?

"It's okay to be happy," she told him. "I promise I won't freak out again."

The corners of his mouth quirked up. "I guess this means we have things to discuss."

She knew exactly what *things* he was referring to. He looked so genuinely excited, so happy, she didn't doubt for one second that he would be a wonderful father. But a husband? She wasn't sure if she was ready for one of those. She didn't know if she would *ever* be ready. The idea of sharing her life with someone, all the compromise and sacrifice it would take…it just seemed like a lot to ask. She was happy with her life the way it was.

That didn't mean she couldn't possibly be happier with Nick there, but what if she wasn't?

As promised, he hadn't said a word about marriage while they waited for the test results. Now he looked as if he was ready for an answer.

"It's nothing personal, Nick. I just…I'm afraid it wouldn't work between us."

"Why wouldn't it? We're friends. We work well together. We understand each other." He leaned in closer, his eyes locked on hers. "Not to mention that in the sexual chemistry department we're off the charts."

God, she wished he wouldn't look at her that way. It scrambled her brain. And she hated that he was right. But good sex—even fantastic sex—wasn't enough to make a marriage work.

He leaned in even closer and she could smell traces of his musky aftershave, see the dots of brown in his hazel eyes. "Can you honestly say you haven't thought about that night at least a dozen times a day since it happened?"

"It wasn't *that* good." She tried to sound cocky, but her voice came out warm and soft instead. It had been more like a hundred times a day.

Nick grinned and leaned forward, resting his hands on the arms of her chair, caging her in. "Yes, it was. It was the best sex you ever had. Admit it."

Heat and testosterone rolled off his body in waves, making her feel light-headed and tingly all over. "Okay, yeah, maybe it was. But that's not the point. I don't want to jump into anything we might regret. What if we get married and find out a month later that we drive each other crazy?"

"Too late for that, sweetheart." He reached up and touched her cheek and her heart shimmied in her chest. "You already do drive me crazy."

Right now, he was doing the same to her. He looked as if any second he might kiss her. And though she knew it would be a bad idea, she wanted him to anyway. She didn't even care that anyone in the office could walk in and catch them. It would take ten minutes tops for the news to travel through the entire building. For the rumors to start. That was exactly what they *didn't* need right now.

She just wished he would make up his mind, wished he would either kiss her or back off. When he sat so close, his eyes locked with hers, it was difficult to think straight.

Which is probably the exact reason he was doing it. To throw her off balance. To make her agree to things she wasn't ready for.

"I mean drive each other crazy in a bad way," she said.

"So what would you like to do? Date?"

"I think we're a bit past the dating stage, don't you? Socially we get along fine. It's the living together part that worries me."

That grin was back on his face, dimple and all, which usually meant trouble. "That sounds like the perfect solution."

Funny, but she didn't remember mentioning one. "Which solution is that?"

"We could live together."

Live together? "Like in the same house?"

"Sure. What better way to see if we're compatible."

She'd never had a roommate. Not since she left home, anyway. Back then she'd had to share a room with three of her sisters. Three people borrowing her clothes and using her makeup without asking. Although, she doubted that would be a problem with Nick. Her clothes were way too small for him even if he wanted to borrow them and when it came to wearing makeup, well...she *hoped* he didn't.

To get any privacy back home she'd had to lock herself in the bathroom, which would last only a minute or two before someone was pounding on the door to get in.

But she had two bathrooms if she needed a place to escape. A full on the main floor and a half down in the finished part of the basement. Granted her house was barely a thousand square feet, but how much room could one guy take up?

Unless he was thinking she was going to move in with him. His condo was twice the size of her house, but it was in a high-rise in Royal Oak, with people living on every side.

No one should ever live that close to their neighbors. It was too creepy, knowing people could hear you through the walls. She dreamed of one day owning an old farmhouse with acres and acres of property. She wondered how Nick, a born and bred city boy, would feel about that. Despite how well they knew each other, there were still so many things they *didn't* know. So much they had never talked about.

Things they could definitely learn if they were living together.

"And if we are compatible?" she asked.

"Then you marry me."

"Just like that?"

He nodded. "Just like that."

She hated to admit it, but this made sense in a weird way.

My God, was she actually considering this? The only thing worse than premarital sex in her parents' eyes was living in sin without the sanctity of marriage. Of course, what they didn't know wouldn't hurt them. Right?

"If we were to do this, and I'm not saying we are, but *if* we did, logically, I think it would be best if you move in with me," she said. "Your condo can get by without you. I have a yard and a garden to take care of."

"Fine with me," he agreed.

"And we should probably keep this to ourselves."

"Zoë." He shot her a very unconvincing hurt look. "Are you ashamed of me?"

Yeah, right, like it mattered. When it came to self-confidence, Nick had it in bucket loads.

"You know how the people in this building can be. I'm just not ready to deal with the gossip. Not until we've made a decision."

"Which will be when?"

"You mean like a time limit," she asked, and he nodded. "How about a month? If by then it's not working out, we give it a rest."

He sat back, folded his arms across his chest and gave her an assessing look. "A month, huh?"

A month should be plenty of time to tell if they were compatible. In areas other than friendship. And the bedroom.

"And if after a month we haven't killed each other, what then? We set a date?"

The mere idea triggered a wave of anxiety. Her heart rate jumped and her palms began to sweat. "If we can make it one month living together, I promise to give your proposal very serious thought."

"And hey," he said with a casual shrug. "If nothing else, we can save money on gas driving to work together, so it won't be a total loss."

"How can you be so calm about this?" The idea of him moving in was making her a nervous wreck.

"Because I'm confident that after a month of living together, you'll be dying to marry me."

She hoped he was right. "What makes you so sure?"

A devilish grin curled his mouth. "This does."

He leaned toward her and she knew exactly what he was going to do. He was going to kiss her. She knew, and she didn't do a thing to stop him. The crazy thing was, she *wanted* him to kiss her. She didn't care that it would only confuse things more, or that anyone could walk in and catch them.

He didn't work into it either. He just took charge and dove in for the kill. He slipped a hand behind her head, threading his fingers through her hair, planted his lips on hers and proceeded to kiss her stockings off. Her body went limp and her toes curled in her pumps.

She'd almost forgotten how good a kisser he was, how exciting and warm he tasted. The memory lapse was purely a self-defense mechanism. Otherwise there would have been a lot of kissing going on these past weeks.

She could feel herself sinking deeper under his spell, melting into a squishy puddle in her chair. Her fingers curled in his hair, nails raked his scalp. His big, warm hand cupped the back of her head with gentle but steady pressure, as if he wasn't going to let her get away.

Yeah, right, like she would even try.

Hearing her office door open barely fazed her, nor

did the, "Zoë, I need—*whoops!*" of whomever had come in. Or the loud click of the door closing behind them as they left. And the very real possibility of the news reaching everyone in the building by day's end.

Nick broke the kiss and backed away, gazing down at her with heavy-lidded eyes. "So much for keeping this to ourselves."

"Yeah, oops." She should care that their secret was out—well, at least one of their secrets—but for some reason she didn't. In fact, she was wondering if maybe he should kiss her again. Her cheeks felt warm and her scalp tingled where his hand had been. She was sure if she tried to get up and walk her legs wouldn't work right.

One kiss and she was a wreck.

"So, when do you want me to move in?" he asked, his dimple winking at her.

How about right now? she thought. But she didn't want to sound too eager. Then again it *was* Friday. That would give him all weekend to settle in.

Oh what the heck?

She looked up at him and smiled. "How about tonight?"

There was a reindeer standing on Zoë's front porch.

Nick stood beside it holding the reins in one hand, a duffle bag in the other.

Okay, it was actually a leash he was holding, and the deer was really a dog. A very large, skinny dog with a shiny coat the color of sable.

"What is that?" she asked through the safety of the screen. Did he really think he was bringing that thing into her house?

"This is my dog, Tucker." At her completely blank look he added, "You knew I had one."

Yeah, she knew, but it never occurred to her that it would be moving in, too. "This is going to be a problem. I have a cat."

"Tucker has a low prey drive, so it shouldn't be an issue."

"Prey drive?" She snapped the lock on the storm door. "Dexter is not prey."

"Tucker is a retired racing greyhound. They use lures to get them to run. Some have higher prey drives than others. Tucker has a low enough drive that he's considered cat safe."

"Cat safe?" She narrowed her eyes at him. "You're sure?"

"He'll probably just ignore the cat." He stood there waiting for her to open the door, but she wasn't convinced yet.

"Will he chew on my shoes?" she asked.

"He's not a chewer. He's a collector."

"What, like stamps?"

Nick grinned. "Cell phones, remote controls, sometimes car keys, but his favorite is slippers. The smellier the better. He's also been known to take the salt and pepper shakers off the table. If anything is missing, his bed is the first place I look."

She looked down at the dog. He looked back up

at her with forlorn brown eyes that begged, "Please love me."

"He won't pee on my rug?"

"He's housebroken. He also doesn't bark, barely sheds and he sleeps twenty-three hours of the day. He's not going to be a problem. In fact, he'll love having a fenced yard to run around."

She looked at the dog, then back at Nick.

"Are you going to let us in? I'm on excessive doses of allergy medication so I can be around your cat. You can at least give Tucker a chance."

He was right. How much trouble could one over-sized dog be?

Scratch that. She probably didn't want to know.

She unlocked the door and opened it. "Sorry about the mess. I didn't have time to clean."

Nick and Tucker stepped inside and the room suddenly felt an awful lot smaller. He unsnapped the leash and hung it on the coat tree and Tucker, being a dog, went straight for Zoë's crotch. He gave her a sniff, then looked up, as if he were expecting something. He was even bigger than he looked standing on the porch.

"He's enormous."

"He's an extra large." Nick shrugged out of his leather jacket and hung it over the leash.

"Why is he staring at me?"

"He wants you to pet him."

"Oh." She patted the top of his head gingerly. "Nice doggie."

Satisfied that he'd been adequately welcomed, Tucker trotted off to explore, his nails click-clicking on the hardwood floor. "Will he be okay by himself?"

"Yeah, he won't get into anything."

She gestured to Nick's lone bag. "Is that all you brought?"

"I have a few more things in the truck. I figure as I need stuff I can run over to my place and pick it up."

"I'm giving you the spare bedroom," she told him.

He flashed her a curious look. "I don't remember agreeing to that."

"I think at this point sex will only complicate things." He'd proven that this afternoon when he had kissed her. Her brain had been so overdrenched in pheromones she would have agreed to practically anything. "We should ease into this slowly. We need to get used to living together. We need to be sure this relationship isn't just physical."

That sexy grin curled his mouth. The guy was unbelievably smug. "You really think you can resist me?"

She hoped so, but she could see by the devious glint in his eye he wasn't going to make it easy. "I'll manage."

From the kitchen Zoë heard a hiss, then an ear-splitting canine yip, and Tucker darted into the living room, skidding clumsily across the floor, long gangly legs flailing. Whining like a big baby, he scurried over to Nick and hid behind him. In the kitchen doorway sat Dexter, all whopping eight pounds of him, casually licking one fluffy white paw as though he didn't have a care in the world.

So much for the dog ignoring the cat.

"He's bleeding," Nick said indignantly, examining Tucker's nose. "Your cat attacked my dog."

"I'm sure he was provoked." She found herself feeling very proud of Dexter for protecting his domain. No big dopey dog was going to push him around. "They probably just need time to get used to each other."

Kind of like her and Nick.

"So," she said, suddenly feeling awkward. "I guess we should get you settled in."

Nick followed her down the hall to one of the two downstairs bedrooms. On the left was her office, and on the right her guest room. He stepped inside, taking in the frilly curtains and lacey spread.

"Pink?" He cringed, as though it was painful to look at. "I can feel my testosterone drying up. Maybe I should just sleep on the couch. Or in a tent in the backyard."

"Don't be such a baby," she said and he tossed his bag on the bed. "I was thinking we could just get carryout for dinner."

He shrugged. "Works for me."

"We can order, and while we're waiting for it to be delivered, we can get the rest of your things out of the truck."

He followed her to the kitchen and she pulled open her junk drawer. It held a menu from every local restaurant within delivering distance. "What are you in the mood for," she asked, and he gave her that simmering, sexy look, so she added, "besides *that*."

He grinned. "I'm not picky. You're the pregnant one. You choose."

She chose pizza. A staple item for her these days. The cheesier and gooier the better.

While they waited for it, they brought in the last of his things, most of which were for the dog who lay snoozing on his bed in the living room, occasionally opening one eye to peek around. Probably to make sure the cat was a safe distance away. Dexter lounged on the front windowsill pretending not to notice him.

It wasn't as if Nick had never been to her house, but showing him around, inviting him into her private domain, was just too weird. He would be using her towels to dry himself, washing his clothes in her washing machine and eating food from her dishes. It was so intimate and invasive. The enormity of it all hadn't really hit her until she'd seen him on the porch. She hadn't realized just how used to living alone she'd become in the past ten years. Most of the single women she knew who were her age or younger were looking for a companion. They wanted Mr. Right. She only wanted Mr. Right Now.

Not that she wasn't going to try to make this work.

The tour ended in the kitchen, and when Nick opened the fridge, he frowned. It was pitifully empty. But the freezer was stuffed wall-to-wall with Lean Cuisine dinners.

He gave her a look, and she shrugged. "There was a good sale so I stocked up."

"There's no real food in here," he said. "Don't you *ever* cook?"

Never. It was one of the few things her mother hadn't made her do. She had this nasty habit of burning things. The last time she attempted to cook herself a real meal, she'd wandered out of the room without shutting off the heat under a greasy frying pan and had set her kitchen on fire. Thank God she had a smoke detector and a good fire extinguisher. "Trust me when I say, we're both a lot safer if I don't cook."

For a second she thought he might ask for an explanation, then he just shook his head. He probably figured he was better off not knowing.

"Besides, who needs real food when you have carryout and prenatal vitamins?" she asked cheerfully.

He began opening cupboards, one by one, taking inventory of their lack of contents, shaking his head. Did he think the real food was going to miraculously appear?

"What are you doing?" she asked.

"Making a mental list so I know what to buy. Which at this point is pretty much everything."

"You can buy all the food you want, as long as you don't expect me to cook it."

"It may surprise you to learn that I'm not half bad when it comes to preparing a meal. It's one of the few things I remember doing with my mom."

Though he tried to hide it, she could see a dash of

wistful sadness flash across his face. The way it always did when he mentioned his mom.

"How old were you?"

"Five or six I guess."

"She was okay then?"

He shrugged. "I don't know if you could ever say she was completely okay. But life would be almost normal for months at a time, then the meds would stop working, or the side effects would be so bad she would stop taking them. Gradually she got so bad, nothing seemed to work. I was eight when social services removed me."

"And you haven't seen her since?"

He shook his head. "Nope."

She couldn't imagine going all those years without seeing her parents. Not knowing where they were or what they were doing.

"I used to get an occasional letter, but not for about six years now. She moved around a lot, going from shelter to shelter. I haven't been able to find her."

"What would you do if you did find her?"

"I'd try to get her in an institution or a group home. Her mental illness is degenerative. She won't ever get better, or even be able to function in society. But the truth is, she's probably dead by now."

He sounded almost cold. If she hadn't known Nick so well, she might have missed the hint of sadness in his tone. It made her want to pull him in her arms and give him a big hug. How could he stand it, not knowing if she was dead or alive? Not knowing if she was out there somewhere suffering. Cold and lonely and hungry.

"Are you worried about the baby?" he asked.

"What do you mean?"

"About the fact that mental illness can be genetic."

Honestly, she'd never even considered that. She didn't know all that much about mental illness, and even less about genetics. "Should I be worried?"

"My mom's illness stems from brain damage she sustained in a car wreck when she was a kid. So no, the baby won't be predisposed to it. Unless it runs on your side."

"My parents had nine kids, which if you ask me is completely nuts. But as far as I know, neither of them are technically mentally ill. Unless it was some big secret, I don't recall *anyone* in my family ever being mentally ill. And it's a big family."

"Speaking of big families, that's something we've never talked about," he said. "If this does work out, and we decide to get married, how will you feel about having more kids?"

Did the phrase, *over my dead body* mean anything to him? And how would he react if she was adamant about not having any more children.

That was something they would worry about later, when it became clear how far they planned to take this.

"I'm not sure," she told him, which wasn't completely untrue. There was a chance, however slim, that she would agree on one more baby.

"It's something I feel strongly about," he added.

She could see that, and she couldn't help feeling they were starting with one strike already against them.

Five

Zoë woke at eleven-thirty Saturday morning with a painfully full bladder and a warm weight resting on her feet. She pried her lids open and looked to the foot of the bed to find a pair of hopeful brown eyes gazing back at her.

"What are you doing in my bed?" Just her luck, Tucker was one of those dogs attracted to humans who didn't like them. She gave him a nudge with her foot. "Shoo. Get lost."

Tucker exhaled a long-suffering sigh and dropped his head down on the comforter, eyes sad. Up on the dresser beside the bed, Dexter watched over them, giving Tucker the evil eye.

"Go sleep in your own bed." She gave him another

gentle shove. He tried one more forlorn look, and she pointed to the door. "Out."

With a sigh he unfolded his lanky body and jumped down from the bed, landing with a thud on the rug, the tags on his collar jingling as he trotted out the door and down the stairs.

She sat up and her stomach did a quick pitch and roll. So far she'd gotten away with negligible morning sickness. A bit of queasiness first thing in the morning that usually settled after she choked down a bagel or muffin.

She eased herself out of bed and shoved her arms into her robe, but when she looked down for her slippers they were no longer on the side of the bed where she was sure she'd left them.

Darn dog.

She shuffled half-asleep across the ice-cold bare floor and down the stairs to the bathroom. She smelled something that resembled food and her stomach gave an empty moan followed by a slightly questionable grumble. She used the facilities and brushed her teeth. She tried to brush her hair into submission and wound up with a head full of blond frizz.

Oh well. If he was going to stay here, he would have to learn to live with the fact that she woke up looking like a beast. It also hadn't escaped her attention that the bathroom smelled decidedly more male than it had the previous morning, and when she opened the medicine chest, she found a shelf full of *guy* things there. Aftershave, cologne, shaving gel and a razor. Along with several other tubes and bottles of various male things.

She shook her head. Weird.

She found her way to the kitchen, doing a double take as she passed through the living room. She blinked and rubbed her eyes, sure that it was an illusion. But no, the clutter was gone. The newspapers and old magazines and dirty dishes. The random tufts of cat fluff had been vacuumed away. He'd even dusted.

A man who did housework? Had she died and gone to heaven, or had she woken up in the twilight zone?

Tucker lay on his bed beside the couch, the tips of two furry pink slippers sticking out from under his belly. *Her* slippers.

"Give my slippers back you mangy thief." Tucker just gazed back at her with innocent brown eyes that said, *Slippers? What slippers?*

Since he didn't seem inclined to move any time soon, she reached down and tugged them out from under him. Lucky for the dog they weren't chewed up and covered with slobber. Regardless, she would have to start keeping them on the top shelf of her closet.

She found Nick in the kitchen standing at the stove, cooking something that looked like an omelet. He wore a red flannel shirt with the sleeves rolled to his elbows, one that accentuated the wide breadth of his shoulders. His perfect behind was tucked into a pair of faded blue jeans that weren't quite tight, but not exactly loose either. On his feet he wore steel-toed leather work boots.

"That smells good."

Nick turned and smiled. "'Morning."

He was showered and shaved and way too cheerful. He looked her up and down and asked, "Rough night?"

"You know those women who wake up looking well-rested and radiant? I'm not one of them."

He only grinned. He probably figured silence was his best defense. To say she didn't look like a troll would be a lie, and to admit it would hurt her feelings.

Smart man.

"Thanks for cleaning up," she said. "You didn't have to do that."

"If I'm going to live here, I'm going to pitch in." He turned back to the stove. "The eggs will be done in a minute and there's juice in the fridge."

Juice?

She had no juice. Just a half gallon of skim milk that went chunky three days ago. Come to think of it, she didn't have eggs, either. Or the bacon that was frying in the skillet beside the nonexistent eggs. Or the hash brown patties sitting in the toaster. "Where did all this food come from?"

"I went shopping."

He shopped, too? She *was* in the twilight zone.

"If you're trying to impress me, it's working." She opened the refrigerator and found it packed with food. Milk, juice and eggs and bags of fresh fruit and vegetables. She wondered if he did windows, too. "What else have you done this morning?"

He grabbed two plates from the cupboard. It sure hadn't taken him long to familiarize himself with her kitchen. "I jogged, showered, cleaned and shopped, and I stopped by my place to pick up a few more things."

"Jeez, when did you get up?"

"Fiveish."

"It's Saturday."

He shrugged. "What can I say—I'm a morning person."

"I'm sorry, but that is just sick and wrong." Not that it wasn't kind of nice waking up and having breakfast ready. She poured herself a glass of organic apple juice—organic?—and sat at the table in the nook. Nick set a plate of food in front of her. Eggs, bacon, hash browns and buttered toast. She wondered if it was real butter. "Looks good. Thanks."

Nick slid into the seat across from her, dwarfing the small table, his booted feet bumping her toes. Invading her space. The man took up so much darned room.

She closed her eyes and said a short, silent, guilt induced blessing. A holdover from her strict Catholic upbringing. Some traditions were just impossible to break.

Nick dug right into his breakfast and, like everything else, ate with enthusiasm and gusto. No doubt about it, the guy enjoyed life to the fullest.

She picked at her food, nibbling tiny bites and chasing it down with sips of juice.

"Not hungry?" he asked.

"Not really." She bit off a wedge of toast. "Mild morning sickness."

"Anything I can do?"

"You could have the baby for me."

He gave her a "yeah, you wish" look.

After a few minutes of nibbling, her stomach gradually began to settle, and she began to feel her appetite returning. Though she didn't typically eat a big breakfast, she stopped just short of picking up her plate and licking it clean. She even reached across the table to nab the last slice of bacon off Nick's plate.

"Not hungry, huh?"

"I guess I was hungrier than I thought."

Nick got up and cleared the dishes from the table. "I was thinking about heading into the office for a few hours. Want to tag along?"

She had enough of the office Monday through Friday. Her weekends were hers. "I don't think so."

Normally she would wait until after dinner to do the day's dishes—sometimes three days later—but out of guilt she took the dirty plates and juice glasses from the sink and stacked them in the dishwasher. "It's supposed to get up in the high fifties today. I was planning on working in the garden. I need to get my gladiola bulbs planted."

"Then I'll stay and help."

She closed the dishwasher and wiped her hands on a towel. "Nick, your living here doesn't mean we'll be attached at the hip. We don't have to spend every second of the day together."

"I'm not asking for every second of your time. But I'm also not looking for a roommate I'll only see in passing." He folded a work-roughened hand over her shoulder. Its warm weight began to do funny things to her insides. "If we're going to do this, we're going to do it right. We're going to be a couple."

A couple of *what,* that was the question.

A couple of idiots for thinking this might actually work? Or a couple of fools for not realizing they were too different for this kind of relationship?

Having a big, strapping man around definitely had its advantages.

It might have taken Zoë two or three weekends to turn over the dirt to create a new flower garden and prepare it for planting. That meant two or three weeks of sore arms, an aching back and dirty fingernails. Nick, macho guy that he was, had nearly the entire area turned over and de-sodded in three hours.

She'd offered to help, but he said he would never let a woman in her condition do a man's job. Normally a comment like that would have gotten him a whack over the head with a shovel, but then he started driving the pitchfork into the soil and she became distracted watching the powerful flex of his thighs against worn denim. The way they cupped his behind just right.

As the temperature climbed up close to sixty, Nick shed first his jacket, then he peeled off his tattered Yale sweatshirt. She found herself increasingly distracted from her chore of picking weeds from the turned soil and dumping them in a bucket to go in the compost pile. She was much more interested in watching the play of muscles under the thin, white, sweat-soaked T-shirt.

What would it feel like to touch him again? What would he do if she got up right now and ran her hand up his back...

She shook away the thought. No. *Bad Zoë.* No touching allowed. Not yet anyway. Not until it was clear this relationship wasn't based solely on sex.

He was just so...*male.* And she was suffering from a serious excess of estrogen or pheromones, or whichever hormone it was that made a woman feel like molesting every man in sight.

One would never guess from the look of him that Nick had been raised among the rich and sophisticated. Not that he gave the impression of being a thug, either. He wore jeans and a flannel shirt the way most other men wore a three piece suit. When Nick entered a room, no matter the size, he filled it. He drew attention with his strength and character. With his unwavering confidence and larger-than-life presence. But he was so easygoing, he could impress without intimidating.

He was also a loyal friend and a fair employer. The kind of man a person could count on.

That didn't mean he was a pushover, though. People didn't mess with Nick. He may have had the patience of a saint, but cross him and watch out. His wick was long, but the impending explosion was catastrophic.

Something bumped Zoë's shoulder and she turned

from watching Nick to find a long snout in her face. Before she could react, Tucker gave her a big sloppy kiss right on the mouth.

"Aaaagh!" She frantically wiped dog slobber off her face with the sleeve of her sweater. "Go away, you disgusting animal!"

Nick turned to see what the problem was. "What's wrong?"

"Your dog just slobbered on my face."

Nick grinned. He probably trained the dog to do that just to annoy her. "That's his way of saying he likes you."

"Couldn't he find a less disgusting way to show affection? One that doesn't involve his spit."

He drove the pitchfork into the ground and leaned on the handle, a bead of sweat running down the side of his face. "I've been thinking about this arrangement we have and it occurred to me that we've been out together lots of times, but never as a couple."

"Like a date?"

"Right. So I was wondering if maybe you would like to go out with me tonight."

"As a couple?"

"I was thinking something along the lines of dinner and a movie."

Interesting. "Like a *real* date?"

"Yep."

She hadn't been on *any* kind of date—real or pretend—in longer that she wanted to admit. Her social life had been less than exciting lately. Most men seemed to want one thing, and they expected it on the first date no less. She obviously had no objections to sex before marriage, but even she thought two people should get to know each other before they hopped in the sack together.

"I get pregnant, you move in, *then* you ask me out on a date. Amazing how backward we're doing all of this, isn't it?"

"Is that a yes?"

"Yes. I'd love to go on a date with you."

He surveyed the ground he had yet to turn over. "This should only take me another fifteen or twenty minutes. Then I'll need to shower."

"Me, too. Why don't I hop in first while you finish up."

She hiked herself up, brushing dirt from her gardening gloves and the knees of her jeans. She knew it was something she would have to get used to, but the idea of showering while he was in her house was a little weird. Maybe if she hurried, she could get in and out while he was still outside.

Unless he wanted to conserve water and shower together…

No. *Bad* Zoë.

She gave herself a mental slap. There would be no shower sharing. At least not yet. But that *was* something couples did, right?

"One more thing," Nick called after her as she dashed to the house. She turned and found him flashing her that simmering, sexy smile.

Uh-oh, what was he up to?

"Since this is a real date, I'll be expecting a good-night kiss."

Nick glanced through the darkness at Zoë. She sat beside him in the truck, her head resting against the window, a damp tissue crumpled in her hand. Since they left the theater, her sobs had calmed to an occasional hiccup and sniffle.

On a first date disaster scale of one to ten, they had ranked a solid eleven. But technically the date wouldn't be over until they got home, so he wasn't going to count his chickens. It could get a lot better—or a lot worse.

Agreeing on a movie had been the first hitch. She had wanted to go to some artsy foreign film playing in Birmingham, and he wanted to see the latest martial arts action flick.

After a long debate-argument, they finally compromised—he being the one to do most of the compromising—and agreed on a romantic comedy.

As a trade-off, she'd let him pick the restaurant this time. He chose a four-star Middle Eastern place in Southfield he'd heard fantastic things about. He'd also learned a valuable lesson. Never try to feed a pregnant woman new, exotic food. When the server had set their plates in front of them, the unfamiliar textures and scents had turned her skin a peculiar shade of green. One bite had her bolting to the bathroom.

She'd had to wait outside while he paid the bill and the waitress packed up their uneaten dinner in carryout containers.

Since they were both still hungry, they had stopped at a fast food drive-thru and ate burgers and fries on the way to the theater.

He didn't normally get into chick flicks, but the film hadn't been as boring as he had anticipated, and their experience at the movie theater had been blessedly uneventful. Until the end, that is, when Zoë dissolved into uncontrollable sobs. Which was a little strange considering the movie had a happy ending. She'd been crying so hard he'd practically had to carry her out of the theater.

He'd gotten more than a few evil looks from female moviegoers—as if her emotional breakdown was somehow his fault—and several sympathetic head shakes from their male counterparts.

He wasn't going to pretend he had even the slightest clue what had happened. Or how to fix it. What he did know was that good night kiss he was hoping for seemed unlikely at this point. As did any possibility of seducing his way into her bed.

Beside him, Zoë sniffed and dabbed at her eyes with a tissue.

"You okay?" he asked, giving her shoulder a reassuring pat.

She wiped her nose and said in a wobbly voice, "I ruined our first date."

Ruined was such a strong word. There had been

good points. Given time, he could probably think up a few. "You didn't ruin anything."

"I got sick at dinner then had a breakdown in the movie theater."

He was going to say that it could have been worse, but they were still a few minutes from home. No point tempting fate.

"What if it's a sign?" she hiccupped. "What if this is God's way of telling us our relationship is going to be a disaster? Maybe this is our punishment for the premarital sex."

He'd never spent much time with a pregnant woman, but he was almost one hundred percent sure this was one of those mood swings he'd heard expectant fathers talk about. "Zoë, I think this has more to do with hormones than divine intervention."

"It was our first date. It was supposed to be special."

It was completely off the wall, but despite the fact that her face was all swollen and blotchy and her nose was running, he didn't think he'd ever seen her look more beautiful.

It wasn't often he got the opportunity to take care of Zoë. She was so damned capable and independent. He liked that she needed him. That she had a vulnerable side.

He took her free hand, linking his fingers through hers. "Just being with you made it special."

She looked up at him through the dark, tears welling in her red, puffy eyes and leaking down her cheeks. "That's s-so s-sweet."

But not so sweet that she would be willing to spend the rest of her life with him.

The words sat on the tip of his tongue but he bit them back. He had no interest in trying to guilt her into marriage. If and when they exchanged vows, he wanted her to mean every word she said.

And if that never happened? If she decided she didn't want to marry him?

Well, they would burn that bridge when they came to it.

Six

Sunday—thank goodness—proved to be a quiet and uneventful day. Zoë woke once again to a hot breakfast, and after the kitchen was cleaned, she and Nick had lounged around, chatting and reading the newspaper. Nick had adopted the recliner and Zoë shared the couch with the dog—who in two days had become her shadow. Later Nick watched football and drank beer while she retaught herself to knit, in the hopes of making the baby a blanket.

It felt so...domestic. And though she had never been a big fan of football—or any sport for that matter—it was nice just being in the same room with him, each doing their own thing. It had been...comfortable.

Isn't that how her parents had done it? When they

weren't working that is, which wasn't very often. Her father would park himself in the La-Z-Boy and her mom would grade papers or do needlepoint.

Maybe that was what all real couples did.

Nick fixed authentic, spicy enchiladas for dinner, which as he promised were delicious. And were probably the reason she woke Monday morning feeling as if someone had siphoned battery acid into her stomach.

She didn't manage to drag herself to work until after ten. She knew there was a problem the instant she stepped into her office and saw Shannon sitting at her desk, a determined look on her face.

The kiss.

She'd been so wrapped up in the living together thing, she had completely forgotten someone saw her and Nick kissing on Friday. Obviously, it had gotten around and Shannon was expecting an explanation.

Zoë shrugged out of her jacket and collapsed into her visitor's chair, since her own chair was occupied. "Go ahead, get it over with."

"It isn't bad enough that you don't tell me you're playing hide the salami with the boss—"

"Charming," Zoë interjected.

"—but this morning I take a call from your doctor's office and I'm told your prescription has been called into the pharmacy. Your prescription for *prenatal vitamins.*"

Oh crud. Zoë felt all the blood drain from her face.

Shannon smiled smugly. "Is there by any chance something you neglected to tell me?"

Zoë winced. The kiss getting out was bad enough. She really wasn't ready for everyone to find out about her pregnancy.

"I admit I was deeply hurt."

She didn't look hurt. She looked as if she was preparing to give Zoë a thorough razzing. That was definitely more her style. Zoë and everyone else in the office had learned not to take it personally. Shannon leaned forward, elbows on the desk, fingers steepled under her chin. "But considering you probably just made me five-hundred and thirty-eight dollars richer, I might have to forgive you."

Five-hundred and thirty-eight dollars? "How did I manage that?"

"I won the pool."

"*Pool?*" Why did she get the feeling she didn't want to know what Shannon was talking about?

"Every time Nick skips out on a fiancée there's a betting pool to guess how long it will take him to find a replacement. I said within a week."

"The office has been *betting* on Nick's dating habits?" How is it that she had never heard about this?

"There's been some obvious tension between you guys since the wedding. Lots of long lingering looks when the other isn't watching. I put two and two together." She flashed Zoë a smug smile. "Looks like I was right, huh?"

She so did not need this hassle. There would be

questions that required explanations she just wasn't ready to give.

Zoë blew out a breath. "Who knows?"

"About you and Nick sucking face? Pretty much the whole office. It was Tiffany that walked in on you."

"I should have known, she never knocks." She also had a big mouth, and Zoë was pretty sure she had a crush on Nick.

"What about the baby? How many people know about that?"

Shannon sat back in the chair. "You see, that's tricky. Without telling everyone, I'll have a hard time proving the entire timeline, and the fact that I actually won. I had to ask myself, what's more important to me? Our friendship or being able to buy that forty inch flat screen television I've had my eye on. And as a result, reap the reward of many weeks of fantastic sex from my very grateful spouse."

"So it all boils down to our friendship or good sex?"

"You may not believe this, but after three kids and ten years of marriage, good sex can be pretty hard to come by."

Which probably meant that her secret didn't have a chance of hell in staying that way. "So what did you decide?"

She grinned. "That our friendship means more to me. But, honey, you're going to owe me big time for this one."

"Thank-you," Zoë said softly, close to tears again. Which was so not her. She never cried.

Would this emotional roller-coaster ride never end?

"That doesn't mean I don't want details. So spill."

"We didn't plan this," she told Shannon. "It was supposed to be a one time thing. A drunken mistake."

"But you got a little surprise instead?"

Zoë nodded. "The whole thing is a fluke."

"This was no fluke, Zoë."

She wished she could believe that. "He asked me to marry him."

Shannon didn't look surprised. "That sounds about right for Nick. What did you tell him?"

"That I'm not ready for that. We've decided to try living together for a while first."

"Which sounds about right for you."

Zoë frowned. "What's that supposed to mean?"

"No offense, but you *always* play it safe. You keep everyone at arm's length."

"I do not!" Zoë said, feeling instantly defensive. "You and I have been friends for a long time."

"And you know pretty much everything about me, right?"

"I guess so."

"And what do I know about you? What have you told me about your family?"

She bit her lip, trying to remember what she might have told Shannon, a sinking feeling in her chest. "You, um, know I have a big family."

"I know there are nine of you, but I have no idea how many brothers or sisters you have. I don't know their names. I know you grew up in Petoskey but you never talk about what it was like there. How it was for you growing up. You never talk about school or friends. *Nothing* personal. To get you to open up at all I have to practically drag it out of you. You have a lot of friends here, but besides Nick, I don't think *anyone* really knows you."

She hated to admit it, but Shannon was right. Zoë didn't get personal with too many people. Just her sister and Nick, and Nick hadn't been by choice. He had just sort of insinuated himself into her life, settling in like a pesky houseguest who never left. And there had always been a bit of resistance on her part. There still was. She always held a tiny piece of herself back.

Was Shannon right? Had Zoë been keeping everyone at arm's length?

An uneasy feeling settled in her stomach. Maybe her aversion to marriage had less to do with her family and was instead just a strange quirk in her personality. Maybe she'd never learned how to let herself open up to people. And if she didn't change, what kind of future could she and Nick possibly have? If they had one at all. If she refused to marry him, would it ruin their friendship? Would they wind up resenting each other?

The thought made her heart shudder with fear.

Nick was such a huge part of her life. What would she do without him?

If they were going to make this work, she would have to learn to open up and let him in.

All the way in.

"I'm not saying this to hurt your feelings," Shannon said, looking apologetic. "I think you're a wonderful, kind person. I consider you a good friend. Which is why I'd like to see this thing with Nick work out. You may not realize it now, but you two are perfect for each other."

"I told him no sex," Zoë blurted out, then turned twenty different shades of red. Why had she said that?

Shannon's eyes rounded. "No sex? Ever?"

"Not ever. Just until we're sure our relationship isn't just physical."

"One night of sex in what, ten years of friendship, and you're worried the relationship is only physical?"

Zoë hadn't realized until just now how ridiculous that sounded. And how equally ridiculous it must have sounded to Nick. What he must think of her.

"Do you think denying him sex is my way of keeping him at arm's length?"

"Honey, it doesn't matter what I think. The question is, what do *you* think?"

She was thinking that insisting they live together first had been her roundabout way of putting off making a difficult decision. One that shouldn't have been difficult in the first place. After ten years of friendship, she should know what she was feeling. Either she loved him or she didn't.

And if she didn't, maybe it was only because she hadn't let herself.

Nick had been incredibly patient with her so far, but

at some point he was going to grow tired of chasing her. How could she risk losing the one man she might have been destined to spend the rest of her life with?

She had to make a decision, and she had to make it soon.

"I don't care what his excuse is," Nick barked into the phone. His foreman, John Miglione, had just delivered the news that one of his employees had left for lunch and failed to return—for the fourth time in two weeks. On top of that the man called in sick at least once a week. There was nothing Nick hated more than firing people, but he needed reliable employees. A smart man knew that to survive in business he should surround himself with competent people. The weak links had to go. "Tell him one more time and he's out of a job."

"Will do, Nick. And there's one more thing."

He was silent for a second, as if he were working up to something, and Nick knew exactly what that something was.

"I know you want to ask, so just go ahead and get it over with."

"Is it true about you and Zoë?"

"That depends on what you heard."

"That Tiffany walked in on you two getting down and dirty."

"Tiffany exaggerates. It was just a kiss."

"Does that mean you two are…"

"Possibly. We're giving it a trial run."

"Well, it's about time."

Nick shook his head. "Do you know that you're the third person who said that to me today."

Zoë appeared in his office doorway—speak of the devil. He held up a finger to let her know he would only be a minute.

John laughed. "Then that should tell you something, genius. Give her a big wet one for me. I'll talk to you later."

He shook his head and hung up the phone, turning to Zoë. "What's up?"

"Is this a bad time?" she asked.

"No. John just called about O'Connell. He didn't come back after lunch—again. He seemed like a decent guy when we hired him. Overqualified even, but he can't seem to get his act together."

"That's too bad." She closed and locked the office door.

Did they have a meeting he'd forgotten? And if so, why lock the door?

Without a word she crossed the room and walked around his desk looking very...*determined*.

Determined to do what, he wasn't sure.

There was definitely something up.

"What's going on?" he asked.

With her eyes pinned on his face, she began unbuttoning her blouse.

Huh?

He watched as she slipped the garment off her shoulders and let it drop to the floor. He was too stunned to do anything but sit there as she climbed in his lap. She straddled his legs, her skirt bunching at her upper thighs, wrapped her arms around his neck and kissed him.

No, this wasn't just a kiss. This was a sexual attack. A wet, deep, oral assault. And he was completely defenseless.

He knew she was passionate, but man, he'd never expected this.

She feasted on his mouth, clawing her fingers through his hair, arching her body against him. She rode him like he was her own personal amusement park attraction.

It was hot as hell, the way she was throwing herself at him, still, something wasn't right. Something he couldn't quite put his finger on.

Something was…*missing*.

He felt her tugging his shirt from the waist of his jeans, fumbling with the buckle on his belt.

What the heck was going on?

He wasn't one to turn down sex, even if it was in the middle of the afternoon in his office. In fact, the idea of sex *anywhere* with Zoë was enough to get his engine primed, but something about this just wasn't right. She was kissing him, rubbing her satin and lace-covered breasts against his chest, yet he wasn't feeling a damn thing. He didn't even have a hard-on.

He grabbed Zoë's shoulders, held her at arm's length and asked, "What are you doing?"

"Seducing you," she said, like that should have

been completely obvious, sounding more exasper-ated than turned on.

"I see that. But why?"

She looked at him as though he was speaking an alien language. "Why?"

"You said you wanted to wait," he reminded her.

"I'm not allowed to change my mind?"

"Of course you are." But he had a strong feeling she hadn't changed her mind, or something had changed it without her consent. It was as if she was going through the motions, but her heart wasn't really in it. "Just tell me why."

She blew out an exasperated breath. "Do I need a reason? Jeez! I thought you would be jumping at the chance. I thought you would have me naked by now."

"Normally, I would. It just feels like…I don't know. Like you're doing this because you have to. Or I'm forcing you or something."

"You're *not* forcing me."

"I'm sorry, but something about this just doesn't feel right."

A delicate little wrinkle formed between her brows. "Are you turning me down?"

It was hard for him to believe, too. In fact, he couldn't think of a single time when he'd turned a woman down. "At least until you tell me what's up. Why the sudden change of heart?"

She slid out of his lap, snatched her shirt up from the floor and covered herself with it. "I thought this was what you wanted."

He could see that he'd hurt her feelings, but he needed to know what was going on. They had to be honest with each other or this relationship would never have a chance.

"Of course it's what I want. But is it what you want?"

She gave him that confused look again. "I don't understand. I'm here, aren't I?"

"Zoë, why did you come in here?"

She tugged her shirt on and buttoned it. "You know why."

"What I mean is, what *motivated* you?"

Her frown deepened. "I wanted to have sex with you."

He sighed. This was going nowhere. "Let's try this. Let me give you a scenario, and you tell me if I'm right. Okay?"

She nodded and smoothed the creases from her wrinkled skirt.

"You were sitting at your desk thinking about me, remembering that night in the hotel. You became so overcome with lust and passion that you couldn't wait another minute to have me, so you raced down to my office."

She just stared at him, so he asked, "Was it something like that?"

She bit her lip. "Um…"

He was a little disappointed, but not surprised. "Talk to me Zoë. Tell me what's going on."

"I thought that if I didn't have sex with you soon, maybe you were going to get sick of waiting.

Maybe you would find someone else. Someone… better."

That had to be the dumbest thing he had ever heard. "Contrary to what you might believe, a man can go three days living with a woman and not have sex." He leaned back in the chair and folded his arms over his chest. "Hell, there have been times I've lasted a whole week. And if it becomes a problem, there's no reason why I can't…take matters into my own hands, so to speak."

Her cheeks flushed pink and she lowered her eyes to the floor. It amazed him that a woman who so excelled at talking dirty could possibly be embarrassed by this conversation.

He patted his legs. "Come'ere. Have a seat."

She hesitated—the woman who had just thrown herself at him with guns blazing—then sat primly on his knee, tucking her skirt around her legs.

This was definitely not going to cut it.

He wrapped his hands around her waist. She gasped as he pulled her snug against his chest, her behind tucked firmly into his lap.

That was much better.

"Okay, now what made you think I would dump you if you didn't sleep with me?"

She looked up at him, so much conflict and confusion in her eyes. "I keep everyone at arm's length."

"Arm's length?" What was she talking about?

"I'm too private. I don't let people in. You're

going to get sick of me shutting you out and find someone else."

Where was she getting this garbage? How could a woman so intelligent act so dumb? "And sex is supposed to fix that?"

She shrugged. "It's a start."

"Do you honestly think I'm that shallow?"

She shook her head, looking guilty for even thinking it.

"If I thought you were shutting me out emotionally, sex ten times a day wouldn't make a damned bit of difference."

She gnawed at the skin on her lower lip. "I guess I never thought of it like that."

"I guess not." He brushed a few wayward blond curls back and tucked them behind her ear. "You must have had a good reason for wanting to wait, and I respect that. If you're not ready, that's okay. I understand."

The crinkle in her brow grew deeper. "That's just it. I'm not sure if the reason I had was a good one. We've been friends for years and managed not to have sex. So why would I think our relationship would only be physical? And it's not like I don't want to have sex. It's all I think about lately. When I'm not sick, or sobbing my eyes out, that is."

A grin curled his mouth.

"I have this really annoying habit of looking at your butt. I never even used to notice it, and now I can't peel my eyes off of it. And I want to touch it. I want to touch you *everywhere*. So why am I still telling you no?"

He shrugged. She was adorable when she was confused and frustrated.

"I'm afraid I'm doing it because I don't let people close to me."

"Maybe it's just that you're dealing with an awful lot right now and a sexual relationship is more than you're ready for."

"You think?" she asked, a hopeful look in her eyes.

"When I make love to you, Zoë, I want it to be like that night in the hotel. I want you to want me as much as I want you."

Her lips curved in a dreamy smile. "It really was good, wasn't it?"

He couldn't help grinning himself. "Oh, yeah."

She cupped his face in her hands. Her skin was warm and soft and smelled like soap. "You know what? You're a great guy."

Then she kissed him. A sweet, tender kiss packed with so much simple, genuine affection it nearly knocked him out of his chair.

Now, this was definitely more like it. He would rather hold and kiss her this way for five minutes than have an entire night of meaningless sex.

That night in the hotel he knew that there was something more between them. Something they had both buried away. Maybe she just wasn't ready to take that last step. But she would be eventually.

He was certain of it.

Seven

When Zoë pulled into her driveway later that evening there was a car parked there.

"Oh, fudge."

That's what she got for dodging her sister's calls. And giving her a key. She should have known that if she didn't come clean, Faith would pop in for a surprise visit.

Maybe she subconsciously wanted her here. Maybe she needed someone to tell her what to do.

She parked her conservative Volvo beside her sister's flashy little crimson Miata. They had always been polar opposites. Zoë the practical, responsible sister and Faith the wild child.

When they were kids, Faith had always wanted to

loosen Zoë up and teach her to have fun, while Zoë ran herself ragged trying to keep Faith out of trouble. If their parents knew how many times Zoë had covered for her when she'd snuck out after midnight to meet a boyfriend or go to a wild party, they would have strokes.

She gathered her things and headed for the front door. She stepped inside and called, "I'm home."

Faith appeared from the kitchen, her flame-red hair cut stylishly short and gelled into spiky points, a drastic change from the waist-length curls she'd had last time. She was dressed in body-hugging black jeans and a stretchy chenille sweater the exact same green as her eyes.

She clicked across the room in spiked high heels and hugged Zoë fiercely. "Surprise!"

"What are you doing here?" she asked, wrapped up in a scented cloud of perfume and hairspray.

"Don't even pretend you don't know why I'm here. You haven't been returning my calls and that always means something is wrong."

"Nothing is wrong, I promise." She stepped back and looked her sister up and down. She looked perfect, as usual. She wore just enough makeup to look attractive, without being overdone. Her acrylic nails were just the right length and painted a warm shade of pink. Attractive, but not overly flashy. Faith has always been the pretty one. "You look gorgeous! I love the new haircut."

"And you look exhausted. But don't even change the

subject. Why was there an enormous dog in your house and what's with all the guy stuff in the spare bedroom?"

"Those are Nick's things. So is the dog." She looked around, wondering why Tucker hadn't met her at the door. She was kind of getting used to the crotch sniff greetings and sloppy dog kisses. "Where is the dog?"

"I let him out. And why is Nick staying here? Is he getting his place sprayed for bugs or something?"

Before Zoë could explain, the front door opened and Nick walked though, his regular old big gorgeous self. She saw him through different eyes now and couldn't help wondering if it would be obvious to the world what she was feeling. Not that she thought there was a snowball's chance in hell of keeping this from her sister now.

"Pork chop!" Nick said, giving Faith a big hug, lifting her right off her feet.

"Sugar lump!" Faith squealed, hugging him back.

Zoë felt the tiniest twinge of jealousy. Faith had always been so outgoing and friendly. So full of warmth and affection. Why couldn't Zoë be more like that?

Nick set her down and took a good look at her. "Wow. You look great."

"Right back attcha, stud. Zoë was just about to explain why you're staying here. Is something wrong? Did you lose your condo?"

"Um, no," Nick said, looking to Zoë for guidance, like she had the slightest clue how to explain this.

Maybe it would be best to just come right out and say it. "The thing is, I'm pregnant."

Faith's mouth fell open and for about ten seconds she looked too stunned to speak. Maybe just saying it hadn't been the best way to go after all. "You're *what?*"

"Pregnant."

"*Pregnant?* And you didn't *tell* me?"

"Sorry. I was going to call you. I only found out for sure a couple of days ago. I've been a bit… confused."

"Which still doesn't explain what Nick is doing here."

Zoë and Nick looked at each other, then back at Faith. Did they really need to spell it out? Were they so unlikely a couple that Faith would never guess it?

Faith looked from Zoë to Nick, then back to Zoë again. Then she gasped. "It's *Nick's?*"

"You have to swear not to say anything to Mom and Dad," Zoë pleaded. "I haven't decided what to tell them yet."

"How did this happen?" Faith demanded.

"The usual way," Nick said, and Zoë felt her cheeks begin to burn with embarrassment.

"When did you two start seeing each other? And why didn't anyone tell me?"

"Why don't I start dinner while you two talk," Nick said. He beat a path to the kitchen like his pants were in flames and he needed a fire extinguisher.

Coward.

"You and Nick?" Faith said, shaking her head, like she just couldn't believe it.

Zoë felt a jab of annoyance. It's not as if she and

Nick were a different species for God's sake! "Is it really so hard to imagine that Nick would be attracted to someone like me?"

"Of course not. I've always thought you and Nick would be a great couple. I just didn't know you thought so, too."

"I didn't," she admitted. At least not consciously. Maybe all this time the idea had been there, lurking in the back of her mind.

"I want the whole story," Faith said, giving her a pointed look. "And I expect *details*."

Zoë knew exactly what kind of details her sister was referring to.

"Then you had better sit down and get comfortable. This is going to take a while."

Nick, Zoë and Faith sat up until well after midnight chatting. They probably would have stayed up all night if Nick and Zoë hadn't had to go to work the next morning.

Since Nick had the guest room, Faith bunked with Zoë. They took turns in the bathroom, changed into their jammies, then climbed under the covers together, giggling in the dark like they had when they were kids. Back then they'd shared bunk beds. Faith on top and Zoë below.

"Are you sure you can't stay for a few days?" Zoë asked. She didn't see her sister nearly as much as she would have liked to. She wished she lived closer. Especially now that Faith was going to be an aunt.

"I really have to get back. I just had to make sure you were okay. I promised I wouldn't be gone long."

"Promised who?"

Zoë could see the flash of Faith's teeth as she smiled. "I'm seeing someone new. No one really knows about it yet."

"And you accuse me of keeping secrets," Zoë admonished.

"Yeah, well, Mom and Dad aren't exactly going to approve of this, either."

"Let me guess, he's Lutheran."

"Nope."

"Jewish?"

"Atheist."

Zoë cringed. "Ooooh, yikes."

"And he's not a he, he's a she."

For a second Zoë was too surprised to reply. A *she?* "You're dating a *woman?*"

"Are you totally grossed out?" she asked, her voice lacking its usual confidence.

"Of course not! I just…I'm surprised, that's all."

"It kind of surprised me, too."

"What happened? Did you just one day decide, hey, maybe I'll try something new?"

"You know me, I'll try anything once. Her name is Mia. Are you sure it doesn't gross you out?"

She wouldn't lie to herself and not admit it wasn't a little weird to think of her sister in a new way, but all that mattered was that Faith was happy. "I promise, I'm not grossed out."

"That's good, because as strange as it probably sounds, I think I might be in love with her."

It must have been serious, because like Zoë, Faith didn't do love. She didn't let herself get tied down. Didn't talk about having a family. Ever. She just wanted to have fun.

The truth was, Zoë felt jealous. Not about the same sex part. She was firmly rooted in her heterosexuality. She liked men, plain and simple.

What she envied was that Faith had clicked with someone and she went for it, no question. Even though she knew it could potentially get complicated, she wasn't afraid to take a chance.

Why couldn't Zoë be like that? Why couldn't she just open up and let this thing with Nick happen? Why was he sleeping in the guest room when he should have been in bed with her?

"I'm thinking of telling Mom and Dad," Faith said.

"Wow, it must be serious."

"I swear, I've never felt like this about anyone. I know they're going to freak, and possibly disown me. I guess it's a risk I'm willing to take. I feel I owe it to Mia not to try and hide it. I don't want her to think I'm ashamed of our relationship. I'd like you to meet her, too. Maybe we could come down and stay for a couple days."

"I'd like that," Zoë said, and realized she really meant it. She wanted to meet the person that had captured her sister's heart. "Maybe next weekend."

They talked for a while longer, until Faith drifted

off to sleep. Zoë lay there awake until after one, her mind unable to rest. She couldn't stop thinking about all the things that had changed over the past few weeks. She felt as if her entire life had been flipped upside down, spun around and set back down slightly askew.

But not in a bad way. Things would never be the same, but she was beginning to realize that wasn't necessarily a bad thing.

She tossed and turned for another few minutes, then decided to try a glass of warm milk to help her sleep. Which was kind of weird since she'd never in her life had warm milk and the idea sounded pretty gross. She climbed out of bed and tripped over Tucker who lay sleeping on her rug. She couldn't find her slippers in the dark, and she didn't want to disturb her sister by switching on the light, so she padded across the cold floor in bare feet. She headed down the dark stairway but instead of her feet taking her to the kitchen, she found herself standing in the partially open door of the guest room. Maybe that had been her intention all along, and the warm milk was just her way of convincing herself to walk down the stairs in the first place.

She could tell by his slow and deep breathing that Nick was asleep.

Instead of turning around and going to the kitchen, she tiptoed into the room. She had no idea what she was doing, or even why she was doing it. But it wasn't enough to stop her.

Maybe everything wasn't supposed to make

sense. Maybe it was okay to do things simply because it felt good.

Nick was turned away from her, on his right side, his wide shoulders bare. She felt a deep ache in her heart, a pull of longing that propelled her closer to the bed. Closer to him. She wasn't here for sex, she knew that much. She just wanted to be near him.

Without thinking, or considering the consequences, she pulled back the covers and very quietly slipped in beside him. The sheets were cool and soft and smelled of his aftershave.

She rolled onto her side, facing away from him, carefully tucking the covers around her shoulders. Beside her, Nick stirred.

"Zoë?" he said in a voice rough from sleep and rolled toward her.

"Sorry. I didn't mean to wake you."

"S'okay," he mumbled and curled up behind her, enfolding her in the warmth of his body, wrapping a thick arm around her. He spread one large hand over her belly, easing her closer, burying his nose in her hair.

Oh, this was nice.

She held her breath, waiting to see what he would do next, what he would touch, if he would kiss her. And to her surprise, he didn't do a thing. He just snuggled up to her and fell back to sleep. It was as if he knew exactly what she wanted without her even having to ask.

She sighed and placed her hand over his, twining their fingers together. This was definitely more effective than warm milk. Already her lids were beginning to feel heavy. The heat of his body soothed her, his slow, steady breathing warmed the back of her neck and the deep thud of his beating heart lulled her to sleep.

It was a good thing she was having the boss's baby. In any other situation Zoë's erratic work schedule would surely get her fired. And so much for them saving gas driving together.

It was past eleven when she finally strolled into work. Her sister had already been gone by the time she got out of bed, but Faith left a note saying she would call so they could talk about her and Mia visiting next weekend. Nick, she added, had made her breakfast before he left for work.

Zoë hadn't heard or felt him get out of bed. Typically sharing a mattress meant a restless night's sleep for her. Last night, curled up in Nick's arms, she'd slept like the dead and woke feeling well-rested for the first time in weeks.

One very good reason to invite him upstairs to sleep tonight. In fact, maybe it would be better if he moved *all* of his things up there. Maybe it was time to begin treating this exactly the way they should, as an intimate, monogamous relationship between two people who cared deeply for each other. Maybe even loved each other. And if she wasn't actually in love with him yet, she was darned close.

She dropped her purse and jacket in her office

then took the hall down to Nick's office, getting more than a few curious looks and several knowing smiles along the way. News of the kiss had definitely made the rounds. And instead of feeling ashamed or self-conscious, she found herself holding her head a little higher, her back straighter. She found herself answering their looks with a smile that said she was proud to be with a man of Nick's integrity, a man who was so admired by his peers.

If they only knew the *whole* story.

She *wanted* people to know. She was proud to be having Nick's baby.

The thought nearly blew her away.

The only logical explanation was that for years there had been feelings between them that they had either been denying or stowing away. And now that those feelings had been acknowledged and set free, they were multiplying at an exponential rate.

Nick's office was empty, and she remembered belatedly that he had planned to work on-site today—an inspection had been scheduled that he wanted to be there for. She felt a dash of disappointment that she would have to wait all afternoon to see him.

She turned to leave and plowed into a brick wall of a man coming from the opposite direction.

"Whoa!" He grabbed her arms to keep her from toppling over on her butt. She recognized him as O'Connell, the man they had hired only a few weeks ago. The one who'd been giving Nick so much trouble. "Sorry," he said gruffly.

"No, it was my fault." She backed away from him. "I wasn't looking where I was going."

He was *enormous,* with long sandy brown hair, a bushy beard and craggy, almost harsh features. He wore the typical construction worker's uniform— work-faded, dusty jeans, a quilted flannel shirt and steel toed work boots.

"He's not in?" he asked in a deep rumble of a voice.

"No. He's on-site. He should be back sometime later this afternoon."

He gave her a solemn nod and started to walk away, his heavy footsteps vibrating the floor under her feet.

"Can I give you a bit of advice?"

He stopped and turned back to her.

"Nick is a patient man and a fair employer, but you're pushing him over the line."

He narrowed his eyes at her, looking downright fierce. She might have been intimidated, but she'd spent the last ten years around men like him. They looked big and tough, but deep down most were just big teddy bears.

"Is that supposed to scare me?" he asked.

"Your references from your last job were impeccable. Your work is quality. So what's the problem? Why do you keep screwing up?"

"You wouldn't understand," he said gruffly, a distinct hint of sadness lurking behind a pair of piercing blue deep-set eyes. She couldn't help thinking there was more to this situation than he was letting show. And a damned good reason why he was missing work.

She could read people that way.

She propped her hands on her hips and gave him one of her stubborn looks. "Oh yeah, tough guy? Why don't you try me?"

Eight

It was nearly three by the time Nick got back to the office and the only thing on his mind, the only thing that had been on his mind all day, was stopping in to see Zoë. He barely remembered her climbing into bed with him last night, so waking to find her curled in his arms had been a pleasant surprise. And if he hadn't had an appointment with an inspector, he might not have gotten out of bed.

He wasn't going to pretend to know what had motivated her to do it. She was the one calling the shots, setting the pace. But he felt as if they had taken a giant step forward last night.

They had made progress.

He headed into his office to drop off his briefcase

and jacket, and found Zoë sitting at his desk. O'Connell, his problem employee, was standing by the door, as if he'd just been on his way out.

"Nice of you to show up," Nick told him, feeling his good mood fizzle away.

"Boss." O'Connell nodded Nick's way then shot Zoë a half smile. "Thanks."

Nick felt his hackles go up. What the hell was that all about? Why was he smiling at Nick's woman? And why were her eyes red and puffy? Had she been crying?

She sniffled and returned the smile, which pissed off Nick even more. "No problem. You just have to promise you won't make a move until I talk to Nick."

"I won't." He gave her a nod, and ignoring Nick, walked out.

"What was that all about?" Nick demanded. "Why are you crying? Did he hurt you?"

She chuckled and waved away his concerns. "I'm fine. This is nothing. Just the usual overactive hormones."

"What did you need to talk to me about?"

"Come in and shut the door."

He did as she asked and walked over to his desk. "What's going on? I don't like you being alone in here with him. I don't trust him."

A grin split her face. "Nick, are you *jealous?*"

"Of course not," he said automatically, then frowned. Damn, he *was* jealous. He was behaving like a suspicious spouse. "I'm sorry."

"He came in to quit," Zoë told him.

"That's convenient. It'll save me the trouble of firing him."

"I told him I wouldn't let him. And you're not firing him, either."

Maybe she was forgetting who owned the company. "Why the hell not?" he snapped.

"This guy came highly recommended from his last employer. They couldn't say enough good things about him. I knew something had to be up."

"And?"

"So I asked. Like we should have a week ago."

"*And?*" he repeated impatiently.

"And it took some prying, but I finally got him to admit why he's been missing so much work."

No doubt O'Connell had tried to con his way into keeping the job, pulling on Zoë's heartstrings. She was emotionally unstable enough these days to fall for just about anything.

He folded his arms across his chest. "This should be good."

"He has a sick daughter."

Nick frowned. That he hadn't expected. A drug or alcohol problem maybe, but not a sick kid. He didn't even know O'Connell was married. "How sick?"

"She has a rare form of leukemia."

And what if it was all bull? "You're sure he's not just saying that to—"

"He showed me pictures," she interjected, her voice going wobbly and her eyes welling with tears again. "Taken in the children's ward of the hospital. She looks like such a sweet little girl. Only seven years old." She sniffled and wiped away the tears spilling down her cheeks. "Sorry. It was just so sad. He got misty-eyed when he talked about her. I could see how much he loves her, and how hard it's been for him."

Nick cursed and shook his head. "Why the hell didn't he say anything?"

"Because he's a big burly macho guy who thinks he can carry the weight of the world on his shoulders. He lost his wife three years ago, so it's just the two of them. They moved here from up north to be close to Children's Hospital in Detroit. There's a specialist there who thinks he can help her. Only problem is, she has to go in for treatment several times a week and sometimes he can't find anyone to help him. Some days she's so sick from the chemo and radiation he can't leave her."

"I would have given him the days off."

"It gets worse. Even with insurance, medical bills are eating up all his money and they're about to get evicted from the apartment they're staying in. Although from what he says, it sounds like the place is a dump and it's in a terrible neighborhood. He said they have no choice but to go back up north so he can move in with his parents."

"And what about his daughter?"

"This treatment is her last option. Without it she'll probably die."

Nick leaned forward in his seat. "What can we do to help him?"

A grin split Zoë's face. "I talked to him about the company possibly loaning him some money."

"And?"

"He says he's already too far in debt." She plucked a tissue from the box on his desk and wiped the last of her tears away. "I think he's too proud to take a handout."

"We have to do something." There had to be a way to help this guy. A way that wouldn't bruise his pride.

He looked over at Zoë and saw that she was still smiling at him, her eyes full of warmth and affection. "What?"

"You're a good man, Nick."

He shrugged. "Anyone would want to help him."

"No, they wouldn't. But I knew you wouldn't question helping him. You would do it without a second thought."

She got up from his chair and walked to the door. He thought she was going to leave, instead she snapped the lock.

What was she up to?

She turned and started walking toward him, the weeping gone. Instead she gazed down at him a heavy-lidded, almost sleepy look in her eyes. This was awfully familiar. Where had he seen this before...?

Oh yeah, she'd been wearing an identical expression that night in the hotel, seconds before they pounced on each other.

Oh man, here we go again.

Her cheeks were rosy, her lips damp and full, like

plump, dew covered strawberries. He didn't doubt they would be just as sweet and juicy.

She exhaled a breathy sigh and fanned her face. "Phew, it's getting awfully warm in here, isn't it?"

It didn't feel particularly warm to him, although, if she was going to do what he thought she was going to do, it would be a lot warmer in a minute or two. "If you say so."

She reached up, her eyes pinned on his face, and began unfastening the buttons on her shirt. Very slowly, one by one, inch by luscious inch, exposing a narrow strip of pale, creamy skin.

He could see in her eyes, she wanted him. She wasn't doing it because she knew it was what *he* wanted. And she sure wasn't in a hurry.

Well, hell, it *was* getting hot in here.

"I don't want to wait any longer," she said in a husky voice.

"What if someone needs me for something?" he asked, figuring it would be irresponsible to not object at least a little. They were, after all, at work.

"They'll just have to wait their turn."

Well then. He leaned back in his chair to enjoy the show, felt his heart rate skyrocket when she slipped the blouse from her shoulders and let it drop to the floor. Underneath she wore a siren-red transparent lace bra that barely covered the essentials. Her skin looked pale and creamy soft, her nipples taut and nearly as rosy as the fabric that did little to cover them. She wasn't what he would call well-endowed, but what she did have was firm and perfectly shaped. Just enough to fit in his cupped hand with barely any overflow.

And he was so hard that any second he was going to bust out his zipper.

Zoë unfastened her slacks and pushed them down. And when he saw the thong she wore underneath he stopped breathing. In the same vibrant shade as her bra, it was so scandalously brief and transparent it left *nothing* to the imagination.

Had she dressed this way for him or did she always wear sexy underwear to work?

She flashed him a mischievous smile. "See anything you like?"

He lowered his eyes to his crotch, to his very obvious erection. "What do you think?"

He followed the movements of her hand as she stroked a path between the swell of her breasts, trailed it down her taut stomach, stopping briefly to circle her navel, then lower still, brushing her fingers over the itsy bitsy patch of lace.

She leaned forward, resting her hands on the arms of his chair, giving him a beautiful view of her cleavage. "Thinking about stopping me again?"

Oh, hell no. He reached up and hooked a hand behind her neck, pulling her face to his, his fingers tangling through the softness of her pale curls. "Kiss me."

Her lips were soft and warm and so sweet as she brushed them against his own. She slipped into his lap, straddling his thighs, pulling at his clothes—

The knob on his office door rattled, then there was a loud pounding. "Nick! Open up!" John called.

Damn it.

"I'm busy," he shouted in the direction of the door. He had a nearly naked, aroused woman in his lap who seemed intent on getting him naked, too. No way in hell he wasn't going to make love to her.

"It's an emergency."

He closed his eyes, let his head fall back, and cursed.

Zoë let go of the hem of his shirt and called, "What happened?"

There was a brief pause, as Nick was sure his foreman was putting two and two together, then he said, "Sorry to interrupt, but I just got a call that there was an accident at the Troy site."

Zoë sighed and Nick cursed again.

"How bad?" he called.

"I'm not sure. I only know they took one of our guys to the hospital."

He scrubbed his hands across his face and mumbled, "I don't believe this."

"Give us a minute," Zoë said, and he looked up at her apologetically. "I know, you have to go."

She climbed out of his lap and grabbed her clothes from the floor. He stood up and tucked his shirt back in.

He watched her dress, knowing his own face mirrored her look of disappointment. "We have piss-poor timing, don't we?"

She buttoned her blouse and tucked it into her slacks. "No kidding."

As she headed for the door, Nick grabbed her arm and tugged her to him. "Tonight," he said, "you're all mine."

Unfortunately *tonight* never transpired.

Zoë ran home to let the dog out at five, then went back to the office and stayed until eight to make up for some of the time she'd been missing and work she'd been neglecting the past couple of days. She expected Nick to be back home when she pulled in at eight-fifteen, but the driveway was empty and the house dark.

The intense tug of disappointment she felt took her by surprise. Coming home to an empty house had never bothered her before. Well, not usually. Sometimes it sucked being alone, but she always had Dexter to keep her company.

In only a couple of days she'd grown used to having Nick around.

She raided the frozen dinners in the freezer, unable to choose between her two favorites.

"What do you think?" she asked the dog, holding them both up. "Chicken Alfredo or lasagna?"

He looked up at her with a goofy dog smile, his long skinny tail wagging like mad and whacking the table leg.

"You want me to make both?"

He barked, which he almost *never* did, so she took that as a yes. She'd never been much of a dog person, but Tucker wasn't half-bad. She couldn't help growing attached to him, especially when he shadowed her every step, gazing up at her with lovesick puppy eyes.

She nuked both dinners and ate in front of the television, tossing bites to Tucker who gobbled them up enthusiastically. When they were finished eating, Zoë stretched out on the couch with the cat curled up on her feet and the dog sacked out on the rug beside her. She channel surfed, running across a show about babies on the Discovery Channel. She settled in to watch it and the next thing she knew, someone was nudging her awake.

Nine

Zoë pried her eyes open, feeling drugged from sleep. The television was off and Nick stood over her grinning, illuminated only by the light in the hallway.

"What time is it?" she mumbled.

"After midnight."

"I guess I fell asleep." She yawned and stretched. "How did it go at the hospital?"

"Nothing fatal. A couple of cracked ribs and a broken collarbone. He'll be off work for a while, but he'll make a full recovery." He extended a hand toward her. "C'mon, let's get you into bed." At her curious look he added, "To sleep. I think we're both too tired for any fooling around."

He was right. It had been a long eventful day for them both.

He took her hand and hoisted her off the couch.

"Are you coming to bed, too?"

"With you?" he asked, and she nodded. "Do you want me to?"

She really, truly did. "I want you to."

He flashed her that dimpled grin. "Then I will."

"I have to brush my teeth first."

"Me, too. You mind sharing the sink, or do you prefer to take turns?"

It's not as if she had never shared a sink before, and often with three or four other people all rushing to get ready before the school bus honked out front. Besides, that was what couples did, right? "I don't mind."

It was a little weird watching Nick brush his teeth. It was one of those normal everyday things that a person did that she never really thought about, but doing it together felt very personal and intimate. Like learning a secret.

She drew the line at staying in the bathroom while he used the facilities—some secrets should stay secret—and went upstairs to change into her pajamas. In her bedroom she found Tucker and Dexter curled up together on her bed.

She propped her hands on her hips and told Dexter firmly, "You little traitor."

Dexter looked up guiltily.

"Get down," she said, tugging on the covers. Like

new best buddies, both animals jumped off the bed and headed down the stairs together.

It would seem that even Dexter had already adjusted to having them here. That had to be some sort of sign, didn't it?

She stripped down and slipped into an oversized, extra long T-shirt with a Happy Bunny logo on the front. She was already under the covers by the time Nick came upstairs. She curled up on her side and watched as he sat on the edge of the bed and first pulled off his work boots and then his socks. Next he unbuttoned his shirt, tugged it off, and draped it across the footboard.

She sighed with pleasure at the sight of all that beautiful bare skin over ropes of lean muscle. Despite his dark coloring and coarse beard, he wasn't all that hairy. Just a sprinkling on his pecs that trailed down into a narrow path, bisecting his abs and disappearing under the waistband of his jeans.

Looking completely at ease in her bedroom, he rose to his feet and unfastened his jeans. He shoved them down and kicked them off, revealing long powerful legs. Men's legs didn't typically do much for her, but as far as she was concerned Nick's were perfect.

Wearing only his boxers, he slipped into bed beside her. He rolled on his side facing her, leaned close and gave her a brief, but incredibly sweet kiss. His chin felt rough against her skin. He smelled of toothpaste and soap and just a hint of aftershave. "Good night."

"Good night." She reached behind her and

switched off the lamp. As her eyes adjusted to the dark, she could see that Nick had closed his eyes. He must have been pretty tired considering he was typically out of bed before 6 a.m.

Yep, she was tired, too. Absolutely exhausted. Much too tired to finish what they had started in his office this afternoon.

So why couldn't she seem to close her eyes? Why was the urge to touch Nick nagging at her?

She didn't want to wait. She wanted sex now, damn it!

She laid a hand on Nick's arm, rubbing from wrist to shoulder. "Nick, you awake?"

He didn't respond so she gave him a gentle shake. "Nick, wake up."

He answered with a half mumble, half snore.

He was sound asleep.

Swell.

She sighed and rolled onto her back. Two days ago she hadn't been ready for sex, now it was all she could seem to think about. If only they could get their schedules coordinated.

Tomorrow, she decided. Tomorrow they were going to get down and dirty and *nothing* was going to stop them.

"I think I figured out a way to help O'Connell," Nick said the next morning at the breakfast table. He'd fixed them pancakes, sausage patties and freshly squeezed juice from organically grown oranges.

The way she'd been eating lately, she was going to gain a hundred pounds before this baby was done cooking.

"How?" she asked, stabbing her third sausage patty.

"Well, his immediate problem is finding a place to live that he can afford, right? Well, I have a two bedroom condo sitting empty in Royal Oak. They can stay there rent free."

"You're a genius! That's absolutely *perfect*. Do you think he'd go for it?"

"Since it's paid off, and I'm not getting any rent for it now, it's technically not a handout."

"I can't believe we didn't think of it before. And it's even closer to the hospital than the place he's staying in now."

"There's only one possible drawback. Unless I want to kick him and his daughter out at some point, you're going to be stuck with me for God only knows how long."

"And that's okay with you?" she asked.

He nodded. "It really is. How about you?"

She smiled. "It's really okay with me, too."

"You're sure? This is a pretty big step."

A step she honestly felt ready to take. She knew exactly what she wanted, and she was going for it, damn it. "I'm absolutely, and completely sure."

He flashed her that dimpled grin. "Should I talk to O'Connell or do you want to?"

"Since it's your place it would probably be better if you talked to him. It might be easier to accept coming from a guy than me." Then she added, "And you should do it right away."

"Just give me a minute to load the dishwasher," he said, carrying their plates to the sink. "Then we'll get out of here."

Suddenly she couldn't wait to get this settled. After hedging all this time, she was so ready to get Nick moved permanently into her home—into her life—she didn't want to wait another minute.

She followed him to the sink and said, "Nick, look at me."

When he turned to face her, she curled her fingers into the front of his shirt, pulled him down to her level, and gave him a long, deep, wet kiss. One designed to let him know exactly how much she wanted him.

His strong arms circled her, pressing her closer. One big hand plunged through her hair to cup the back of her head while the other traveled downward to fit itself comfortably over her backside.

Zoë pressed her body against him, feeling as if she couldn't get close enough. As if she would *never* be close enough to him.

She knew in that second, without a doubt, she was in love with this man. She was going to marry him, and they were going to have a family. She suddenly understood the appeal of marriage and babies.

Because the babies she had would be Nick's. And it would be his arms she would wake in every morning.

Nick pulled away and flashed her a hungry grin. "Wow, what was that for?"

"It was just a sample of what you have to look forward to later."

He stroked the side of her throat with his thumb, his eyes dark with desire. "I can't wait."

"Me, neither. And the sooner we get to work, the sooner we get to come home."

After only a minimal amount of coercion on Nick's part, and a bit of hedging from O'Connell, he accepted Nick's offer and agreed to move in right away. When O'Connell thanked him, his eyes were filled with such deep gratitude and utter relief, it nearly choked Nick up.

No doubt the guy really loved his little girl. Nick couldn't imagine being in his shoes, the life of his child hanging in the balance. Living with the fear that he couldn't afford the medical treatment needed to save her. Especially after having lost his wife to cancer.

After O'Connell left to pack, Nick sat at his desk thinking about how precious life really was. He tried to imagine it without Zoë. The idea made him sick inside. She was indelibly etched into his life. He had a bond with her that he'd never felt with another woman. That he'd never felt with *anyone*.

"I guess things went well."

Nick looked up to see Zoë standing in his doorway, a big grin on her face. Damn she was pretty. She had that ethereal glow of good health that pregnant women were supposed to have.

She looked…happy.

"What makes you say that?" he asked.

"O'Connell just came up to me in the break room and gave me a bear of a hug and a big kiss." She laughed. "You should have seen the jaws drop. Everyone is going to think I'm cheating on you."

Nick's brow furrowed. "He kissed you?"

"Relax," she said, her grin widening. "It was only on my cheek. And he *smiled*, Nick. Up until that moment I didn't even know he had teeth!"

He didn't like the idea of anyone but him kissing her, but she looked so happy, he felt a grin of his own tugging at the corners of his mouth.

"We really helped him," she said.

He nodded. "We really did."

She crossed the room and slid into his lap, weaving her arms around his neck. "It feels good."

"It certainly does," he growled, tugging her more firmly against him.

She kissed him, drawing his lower lip between her teeth and nibbling. Damn did he love when she did that. She tasted like sweet tea and raspberry-filled donuts.

"Maybe we should lock the door and celebrate," she said, rubbing herself against him. Driving him crazy was more like it. And God it was tempting. After so many near misses, all he had to do lately was look at her and he was instantly hard. He really needed to get this woman into bed. But he wasn't interested in a quickie at the office, when he made love to Zoë, he planned to take his time.

Meaning it would have to wait. *Again*.

"No time," he told her. "We have to get over to my condo and pack up my things. I told him he could move in right away."

She gave him an adorable little pout, then sighed and said, "Well then, I guess we had better hurry. And I don't care if we don't get home until 2 a.m., we are getting naked tonight."

Sounded like a good plan to him.

It was after eight when they finally got Nick's things loaded in the back of his truck and headed home.

Home. The word had a totally different meaning to her now.

While helping him pack, Zoë made a startling and somewhat disturbing discovery. Nick had no pictures from his childhood, no family mementos. Nothing to indicate he even had a family. It was as if he had no past at all, or at least not one he had any desire to look back on.

She had boxes and boxes of photos and old birthday cards, pictures her younger siblings had drawn for her, and even a couple of their baby teeth. She had at least one or two items from each member of her family.

Only then did it truly sink in, did she realize what it must have been like for him growing up. How lonely he must have been, and why having a family was so important to him now.

He'd never truly experienced a *real* family and now she wanted to be the one who gave him that. She wanted to be the one who finally made him feel complete. She planned to spend the rest of her life making up for every lonely day, every isolated minute he had ever spent. Even if that meant having another baby. Or even a third.

Which, of course, would necessitate them getting a bigger house. She wondered if he would mind moving into a more rural setting. Maybe Romeo or Armada. They could have a huge yard for Tucker and the kids to play in. She could have an enormous flower garden, and maybe start growing vegetables. She could can pickles and jam, the way her grandmother used to. Maybe she could even take an extended leave from work and try the stay-at-home-mom thing for a while. Or at the very least work part time from home.

A world of opportunities she'd never even considered had opened up to her and she couldn't wait to see just where life would lead her.

"You're awfully quiet," Nick said, as he backed his truck into the driveway and parked beside her car. "Everything okay?"

She turned to him and smiled. "I'm just conserving my energy for other things."

He put the truck in park and killed the engine. "I want to say to hell with the unloading, but everything I own is sitting back there. I could probably just toss it all into the garage."

"The lock on the door is broken." It wasn't as if she lived in a bad neighborhood. Birmingham was considered upscale by most accounts, but there was no point taking chances. "If we move fast, we can get the boxes unloaded in no time. Consider it foreplay."

"You don't pick up anything heavier than a phone book," he said firmly and she rolled her eyes. He was such a guy.

They climbed out and he opened the tailgate while she unlocked the front door. She could hear Tucker inside, hopping around excitedly like an overgrown rabbit. They had stopped by home only a couple of hours ago to feed him and let him out, but he greeted her as if she'd been gone for days.

"I know, I know," she said, patting his head as she pushed her way through the door. "We missed you, too, you big oaf."

She grabbed Tucker's collar so he wouldn't bolt and held the door open for Nick. He brushed past her with two boxes marked Bedroom. He carried them down the hall and past the stairs.

"Where are you going with those?" she asked.

He turned to her, a puzzled look on his face. "To the bedroom."

"But our bedroom is upstairs."

A slow grin curled his mouth. "*Our* bedroom."

"Our bedroom," she repeated. And because she knew what was coming next, she added, "And yes, I'm sure."

Savoring the mildly stunned, incredibly happy expression on his face, she headed out the door to grab more boxes. If he thought he was happy now, he should just wait until she'd gotten her hands on him.

After she was through with him, a bulldozer couldn't pry the smile from his face.

"That's it," Nick said, closing and locking the front door.

They had hauled everything inside in under twenty minutes and the anticipation was killing her.

Now it was time to get to the good stuff.

"You know what that means," Zoë said, looking up at him from under lids that were already heavy with pent-up lust. Her legs and arms felt warm and weak and her head felt dizzy. She couldn't recall a time in her life when she'd been more turned on by the idea of making love to someone.

She took off her jacket and tossed it over the back of the couch. With a look to match her own, Nick did the same.

As she pulled her shirt up over her head, every inch of her skin buzzed with sexual awareness. The brush of lace from her bra teased her already sensitive nipples. The vee of skin between her thighs ached to be caressed. Even her hair felt alive and tingly.

Nick yanked his shirt over his head and dropped it on the floor. His skin looked deep golden tan in the dim lamplight. Her heart tapped out a wild beat as he walked toward her, unfastening his jeans. She couldn't wait to get her hands on him, touch and taste every inch. How could she have denied herself this? Why hadn't she realized how good it would be?

He stopped in front of her and she felt dizzy with

anticipation, every cell screaming to be touched. He lowered his head to kiss her and she rose up on her toes to meet him halfway. Their lips touched and she went hot all over, as if someone had replaced the blood in her veins with liquid fire.

He unfastened her jeans, shoving them down and she stopped kissing him just long enough to wiggle out of them and kick them into the dark corner beside the couch.

Her heart beat harder, in perfect time with the sudden loud pounding on the front door.

Nick groaned and pressed his forehead to hers, his breath coming hard and fast. "I don't *believe* this."

She didn't have a clue who it could be this time of night, but whatever they wanted couldn't possibly be as important as her getting into Nick's pants this very second.

"They'll go away." She slipped her hand inside his open fly and stroked the firm ridge of his erection through his boxers. He closed his eyes and groaned. He lifted her right off her feet and backed her against the wall separating the kitchen from the living room. She hooked her legs over his hips and gasped as the length of his erection rocked against her, her breasts crushed into his chest.

She kissed him and his mouth tasted hot and tangy. She felt as if she couldn't get enough, as though she could eat him alive and crawl all over him. She clawed at his jeans, shoving them and his boxers down, then cupped his bare behind, digging her nails into his flesh, feeling wild and sexy and completely out of control. No man had ever made her want to let go this way, to give so much of herself.

The pounding on the door persisted for a minute or two, then through a haze of arousal Zoë heard the jingle of keys, and the rattle of the doorknob being turned. Nick must have heard it too because he stopped kissing her and went stone still.

It happened so fast, neither had time to react. One minute they were alone, the next her sister was standing in the open doorway staring at them, mouth agape. Thank goodness there weren't many lights on, but there was no mistaking exactly what was happening.

For several seconds time stood still. No one moved or said a word. Faith looked down at Zoë's hands, still clutching Nick's behind. She said, "Nice ass," then burst into tears and walked back out the door.

Ten

"I'm so sorry," Faith hiccupped for the umpteenth time since Nick and Zoë had yanked their clothes on and tugged her back inside the house. Zoë sat on the couch by Faith. Nick stood across the room wearing a typical male slightly confused, mildly alarmed expression, looking as though any second he might bolt.

Faith was not the crying type, not even when she was a kid, which led Zoë to believe something really awful had happened. At first Faith had been crying too hard to string together a coherent sentence. They were only able to assess that she wasn't in need of medical attention and no one had died.

Faith sniffled and tugged another tissue from the box in her lap. "I can't believe I fell apart like that, and I really can't believe I walked in on you right in the middle of…well, you know."

"Stop apologizing," Zoë told her. "Tell us what happened."

Faith wiped away the mascara smudges under her eyes. "I am such an idiot."

Nick pushed off the wall where he'd been leaning. "Why don't I leave you two alone to talk."

Before Zoë or Faith could answer, he was on his way up the stairs.

"Wow," Faith said. "I sure scared him off."

Zoë shrugged. "What can I say, he's a guy. He's been getting more than his share of emotional stuff from me these days. I think he's suffering from an overload."

Faith sat there for a second, quietly toying with the tissue, then she looked up at Zoë and said, "I got dumped."

"Oh, Faith." Zoë rubbed her sister's shoulder.

As if Tucker could sense her unhappiness and wanted to help, he walked over to the couch and laid his head in Faith's lap, gazing up at her with what Zoë could swear was a look of sympathy.

Faith sniffled and scratched him behind the ears. "I told her I loved her, and I wanted us to move in together. I told her I was going to tell my parents the truth, no matter the consequences, and she told me I probably didn't want to do that. Then she said she decided to go back to her husband."

"I didn't know that she was married."

"Neither did I. Long story short, Mia said she had

just been experimenting, and basically trying to make her husband jealous. And I guess it worked. He wants her back." Faith sniffled and wiped away fresh tears. "She was so…*cold*. Like she never cared about me at all. Like I was some high school science experiment."

"Oh, sweetie, I'm so sorry. I know how much you cared about her."

"I feel so stupid. But I can't help thinking I deserved this."

That was just crazy. "How could you possibly deserve to be treated this way?"

"Do you know how many men I've dumped who claimed to 'love' me?"

"Honey, you deserve to be happy just as much as anyone else."

"Speaking of being happy," Faith said, brightening. "It looks like things with you and Nick are going pretty well, huh?"

Zoë felt guilty admitting how happy she was in light of her sister's heartache, but she couldn't contain her joy. "I'm going to tell him yes. I'm going to marry him."

"Oh my gosh!" Faith squealed excitedly and gave her a big hug. "I can't think of a more perfect man for you." She held Zoë at arm's length and grinned. "Not to mention that he has a mighty find rear end."

Zoë grinned. "No kidding."

"Speaking of that, I should go and let you guys get back to business. I can stay in a hotel."

"You're not staying in a hotel. The spare bedroom is free now. Stay as long as you like."

"I don't have to be to work until Monday, so maybe I will hide out here for a couple of days, if you don't mind."

"We would love to have you," Zoë said, rising from the couch, anxious to get upstairs and finish what she and Nick had started. "Maybe we can go shopping tomorrow. Spending money always helps me chase away a bad mood."

"Just so you know, I'll be sleeping with these on." She held up a pair of headphones and an MP3 player, and grinned mischievously. "So be as loud as you like. I won't hear a thing."

When Zoë finally made it upstairs, Tucker on her heel, Nick was sitting in bed, bare-chested and gorgeous, reading a hardcover novel.

"Everything all right?" he asked.

"She got dumped."

"That's kind of what I figured." He closed the book and set it on the nightstand. "Is she okay?"

"Bruised but not broken." She peeled her shirt off and tossed it in the general direction of the hamper, missing her target by several feet. "I hope you don't mind, but she's going to stick around for a couple days. I don't think she wants to be alone."

"Of course I don't mind. But I guess that nixes tonight's scheduled activities, huh?"

She peeled off her jeans and dropped them

where she stood. "I don't care if the house burns down, nothing is going to stop me from getting you naked tonight."

"That's convenient." He flashed her a sexy, dimpled grin, and tossed back the covers. "Because I'm already naked."

Holy moly! Naked and *very* aroused. She raised a brow at him. "Did you start without me?"

"It won't go away. I need you to put me out of my misery."

"It would be my pleasure." She walked around to his side of the bed, dropping her bra and panties along the way. The way his eyes raked over her—she felt as if she were the sexiest, most desirable woman on the planet.

He patted his thighs. "Come'ere."

She climbed in his lap, straddling him. His crisp leg hair tickled her skin as she lowered herself onto his thighs. His body felt warm and solid as he looped an arm around her waist and drew her closer.

"Here we are," he said, tucking her hair back behind her ears.

Finally. "Just you and me."

He stroked her cheek, his eyes searching her face. "I want you to know that there is no one else on earth that I would rather be with right now. That I would *ever* want to be with."

His words warmed her from the inside out. There was no one she would rather be with, either. "Me, too."

She still wanted him, couldn't wait to feel him

inside her again, but that sense of urgency was gone. Now she wanted to take her time, savor every minute. He must have felt the same way, because for the longest time they only played with each other, kissing and stroking and tasting. Exploring each other as if it was the first time, yet she felt as if they had learned each other a hundred years ago.

How could something be exciting and new, yet this comfortable and familiar?

"I love the way this feels," he said, using his thumbs to gently caress the smooth skin at the junction of her thighs. He watched his movements, as if he found the sight of it fascinating. His featherlight strokes made her hot and cold at the same time and her head started getting that dizzy, detached feeling.

She rose up on her knees to give him a better look, gripping the headboard on either side of him and he groaned his appreciation.

He leaned forward, his hair brushing against her stomach and touched her with his tongue. Just one quick flick, but his mouth was so hot, the sensation so shockingly intense, she gasped with surprise and jerked away.

He looked up, a grin on his face, and said, "Delicious."

She might have been embarrassed, but she was too turned on. He cupped her behind in his big, warm hands and pulled her back to his mouth, lapping and tasting while she balanced precariously between torture and bliss. Every slow, deep stroke of his tongue took her higher, until she could hardly stand it. She wanted to grab his head and push him deeper.

She wanted more, and at the same time she was on total sensory overload.

She was aware of the sound of her own voice, but the words were jumbled and incoherent. The wet heat of his tongue, the rasp of his beard stubble on her bare skin—it was too much.

The pleasure started somewhere deep inside, in her soul maybe, and radiated outward. It gripped her with such momentum, time seemed to grind to an abrupt halt. Every muscle in her body clenched tight and her eyes clamped shut. Her hands tangled in his hair, trapping him close as she rode the waves of pleasure. Her body shook and quaked for what felt like forever.

Her heart throbbed in time with the steady pulse between her thighs. She didn't know if it was Nick's incredible skills or the pregnancy hormones, or maybe even a combination of both, but she had never come so hard in her entire life.

She sank down into his lap and rested her forehead against his shoulder, wanting to tell him how out-of-this-world, amazingly and unbelievably sensational he'd just made her feel, how she was pretty sure she'd just had her first out-of-body experience, but she was barely able to breathe much less use her mouth to form words.

So instead, she kissed him, tasting herself on his

lips and finding it unbelievably erotic. She reached down between them and wrapped her fingers around the impressive girth of his erection. He groaned low in his chest and kissed her harder.

She stroked him slowly, felt him pulse in her hand. He was hot to the touch and velvet smooth. She wanted to take him into her mouth, but when she made a move to bend forward he caught her head in his hands, tangling his fingers through her hair. "Don't."

"I want to."

"I want to make love to you."

"Can't we do both."

He shook his head. "I'm so hot for you right now, it's going to have to be one or the other, and I need to be inside of you."

Well, if he put it that way. Besides, what was the rush? They had the rest of their lives to try anything they wanted. And though she had never been particularly creative or adventurous in bed, she wanted to try it all with Nick.

"You know the best thing about pregnant sex?" he asked wrapping his hands around her hips.

"Huh?"

He fed her a mischievous grin. "No need for a condom."

Nick guided her and she lowered herself on top of him. He sank inside her slow and smooth and oh so deep.

He hissed out a breath, his grip on her tightening. For a moment they sat that way, not moving, barely even breathing. It was almost scary what a perfect fit they were, how connected she felt to him. There was no doubt in her mind that Nick was the man she was supposed to spend the rest of her life with. She wanted to have babies with him and grow old with him.

And she wanted him to know exactly how she was feeling. "Nick, I love you."

He smiled, caught her face between his hands and kissed her, tender and sweet. And she couldn't stop her body from moving, from rising and sinking in a slow, steady rhythm. She watched with fascination as a look of pure ecstasy washed over his face. He let her set the pace, let her do most of the work while he kissed and touched her and whispered sexy, exciting things to her. She found herself answering him, using words she never would have expected to come out of a good Catholic girl's mouth. Dirty things he seemed to love hearing.

He reached between them, caressing the sensitive bud he had so skillfully manipulated with his tongue, and the reaction was instantaneous. Pleasure slammed her from all sides, hard, deep and intense. Forget an out-of-body experience. She wasn't even on the same planet. Only when she heard Nick groan her name, when his body rocked up to meet hers, did she realize she'd taken him along for the ride.

They sat there for several minutes afterward, catching their breath. She kept telling herself she should move, but he was still hard and he felt so good inside her. She waited, watching the minutes tick by on the alarm clock, two, then three, then five, but it still didn't go away. In fact, instead of getting soft, she was pretty sure he was getting harder.

Just for fun, she wiggled her hips and he answered her with a rumble of pleasure.

"You weren't kidding about it not going away." She sat up and smiled. "I'm impressed."

"You know what that means," he said, returning her smile. "We'll just have to do it again."

"Do you remember when we first met?" Nick asked. Zoë lay in his arms her head resting against his chest. She smelled so warm and sweet and girly. It was getting late, and they both had to get up and go to work, but his mind was moving a million miles an hour.

"Of course. I came for an interview, and did a pretty fair job of lying through my teeth."

He played with her hair, looping a curl around his index finger then letting it spring free. There were so many places on her body to play with, so many things to touch. He was pretty sure that tonight he'd managed to play with or touch just about every single one. As far as sex went, Zoë didn't seem to have a single reservation or hang-up. He could do or try pretty much anything and she was always ready for more. Things so forbidden and intimate he'd never had the guts to try them so early in a relationship. Of course, they'd had ten years to develop a deep sense of trust.

It had just taken them a while to get to the good stuff.

"I knew an eighteen-year-old couldn't possibly

have the experience you listed on your application, but you looked so young and vulnerable. I couldn't turn you away."

She looked up at him. "Are you saying you took pity on me?"

He grinned. "Pretty much, yeah."

She propped her chin on his chest. "As much as I wanted to get away from my family, those first few months were hard. I never anticipated how lonely I would be. You were incredibly patient with me considering how bad I stunk as a secretary."

He chuckled. "But you tried so hard, I didn't have the heart to fire you. I knew deep down that you were special. And you were cute."

"I never told you this, but I had a major crush on you for the first year."

"I could kind of tell."

She looked surprised. "Really?"

"Yeah, and I was tempted, believe me. But at the time I wasn't looking for a relationship, and I didn't want to risk killing our friendship with a one-night stand. I liked you too much."

"Want to hear something weird. Almost every boyfriend I've had over the years has felt threatened by my relationship with you."

"Want to hear something even weirder? I've had the same problem with *every* one of my girlfriends. It was as if they couldn't believe a guy like me could have a woman as a good friend."

"Maybe they were seeing something we didn't."

"Maybe." He stroked the wispy curls back from her face. "I never told you what Lynn said right before our wedding, the real reason she decked me."

"What did she say?"

"As we were getting out of the car in the courthouse parking lot, she told me that she would only marry me if I fired you."

Zoë's eyes widened. "You're kidding!"

"She didn't want me seeing you anymore, either. I had to break all ties with you."

"That's crazy. What did you say?"

"At first I thought she was joking, and when I realized she was serious, I was too stunned to say anything. It's not as if I wasn't already having major doubts, but up until that moment I had really planned to go through with it."

"Yet, you waited until the last minute to dump her."

"She was so…manipulative. I guess I wanted to punish her, or knock her down a few pegs at least. You should have seen the smug look on her face when we were standing there. When I backed out, I was more or less saying that I was choosing you over her."

"That had to sting." She sounded sympathetic, but he could tell she was getting a lot of satisfaction from this. She liked hearing that he'd picked her over the woman he'd asked to marry him.

"I'm ashamed to admit it, but I actually enjoyed dumping her."

"That makes two of us, because I enjoyed it, too."

"Now I'm exactly where I'm supposed to be." He

spread his hand over her flat belly, where their child was growing. "Here with you and the baby."

Zoë sighed and rested her head on Nick's chest, cupping her hand over his. So was she, exactly where she belonged. And she wanted to tell him so, right now. But after making him wait for an answer to his marriage proposal, somehow just saying yes didn't seem good enough.

Nick," she said, stroking the tops of his fingers.

"Huh?"

"Would you marry me?"

He was silent, so she looked up and saw that he was grinning. A great big dimpled grin full of love and affection. He had gotten the message loud and clear. He leaned forward, caught her face in his hands and kissed her. *"Absolutely."*

A part of her sighed with relief. Not that she thought he was going to say no. Maybe it was because things were finally settled, it felt as though her life was back on track.

Yet there was something else. A niggling in the back of her mind. A tiny seed of doubt. "I think we should do it soon," She said, feeling a sudden urgency to get this settled. To get on with their life together. Like maybe deep down she thought he might change her mind. "You know, because of the baby."

"How soon?"

"How does next Friday work for you?"

His smile got even bigger. "Friday would be perfect."

"Something really small, like the justice of the peace?"

"Whatever you want."

She settled into his arms and snuggled against him, knowing deep down to her soul that she was doing the right thing, and hoping he felt the same way.

He was quiet for several minutes then asked, "Can I tell you a secret?"

"You can tell me anything."

"I've never once told anyone I love them."

She propped herself up on her elbow to look at him. His eyes were so…*sad*. "How is that possible? You were engaged two times."

"Weird huh?"

"You didn't love them?" A part of her wanted him to say he hadn't. The selfish part that wanted him to love only her.

"I don't know. Maybe I did in my own way. Maybe I'm not physically capable."

Maybe growing up the way he had, had damaged him somehow. How terribly sad that a person could go through their entire life never feeling real love.

"I'm a different person with you, Zoë. We're going to be a family."

She let her head drop back down, breathed in the scent of him, felt his heart thump against her ear.

A family. Her and Nick.

Did that mean he loved her? And if he did, why didn't he say the words? Was he really not capable? Or was admitting that to her just the first step? And

if it had been, at least it was a step in the right direction.

He was quiet for a while, then his breathing became
slow and steady and she knew he had fallen asleep.

He did love her. And it wasn't just wishful
thinking. She knew it in her heart. She sensed it when
he looked at her, could feel it when he touched her.
When he was ready, he would tell her.

She would just have to be patient.

Eleven

Zoë felt like death warmed over the next morning at seven when Nick nudged her awake. She managed to pry one eye open far enough to see that he was already showered and dressed and far too awake considering how late they had fallen asleep. And it must have been pretty obvious that she was in no shape to go to work, because he just kissed her, tucked the covers up over her shoulders and said he would see her later.

She fell back to sleep and had strange, disturbing dreams. She dreamed it was her wedding day, and she was walking down the aisle, her arm looped in her father's. Instead of a white gown, she wore the dress she'd worn to both of Nick's weddings, complete with broken straps and stains, and it had been dyed crimson—the same shade as her sister's car.

Not that anyone seemed to think that was out of the ordinary. Row upon row of people dressed in white sat on either side smiling and nodding. Bunches of blood-red roses decorated the aisle, giving everyone a pale, ethereal look.

Her mind kept telling her that everything was normal, but something didn't feel right.

She could see Nick waiting for her by the altar, wearing the same suit he'd worn at his last wedding. He was smiling, but it looked unnatural and plastic, as if he was being forced to stand there against his will. She kept walking toward him, telling herself everything was going to be okay, but instead of getting closer, the longer she walked, the farther away he was getting. The cloying scent of roses crowded the air. But instead of smelling like flowers, it smelled metallic, like blood. It burned her nose and made her stomach ache.

Something definitely wasn't right.

She started walking faster, trying desperately to reach him, but Nick was fading from her vision. Disappearing. She called out to him, but he didn't seem to hear her.

She broke into a run but her legs felt heavy and weak and cramps knotted her insides, doubling her over. The fog grew thicker, closing in around her like wet paper. She clawed her way through it, felt it filling her lungs, constricting her air. She couldn't see, couldn't breathe, could hear nothing but the frantic pounding of her heart.

She called for him again but it was no use. Nick and her father, the smiling people, they were all gone. She was all alone with the sick feeling that she'd just become number three. Nick had left her at the altar, just like the others.

She felt a firm hand on her shoulder and someone called her name.

Zoë shot up in bed, disoriented and out of breath.

"Hey, you okay?" Faith stood beside the bed, a look of concern on her face.

"Bad dream." Her voice sounded weak and scratchy.

"You called for Nick. He already left for work." She touched Zoë's forehead. "You're all sweaty."

Faith was right. The sheet was clinging to her damp skin and her hair felt wet. She felt hot and cold at the same time and everything was fuzzy and surreal.

Zoë blinked several times and fought to pull herself awake, but couldn't shake the sensation of being caught somewhere between sleep and consciousness. It took a minute to realize that the cramps in her stomach hadn't faded with the dream.

It wasn't real, she told herself. She was fine. But the pain was very real and too intense.

Fear skittered across her spine, and her heart gave a violent jolt in her chest.

Faith looked downright scared now. "Zoë, what's wrong? You're white as a sheet."

Everything was fine. The baby was fine, she assured herself, but the tips of her fingers had begun to go numb with fear. She felt as if she couldn't pull in a full breath.

That was when Zoë felt it. The warm gush between her legs.

No, this was not happening.

She and Nick were going to get married. They were going to have a baby together.

"Zoë?" Faith's hand was on her shoulder again and there was real fear in her voice. "Talk to me."

The pain intensified, cramps gripped deeper.

No, no, no, this couldn't be happening. She had to find a way to stop it. She had to *do* something.

She looked up at her sister, tears welling in her eyes. "I think I'm losing the baby."

Nick stood impatiently waiting for the hospital elevator to reach the third floor. He didn't have a clue what was going on, only a message from Faith telling him to get to Royal Oak Beaumont Hospital.

He'd been out of the office all morning, and because he had forgotten to charge it last night, his cell phone was dead. He was unaware of any problem until twenty minutes ago when Shannon accosted him on his way to his office.

He'd tried both Faith's and Zoë's cell phones before he left but neither was answering.

There had to be some rational explanation, he kept telling himself. Nothing was wrong. He was sure that she was fine.

And still a knot of fear had lodged itself in his gut. What if she wasn't fine? What would he do then?

The elevator dinged and the doors slid open. He

crossed the hall to the nurses' station and gave the nurse, an older woman with a fatigued face, Zoë's name.

"Room thirteen-forty," she said in a voice that mirrored her tired expression. She motioned with a jerk of her thumb. "That way, around the corner."

He started down the hall, his heart beating faster and harder with every step.

She was fine. Everything would be okay.

He rounded the corner and saw Faith standing outside one of the rooms. When she turned and saw him coming, he could see by the expression on her face that everything was *not* okay.

His heart took a sudden dive and landed with a plop in the pit of his stomach.

"What happened," he demanded. "Is Zoë okay?"

"She's fine," Faith said. "They're going to keep her overnight just to be safe."

Relief hit his so hard and swift his knees nearly buckled. He braced a hand against the door frame to steady himself. He hadn't realized until just then how scared he'd been. He didn't know what he would have done if she'd been hurt or sick.

So why was she here?

Then it hit him. He'd been so worried about Zoë, he'd completely forgotten about the pregnancy.

"The baby?" he asked.

Faith paused and bit her lip, looking exactly like Zoë did when something was wrong.

Damn it.

They had lost the baby.

What was this going to do to Zoë? Lately she had really warmed to the idea of becoming a mother. He knew this was going to be tough for her to handle. She would feel so guilty. And what if it had something to do with last night? He would never forgive himself if this was his fault.

Right now, he just needed to see for himself that Zoë was okay. "Can I go in?"

"Of course. She's been waiting for you."

Taking a deep breath, he walked past Faith into the room. Zoë sat in the bed wearing a hospital gown looking so small and vulnerable. So alone and numb.

"Hey," he said, walking over to the bed. As he got closer, he could see that she was holding back tears, fighting to keep it together.

It was just like her to think she had to be strong for everyone else.

She looked up at him, her eyes so full of hurt. "We lost the baby."

He had known, but hearing the words felt like a stab in his gut.

"She told me. I'm so sorry I didn't get here sooner." He sat on the edge of the bed and she sat stiffly beside him. She was so tense, one good poke would probably snap her in half. Did she think he was going to make her go through this alone?

"I'm so sorry," she whispered, her voice trembling.

"Zoë, it's okay. It's not your fault." He put an arm around her and nudged her toward him, and everything in her seemed to let go. A soft sob racked through her and she dissolved into his arms. She cried quietly for several minutes and he just held her. He had no idea what to say, what to do. He didn't even know what had happened.

"I-I thought you might be mad," she finally said, her voice quiet and miserable.

He grabbed a tissue and handed it to her. "Why would I be mad?"

She shrugged and wiped away the tears. "I know how much you wanted this."

"But your being okay means a lot more to me."

"It's so weird. I was so freaked out about being pregnant, now I feel so…empty. I really wanted this baby, Nick."

"I know you did." He stroked back a stray curl that clung to her damp cheek. He didn't even want to know, but he had to ask. "Do they know what caused it? I mean, last night…"

"It wasn't that. They did an ultrasound and I could tell by the look on her face that the technician saw something wrong, but she wouldn't say what. She said the doctor would be in soon to see me. That was like an hour ago."

"I'm so sorry I wasn't here for you." Nick rubbed her back soothingly. Sometimes he forgot how petite she was. How vulnerable. His first instinct was to protect her. To say anything to make her hurt less. "I'm sure everything is fine."

"What if it isn't?" she said, sounding genuinely frightened. "What if something is really wrong? I thought I never wanted kids, but the idea of never being able to—" Her voice hitched.

"There's no point in worrying until we know what's going on."

But that got Nick thinking, what if she couldn't have kids? What if they could *never* have a child together? After all these years of longing for a family, waiting for just the right time, could he marry a woman who was infertile?

The answer surprised him.

The truth was, it didn't make a damned bit of difference, if the woman he was marrying was Zoë. Maybe at first his desire to marry her was partially due to the pregnancy, but not any longer. He wanted her.

Baby or no baby.

Before he could tell her that, Doctor Gordon walked in, Faith on his heels. Zoë wrapped her hand around his and squeezed. He could feel her trembling.

"First, I just went over the results of the ultrasound. I want to assure you that neither of you is in any way at fault. There is a thin membrane that has separated Zoë's uterus into two sections. This constricted the baby's growth, causing the miscarriage."

He went on to explain that she was actually lucky that the egg had implanted itself on the smaller side. Had it been on the other side it's quite possible she could have progressed well into the fourth or even fifth month before miscarrying, which would have been a much more devastating loss.

Nick found it tough to think of losing a baby as a good thing, but what the doctor said made sense.

Zoë didn't say anything, just kept a death grip on his hand, so Nick asked what he knew she was probably afraid to. "Is this something you can fix?"

"I can perform a simple outpatient procedure to remove the membrane," he said. "With no complications, recovery time is usually only a week or two."

"And then she'll be okay? She'll be able to get pregnant?" He wanted to know more for Zoë's sake than his own. He didn't want any question in her mind.

"Did you have any difficulty conceiving?"

"Nope," Zoë and Nick said in unison and the doctor cracked a smile. Getting pregnant had been the easy part.

"Then I see no reason why, with the surgery, she wouldn't be able to conceive and carry a baby to term." He flashed Zoë a reassuring smile. "I think you're going to be just fine."

The grip on Nick's hand eased. He could almost feel the relief pouring through her. He knew how doctors worked. In this litigious society they didn't give false hope. Zoë would be okay. They would get past this. She would have the surgery and they could try again.

"I'd like to see you in the office in two weeks," Doctor Gordon told Zoë. "If everything looks good we can schedule the procedure."

Zoë and Nick each asked a few more questions, then thanked him. When he was gone, Faith walked around the bed and gave Zoë a big hug and a kiss on the cheek. "I'm glad everything is okay."

"Thanks," Zoë said, and some unspoken under-standing seemed to pass between them.

She had no idea how lucky she was to have that kind of bond with someone. To have family. Now he would know, too. When they got married, her family would be his.

"I'm going to run down to the cafeteria and give you guys some time alone," Faith told them. "I'll see you in a bit."

After she left, Zoë said, "So, I guess you're off the hook, huh?"

She couldn't possibly mean what he thought she meant. Nick took her hand and held it. "Which hook would that be?"

"There's no baby. You don't have to marry me now."

"I'm going to pretend you didn't say that."

"What if I can't have another baby, Nick?"

"That's too bad, sweetheart. You're stuck with me." A tear rolled down her cheek and he brushed it away with his thumb. "You heard what the doctor said. There's no reason to worry about that now. You'll have the surgery and everything will be fine."

She nodded, but didn't look completely convinced.

"There is something missing, though," he said.

She frowned. "Missing?"

"We still have to make it official." Enjoying her puzzled look, he reached into his jacket pocket and pulled out the small velvet box. He lifted the lid and watched her jaw drop when she saw the two carat marquee cut platinum diamond engagement ring that had taken him three hours at six different jewelers to choose.

"Oh my God," she breathed, looking genuinely stunned. "You got me a ring?"

"Yeah, and it took me all morning to find the perfect one." He took the ring from its satin bed. She held her breath as he slipped it on the ring finger of her right hand. It was a perfect fit. Feminine but not too flashy.

She held up her hand and the stone shimmered in the fluorescent lights. "How did you know what size?"

"I borrowed a ring from your jewelry box before I left this morning. Do you like it?"

"It's exactly what I would have chosen." Tears welled in her eyes. Happy ones, he hoped. Then she looked up at him with a watery smile. "It's perfect, Nick."

"So now it's official. And since there's no rush, we can wait and plan something nice if you want. Something bigger. I hear most women spend their lives planning their wedding day."

She shook her head. "Not me. I don't need a big wedding. And I don't want to wait. I want to do it next Friday, like we planned."

"Are you sure you'll be feeling up to it? You've been through a lot today—"

"I feel better already knowing everything is going to okay. I want to try again as soon as the doctor says it's safe. I want us to have a baby."

He squeezed her hand. "Whatever you want."

"And I want more than one. At least two, maybe even three."

Wow. When she changed her mind, she really did a complete one-eighty. "We'll never fit a family of five into your house or my condo. I'll have to build us something bigger."

"With a yard big enough for Tucker and the kids to play in? And a huge garden?"

"Whatever you want."

"That's what I want," she said, wrapping her arms around him and hugging him tight. "That's exactly what I want."

She looked happy, and sounded happy, so why did Nick get the feeling something wasn't right?

Twelve

Zoë took the rest of the week off and though Nick thought she needed more time, she was tired of sitting around feeling sorry for herself and went back to work Monday morning.

It had been the right thing to do. Four days later she felt as though she had begun to heal both physically and mentally. She felt ready to move on.

She kept reminding herself what the doctor said, how much worse it would have been if she'd been four or five months along. The baby would have been almost fully developed. A little person. They would have known if it was a boy or a girl.

And they would have spent the days following

the miscarriage not recovering, but planning a funeral. The idea gave her a cold chill.

So really, losing the baby so early, when it was just a speck of life she hadn't even felt move, was a blessing in disguise.

As badly as Nick wanted children, she had expected him to be really upset, but he had seemed more concerned about her health than the fact that they had lost a child. Not that he hadn't made it clear he was concerned about future fertility issues, and he seemed so relieved when the doctor said the surgery would probably fix the problem.

She couldn't help wondering, what if it didn't? Nick hadn't even been willing to discuss it. What if something went wrong and she could never have kids? How would Nick feel about marrying her then?

Of course, by then they would already be married.

Maybe that was why he'd suggested putting the wedding off for a while. Maybe he wanted to be sure she was okay before he tied himself down to her. Maybe he didn't want to marry a woman who couldn't give him children.

She closed her eyes and shook her head.

That was ridiculous. He'd gotten her a beautiful ring and he'd been unbelievably sweet the past few days.

At the hospital, all she had wanted was to come home, but when she got home, it felt as though everything had changed. Getting back to her regular routine had been so difficult. He had stayed beside her the entire first day after it happened. He'd brought her tea and held her when she cried, which was almost constantly.

Why would he do any of that if he didn't want to marry her? If he didn't love her?

And if he did love her, why didn't he say it?

"Hey Zoë, how ya feeling?"

Zoë looked up to find Shannon standing in her office doorway. Again. It was her third time today checking up on Zoë and it was barely three o'clock. She'd been doing this all week, watching over Zoë like a mother hen. "You can stop hovering. I'm fine."

She flashed Zoë a squinty-eyed assessing look. After a few seconds, her face softened, as if she was satisfied that Zoë was being honest. "You know where I am if you need me," she said, then disappeared down the hall.

Word of what happened had traveled through the entire office in record time. She'd received several flower arrangements and sympathy cards over the weekend. They had been addressed to both her and Nick, so that cat was definitely out of the bag. Not that she cared. Everyone would have found out soon enough. They also knew that she and Nick were getting married.

Several men in his crew had wanted to throw him a bachelor party tonight, but he said that in light of what they had just been through, he didn't think it was appropriate. Zoë had said the same thing when the girls in the office had approached her about a trip across the Ambassador Bridge to the male strip club in Windsor.

She just wanted to get this wedding over and done with. Every day she waited she was more anxious, more worried that she would make it all the way to the altar only to have him say he couldn't go through with it.

Or what if he didn't show up at all? They were taking the traditional route and spending the night before their wedding apart. Nick's idea. She was staying home and he was bunking with O'Connell in his condo. Maybe she should have insisted they drive together, so she could at least be sure he would make an appearance.

She nearly groaned out loud.

This was ridiculous. She was being silly and paranoid. Of course he was going to show up. Not only was he going to show up, but he was going to marry her. Even if he hadn't actually said that he loved her.

In less than twenty-four hours she would be Mrs. Nick Bateman. Someone's *wife*. A month ago that fact would have given her hives, but for some reason the idea of getting married didn't seem all that weird to her anymore. She'd changed over the past few weeks. Being with Nick had made her realize that sharing her life with someone didn't mean sacrificing her freedom. It didn't mean compromising herself as a person.

She didn't even mind having his big dumb dog around. In fact, they felt a lot like a family. And someday their little family would grow to include children. A little boy with Nick's dimples and hazel eyes, or maybe a little girl with Zoë's curly hair and stubborn streak.

The possibilities were endless.

Tiffany from accounting barged into her office without knocking—the way she always did—and dropped an invoice on Zoë's desk.

"I need this approved," she snapped.

Nice, Zoë thought. It was common knowledge that Tiffany had been after Nick for the better part of her first six months working here. According to Shannon, Tiffany had been convinced she was next in line after the Lynn relationship had tanked, but Nick had completely blown off her very obvious advances. When she reduced herself to bluntly asking him out, he'd told her very politely—because that was his way—to give it a rest.

She was young, big-breasted and beautiful, and probably not used to men telling her no. Since she had caught Zoë and Nick playing tonsil hockey in the office that day, her panties had been in a serious twist and Zoë had been on the receiving end of a whole lotta attitude.

What Tiffany didn't seem to realize is that Zoë had the authority to fire her jealous little behind— and probably would have if the girl wasn't such a hard worker.

"I'll get this back to you by Monday," Zoë said, hoping Tiffany would take the hint and leave.

She didn't.

"So, tomorrow's the big day, huh?"

"Yup," Zoë replied, pretending to be engrossed by the open file on her computer screen. If you ignored a pest, it was supposed to go away, right?

"Considering Nick's reputation, aren't you nervous?"

Just ignore her, she told herself. She's only trying to get a rise out of you. She looked up, forcing what she hoped passed for a patient smile, but probably looked more like a grimace. "Tiffany, I'm a little busy here."

Tiffany went on as if Zoë hadn't already, in a round about way, told her to get lost. "I'm just worried about you. I'm sure you're feeling vulnerable right now."

Oh please! Now she was going to pretend to be concerned for Zoë's welfare? What an absolute crock.

"I appreciate your concern." *Not.* "But I feel a little uncomfortable discussing personal matters with you."

"You have to be at least a little worried," she persisted. "I mean, before he had a reason to marry you. And now, well…" She trailed off and let the statement hang in the air for Zoë to absorb.

And it did. Zoë had to struggle against the urge to vault over the desk and claw Tiffany's eyes out.

What Tiffany was really saying, was that Zoë was no longer pregnant, so Nick would have no reason to marry her. She couldn't deny the trickle of icy fear that slid through her veins. Because nothing Tiffany said was untrue. Bitchy and rude, yes, but not necessarily inconceivable.

"It would be bad enough being left at the altar, but what if he didn't even show up?"

Zoë's fists clenched tightly in her lap. *Don't kill her. Don't kill her,* she chanted to herself. But oh how good it would feel to blacken one of her pretty blue eyes. Or hell, maybe both of them. Tiffany may have been eight years younger and a head taller, but Zoë was pretty sure she could take her.

"Shut up, Tiffany," Shannon snapped from the doorway, appearing like an angel of mercy. "You're just jealous because you asked Nick out and he turned you down flat."

Tiffany's cheeks blushed a bright crimson and she shot Shannon a nasty look. "My money is on Nick dumping her. I guess we'll just see, won't we?"

She stomped from the room and Shannon mumbled, "What a bitch."

Zoë leaned back in her seat and exhaled deeply. "If you hadn't come in just now, I could see a possible assault charge in my very near future."

"Don't listen to her, Zoë. She has no idea what she's talking about."

"What did she mean by her money?" Zoë asked, even though she already had a pretty good idea.

"Just ignore her."

"What did she mean, Shannon?"

Shannon bit her lip, looking very uncomfortable. "I wasn't going to tell you…"

"It's another pool, isn't it?" Just what she needed, the employees betting on her getting her heart sliced and diced.

Shannon nodded, and Zoë's heart plummeted. She felt like going home, crawling into bed, covering her head and staying there forever.

"What are they betting on exactly this time?" she asked, trying to keep her voice light. Pretending that she didn't feel hurt and betrayed by people she considered her friends.

"They're betting on whether or not Nick will marry you, dump you at the altar, or not show up at all."

Zoë felt physically ill. Her voice shook when she asked, "Where did you put your money? Do you think he's going to dump me?"

"I didn't bet on this one, but if I had, I would have put my money on Nick marrying you. No question. In my life I've never known two people more perfect for each other."

"You don't think he was marrying me because of the baby?"

"As far as I'm concerned, the pregnancy just sped things up a bit. I don't doubt that he wants kids, and maybe that had been a motivating factor before when he asked those other women to marry him, but this is different. I know it is."

Zoë wanted to believe that, but she had to admit, she had doubts. Maybe if he would just tell her he loved her.

If by some miracle he didn't leave her at the altar, if they actually got married, did she want to spend her life with a man who just liked her a lot? Didn't she deserve better than that?

"It's all going to work out," Shannon assured her.

She used to think so, now she wasn't so sure. The question was, what did she plan to do about it?

"Are you sure you don't want me to be there?" Faith asked for the billionth time. "I could hop in the car and if I do ninety all the way I can be there just in time for the wedding."

Three hours, Zoë thought. She was marrying Nick in three hours. It seemed so unreal.

She'd slept in fits and bursts last night and crawled out of bed before the crack of dawn. She was too nervous to eat. Too distracted to do much more than sit at the kitchen table sipping her tea and skimming the newspaper.

According to the *Oakland Press,* the temperature would reach the midsixties with sunny skies all day. She couldn't ask for better weather.

It was her wedding day for heaven's sake! She should be happy. So why couldn't she work up a bit of enthusiasm? She hadn't even managed to drag herself into the shower yet and the dress she and Shannon had spent all day Wednesday shopping for still hung wrapped in plastic in the backseat of her car.

"Zoë?" Faith asked.

"I'm not even sure if I'm going," she admitted.

"Don't even talk like that. I've never seen you so happy. I know you've been through a lot in the past week. Maybe Nick is right, maybe you should wait a while and plan a real wedding. One your family and friends can attend."

And risk being dumped at the altar in front of the entire Simmons clan? Don't think so.

"I've just got prewedding jitters," she told her sister, so she wouldn't actually jump in the car and come down. "Everything will be great."

"Nick loves you."

"I know he does."

But therein lay the problem. She really *didn't* know. Nick hadn't said so, and she'd been too much of a chicken to come right out and ask him.

What if he said no?

Sorry, Zoë, I'm not capable of love, but I sure do like you a lot.

"I have to let you go so I can get ready," Zoë said.

"You're sure you're okay?"

"I'm fine." Lie, lie lie. She was *so* not fine.

"You'll call me later and let me know how it went?"

"I promise."

She hung up the phone and sighed, still not ready to drag herself to the bathroom for a shower. Instead she made herself another cup of tea and sat back down at the table.

Two hours later she was still sitting there, and only then did it sink in that she couldn't do it. She couldn't marry him.

The question now was, what would she tell Nick?

Thirteen

Nick stood in the lobby of the courthouse, alternating between watching the door, checking the time on his watch and pulling his phone from his pocket to make sure it was still on. His starched shirt was stiff and uncomfortable under his suit coat and his new tie was beginning to feel like a noose around his neck.

He'd tried Zoë's house phone and cell but she hadn't answered. He'd even called Faith, then spoke to Shannon in the office, but no one had heard from her for hours.

A smart man, a *realistic* man, would have left a long time ago. Right after he realized his fiancée was, in fact, not going to show up for their wedding.

He should have been at least a little angry at Zoë

for leaving him high and dry, but the truth was, he had it coming.

He deserved this.

In fact, he was glad she'd done it. It was the push he'd needed to realize just how much of an ass he'd been.

What reason had he given Zoë for believing he would marry her? Hell, as far as she knew, he might not have even shown up. Sure he'd said he wanted to marry her, but he'd fed the same line to two other women.

What he had failed to do was prove to Zoë that she was different. That she was the *one*.

He loved her, and he should have told her so.

And it's not as if he hadn't had chances. That night when they had made love and she had told him she loved him, he could have said he loved her, too. And later, when he'd admitted to her that he'd never said the words. He could have told her then.

He could have said it in the hospital, or any time the entire next day they had spent side-by-side, mourning their loss. So many times the words had been balanced on the tip of his tongue, ready to be spoken, but something always stopped him. He had always held back.

Maybe that was simply what he had taught himself to do. His mother had been the only one who loved him and she'd left. By no fault of her own, but that hadn't made it hurt any less.

His aunt and uncle might have loved him, but if they had, they never said so. As he grew up, it was just easier not letting anyone get too close. Not letting himself fall in love.

Talk about a cliché. But clichés were born for a reason, weren't they? Maybe deep down he was still that little boy who was afraid to get his heart broken again.

But it was too late, he was in love with Zoë. The only thing he'd accomplished by keeping that to himself was hurting her.

"I love her," he said to himself, surprised to find that it wasn't that hard to say at all. In fact, he liked the sound of it, the feel of the words forming in his mouth.

It felt...natural.

He pushed off the wall and headed for the stairs, knowing exactly what he needed to do.

It was time he said goodbye to the little boy and started acting like a man.

Zoë wasn't sure how long after their scheduled wedding Nick finally showed up. She sat alone on the swing in the backyard, still in her pajamas, with her legs pulled up and her knees tucked under her chin, wondering if he actually *would* show up. Maybe he was so angry he would never speak to her again.

But then the backdoor had opened and Nick walked through, still dressed in his suit. He crossed the lawn to the swing, hands tucked in the pockets of his slacks, looking more tired than angry.

And boy did he look good in a suit. Almost as good as he looked out of it.

What was wrong with her? She just stood the guy up and now she's picturing him naked?

"You seem to have forgotten that we had a date this afternoon."

She cringed and looked up at him apologetically. "I am so sorry, Nick."

"No." He sat beside her on the swing, loosening his tie. "I'm the one who's sorry."

He didn't hate her after all, not that she ever really believed he would. Maybe she thought she deserved it. "This is completely my fault. I guess I just…got scared."

"Scared that I would back out at the last minute. Or possibly not show up at all?"

She nodded, thankful that he said it for her. And even more thankful that he understood.

"I gave you no reason to believe otherwise." He took her hand and held it, lacing his fingers through hers. "Which makes this entire mess very much my fault."

"I should have trusted you."

He laughed, but there wasn't a trace of humor in the sound. "What did I ever do to earn your trust? Ask you to marry me? Stick a ring on your finger? Well, so what? I did the same thing with two other women and I'm not married to either of them, am I?"

Jeez, twist the knife a little deeper why don't you? Was he *trying* to make her feel worse?

"Um, I'm not quite sure what your point is, but for the record, this isn't helping."

"My point is, I knew exactly what you needed

from me, but I was too much of a coward to give it to you. That line I fed you about the ring making it official was bull. The only way to make this relationship official is for me to stop acting like an ass and tell you how I feel."

"I could have asked," she said.

He shot her a look. "You shouldn't have to."

No, she shouldn't, which is probably why she hadn't. Call her stubborn and a little old-fashioned, but she believed that when you felt a certain way about someone, you told them so.

He cupped her chin in his hand and lifted her face to his. "I never thought it was possible to love someone as much as I love you. Maybe that's why I didn't let myself trust it."

She could feel tears welling in her eyes and burning her nose, and she didn't even have those pesky hormones as an excuse this time.

He kissed her gently. "I love you, Zoë. With all my heart."

She closed her eyes and sighed. No words had ever sounded sweeter or meant so much. Because she knew they came directly from his heart. "I love you too, Nick."

"I have a favor to ask. This is going to sound a little strange, but I'm asking you to trust me."

"Okay."

"Could I possibly have that ring back for a minute?"

It was a little strange, but she trusted him. She slipped it off her finger and set it in his hand.

"I figured it was about time I do this right." He slid off the swing and got down on one knee in front of her. Zoë held her breath and the tears that had been hovering inside her lids began to spill over. "Zoë Simmons, would you do me the honor of becoming my wife?"

"Absolutely," she said. He slipped the ring back on her finger and she threw her arms around his neck and hugged him.

"I know you didn't want a big wedding, but I don't think you have much choice now."

She pulled back and looked at him. He had a very sly, devious grin on that gorgeous face. "Why?"

"Because when I hung up the phone after asking your parents' permission to marry you, they were already working on the guest list."

Her mouth fell open. "You called and asked their *permission?*"

He grinned. "I told you, I wanted to do it right this time."

Oh my gosh, she was now officially daughter of the year. And only a couple of weeks ago she'd been worried about excommunication. "So what did you say?"

"I told them I was in love with you, and I wanted their permission to marry you."

She couldn't believe he'd actually asked permission. "What did they say?"

He grinned. "They both said, it's about time."

Epilogue

Nick trudged down the stairs to the first floor, side-stepping to avoid the half-naked Barbie doll lying in the hallway and kicking aside a handful of Matchbox cars in the den doorway. This all should have been picked up by now.

When he saw the video game on the television screen, he knew why it wasn't.

He crossed the room and shut the television off and received a collective, *"Daaaaaaad!"* from their oldest children, nine-year-old Steven and eight-year-old Lila.

"Don't dad me. You're supposed to be cleaning up your toys. It's almost bedtime."

Six-year-old Nathan, who had inherited not only his father's dark hair and hazel eyes, but also his clean gene, was already working diligently to get all the LEGOS put back in their bin.

"Jenny burped," he said, pointing to the six-month-old tucked under Nick's left arm. The one struggling and squirming to get down and practice the new crawling thing she'd mastered just yesterday.

He didn't have a burp cloth handy, so he wiped away the spit-up with the hem of his shirt, wondering if a day had passed in the last nine years when he hadn't walked around with the remains of someone else's dinner on his clothes.

"Daddy!" four-year-old Olivia, the outspoken one of the bunch, screeched from the doorway, not three feet away. She had two volumes. Loud, and *really* loud. "Mommy is in the kitchen eating cookies again."

He crouched down in front of her, and being closer to the floor and freedom, Jenny let out an earsplitting squeal and struggled to get loose. "Liv' honey, what did Mommy and Daddy tell you about tattling?"

Olivia's lower lip curled into her signature pout. "I want cookies, too."

"Not before bed."

"Then why does Mommy get to eat cookies before bed?" Nathan asked.

"Because she's a grown-up," Lila said, giving him a shove as she walked past him. "She can eat cookies whenever she wants."

"You can have cookies tomorrow," Nick told her.

"She ate like the whole box," Steven mumbled. "There won't be any left tomorrow."

"Hey, mister, I heard that." Zoë stood in the den doorway, hands on her hips. Her hair hung in damp tendrils from a recent bath and her pink robe was conspicuously dotted with cookie crumbs. "Lila, can you please watch your sister for a minute? Daddy and I need to have a quick meeting."

"Sure, Mom!" she said, brightly, taking her baby sister from Nick's arms. Watching Jenny meant she didn't have to clean.

Zoë motioned him out of the room, mumbling, "Five kids. Whose bright idea was that?"

It hadn't actually been anyone's *idea*. After Steven and Lila, who were both carefully planned, they figured they had their boy and girl, so they were all set. But then Lila had started getting a little bit older and Zoë started having those baby cravings again.

They were a little lax with the contraceptives thinking that if it was meant to be, it was meant to be, and along came Nathan nine months later. Olivia was their first real oops baby, and the result of a bit too much champagne on New Year's Eve.

Jenny, oops baby number two, had been conceived when they thought they were being careful. Obviously not careful enough, her doctor had said when the test came back positive.

After Jenny was born, to avoid any further oopses, her doctor had finally put her on the pill. It was wreaking havoc on her menstrual cycle, and she'd been awfully weepy lately, but thank God it appeared to be working. Their only other option had been a vasectomy. Either that or he would have to move into an apartment down the street since after almost eleven years of marriage he still couldn't seem to keep his hands off her.

She led him to the first floor meeting room—the half bath next to the kitchen. One of the few places besides their bedroom that they could truly be alone.

She turned to him, her cheeks rosy from her bath, her eyes bright. It amazed him sometimes how much he loved her. It was as if, once he opened up his heart to her, it went a little crazy making up for lost time.

Each time he thought he couldn't possibly love her more than he already did, he would hear her reading Olivia a bedtime story, changing her voice for all the different characters, or he would catch her blowing raspberries on Jenny's belly while she changed her diaper. There were a million little things she did that made him love her more every day.

He might have been worried that he loved her too much, but she felt the exact same way about him.

"What's up?" he asked.

She blew out a big breath and said, "We have a problem."

He frowned. "What kind of problem?"

"Well, not a problem exactly, more like a slight inconvenience."

He folded his arms across his chest and sighed. "What did they break this time?"

"Nothing was broken. You know how my periods have been screwy since Jenny was born."

"Yeah?"

She bit her lip. "And, um, how I've been feeling a little yucky lately? Really tired and kinda nauseous."

Uh-oh, he had a feeling he knew where this was going. "I thought that was from the birth control."

"So did I. At first."

"But?"

"But then I noticed that it had been a while since I had my period."

"So what you're saying is, you're late."

She nodded. "I'm late."

He took a big breath and blew it out. Here we go again. "How late?"

"Two weeks, maybe three."

He raised an eyebrow at her. "Which is it, two or three?"

She bit her lip again. "Um, probably closer to three."

"Does this mean I need to make a trip to the pharmacy and get a test?"

"I went four days ago before I picked the kids up from school."

"*Four* days?"

She shrugged. "Denial. I finally worked up the courage to take it tonight after my bath."

Asking was merely a formality at this point. "And?"

She sighed. "Oops."

He tried not to smile, but he could feel a grin tugging at the corners of his mouth.

She rolled her eyes. "I know you're happy about this so you might as well just go ahead and smile."

He gripped the lapels of her robe and tugged her to him, brushing a kiss across her lips. "I love you."

"Six kids," she said, shaking her head. She looked a little shell-shocked, but he could tell she was happy, too.

The truth was, they could have six more and she wouldn't hear a complaint from him. He had plenty of love in his heart to go around.

"Not bad for a woman who once said she never wanted kids."

"Steven will be barely ten when the baby's born meaning we will have six kids under the age of eleven." She ran her fingers through the hair at his temples that had just begun to turn gray. "We must be completely nuts."

"Probably," he agreed, but insanity was highly underrated.

"I guess this is what I get for marrying a man who wanted a big family, huh?"

"Yeah, because you know what they say."

She thought about it for a second then said, "Fools rush in where angels fear to tread?"

He grinned. "Be careful what you wish for, you just might get it."

* * * * *

Memo: Marry Me?

JENNIE
ADAMS

Jennie Adams believes a little of the author's life appears in every book. In the case of Lily Kellaway in this story, it's list-making and a deep admiration for those who face adversity on a daily basis and somehow remain so strong. This book is Jennie's tribute to you all.

Jennie loves to hear from her readers, and can be contacted via her website at www.jennieadams. net

For Cheryl, whose courage, humour and strength inspire me constantly, and inspired the idea for Lily's story. Thanks for the working lunches, the laughs and the internet jokes. You're a champion.

For Mary Hawkins. The mountains are inevitable. Thanks for climbing a little of this one with me.

And for my editor, Joanne Carr. Thanks so much.

CHAPTER ONE

'ARE you Zachary Swift?' Lily stood in the doorway of the spacious eighteenth-floor Sydney office, and pushed words up through a throat filled with fear. She hoped she sounded calm and rational, and not worried sick. 'I'm Lily Kellaway, owner and manager of Best Secretarial Agency. I'm here in response to your…concerns about my employee.'

He could refuse to speak to her. Could have her and her agency blackballed, and end her career just like that. Lily knew it, feared it, but if she wanted any chance to make this situation right she had to sound confident, a woman who could and *would* make things better.

'I'm Zach Swift, yes, and it's no idle accusation against Rochelle Farrer.' He sat at his desk, broad shoulders pressed into a black leather chair, confidence and assurance written in every line of his body.

Sydney's leaden April sky loomed behind him, viewed through a bank of plate-glass windows. Through a long, slim grill above those windows, the sounds of a city that never stopped emphasised his decisive words—vehicles possessing the roads below, the blast and clang of construction, a siren's blare.

Firm, determined sounds, when Lily only wanted to hear his deep voice softening, inviting her in to discuss this problem face to face.

'I don't dispute your accusation.' She wished she could disprove it, but, sadly, it was all true. 'But it's one that can be addressed. Amends can be made. The situation can be fixed.'

'Is that why you're here? To try to fix what happened? There's no turning back the clock.' Dark brows drew down. His lean, tanned face revealed his irritation. 'I think I made my feelings quite clear when we spoke by phone half an hour ago.'

She recalled the shock of that phone call very well. Dismay and embarrassment had robbed her of the ability to reason with him. While she'd still been floundering, he had told her he wanted nothing more to do with her agency, and had hung up.

'You raised certain issues when you phoned.' The empty secretary's desk in the reception room at her back mocked her. Her fingers clenched around the notebook held in her left hand, and she prayed that he would listen. 'I'd like the chance to address those issues, now that I've had time to assimilate what's happened.'

Please, God, she wouldn't forget the speech rehearsed three times on the frantic taxi trip here.

'What's to address? I sacked your employee. I've sacked your agency. End of story.' With an irritated growl, he rose and stalked across the thick beige carpet until he stood before her.

Over six feet of annoyed, affronted male, and her agency was responsible for his anger. She quaked. But something else happened, too. Something quick and unexpected when her gaze zeroed in on thick-fringed hazel eyes. A mixture of curiosity and interest flowed through her, locked her breath in her throat. Shock and dismay followed. She couldn't be attracted to him? It must be some sort of nervous reaction, surely?

Yes, that must be it, and just as well, because all other facts aside she was too busy for a relationship with a man right now. Busy. Inadequate. Just look at your relationship with your parents, a silent voice interjected. 'All I ask is a few minutes of your time. If you'll hear me out, those minutes will be well invested.'

'Will they, Ms Kellaway? You seem very sure of that.'

Lily adjusted the weight of the tote bag slung over her shoulder, tugged her green skirt into place and smoothed the matching blazer. 'I have a solution.'

'Do you? For the past week I've been sexually stalked while your employee ignored her duties.' His narrowed eyes revealed his distaste. 'My working life has been thoroughly wrecked, culminating in this morning's episode. *Your* agency is responsible for that, and you want to *solve* my problem?'

Lily drew a sharp breath. Something mellow and male drifted across her senses. Cedar wood and citrus, heated by warm man. 'I do apologise…' The words trailed off as her attention seemed to shift of its own volition to the black leather sofa in the corner.

He followed her gaze, and his lips thinned. 'Were you aware I would walk in on that particular sight today? Perhaps your agency condones such behaviour in its temp secretaries?'

'I was certainly *not* aware that Rochelle had behaved in

such a way, or that she might do so.' Lily had no doubt that this indelible piece of conversation would stick like a barnacle to the inside of her head. 'If I'd known, I never would have employed her. Until now, I've not had a whiff of trouble from any of my employees.'

'Then how did it happen, Ms Kellaway?' He strode away, clasped the edges of the desk in long-fingered hands. An intense and focussed scrutiny demanded her answer. 'How was it that I walked into my office this morning to find Rochelle Farrer waiting naked for me on my sofa?'

Lily's hand shook as she snared a few errant strands of hair and pushed them back off her face. Rochelle had believed if she'd stripped off and waited this man would leap at the chance to have her, and afterwards to keep her. She hadn't hesitated to say so, when Lily had confronted her by phone as she'd rushed here to try to put things to rights. 'Rochelle…appeared to be under the misapprehension that she could, uh—'

'Marry a rich husband and live off his wealth for the rest of her life?' He inserted the words with freezing helpfulness. 'And she only needed to throw herself at her potential victim to get her wish?'

'Well, yes.' Lily's mouth tightened into a stiff pucker. He might be angry, but the interview with Rochelle hadn't exactly been pleasant for her, either! 'I didn't know Rochelle would sell herself that way for the chance to become a wealthy man's wife. When I interviewed her, she seemed very genuine and businesslike.'

His prolonged silence made her want to fidget. And she wanted desperately to use her notebook to try to get down what they had said so far.

At least she only had to be here long enough to get him to agree to take Deborah on. Then she could return to the safety of running her agency from her small apartment. To days filled with the transcription typing that allowed her to remain out of harm's way, where her shortcomings couldn't get her into trouble. To only venturing out when she felt up to the challenge.

He examined her with disconcerting thoroughness. Eventually, he dipped his head slightly in acknowledgement. 'Surprisingly, I believe you.'

'Thank you.' Her knees sagged with the weight of that gratefully received reprieve. 'I'm so pleased to hear you say—'

'Not that it changes anything.' He burst her bubble of hope expertly and without waste of words. 'Rochelle didn't exactly deliver on your agency's promise of "a reliable secretary with previous experience in busy, challenging office environments", did she?'

'No. She didn't.'

And, while Lily stood in his doorway and attempted to sort this out, she was at a distinct disadvantage. 'I respect your concerns, and the distaste you must feel for all that you've been through. But I have an offer to make that can turn this situation into something more positive. I believe it will be in your company's best interests to hear it.'

After a long moment, he sighed and waved an arm towards the studded visitor's chair that faced his desk. 'All right, I suppose I can spare you a few minutes in comfort. If we're lucky, the phone might even stay quiet for that long.'

He didn't clarify, 'a few minutes to settle this permanently before I contact a more reliable agency and get them to send me a decent secretary', but she had no doubt he thought it.

'Thank you.' She started towards the chair. 'All I want is enough of your time to allow me to resolve this matter.'

'As far as I'm concerned the matter is…' His words faltered. His gaze locked on the movement of her hips beneath the conservative green skirt. His eyelids dropped, but not before she saw the mixture of knowledge and curiosity that confirmed his interest in her—willing or not.

If she'd felt a certain tingling *something* just now too, well, that was because being here gave her the fidgets. It was nerves that sent ripply feelings down her spine, and made her skin feel too tight, certainly not some reaction to him.

Even as she denied any interest in him, a small part of her catalogued the harsh face with its angry frown line and strong jaw, and the thick, dark brown hair.

Lily shook her head and dragged her thoughts back to business. She would finish this. Then she would leave, with a dignified, impersonal handshake. This…interest, or whatever it was, would quickly be forgotten.

'I hope you don't expect to be paid for the week Rochelle stalked me around the office, ignored her work and made a mess of everything?' Zachary gifted her with a glare from beneath his brows.

'Certainly not.' That loss of revenue was only one of her worries right now. 'I would never ask such a thing of a valued employer.'

'But you're here to ask something.'

'Yes, and please believe me when I say I do realise how serious this is.' This was the most important part of her speech. The part that had to convince him to give Best Secretarial Agency a second chance.

Yet now she struggled to drag the words from the recesses of her mind, and panic rippled. She needed this man's forgiveness. If not that, then at least another chance to show him that her agency could live up to expectations.

'You have every right to be affronted and offended. Repulsed, even.' Her pencil flew across the notebook, recorded the basics of the conversation in the special, easy code learned through endless repetition.

If the matter is in any way important, always keep a record. Even before her mentor had told her that, she had done so. Religiously, in fact, since she'd discharged herself from the hospital. Since she'd walked away from her parents' shame, and from her broken dreams.

Zach inclined his head. 'It was a shock to enter my office and find…that. If I'd had anyone with me—'

'It would have been even worse. I agree. And I didn't mean you'd be *repulsed*, repulsed. That is, I'm sure the media testimonies to your, um, interest in women are true.'

Oh, good heavens. Did she have to go on about that? She really needed to focus!

'I'm relieved to know that the Powers That Be acknowledge my healthy heterosexuality.' Sarcasm dripped from each word, but something in his glance revealed that at least some small degree of that healthy maleness was currently focussed on her.

She came back to earth with a thump when he finished saying something and waited expectantly.

Press rewind, and play back—no. Nothing. Whatever his words, she couldn't remember them. Just that one little slip in concentration…

A familiar icy feeling stole through her.

Drat it, Lily. Keep your mind where it should be! Give yourself at least half a chance to get a positive outcome from this.

'Yes, well, um…' Oh, why had Rochelle done this awful thing? And with absolutely no sense of shame or remorse, before or after the event. 'I apologise fully on behalf of Best Secretarial Agency for this unacceptable occurrence. I've let Rochelle go.'

'I doubt you'll consider it a loss.' His mild nod of approval was at least something.

'No. Most likely not.' She might as well be honest about that. Her pencil continued to fly. 'But let me present my offer.'

He leaned forward, his expression intent and far from acquiescent. 'I'd appreciate it if you'd keep it short.'

'You're in need of a replacement secretary. I'm ready and able to provide one.' Each fact went into her notebook. 'To ensure there will be no further difficulties, I want to send Deborah Martyn to you. Deb is my second-in-command, a middle-aged, reliable woman with a lot of office experience behind her.'

She drew a hurried breath and went on. 'I can have Deb here within…' She checked her book rapidly and found the note stating Deborah's availability. 'Within the hour. As an added incentive, I'd like to offer an extra two weeks of work, free of charge, after the end of the existing contract. It can't be easy to obtain a good secretary at a moment's notice. This will save you the time and effort of that search.'

Her breath stuck in her throat until she forced her lungs to move again. 'I presume you haven't already made alternative arrangements?'

'I haven't had time.' He gave a mirthless laugh. 'Let's say I agreed to consider a replacement, which I haven't.'

She had expected some opposition, and sat forward, pencil poised. 'Yes?'

'I don't think it would be wise to take on another unknown female, after the problems I've just experienced. Now if, instead of Deborah Martyn, you could give me a male secretary? Skilled? Fully experienced?'

He emphasised each question with a tap of his finger against the blotter on his desk. 'Preferably one with a wife and kids at home. Someone you can guarantee will be here to work and nothing else. I might consider that. *Might.*'

No male employees, married or otherwise, existed in her retinue of available staff. She had no one to offer but Deborah—a wonderful worker, but definitely female. 'Not a male, no, but I can assure you Deborah is a very happily married—'

'Woman?' He ran a hand over the back of his neck, said it as though the very word were a plague. Yet his gaze lingered on her.

'A very responsible woman,' Lily began, only to be stopped by an upraised hand.

He shifted his focus beyond her to the outer office. 'From my standpoint, it would seem safer to approach a different agency. One more established, perhaps, so that the reputation it's built can truly be trusted.'

'Please. I want the good will of your company.' She had told herself she wouldn't beg, but knew she was close to it right now.

The 'girls' relied on her to keep them in work. All five were great women, and all needed the money brought in through their efforts. They were a tight little band, formed within the first month of the agency's opening nine months ago. Rochelle had come later, and had never really fitted in. Lily should have asked herself the reason for that, should have remembered to check all Rochelle's references thoroughly, and perhaps she might have thought twice about taking Rochelle on at all!

Now she owed it to her girls to fix this problem. And she admitted she needed to do this for herself, too. What would she have left if her agency went under? 'I'll do whatever I need to, in order to regain your good will.'

'No. I'm sorry.' He got to his feet. 'I appreciate the offer, but I can't accept it.'

He couldn't end the interview. Not yet.

'I'll raise the added free service to a month.' Lily stood, too. How her budget would stretch to such a commitment, she had no idea, but she had to convince him.

'You're certainly determined.' His gaze bored into hers with shrewd evaluation, and again with that hint of not entirely concealed male interest. 'And probably worried sick that I'll sue your company.'

Her heart fluttered in response to that look, but the flutter stopped abruptly as she absorbed his words. She feigned a calm she didn't feel. Shook her head. 'Not at all. I—'

She had considered it. Indeed, she had almost made herself ill thinking about it on the way here. If he took legal action, her agency could be deemed culpable of all sorts of awful things and might sink in a sea of murky corporate waters, never to be seen again.

If he denigrated her agency to his business colleagues, that alone would bring about the same result. Neither option was acceptable. 'Is that what you have in mind?'

'No.'

Just that. Flat. Unequivocal. Decided, she suspected, before he even brought the matter up.

He went on, a considering look in the backs of his eyes. 'But I'm impressed by your commitment to your agency, and by your resourcefulness. I've decided there *is* a way you can placate me.'

'Anything.' Words poured out. 'A line of dedication to you on my tombstone. Jemima's firstborn kitten—if I don't manage to get her spayed before that happens. All Betty's eggs for a year.'

She sounded too desperate, managed at least to stop herself before she admitted to her eBay addiction, too. Heat stung her cheeks. 'Well, naturally you wouldn't care about any of that, but what did you have in mind? If it's within my power to do so, I'll make it happen.'

'Jemima? Betty?' He murmured the names, and for a brief moment warm humour lit his eyes.

There was something so appealing about a man who could smile…

Then he shook his head, and the expression vanished. 'Initially, all I thought I wanted—needed—was someone to keep things in basic good order while my regular secretary took her long-service leave.'

'Yes.' Her vigorous nod made her hair swing against her

cheeks. 'I understood those were your requirements when you first contacted us.'

He took a step forward. Reached one hand towards her cheek, stopped, shoved both hands into his pockets. 'Things have changed.'

'I'm afraid I don't quite understand.' She tightened her grip on the red and black pencil. Had he really been about to stroke her face? Her skin begged her to make it happen.

'A woman in your position would have to be well-versed in all aspects of office skills?' he prompted.

'Well, yes, I am.' Her pencil traversed the page at warp speed, making her odd-looking squiggles. Why make this personal—about her, specifically? Fresh unease built up.

'You'd have worked on a number of temporary jobs, Ms Kellaway?' A muscle in his jaw tightened, and his dark gaze shifted just once to her mouth before moving away. 'Do you still do that?'

It took all her effort not to raise a hand to her lips. To touch them, as though, by simply looking at them, he had changed their texture or shape and she needed to feel that change for herself. 'I keep my hand in, yes, with short assignments that don't take too much away from my other responsibilities.'

Assignments that allowed her to appear in a good light to those business people she chose for the purposes of keeping her skills fresh. 'My commitment to the agency doesn't allow for more than that.'

That was true, too, if not all of the truth.

'If circumstances demanded it, you could do more. You would adapt. I suspect you would be good at that.' His words held a husky timbre that made her wonder just what sort of adaptation he was thinking about.

Then he gave a brief nod. 'So here's *my* proposition. I want you in this office, to sort out my problems and deal with my backlog.'

With each statement, her eyes widened. A mixture of anxiety, incredulity and fear stormed through her. He wanted *her*? She could stay here for a couple of weeks, but even that wasn't in her plan. 'I can't leave my work—'

'You'd be surprised what you can do, Lily Kellaway, if the need and the motivation are there.' Unshakeable demand in each word, he continued. 'I want you to make my office run the way it has done for the past eleven years, with barely a hiccup to disturb me. When Maddie comes back, I want things to be so shipshape, she won't even know she's been gone.'

'Really. I'm sorry.' Lily had wanted a second chance, but not like this. She would make a fool of herself, would reveal her weaknesses in front of him. No. It was out of the question. As was explaining her reluctance to take up what he must see as a reasonable challenge. 'But I couldn't—'

'Yes, you could, and you will. You're the right person to take it on, because you care enough about the outcome that you'll make sure it all works out.'

He didn't move, but she sensed the mental dusting of hands as he presented her with what he must view as a *fait accompli*. If he had any lingering concerns about feeling attracted to her, they were well buried.

Perhaps he had simply shut that attraction off? Not that she couldn't do the same. The stress of this situation had blurred her ability to act decisively, that was all.

He went on, his voice deepening with each word. 'I'm sure your organisational skills will be more than up to the task, and it's only a few months when all's said and done.'

'Only a f-few months.' He really wanted her to do this work herself. Had made his mind up and would refuse to accept anything else. As for her organisational skills, she choked back a bitter laugh. Lily organised her life to death, and it still wasn't enough.

The inescapability hit her. The notebook slipped from her fingers and fell to the floor. Pages fanned out like a startled lizard's ruffle. Her carefully controlled world fell on its ear at the same time.

With the addition of the month she had stupidly tossed in, it would be three months and three weeks. She couldn't afford to be here anywhere near that long.

She would have to prevaricate. Would have to accept his ultimatum for now, and convince him later to take Deb in her place.

'You don't have any choice, you know.' He retrieved her notebook and gently passed it to her.

The book was a symbol of her weakness, if he had but known it. Within its pages she attempted to maintain control of her life. Everything from shopping lists, to appointments, to work demands, to names of people she might need to call again.

'I've quite made up my mind, you see. So put your wonderful Deborah in charge of your agency. Let her do whatever it is you usually do.' His tone lowered to calm, focussed intent and he went on. 'And you, Lily Kellaway, give yourself to me.'

CHAPTER TWO

ZACHARY Swift had given Lily fifteen minutes to organise her agency matters. Lily's small electronic timer counted down the seconds even now. As a result, her phone conversation with Deborah was limited. It would help if she wasn't so aware of Zachary, seated in his office with the door open, working through twin mountains of paperwork with a determined diligence. She even liked that about him—drat the apparently hard-working man!

'I'll look after everything, Lily. Don't worry.' Deb's words barely registered.

It was difficult to notice anything but the man in her peripheral vision.

He glanced up as though sensing her gaze on him, and she felt heat warm her cheeks as she quickly looked away.

'Thanks, Deb.' Lily couldn't afford *not* to take notice of this conversation. She jotted Deb's agreement to take over until further notice into her diary. 'You have the key to my office and the tapes...'

Where had Lily left the tapes? She couldn't visualise them. 'They should be beside the computer. If they're not, I might have left them in the top drawer of the desk. Re-direct the phone to your place. I'll call you tonight to catch up properly.'

The moment Lily ended the call, she scribbled self-help instructions on several sticky notes and slapped them into place above the phone, on the filing cabinet, over the dictation machine. She wished she could put up 'Don't be Aware of the Boss' notices, too.

And she was wasting mental energy when her fifteen minutes were almost up! She needed to take stock. Put steps in place to ensure she could emulate the operation here and seem reasonably competent during the standard 'unfamiliar territory' phase. But surely once things settled down a bit Zachary would be ready to take Deborah in her place?

'Do you have everything organised with your assistant, so you can focus solely on your work here from now on?' He stood in his office doorway, shirt sleeves rolled up, tie loosened.

What if she couldn't turn off the way she noticed him? What if this awareness of him didn't go away? Just kept increasing and deepening, as it was even now? 'Yes. It's all organised, although it involved a certain amount of reshuffling.'

She wished he would comb his ruffled, unruly hair. And, while he was at it, don the jacket he had removed the moment she'd agreed to his demand.

'I'm glad you're organised, because you'll need to be to do a good job here.' His mouth lifted at the corners as though to soften the challenging statement.

Why did he have to attract her, anyway? He was *so* not her type. If she ever took another man into her life—which was highly doubtful—he would be gentle, perhaps scholarly or poetic.

A man who would dress in twill trousers and mis-shapen pullover sweaters, not power business-suits of darkest grey that emphasised every muscle and sinew.

'I'll do the very best for you that I can, Mr Swift.' She deliberately avoided mentioning duration of time, and tried not to let anxiety get the better of her. She should be able to fool him long enough.

Her mentor at the institute might have said she should be open about her limitations, should tell people up front. But he didn't know what it was like to see the change in their faces, to read the pity, and worse, in their eyes.

And she would get over this mild, unexpected reaction to Zachary Swift. She would! She flipped her diary open and put it in a prominent place where she would be sure to see it at frequent intervals. 'I'll go through all this clutter, sort it out, and get to work on the most urgent of it.'

'Zach will do.' His hands rested loosely at his sides. 'And the clutter will have to wait a bit longer, I'm afraid.'

'If not this muddle...' She waved a hand. 'What do you want me to tackle first, exactly?'

'There's a group of proposals on tape on the desk some-where that should have been done Friday.' He lifted a pile of papers as though to search for the tape, seemed to think better of it, and replaced them. 'Standard beginning for each one, but individualised for the last couple of pages. And a meeting scheduled for 12.30 today in the conference room for ten people, plus us.'

'No problem.' Just a heap of overdue proposals and a lunch meeting to prepare for all in the space of, oh, what—an hour and a half? Panic snapped at her heels, scrambled up her ankles and sank its claws into her calves. She swallowed hard, and forced a calm tone she didn't feel. 'I'll attend to typing the proposals. What's required for the meeting?'

'I'll want a copy of the proposals for each guest, plus one of each for myself. You'll also organise the meal, and take notes of anything pertinent said while we meet. Is that all clear?' He glanced up in time to catch her scribbling furiously into her notebook, and his face softened a little. 'You're certainly diligent, taking notes of everything…'

'It's the way I work.' She tipped her chin up and hoped he wouldn't question her about it. 'I'll get started straight away. If that's all for the moment?'

As soon as Lily said the words, she wanted to hyperventilate because she'd gone blank. She couldn't remember any of his instructions. Not a one. They'd fallen into one of those holes inside her head, and disappeared. If her notes didn't make sense once he turned his back, she was toast.

'That's all.' He started to turn away, and then stopped. For a moment he watched her, as though he wanted to puzzle her out. 'There are millions of dollars tied up in today's meeting. The largest project belongs to a man who can be difficult. I don't want him to have a reason to criticise my company.'

In other words, Lily had better not let Zach down! She focussed on breathing deeply in and out. 'I understand.'

He must have believed the act, because he gave a short, satisfied nod. 'I'll leave you to it. I trust I'll have the proposals very soon.' He walked into his office and shut the door.

Please let me get these things done in time. Lily re-read her notes. Fortunately, they made sense. Then she scribbled the meeting details onto the wall chart and into her diary, sticky-noted the need to find, type and collate the proposals, and dived for the phone book.

Thankfully she could cajole people when needed. That is, people other than the unshakeable Zachary Swift. Minutes later, with the meal agreed upon and delivery promised by 12.15 for a 12.30 start, she began to type.

The proposals were out, copied and onto Zach's desk with just minutes to spare. A convincing summation of several of Swift Enterprises' recent success stories, and individual offers to each company or business.

If his guests weren't duly impressed, well, Lily was. He dealt in *big* business. The knowledge of his prowess was quite...stimulating. *Intellectually.*

Even as she thought it, she studied his down-bent head from her vantage point in front of his desk, and acknowledged that no other male had appealed to her as much or as quickly as he had. What was wrong with her? Since moving to Sydney she had avoided even the slightest interest in men. It hadn't been difficult to make that choice until now.

'Good work.' Zach skimmed the final page of the last copy, and rose to his feet. 'Very accurate. Your typing speed must be as fast as your short—eh, note—taking.'

So he had noticed already that her code wasn't the usual shorthand script. If he asked, she would explain it as a newly developed recording style, which was nothing but the truth. Sort of. But it worried her that he had picked up on that so quickly. What else might he see and wonder about?

When he stretched to relax his shoulders, she tried not to let her gaze be drawn to him. But she failed dismally. The man appeared to have some rather nice muscles under that suit, and something in her feminine make-up was attracted by that knowledge. In defence against her own thoughts, she crossed her arms.

'I'm glad you're happy with my work, although I know Deborah would have done just as well.' She had to get that in, the first building block towards her own imminent exit. 'These offers will mean a lot of new work, if they're all accepted.'

His gaze tracked over her hair, then her shoulders, before taking a leisurely path downward, and back up again. It was cold comfort to her to know that in this case, unlike when they'd discussed the Rochelle debacle, the attraction appeared to be mutual. She didn't *want* to want him, whether it was reciprocated or not.

He seemed to catch himself, and his glance shifted to the windows. 'Yes, but we're geared to handle that sort of influx. It's what my finance and planning gurus thrive on.'

His forehead creased in thought. 'This lot are an interesting mix of people. It's not always those in financial trouble who need a partner or to sell out. Two of them, for example, are estate inheritances.'

'Estate inheritances.' She repeated it while her fingers itched foolishly to smooth the attractive wrinkles from his brow. 'Stuck suddenly with a monstrosity they're not prepared to take on? Yes. I can understand why some people would simply want out. And you can make all these businesses profitable?'

He turned, his eyes lit with interest. 'I've already suggested other avenues for the ones that wouldn't have been.' Her temporary boss smiled, moved to sit on the edge of the desk, and leaned back just enough that she had a breathtaking view of the cleft of his chin and the long, tanned neck. 'You think like a businesswoman. I can see you're going to be even more of an asset than I'd hoped.'

'Well.' She tried to ignore the view, the elevation of her pulse. The warm feeling it gave her to receive his praise, however prosaic. She didn't plan on being here long enough for him to appreciate her very much! 'We'd best make our way to the conference room.'

'Let's hope they're all on time for the meeting. What did you choose for the food?' He rose, scooped up the pile of meeting notes and handed them to her.

Their fingers touched. Warmth. The slightest sandpapery feeling as his skin grazed hers. She experienced a swift, sharp wish to feel those fingers stroke her forehead, her jaw, her neck.

His gaze locked on her face, roved it, touched her eyes, nose, and lingered on her lips. 'Lily…'

'We…ah…' Her mouth dried. This was *not* anticipation, and he was *not* about to kiss her. For heaven's sake. When had she developed such an overactive imagination? She hurried into her office. Anything to gain a moment's reprieve.

And he had asked a question. The food! He had asked about the menu. The food…

Something good that would keep people happy.

That was all she could recall. So innovate, Lily! 'You'll like what I've chosen. Just wait and see.' There. Good enough, but she should have written the choices down as she'd agreed to them. 'I just need to get a couple of things and I'll be ready.'

'Good afternoon. It's a pleasure to meet you.' Lily's mellow words sounded calm. Unfazed. She looked completely relaxed as she worked to put their visitors at ease.

But Zach stood at her side at the entrance to the conference room and felt the tension that radiated from her. He nodded, smiled, shared a few words with each delegate, but he wasn't relaxed either. Wasn't calm. He hadn't been since that accidental touch as he'd handed her the approved proposals for this meeting, when a flood of heated response had rushed his system.

Indeed, he had wanted her from the moment they'd met, and he would be a fool to pretend otherwise. He might not like the knowledge, but he prided himself on facing the truth. Now he just had to find some way to overcome this unwelcome interest in her.

Since Lara had showed him five years ago what his life had to be, he had dated women casually. No friendships, no commitments, no compulsions driving his interest. He wasn't about to alter that credo. He couldn't.

But he and Lily stood so close now that they breathed the same air. And all he wanted was to snatch her up and get answers to the questions that pounded through his bloodstream. If he kissed her, would the lips that drew his gaze press in passion against his?

If he drew her close, would their bodies fit as though meant to be together? Would it feel right? Would desire flame in an instant, or ignite slowly? It was ridiculous. Too much. They had only just met, yet he couldn't seem to stop the distracting thoughts.

'Wallace. Please make yourself comfortable with the others.' He gestured towards the oval table laid for the upcoming meal, but part of his thoughts remained with the woman at his side.

She smelled of lily of the valley. Had she always worn

her signature scent? He wanted to search out every pulse point and hidden place that carried it.

He suppressed a groan, and stuck out his hand as the final delegate arrived. 'Hardy. Welcome.'

'Am I?' Hardy gripped his hand with more force than was necessary. 'We'll soon see when I read the proposal you've concocted.' The man puffed out his ample girth. 'It had better impress me, or you can forget any chance of a sale. I'm only *considering* this move. Haven't decided yet.'

'Whatever decision you make will be respected.' But they both knew Hardy's trophy wife had run the company into the ground since he'd bought it for her.

'Hmph.' Andrew Hardy's gaze narrowed. 'Fashion can be a fickle business, might well turn around of its own accord before too long.'

'Anything's possible.' Zach tried not to show his disbelief.

When Hardy spotted Lily, his demeanour changed. Predatory interest rose in the florid face. 'And who might this beauty be?'

Mine. The thought was instantaneous. Unsettling. Possessive. Outrageous, because he and Lily had met only hours ago. 'Hardy, this is Lily Kellaway, my assistant. Lily, meet Andrew Hardy.'

The words fell from his mouth with bland disinterest. But his body growled, a rumble of warning deep within, and his gaze communicated that warning to Hardy. The man's eyes widened, then narrowed as he absorbed the silent message.

'Nice to meet you. I hope you enjoy your time with us today.' Lily's smile didn't reach her eyes. With her free hand, she pushed a folder towards the man's mid section.

The aggressive heat in Zach eddied away. She hadn't been taken in by Hardy's façade, had recognised something in the known womaniser that made her cautious.

'You'll find the proposal for your business in there.' Lily waggled the folder. 'You might care to take your seat and peruse it while lunch is being served.'

She was as cool as green salad. Zach suppressed a grin as Hardy stepped back to clasp the folder. A moment later, he had moved on.

They took their seats at the table. Lily sat at his right, and it felt as though she belonged there.

'Now that they're all seated, can you name them again for me, please?' She turned her face to his. 'Start with the person on my left and work your way around the table. Don't leave anyone out.' Her notebook rested on her knee, her pencil at the ready once again.

If he hadn't seen her hand clenched around that notebook, he wouldn't have known she was anything less than utterly confident. The knowledge that she was uneasy, a little uncertain, only made her more human in his eyes, more appealing.

Zach lowered his head to murmur the name and a short description of the business of each person. She scribbled it all into her notebook, and nodded now and then to show she was keeping up.

He could brush her ear with his lips, and he doubted anyone would notice. His breath soughed across the object of his thoughts. She shivered, gave a soft gasp and looked up into his eyes.

So responsive. His gaze moved over the honey-gold hair, then shifted to her mouth, to kissable lips and a short, straight nose. To blue eyes the colour of deep tropical seas beneath a hot sun. Without conscious thought, he supplied the final name and relevant details.

She noted the information in her book, released her breath on a choppy sigh and leaned back. 'Thank you. That will make it easier to match up any comments I need to record.'

Did she know that her eyes took on a dreamy hue when she looked at him? Not avaricious or predatory, like Rochelle's, but something soft, almost vulnerable, and definitely sexy.

'Now, you wanted to know about the menu.' Lily's lashes fluttered as she whipped out a hand-written sheet of paper Zach had watched her garner from one of the waiting staff when she'd first entered the room. She dropped her gaze to the sheet. 'We discussed a few options, but what I chose in the end was seafood cups and mini beef-and-vegetable pies for starters…'

'Which gives us a chance to sample both red and white wines.' Zach no longer wanted to hear about the menu. He let his gaze linger on her. He wanted to kiss her instead.

She outlined the rest of the menu, and looked into his eyes. Warm spots of colour formed on her cheeks, but she only murmured, 'Your wine bill will be sky high. I thought you'd want the best.'

He dipped his head. 'Money is no object in this exercise.'

The guests perused their proposals while the meal was set out. Lively discussion ensued. Zach did his best to throw himself into it and put thoughts of Lily Kellaway's soft skin, and his desire to touch it, out of his mind.

'Once a proposal is accepted, it's handed to one of my

team of experts.' He leaned forward as he explained the procedure to the man seated across the table from them. 'They either supervise the buy-out, or move straight in to manage the re-shaping if it's a share situation. No time is wasted. We're about making things work in the fastest, surest way we can.'

Over the entrées and a fine Sauvignon Blanc, Lily scribbled into her notebook, and picked at delicate prawns and Tasmanian scallops. Zach answered questions, parried comments and told himself he was doing well.

But all the while he was aware of her. In every break in discussions, his gaze went to her unerringly.

He looked at her now, and felt each bite of food she took explode on his own tongue, wanted to meld those tastes in exploration of her mouth. 'You chose the caterer well. Is it one I'd know?'

'Possibly not.' She glanced at the group discreetly situated at the far end of the room, then looked at him again. 'They—they're sort of like a galloping garçon. Zippy little van, go anywhere in a hurry. Several local offices have used them.'

'And you know this because you phoned other secretaries, rather than going at it blind and ringing restaurants and caterers first. Clever.'

Clever, determined, so eager to do her work well, that he couldn't stop himself from wondering if she'd be equally as enthusiastic and unwavering about pleasing a man under the enveloping cloak of a long, sensual night. It wasn't a question he should be considering.

But his praise brought her gaze back to his face with startled gratitude.

'I have to— I try to think outside the box.' She made it sound like an impediment, and hurriedly took a taste of saffron-rice paella, closing her eyes to savour the sharp, tangy fragrance and taste.

Despite his best intentions, his lids drooped as he watched her enjoy the food.

'Mmm.' She glanced at her plate. 'I have to admit, this is very pleasant.'

He ate *salade de boeuf* with buttermilk mash, and noted the fineness of her bone structure, the delicate shoulders beneath the blazer. His body twitched. Yes, this was pleasant—in a torturous sort of way.

Her attention focussed on him. The colour in her face deepened, and she looked quickly away again.

'You've done a good job with the lunch, Lily.' He tried to bring his thoughts back to business. Was it to be like this any time they got closer than the width of a desk away from each other? 'If the rest of your work for me is equally as professional and useful, I'll be very pleased, indeed.'

She straightened in her chair, primmed her mouth and clutched at her notebook again. 'You can rely on Best Secretarial Agency to take care of your business needs. You won't be let down again.'

When the desserts arrived, conversation lulled in favour of enjoyment of the delicate fare. Lily relaxed, let go of the deathly grip on her notebook and turned her attention to her food.

Instead of relaxing with her, Zach's tension increased. *Why* hadn't he been able to banish personal thoughts of her from his mind?

Maybe it wasn't his mind that was causing the problem.

Maybe he needed to indulge his curiosity. He twirled the stem of his wine glass between his fingers. One little taste test. Just to see. So he could put it out of his thoughts once and for all…

'The coffee crème is delicious.' She turned to him and smiled. A simple smile, yet he wanted to rush her into the supply closet at the rear of the conference room and kiss her among the broom sticks, buckets and mops.

He was losing his mind. Could only think of tasting *her*, nothing else, even though every fibre in his being warned him it was dangerous to think this way. Even for a moment. 'Um—'

'I hope the lemon panna cotta and fruit coulis equals it.' She dipped her spoon into the confection again. 'Would you like me to ask the caterers to give you a serving of the coffee crème, too? I'm sure they'd have some spares, if you'd like to try both.'

'No. Thank you.' He cleared his throat, forced civil words out, couldn't quite hide the deeper timbre of his voice. 'I'll be fine with…what I have.'

He tried his lemon panna cotta, praised her choice and tried not to think about her mouth. They were in the middle of a conference meeting, and his awareness of her was off the scale.

She blinked. That rapid flutter again of her lashes. 'That's very good. I'm glad you're enjoying your… dessert.'

'Yes.' The coffee arrived. With relief, he turned to the man on his right and engaged him in conversation until things began to wind down.

Finally, the time came to deliver his short closing speech. He got to his feet. 'You'll all need time to think, to confer with colleagues, to run the figures. I suggest phone conferences tomorrow and Wednesday to conclude our business. Phone Lily in the morning. She'll let you know what time slots are available.'

From the corner of his eye, he saw Lily scribble something in her notebook and underline it.

With murmured thanks, the guests moved out. Zach saw them off at the door while Lily set the caterers to work on the clean up. She returned to his side just as Hardy clamped an unlit cigar into his mouth and said around it, 'A phone conference doesn't suit me. Come to my office tomorrow at 4.00 p.m. I'll give you my answer then.'

'I'm not available at that time.' Zach tried to instil regret into his tone. 'Nor will I be available for anything but phone conferences for the rest of the week. You'll understand that I'm busy.'

As a concession, Zach acknowledged the other man's probable commitments. 'I'm sure you must have a full schedule, too. Perhaps you'd like to call on Thursday or Friday. I'm prepared to extend the deadline for you.'

'We'll see.' Hardy barged out the door, proposal tucked beneath his arm and a scowl on his face.

'Nice exit.' Lily's chuckle washed over Zach, sensual and free. She looked into his eyes, the smile still lingering on her lips. 'Do you think he'll accept your proposal?'

'I expect he will, eventually.' He dipped his head closer to her face. Wanted her. Didn't want to.

She gasped. A soft sigh of sound that revealed her reaction to him. 'Well, um, I'll just have one last word with the caterers, then. To make sure they're, um, all finished catering.

'Don't wait for me. You go on back.' She drew in a shaky breath. 'I'll join you when I've calmed—in a minute. *I'll join you in a minute.*'

He left. It was either that or snatch her into his arms and kiss them both senseless, momentary acquaintances or not.

CHAPTER THREE

'CAN I help you?' Lily closed the filing-cabinet drawer, and offered a questioning smile to the boy who stood in school uniform in the middle of the reception area of her office, his shoulders hunched, his profile to her.

Two and a half weeks had passed since she'd started work at Swift Enterprises. Two and a half weeks filled with a growing, unspoken awareness between her and a man unlike any she had known.

Clients had come and gone. Lily had managed the appointments, ploughed through the pile-up of work, and hadn't bungled anything too badly. Earlier today, Hardy had finally signed on the dotted line, yielding to what he knew was a great deal, just as Zach had predicted he would.

Lots of things had happened, but this was the first time Lily had seen a child in the offices. The boy should have seemed out of place, yet somehow he didn't.

'Oh, hi. I didn't see you there. Is Zach ready?' He turned fully to face her, slung his backpack onto one of the chairs and pushed his hands into his pockets in a gesture she had seen Zach use countless times. 'He said we'd have to go by four o'clock.'

'And it's almost that now, isn't it?' Slowly, she returned to her desk as she tried to assimilate what she was seeing. This boy was the image of the man on the other side of the closed office door. The same thick-fringed hazel eyes, same hair. Same mannerisms, same frown. Everything. It was all there.

Zach's son?

The possibility hadn't occurred to her until now. Faced with it, she felt…unnerved. Her mind leapt immediately ahead. Where was the mother of this child? What relationship did Zach have with her? Why didn't the boy call his father 'Dad'?

And what game had Zach been playing with *her*? He was a well-known and, it was assumed, *carefree* bachelor, and had been sending out 'attracted to you' signals since they'd met. Those signals had only grown stronger on both sides, she had thought, even though Zach had been clearly fighting them all the way.

She'd had no intention of acting on them, either, of course. Had intended to put a stop to her side of things just as soon as she worked out how. Hadn't she?

Of course she had! But what had Zach been thinking?

'Um, your fath— Mr Swift—is taking a phone call.' The boy shouldn't be made uncomfortable because of her surprise and shock. And she *was* shocked. 'I'm sure he'll be finished his call in a moment.'

The boy nodded. 'I'll just wait, then.'

'Yes. Make yourself at home.' She pretended to go back to work, but all that showed up on her screen as she typed was meaningless gibberish.

At times recently, she had wanted to yield to Zach's

interest, and to her own. To step forward instead of stepping back, just once, and see what happened. She shouldn't have wanted that. She was living a deception. He wouldn't want her if he knew her secrets, and she needed to protect herself, too.

But it appeared he also had secrets.

Zach opened his door and came out. He glanced at her, and his eyes flared with familiar heat.

Then he turned and spotted the boy. His face softened in affection and pride. In two strides, he had the young man in a headlock, ruffling his hair as he hugged him close. 'Dan. Good lad, you're right on time. You didn't have any trouble with the buses?'

The boy wrapped wiry arms around the man, pushed his head into his chest and put all his effort into getting loose. He grinned when he broke free. 'Nope. I'm ready to go. You're getting weaker, you know. You barely held me that time.'

A bittersweet smile touched Zach's face. 'You're the one getting stronger. You're growing up too fast.'

Zach made a show of getting his briefcase, but Lily saw the tenderness he tried to hide and, despite her confusion, her heart softened. Zach clearly loved this child.

He rattled off a few instructions to her before he turned back to Daniel. 'Did you two meet? This is Lily. She's filling in while Maddie is away. The other secretary…' he cleared his throat '…didn't work out, so Lily has taken over.'

Lily finished jotting his instructions into her diary. She closed it and looked at the boy. 'Hello again.'

'I'm Daniel.' He shook her hand, mumbled, 'You're prettier than the last one,' and turned a little red in the face. 'I mean—'

'Thank you.' She turned back to her desk to save him from further embarrassment. And to avoid having to look at Zach. 'I won't keep you both. You clearly have somewhere you need to be.'

A slight frown between his brows, Zach nodded. Then the boy drew his attention.

'Mum said you're invited to dinner again tonight, if you want. She's running errands this afternoon, but she'll bring home something nice.' Daniel gathered his school bag and slipped it over his shoulders. He gave Zach a bit of a glare. 'I could go to the orthodontist by myself, you know. If I can manage a couple of buses, I can manage—'

'All the buses. Yes, but I promised when you first got the braces on that I'd take you to every appointment.' Zach ruffled the dark hair again. 'And I always—'

'Keep your promises, I know. But I'm not a baby. You don't need to mollycoddle me.' The boy sighed, and made for the door.

Lily watched him, and tried to contain the anger and dismay that had filled her at Daniel's innocent words. Zach was still involved with the mother of his child! He had been toying with Lily. She felt stupid for not having realised his interest wasn't sincere. Felt second-rate, as she had when Richard had ended their engagement.

'I'm not mollycoddling.' Zach waved Daniel off. 'Go on ahead. I'll catch up with you at the elevators.'

As the boy left, Zach turned back into the room. 'Is everything all right? You seem agitated.' A rather ferocious expression closed in on his face, and he said without any inflection at all, 'Don't you like children?'

'No, it's not that. Everything's fine.' His protectiveness

of the boy made Lily ache for things she didn't have, for family to stand by her. But it didn't change the fact that Zach was now clearly and utterly out of bounds to her. And, right now, she really didn't like him very much. At all!

She busied herself putting a dictation tape into the machine, fiddled with the wishbone earpieces, then placed her hands in readiness against the keyboard. As she did so, she realised the child's name had slipped from her memory. She sought for it, but didn't find it. Darn it! 'It was nice to meet your son, but shouldn't you be going?'

'Ah.' His eyes narrowed as he studied her. 'I think you've just explained the sudden chill in the air. If there's a child, there's got to be a mother, and therefore—'

'You're having dinner with that mother. You're clearly very close.' Oh, couldn't he just go? She didn't want to have this discussion. 'It's got nothing to do with me.'

'Hasn't it? You and I have been—'

'Hurry up, old man. We'll be late!' The warning floated down the corridor, affection wrapped up in the cheeky words. A moment later, the boy poked his head back into the room. 'Are we leaving some time this millennium, or what?'

Zach hesitated, gritted his teeth and strode to join the boy. 'Yes, Daniel. We're leaving. Let's go.'

Daniel, Daniel, Daniel. His name is Daniel. Lily pretended not to watch their exit. As soon as they left, she wrote the boy's name down, although she suspected it would now stick firm for her. Usually, if she could get a piece of information beyond that short-term memory area, it stayed with her for good.

An hour later, after swinging from chagrin to anger and back again, she was doing her best to force Zach Swift out of her mind. She would go on doing that until she crushed every memory of the attraction she had experienced towards him. Utter rejection should have been her response from the start.

As she began to pack up her desk, a middle-aged woman stepped into the room. 'I hope I didn't startle you, dear. Are you about to leave?'

'Hello. Yes, it's almost closing time, but is there some way I can help you?' Lily pushed the last of the folders into the drawer and gave the woman her full attention.

'There is, I hope, but this isn't really a business matter.' The lady smiled. 'Let me introduce myself. I'm Anne Swift, Zach's mother.' She stuck out a hand.

Lily snatched up a sticky notepad and scribbled 'Anne Swift' onto it, then took the other woman's hand and looked into kindly yellow-green eyes. She couldn't help returning the warm smile she found there, even as her picture of Zach shifted for the second time this afternoon.

She had assumed he had no family at all. That he lived for his company, utterly focussed on making money. Lily had even felt a connection, because she didn't have any significant family ties either. Not any more.

Within the space of an hour, Zach had a son, a mother of that son, and a mother of his own.

'I'm afraid Zach's not in. He took Daniel to an orthodontist appointment.' *And, later, he's going to have dinner with the mother of his child. They'll probably make love once Daniel's asleep.*

'Just as I hoped. I timed it so he would be gone when I got here.' A warm chuckle erupted from the small, well-rounded frame. 'Now, I know you're just new, dear, but I need you to join me in a teensy-tiny conspiracy against my darling son.'

Well, that sounded interesting, if rather dangerous! Why would Zach's mother want to conspire against him? 'I'm not quite sure I can help you…'

'You can, and it will be for his own good.' Anne gave her merry laugh again. 'I just need to explain. Come to coffee with me?'

The next morning, Zach greeted Lily with a watchful expression. Lily didn't know what to think. During their stop for coffee, Anne Swift hadn't mentioned anyone special in Zach's life. But, then, Zach's mother had been focussed on other things and perhaps had seen no reason to say anything.

I hope Anne enjoyed her meal, anyway.

The older lady had bought enough take-out containers of food during that jaunt for coffee to supply several hungry eaters. Perhaps she froze portions for herself. Or maybe she had invited guests that night.

'Re-direct the phones. We'll go to lunch early.' Zach spoke in a silken tone from his position in the doorway that connected their two offices. His words made her jump, because for once she'd had no clue of his nearness.

He shifted his stance slightly. 'There's a pub not far from here that serves good, fresh battered fish and chips.'

'I can't.' Lily didn't quite meet his gaze, stared instead at a spot on the wall behind him. *I won't make myself vulnerable to you by getting too close.* 'I'm busy.'

'Let me make this clearer. It's not an invitation, Lily.' He looked down his nose at her, let her see the glitter of anger and frustration for a moment in his eyes before he hooded them. 'Your presence is required.'

Maybe this wasn't personal. Maybe she had done something, made some mistake here in the office?

Her mind raced with possibilities. She'd been skirting around him since she got here this morning. Had that made her lax in her duties somehow? Or had her shortcomings found her out?

Zach hustled her out of the office while she was still worrying. He rattled off their order to the bistro lady at the pub without consulting Lily for her choice, then led Lily to their allocated table and proceeded to drum his fingers on the polished surface.

'What if I hadn't wanted whiting fillets?' She took the paper serviette from around her cutlery, and set everything just so in front of her. It might not be smart to goad him, yet she couldn't help herself. 'I might have preferred the roast pork, or the chicken pot-pie.'

His fingers came to an abrupt stop. He said, apparently out of nowhere, 'Did you know that Daniel loves fish and chips?'

'Does he?' She kept her voice neutral, but wondered about that smooth-as-glass tone of his. 'That's nice.'

Their meals and drinks arrived. He held her gaze over the rim of his beer glass until they were alone again. 'Daniel and I live just around the corner from each other. He stays overnight with me often, drops in evenings and weekends during the day. It's pretty much open house to him any time I'm home.'

What about Zach staying the night with Daniel's mother, or vice versa? Not that Lily cared about his bed partners, she told herself fiercely. And he was baiting her right now. She was sure of it. She glared at him, and took a defiant sip of her lemon squash.

Not another word would pass her lips on the topic. If he had something to say, then let him say it.

After eating most of the meal in loaded silence, she began to toy with her half-empty sachet of tartare sauce. Anything to keep her gaze from his, really, but in the end she couldn't help it. Her resolve teetered, and fell. 'You mentioned Daniel. What about his mother? What's her name?'

'His mother is the same one I have, actually. I wondered how long it would take you to ask.' He speared a chip with his fork, seemed to take delight in the aggressive movement. 'Our mother is Anne. Anne Swift.'

While he ate the chip, Lily drew a deep breath of pub-laden air and tried to assimilate this news. Zach and Daniel were brothers. There *was* no woman with a long history of involvement with Zach. Lily had jumped to a massive conclusion.

Her heart began to beat out an uneasy, rapid rhythm. 'But that's not, that can't be—'

'Daniel was a change-of-life baby, conceived three months before our father died.' He laid down his cutlery, drew two well-thumbed photos from his wallet and flipped them one after the other across the table to her.

'The first is of me and my parents the year before Dad died. It was an aneurysm.' He spoke without particular inflection, but his fingers clenched. 'He didn't suffer. It was very fast.'

'I'm so sorry.' She suppressed the urge to touch his hand, and repeated the information over in her head because she couldn't bear it if she were to forget this later. At times like this she hated her impediment!

'I miss him.' The understatement somehow made Zach's loss all the more real to her. His gaze dropped to the other photo. 'The second is Mum, Daniel and me. It was taken last year when we visited the Imax theatre here in Sydney for a treat for Dan's birthday.'

'In the first, you look about eighteen.' He looked young and happy, as Lily had felt before her accident. She was still happy, she told herself, but for ever changed, just as Zach must have been by his father's death.

But Zach hadn't started this conversation to elicit sympathy. He had wanted to confront her mistake, to make a point about her jumping to conclusions. That was clear to her, and not entirely fair. 'Why didn't you say something when I—?'

'Drew that conclusion with no help from me? By the time I realised what you thought, Dan had interrupted and I had to go.' He reached for the photos. Their fingers touched, and he kept his grip on hers. 'And then I wondered if it might be best to let you believe it.'

Anger gave way to something different. Something deeper. She sought the answer in his eyes, and found a wary, reluctant awareness that echoed deep inside her.

'Yet you've told me. What changed your mind?' She pulled her hand free, and hoped he couldn't see how much she had wanted to leave it in his grasp.

'Honesty.' His gaze remained steadfastly on hers. 'I don't like deceptions.'

Deceptions such as secretaries not confessing their limitations to their boss, and planning to get out of working for him, even though he'd insisted on it? But her situation was different.

His body tensed as he studied her. 'I couldn't let you believe I was committed to some phantom woman. But you and I have been aware of each other, and it's best if you know that I'm not willing to get involved with you.'

'You don't want a relationship?' He had some nerve, making these assumptions, when all she had done was reciprocate his own interest. 'What makes you think I would want to get involved, either? I don't want *any* kind of entanglement!'

His mouth pulled into a scowling line. 'I tried commitment once, Lily. What I had to offer wasn't enough. I had to let it go.'

'You'd have a lot in common with my ex-fiancé, then.' Her words came, uncensored, straight from the hurt she'd been through. 'It turned out he couldn't cope with commitment, either. That experience pretty much cured me where men and relationships are concerned.'

His gaze whipped to her eyes. 'I didn't know you'd been engaged. Perhaps you and I have more in common than you think.' His mouth turned down, as though his thoughts weren't happy ones. 'I was engaged once, too, five years ago. When my fiancée needed things from me that I couldn't give her, we both got hurt. That experience made me accept my limitations. I can't give a woman more than a token, fleeting interest.'

Just for a moment, Lily almost felt that his eyes asked for understanding, that she saw regret in the hazel depths.

'There are things in my life that just make it impossible for me to give more. To have—' He dropped his gaze abruptly to the table top. When he lifted it again, his face was a strong mask, etched in determination. 'I wouldn't change anything.'

If anything, his expression became fiercer. 'I'm not willing to find myself backed into a corner by a relationship with a woman again, that's all!'

Well, she didn't want those feelings, either. She didn't welcome them any more than he did.

'You speak as though there's a risk we might actually get entangled.' They shared an awareness and interest. Strong, yes, but not impossible to overcome. 'But we're quite safe. Neither of us wants this. We certainly don't have to act on it.'

She forced a smile. 'Those sparks in the air have been hanging around, it's true, but, now we've talked about it, we can put it behind us and get on with a proper, uncomplicated working relationship until I leave—for as long as it's needed.'

With a determined toss of her head, she rose. 'Shall we go back to work?'

'Just like that, and it's gone and we forget it was ever there?' He gave a humourless laugh, put the photos away and got to his feet, too.

'Yes. Just like that.' She hurried through the bar and out onto the street, and hoped her words would prove to be true. If they didn't, she was in big trouble.

CHAPTER FOUR

NOTHING was ever easy. Lily twisted the straps of her 1968 hand-beaded bag—Australian eBay, $2.95 plus postage—in her lap and just knew this whole thing was a big mistake. It was Friday evening, the official end of her working week. She should have been at home resting up with a favourite DVD movie. Or out with the girls, having a bit of uncomplicated fun.

She glanced at the man seated in the rear of the taxi beside her. Tonight, in evening clothes, Zach looked as though he could take on the whole world and win.

Dark trousers hugged his strong thighs. A matching jacket rested casually over the crook of one arm. The formal shirt, pristine white, pleated, and such an exact fit that it was probably custom-made, accentuated the broad chest and shoulders.

Against her will, she wanted to touch him. To feel whether his body was as firm and solid as it looked, wanted to embrace his power.

Lily should never have agreed to this. It was the baklava. Anne Swift had led her into temptation with food for the gods at that Greek restaurant right near Zach's office building. Then, when Lily's guard was down—and she'd been on a nice sugar buzz and had taken her first sip of the best flat black ever—*bam*, Anne had gone in for the kill.

Anne had had a persuasive way about her, but what did Lily know about families doing well-intentioned things to make each other happy? She should be focussing on not wanting Zach!

The taxi turned a corner. Her thigh bumped against his leg. She drew a sharp breath.

'He probably hates surprises,' she mumbled towards the window.

I do not want to say Happy Birthday and brush my lips against his cheek. I do not want to be here, at all!

But Lily had agreed to schedule and attend this 'business meeting' tonight as a ruse to get Zach here for the surprise his mother had taken such trouble to plan.

'Would you please face me, not the window, if you insist on muttering? At least give me the chance to try to lip read.' Zach's voice rumbled with something just dark enough to facilitate a fresh batch of shivers down the length of her spine.

The same dark something she had seen when she'd emerged from their office cloakroom dressed for the evening. There hadn't been time to go home to change. They had left straight from work, but not before he'd seared her with just the same look she was receiving now.

She cast about for some excuse for her mumbling, for some distraction from her awareness of him. Their arrival at the exclusive harbour-side address saved her.

The Opera House shimmered in the distance. Cars crawled like busy, multi-coloured ants across the harbour bridge. Boats of all shapes and sizes dotted the water.

It was beautiful, sultry, a living, breathing part of the city that couldn't help but entice. At another time, her surroundings would have worked wonders on her mood. 'We're here. And right on time to see your *client*—Mr Goodman. For the *business discussions* he scheduled.'

Oh, she had worked hard to make sure she retained this name and the business-meeting ruse that went with it!

Zach wondered why Lily's voice had been breathless, and sounded patently relieved. Not to mention her emphasising half her words as though she believed he had suddenly lost most of his comprehension skills. 'It's a co-incidence that Vince chose this venue. I'm a part owner,' Zach replied.

Was she relieved because they could finally quit the confines of the rear seat of the taxi? Because they wouldn't have to be in such close proximity any longer? Was she as sensually charged with awareness of him as he was of her at this moment?

So much for her idea that they could bury their attraction to each other.

Lily nodded with what seemed to be unnecessary enthusiasm. 'Yes, your moth—that is, *Mr Goodman* mentioned you were a part owner in the restaurant.'

'The owner had allowed the place to lose its verve. He didn't want to sell out, so I bought a share, helped him improve the appeal to the public.' He didn't care about that, only wanted to thread his fingers into her upswept hair, to touch her scalp and feel it tighten beneath his hands.

She wasn't right for him. More to the point, he could never be right for her. The woman had a cat and some sort of egg-producing fowl, for heaven's sake. Five years ago, he hadn't even been able to meet Lara's demands. And his ex-fiancée's idea of home-making had been to take a page from *Homes of the Rich and Beautiful* and have a team of decorators apply it to her apartment.

Zach paid the driver, and helped Lily out of the taxi. Got distracted by a glimpse of long leg beneath the shimmering dress.

'You look sensational tonight.' He growled the words from deep within. 'You might as well know, I want to examine every part of you. At my leisure, and preferably in private.'

'It's—you can't simply up and say—' She sputtered to a stop, but twin flags of colour flared in her cheeks and her eyes glittered.

'Then I'll just look.' He did exactly that, taking his time to examine every inch of her. The dress was a shimmering blend of autumn shades that shaped to her torso and hips, and flared just enough from knee to ankle to make movement possible, with a slit that ended mid-thigh.

High in front, a small V-dip in the back, it was perfectly respectable and rather old-worldly. But it caressed her in ways that made his hands itch to do likewise.

'Dressed as you are, and with your hair piled up so that your neck seems smooth and endless, is it any surprise that I want to draw you back into the cab and kiss you until we both run out of breath?'

'You have a b-business meeting,' she stammered, and clutched her evening bag in both hands as though to shield herself from him.

Or maybe to stop those hands from doing something they shouldn't—like reaching out to him? Their gazes clashed, and he saw the trammelled awareness in her eyes, and wanted to tell her to let it go free, to let it lead her…to him.

It was madness. But maybe it would happen, be unleashed, before either of them would be able to move beyond it.

For surely, if they gave in to this mutual interest, the results would be less than he imagined. It couldn't possibly be all that his body and his senses told him he could find with her. 'We need to deal with this, Lily. Because it's pretty clear it won't deal with itself.'

'We can't. We've already agreed neither one of us wants any type of relationship.' She took several hasty steps away from him. 'We need to go in now. We don't want to keep your associate waiting.'

'We'll go in, but this isn't resolved.' He yielded for the moment, but he made no attempt to shield her from the purpose in his gaze. There *would* be a reckoning of some sort, and it would be soon. 'I still don't see why Goodman couldn't have seen me during the day.'

The man was an acquaintance of his mother. He and Zach had done business before. Across a desk in broad daylight. It was Zach's thirtieth birthday today, and, although he admitted that the sight of Lily in a clingy dress was a nice gift, he could think of things he would rather have done with his evening.

Like take Lily somewhere secluded and let nature have its way with both of them…

'Mr Goodman must have been busy during the day, I suppose. Let's go. It's, er, this way, by the look of it.' Lily gave him one short, agitated glance, then turned and hurried towards the entrance to the building.

She had freckles dotted across the milky satin of her

shoulders. Freckles that seemed to invite him to lean closer, to press his lips to each little dot, to taste the freshness of soft, sweet skin.

Zach groaned, and to cover the sound broke into speech. 'Have you been here before? You seem to know exactly where you're going.'

His formal clothing was strangling him. The need to touch Lily was strangling him. Just a couple of short steps and he could have her in his arms.

'I haven't been here before, but I've heard the views from the restaurant floor are spectacular.' Lily pushed the door open and stepped inside.

When they left the elevator on the top floor, the owner himself met them. He whisked them towards a set of concertina doors without giving Zach a chance to even enquire after the business.

'It appears you're headed for the function room.' Zach wondered at the very obvious mistake, and at the man's sense of suppressed urgency. 'We're to meet someone in the restaurant itself—'

Without responding, the owner flung the doors open.

'Happy Birthday!'

'Surprise!'

The room erupted with noise and cheers.

'I've been had.' Zach turned and drew Lily to his side. A brand of ownership? A promise that their shared attraction *would* be addressed? He didn't know, knew only that it was right for his fingers to wrap around Lily's arm as he took in his mother's wide smile, Daniel's grin, and the sea of familiar faces.

Wall-to-floor panes of glass beyond them revealed the

harbour in all its splendour. The magnificence of it shone for a moment in Lily's eyes. He could drown in her. Too easily.

The restaurant owner stepped forward, grinning, and offered a hearty handshake. 'It's too long since you've visited your investment. Enjoy your night.'

Then his mother gave him a quick, one-armed hug. 'Happy Birthday, darling. Are you utterly surprised? Vince thought it a great lark. He *does* have a business proposition to discuss, but Lily has booked an appointment.'

'I didn't suspect at all.' His focus on Lily had dulled his awareness of other things. Even now, the feel of her arm beneath his fingers tantalised him.

When had his mother approached Lily about tonight? All Zach had known was Goodman's demand for a dinner meeting. Complete with secretary to take urgent and important notes!

He turned to look at her again. The results of his hold on her carried a slow burn through his system. 'But I think my new secretary probably has a few things to answer for.'

She dutifully laughed, but for a moment her eyes held a stark vulnerability. Why? He didn't know, but he wanted to take that pain from her. A wave of protectiveness and possessiveness washed over him.

He didn't consider how his actions might look to the many people who observed them. He just reached for her and accepted this had to happen. 'I think you owe me a birthday salute, at the least, for tricking me this way.' What harm could it do to kiss her here, in a crowded room?

She stiffened at his side. 'Oh, no, I don't think it would be a good idea.'

'I do.' He settled his mouth on hers without giving her

a chance to protest further. Without giving himself time to think about it any more, either. Cupped her face in his hands, and tasted the soft fullness of her lips beneath his.

That was all he intended. A simple taste. A chance to prove this wasn't so amazing. That he could walk away and not regret it. But she melted into him, into their kiss.

And he fell into a fathomless ocean of sensation and feeling. Her hands on his forearms, burning through the cloth of his coat. The soft, blurry fragrance of her perfume filling him as he breathed her in. Her mouth moving with his as though they'd always been together.

A feeling of such rightness and of emptiness finally being filled swept over him. He held back a gasp. It took all his will not to drag her in until their bodies melded utterly and he forgot everything. All he had proved was how right they were with each other, and he didn't know what to do about that.

He forced his hands to relax their grip on her arms. His mouth to take one last, lingering taste, then disengage.

The silence immediately near them filled suddenly with chatter and laughter. He didn't know if talk had actually stopped, or he just hadn't been able to hear it while she'd been in his arms.

'You shouldn't have done that.' She whispered the reprimand. Her flushed face revealed the same shock he felt.

The slight puffiness of lips well kissed wrenched a gasp from deep inside him—he held it back, but could do nothing about the gaze that caressed her from head to toe.

'Happy Birthday, Zach.' She pinned on a tremulous smile that might have been meant to convince onlookers that the kiss had been a casual salutation.

Would they believe her? Or would they perceive the depths of the exchange in the same way he had experienced those depths just now?

Lily took a shaky step away from Zach, then another. 'I hope you enjoy your…celebration.'

All Lily wanted to do was to back away and keep on going. Her heart pounded, her hands shook.

Zach had kissed her in front of a room full of people. Had touched her and drawn a response she'd thought had died the day Richard Pearce had abandoned her to a hospital ward, and a future he no longer wanted to share.

No. That wasn't right. She had *never* felt this way. Not with Richard. Not with any man. Did the people around them know it? Could they see Zach had unlocked something inside of her that could carry her away? Make her ignore everything that mattered?

Anne Swift caught her hand in hers and gave it a squeeze. 'Thank you so much for your help. I couldn't have pulled this off without you.'

Her friendliness and the absence of any kind of surprise or dismay gave Lily hope that the kiss *hadn't* revealed as much to others as she had thought it might have.

Anne turned slightly to include someone standing at her side. 'You've met my second son, I think?'

'Yes.' Lily offered the boy a smile. She hoped it looked genuine, because she regretted her impulsive thoughts the last time she'd seen him. 'Daniel and I met at the office.'

'And how are you enjoying the job?' Anne asked. 'Was it difficult to come in part-way through and take over from, oh, what was her name?' She laughed, and waved a dismissing hand. 'My memory isn't what it used to be.'

Lily bit down on a half-hysterical laugh. *Tell me about it!*

'Her name was Rochelle.' Lily tried not to go sour-faced at the name. 'And I'm only filling in for a short time at your son's office.'

'You're filling in for the length of our agreement, so quite a bit longer yet.' Zach spoke right beside her. 'You're mine for that time, Lily, and I plan to hold you to every one of the agreed days.'

'Well, I've done my best to get things in order in the office.' She forced herself to treat his statement at face value, but her skin prickled as she absorbed his quiet words, and their double-edged meaning.

He couldn't mean to pursue their attraction further? The one kiss had been devastation enough.

She had to get out of this man's orbit. The sooner, the better. 'I'm sure any of my staff would be able to take over and keep things going quite seamlessly from this point.' If she could bring Deborah in…

His instant, narrowed gaze bored through her. 'But that's not going to happen, my dear. Now, let's go mix with the crowd. I'm sure lots of these people would like to meet you.'

My dear. Oh, it had been nothing but a throwaway line. Yet, even as she told herself this, she reacted to the heat of awareness in his gaze.

'I was about to leave, actually. This is your night. The business dinner was just a ruse to get you here. You don't need me hanging around.'

'Nonsense. If you think I'll let you go now…' A certain tautness of his features made his determination clear. 'Besides, a lot of these people are business contacts. You might pick up some interest in your agency. That's what you want, isn't it? To build up business?'

'Naturally, I do.' She couldn't very well say anything else. 'But I can't push my agency down people's throats at your party.'

He took her hand and tucked it through the crook of his elbow. 'You could if you wanted to. But, if not, then just enjoy yourself and don't be a drama queen about it, there's a good girl.'

Ooh! While she was struggling to overcome her flash of ire, he excused them to his mother and brother and started around the room, introducing her to uncles, aunts and cousins, and more business colleagues than she could count. She would never remember most of them.

And Zach still wasn't willing to let her bring in a replacement for herself. What would she do?

'You seem to have quite a few relatives. I'm surprised at how many have travelled to be here.' That made it sound as though Zach wasn't worth making the trip for, and this wasn't *her* family they were talking about.

'Sorry. That came out all wrong. Why don't I go mingle for a while by myself?' she suggested rather desperately. 'Let you get on with enjoying your guests?'

'Why not stay with me? I'm enjoying your company, and it's my birthday. Don't you want to keep me happy?' Aside from the hand that tucked her against his side, he didn't touch her. But his glance held heat.

'I shouldn't.' But she stayed. She was too weak to say no again and walk away. And she convinced herself it would be fine. They'd shared a kiss. But, when his common sense returned, he would have no desire to repeat it. Why would he?

They ate sumptuous finger food passed around by discreet waiters, and more food piled onto a groaning buffet table. During the informal toasts there were a lot of jokes about football. Perhaps Zach had played in high school or something. He certainly had lovely shoulders for the game.

When Zach spoke, she was thinking about those shoulders bared and raised above her. Stark, illicit thoughts that shocked and enthralled at once.

'Come dance with me.'

'You should dance with some of your guests.' Her voice sounded almost normal. She hoped he couldn't see the desperation and lingering desire for him in her gaze.

She couldn't dance with him. Couldn't be held close against the solid wall of his chest without revealing just how much she wanted to be that close, and stay that way for as long as she possibly could.

Darkness had set in. The harbour outside sparkled with twinkling lights. There was far too much of the fairy tale about this night already for her to risk a dance with the prince of the evening.

'I'd rather dance with you.' Before she could argue, he led her onto the dance floor.

She belatedly realised that she had imagined something quite different to the reality. All over the floor, people were grooving down to a fast-paced song from a 1980's movie. This would be no smoochy, mouth-watering moment, and she felt momentarily chagrined by the turn of her thoughts.

Yet the dance moves, that felt natural in the privacy of her living room or when she went out with the girls to a club, seemed quite different with Zach's gaze locked on her.

Every move she made felt sensually charged. Every

move *he* made seemed designed to make her more aware of him. Nobody around them was taking the slightest bit of notice, yet she felt so conscious of the tension between them that it was a physical sharpening down her spine.

And he felt it, too, all of it. She knew it, because he didn't bother to hide the heat in his eyes when their gazes locked. That blatant barrage of sensual interest stole her breath.

Almost at the end of the number, he moved close, his hands firm on the swell of each of her hips as he drew her in. He wasn't watching her body move. Not now.

Instead, he looked into her eyes, and his *burned*, and she knew she was going to melt, utterly, and she wouldn't be able to do a thing to stop it. Not one thing, despite all her determination and her need to watch out for herself. And her memories, and the hurt, and all the things she couldn't trust herself to remember any more.

A smattering of applause indicated the end of the song. Zach lowered his hands. She realised hers were on his waist, let go and stepped back.

'You make shaking your hips an art form.' He smiled, making light of it, but his eyes didn't. They smouldered with dark feelings that showed her she hadn't seen past the first edge of this man. Not really, even though she had worked with him for three weeks and been aware of him for every moment of that time.

'Why don't you ask my brother to dance while I take Mum onto the floor? Dan's a bit shy about girls, but it would do him good to get out there with someone pretty and confident about herself.'

Zach's arms were locked to his sides, as though he didn't trust himself not to haul her back to him.

Confidence had been hard won in the last twelve months, but Lily thought: *you make me feel as though I am those things*, then turned and saw Daniel standing at the edge of the floor tugging at that collar again.

He was just a boy. Not yet in high school, probably. Without realising it revealed her own insecurity, she said, 'Will he let me that close, if I ask him?'

CHAPTER FIVE

'Yeah.' Zach answered Lily's question in a tone gravelled by the suppressed need inside him. 'I don't think Daniel will be able to do anything else.'

Lily didn't hear his words. She had already walked away, and that was probably just as well, because Zach really wasn't himself. He hadn't been himself since she'd walked into his office that first Monday and started to re-order his working life, as a matter of fact. And his comment hadn't been about Daniel, but about himself.

He had kissed Lily. Madly, deeply, in front of a room full of people. He wanted to do it again, in private, and never, ever stop. He couldn't convince himself to let it be. So he'd sent her away to dance with his brother, but so far separation didn't seem to be helping.

Lily headed straight for Daniel, hips wiggling, one arm stretched out to the boy as her finger beckoned him forward. It had the desired effect.

Daniel broke into a grin and was soon on the floor, laughing and showing her a few moves that weren't too bad for an eleven-year-old whose feet tended to get in his way. Zach closed his eyes on a familiar ache.

He was so proud of that kid.

With the need to whisk Lily out of the party and straight to the nearest available bed still thrumming deep in his veins, Zach tugged his mother onto the floor and tried to behave normally, instead of as though every nerve ending burned.

He had never wanted anyone this intensely. He would have taken anything Lily was willing to give him, if she had continued to look at him that way much longer after their shared kiss.

'Thanks, Mum.' He schooled his tone to sound nothing but cordial. 'This was nice of you.'

'I had a little help.' His mother let him twirl her out on the end of his arm, then pull her back in again, her laugh an echo that had lifted his spirits for as long as he could remember. 'Thank goodness Lily came along in time, because there's no way I could have asked that Rochelle creature.'

His mother didn't know about the sofa incident, but Zach could feel his ears burning anyway. 'Yeah, well, Rochelle's gone now, and I've got Lily instead. I hope she didn't have to do too much to help organise tonight.'

Again the protectiveness surged. He didn't want to add to Lily's worries, even though he was the one who had insisted she stay and work for him.

It's not the same thing.

His gaze moved automatically to Lily and Daniel, but it wasn't his brother he watched. It occurred to him that he might be truly out of his depth, but he pushed the idea away. This was a heady attraction, that was true, but it could be only that. He had learned his lesson with Lara.

'No, dear. I didn't make unreasonable demands on your Lily. All she needed to do was get you here.' The number ended and they made their way off the floor. 'Lily did seem a bit taken aback when I first outlined my plan. Does she have much family herself?'

'I don't know.' Suddenly it seemed wrong that he didn't, yet why should it? 'She'll be gone soon. I really don't *need* to know.' But the words rang hollow, because he did want to know about her. He wanted it all. Her history, her secrets.

'I'm not sure if I know what I want,' he muttered, unaware he had spoken aloud.

'Well, my darling, I never thought you would go unscathed for ever. Now, remember we've got the barbecue tomorrow evening. That's still on, despite tonight's surprise. It'll be nice for the rellies who've travelled. Meanwhile, I think I'll start shooing people so we can all get some sleep before then.' And, with that curious mixture of remarks, his mother took herself off.

Zach moved off the dance floor slowly. He wanted Lily. That *was* all. Wasn't it?

Daniel brought Lily off the dance floor to join him, his elbow stuck out stiffly so she could grip it with her fingers. She did so with a soft smile on her face that caught at something deep inside Zach.

'Well done, Dan.' Zach's voice softened. 'I wish Dad could see you. He'd be really proud.'

'I wish he was here, too.' Daniel dropped his elbow, allowing Lily to step away, and his face tightened.

Zach kicked himself for reminding the kid of what he didn't have. He did his best to be father *and* brother to him, but he knew it was a poor second. 'Dan—'

'Did you read the brochure I left on the table at your place? The one about Sarrenden College? They've got the best mechatronics program in Australia, starting right from the first year of high school. The program's brand new.'

'I saw it, but it's in Melbourne, and we live here.' The building of all things mechanical and electronic was Daniel's latest obsession, and Zach was quite willing to indulge him, although Dan's interest would probably soon wane. 'We'll have to see if there's something here in Sydney. Maybe some after-school classes you could go to.'

Daniel's mouth tightened. He muttered, soft enough that only Zach heard, 'You don't understand.'

'Mechatronics is quite cutting-edge stuff, isn't it?' Lily addressed her question to Daniel. 'Wasn't one of last year's Youth Australia Innovation awards given to someone working in that field?'

Daniel's face lit up. 'Yeah. They designed this really cool computerised exercise "pet" that goes out with the person when they walk or jog. It has all-terrain capabilities, and it measures heart rate, blood pressure and a heap of other stuff. It "woofs" if anything is wrong with the person.'

'Speaking of exercise, do you want to take a run with me tomorrow morning?' Zach asked. 'I need to keep my fitness up for the match on Sunday.'

'Touch footy.' Daniel pulled a face. 'It's not *real* football. It's just a bunch of you and your suit friends running around pretending to be fit. Hockey's better.'

'Ah. The football jokes are explained.' At Daniel's side, Lily stifled a chuckle behind her hand. But the crinkling around her eyes revealed her amusement.

Since hockey was the only sport Daniel's senior class played at competitive level, Zach was reluctant to concede the point. 'Maybe, but in touch footy we still get to dive around in the mud if it's rained, and yell and swear a lot.'

A grin tugged at Daniel's mouth. 'I'll run with you,' he relented. 'But I'm not going to the game. And, right now, I'm going to find more food before they take it all away.'

'Off you go, then.' He gave Dan a friendly push towards the buffet table. 'There's still a bit of birthday cake left, I think.'

The hordes shooed rather well under his mother's efforts. Zach got caught up in a little flurry of goodbyes and good wishes. It was towards the end of this that he spotted Lily sidling away, and the feelings inside him roared in protest.

Not like this, just slipping away as though she meant nothing, as though the night and their shared kiss had meant nothing. As though either of them really believed this was over or in any way resolved. The buzz in his system assured him it was not.

His mother gathered Daniel and made her way to the elevator. Zach walked straight to Lily. He had her elbow in his hand before she noticed his presence. 'After a taxi? I'll get one.'

'Thank you, but there's no need to trouble yourself.' By the time she finished speaking, he had hustled her not towards the lift, where others waited to make a leisurely descent to the floor below, but to the ornate staircase. He didn't want to share her, even in this small way.

They descended without speaking. Her heels clacked on the parquet steps. Their clothing rustled as they moved. It was oddly intimate, and his hand moved from her elbow and found its way to the small of her back as they stepped outside into the night.

The evening was warm with the promise of rain whispering on the sea breeze. After the rain, the temperature would drop, but for now the air caressed them, and drifted the scent of her perfume to him. Waves lapped against the wharf, adding to the feeling of intimacy.

Desire had him in its grip. He should leave her now, but he would see her home.

Among departing others, they were silent as they made their way to a row of cabs.

When they reached a vacant taxi, Lily gave a sigh that sounded rather relieved, and turned to him. 'Well, Happy Birthday again, and I guess I'll see you on Monday when things will be back to business as usual—although I do want to talk to you about the future in respect of that. I want to put Deborah—'

'We're not going there.' She wanted to cut and run? Not likely, and he might as well kill the idea now. Lily was a great secretary. He had no intention of losing her.

Besides, she was nervous. Aware. As awash in all of this as he was. And he couldn't help but revel dangerously in that knowledge. He swept her before him into the rear seat of the cab and followed. 'Give the driver your address, there's a love.'

'Oh, but I—'

'Or we could go back to my place.' He wouldn't take her there. If he got her inside the doors of his home, he wasn't sure he could trust himself to let her go again. And, for all that he wanted her, that warning voice still had *some* volume remaining.

She must have taken his threat to heart, because she rattled off her address, a not particularly auspicious suburb near enough to the city centre to make commuting acceptable. What was her home like?

'You've not mentioned your family since you started working for me.' His mother's earlier question hovered in the back of his mind.

'There's not a lot to say.' Her tone held a curious flatness. 'I'm an only child. My parents don't live in Sydney. We keep in contact by phone, mostly. We're all busy with our own pursuits.'

Too busy to see each other in person at least sometimes? Was that by choice? If Lily were part of his family, he would want more than phone calls.

He might have questioned her more, but she looked at him then, and all he saw was the luminous quality of her eyes rendered almost indigo in the darkened interior of the cab. The need to kiss her rushed through him once again.

By the time the driver stopped outside a modest group of four old but large-looking flats in a quiet street, tension had filled the back of the cab.

Zach caught the driver's eye in the rear-view mirror. 'Keep the meter running. I won't be too long—'

'You don't need to be any time at all.' Lily's mouth was a mutinous line.

'A few minutes, perhaps.' Just long enough for a kiss goodnight. For a kiss without a room full of people to bring it to an end. A kiss that *he* ended, to prove that he could. To prove he had control over this. 'Which one's yours?'

'It's the first on the left, the one with the two external doors.'

'One for your home, and one for your office that can be accessed both from within and without?' He followed her up the short path, noted the splashes of brightly coloured flowers in beds on either side. He took her key from her and pushed it into the lock of the second door.

'Yes.' She gave a strained nod. 'That's right.'

A sticky note just below her lighted doorbell said 'catch the cat'. He read the words. Lily did, too, but they made little sense until he swung the door open and Lily bent, and with a deft movement snatched up a ball of tortoiseshell fluff as it tried to catapult itself past them.

'Jemima,' he said absently, and wanted to be held as closely. He wanted to be treasured by Lily, he realised, and shifted uneasily.

'If she got out, she might get run over. How do you know her name?' The question dropped with utter surprise from her mouth as she stepped inside and put the cat down.

He followed her in. 'You offered me Jemima's firstborn kitten if I'd give your agency another chance. You have a duck or a chicken, too, I think.'

'Oh. Oh, of course.' She swallowed. The cat wrapped around her ankles, then sat quietly on the floor beside her feet. 'Are you very fond of cats? I was going to get her spayed.'

She must be really rattled to be unable to remember their earlier conversation.

'You mentioned that.' His pulse quickened. 'In any case, I don't want a kitten.' What he wanted was Lily.

'I see.' She let out a breath, but her body remained tense, and her eyes...

She gave a nervous cough. 'Well, goodnight. Thank you for seeing me home.'

A glow of moonlight shone through the window behind

her. He had seen nothing of her home besides the small bit of foyer they stood in and that extra door outside.

He wanted to see more, but most of all he wanted her. A growl erupted in his throat while his hands reached and pulled her forward. 'Lily. Tell me you want more than a taste of this. Tell me you've been thinking about it all night, too.'

Her skin was softer than he had even imagined. He discovered it inch by inch with the tips of his fingers. Touched the freckles he had fantasised about. A faint tremor followed the touch of his hands, a reaction that thrilled through him as well.

'I haven't wanted to think about it, but I have.' Her admission was reluctant but she remained before him, unable or unwilling to step away from his touch.

That small fact lodged inside him and took hold. He fingered the fabric of her gown where it clung lovingly below her neck. 'I like your dress. It reminds me of things the ladies used to wear to dinner when they came to our house when I was very small.'

Most of all, he liked the feel of the dress beneath his hands, and the thought of what she would feel like without it.

'The dress…the dress, ah…' Her words were breathless, strained with the same anticipation that had him in its grip. 'I, um, I won it on an eBay auction. UK, actually. I got Betty, my chicken, that way too. Not from the UK, from an online auction. Someone was going to *kill* her if I didn't buy her, and she lays the best eggs and is no trouble.'

She was full of surprises, full of adorable nervous talk,

but right now there was only one thing about her that he wanted to know. One thing he wanted to unravel once and for all. 'I'm going to kiss you now, Lily. You might like to stop chattering while I do it.'

'Right.' The word was a sigh of defeat, or perhaps just acceptance as he pulled her close, and her hands rose to his chest to curl into the fabric of his formal jacket.

He wished the jacket away, and the dress shirt along with it. Zach wanted her touch on his skin, wanted it so much.

'Fall into it with me, Lily.' He lowered his head. 'If we must do this, let's do it together.'

'Together...' Lily was too fragile to risk being burned, and she suspected that could very easily happen, yet something inside her made her lift her face.

Warm lips closed over hers as though he had no choice about this, either. As though something deeper than conscious decision drove him.

His mouth was firm and delicious, and he gave it to her with an intimacy that wrapped dangerously around not only her senses, but her emotions. Her protests and concerns faded away in the face of his determined ministrations.

The kiss changed. His lips gentled against hers, and a wave of tenderness poured over her, through her. This shared intimacy reached right to the depths of her. Seemed more moving than any kiss she had shared, ever, and for a few wildly free moments she opened her heart to him.

She hadn't believed there could be more than their first kiss, but it had only been the prelude to this. To reconnecting to full, glorious life again in a way she hadn't done since a fateful kayaking trip twelve months ago.

A sigh slid through her lips, and her body relaxed into

the firmness of his. Instead of fire he had given her a haven, and she wanted that so much.

And he kissed her. Oh, he kissed her so beautifully, as though he couldn't go another minute without having her lips pressed beneath his. As though he needed to have this, and couldn't live if it were denied him.

He kissed her as though she mattered, and she kissed him back. Yielded and demanded just as he did. She set aside everything. Her struggles, the fear that she could never be worthy.

She forgot that this feeling of rightness couldn't possibly be more than a fantasy, a chimera of her making. An illusion drawn from the desires of her heart, not from reality. But eventually that knowledge pushed its way forward, demanded to be heard.

This might feel real, but it wasn't. Because she wasn't the whole person Zach thought her to be.

And he didn't want her in the way she longed to be wanted. Not with his heart and his soul and his feelings.

Hadn't he told her, that day at the pub, that he didn't want any kind of commitment with a woman? That he would never try that again? Lily remembered *that* quite clearly!

So what was she doing here, in his arms, laying herself emotionally bare while he couldn't possibly be engaged in the same way? If he knew her secrets, there was no way that he *could* want her like that.

Her eyes stung and she drew back, cursing her vulnerability and the ease with which she had chosen to ignore all that had shaped her life since she'd come to Sydney. 'I shouldn't have allowed this.'

Especially not here. This was her home. The one place

she could be herself—if she shaved one leg twice, or thought she had washed her favourite pair of jeans and she hadn't, there was only her to know.

'You can't be here, Zach. I can't let you into this part of my life.' And if he started looking around, walked into the heart of her apartment and saw the reminder notices she'd posted up everywhere just so she could manage the most everyday of things—check for eggs after breakfast, wash clothes on Saturdays, buy groceries Sundays—he would see that it was no ordinary life. 'Please, will you—?'

'Stop? Leave?' He stepped back, his chest rising and falling with each sharp breath. He ran one slightly unsteady hand through his hair. Shadows filled his eyes, sharpened his features. 'God knows I don't want to, Lily.'

She searched his face for reasons for that reluctance. The sting of desire coloured his cheeks, formed his features in tightness, particularly around his mouth and nose. His mouth looked both softer, and tougher, than before. And in his eyes...

Banked heat. Shadows. She didn't know what they meant, but, even as she looked, his body tensed and a hooded expression came over his face.

'You want physical satisfaction.' She schooled her voice to sound simply as though she were stating a fact. She wanted fulfilment with him, too, but she wasn't wired for only that.

'This is just an attraction thing, a physical thing. If it was more...' She trailed off, and, yes, some small, hidden portion of her soul wanted him to say she was wrong. That he *did* have feelings for her and wanted to pursue those feelings, and that was what this had been all about.

He didn't. He just watched her silently, every muscle

clenched, that harshness of their first day's meeting back on his face. He balled both fists at his sides, took a step towards her. Then he seemed to fight with himself for a moment before he stepped back again.

A small, silent cry reverberated inside her because of that rejection, even though she had expected nothing else. 'I think you'd better go.'

He hesitated, half-turned, one hand gripping the door frame. But eventually, just as she had known he would, he went.

Lily busied herself with the nightly routine of settling her animals, ensuring all was locked up securely, and with her notebook by the bed before she climbed in.

If she lay awake staring at the ceiling most of the night, well, that was her concern, and the time wasn't wasted. She used it to remind herself of the importance of getting out of Zach's orbit. Not just because of what had happened tonight, but for the sake of her agency as well.

First thing Monday morning, she would tell Zach he had to accept Deborah in her place at the office. Surely, given what had happened tonight, and given that she had got things in order in his office for him, Zach would agree?

Then Lily would put any lingering feelings for him behind her and get on with her life. And the damaged state of her brain and memory would remain her painful secret.

CHAPTER SIX

'I need to talk to you. I've been thinking all weekend, and I've decided—'

'I'm glad you're here early, because we've got a hell of a day—' Zach broke off.

Shoulders tensed and thrown back, Lily strode to stand directly before his desk, her chin hitched high. She wore a simple navy dress in some sort of knit fabric. Was she aware that by its plain severity it made him want to see what lay beneath? He schooled his features to reveal nothing of his thoughts.

'When we first discussed replacing Rochelle, I mentioned bringing Deborah Martyn in here. I know you weren't initially keen on the idea, but now that I've straightened out the office and have things running efficiently…' She smoothed her hands down the sides of her dress. Tension bracketed the mouth that had melted under his on Friday night.

'You want me to take Deborah in your place.' He almost kept the growl from his tone, but couldn't stop himself from rising from his chair. A moment later, he leaned against the edge of the desk near to where she stood.

Close. Casual. Yet his body thrummed in recognition of hers. A silent warning reverberated through him as he faced her: *She wanted him to leave?* 'It's not going to happen, Lily.'

He reached out to toy with the small dictation recorder resting on his desk. Flipped the cassette lid open, closed it again and finally tossed the article aside. 'We've covered this ground.'

'I know, but that was at the beginning. There's no reason she shouldn't step into the role now.' Wariness haunted her gaze, tightened the muscles of her face and neck. 'I've discussed it with Deb, and she's able to replace me as soon as I give her the word. You won't suffer any lag time. Indeed, I'll stay here for an hour or so once Deb arrives. Show her the ropes. Let her know how everything works.'

'You'll give me a nice clean-cut change over, in fact.' He came to his feet. Made no concession to how close together that put them. Said in tones of gravel and sandpaper, because this was what it was all about and they both knew it, 'If you want me to apologise for kissing you—'

'It's got nothing to do with that.' She tipped her head back but otherwise held her ground.

Her strength fired through him, made him want her all the more. The defiance and denial fooled neither of them, but he admired it.

'I think it does.' His weekend had been haunted by memories of holding her, kissing her. Zach needed to get those memories under control, bring what had happened back into a sense of reality, instead of viewing it as utterly mind-blowing.

He turned his head to look out the windows. The washed-out horizon met his gaze. No, he wouldn't let her go. It wasn't that he *couldn't*. He wasn't willing to accept the disruption to his work place. There was nothing emotional in either his decision, or the way he had reacted when he'd kissed her. He was too smart to let there be. Wasn't he?

When he turned back to her, his face was schooled to show only rejection of her desire to leave. 'We had an agreement, Lily. You must know I won't let you break it. Don't you think the weeks you've spent learning your way around the office count for anything?

'A new person, no matter how good or how skilled, would still need to orient themselves. I'm not prepared to lose valuable time to that. You agreed to my terms.' He reminded her of it quietly. 'If you break them, I *will* consider you in breach of contract with my company.'

'You kissed me.' Her accusation came on a ragged whisper. 'You broke your own rules.'

'We kissed each other. It was mutual. If it happens again, it will also be mutual.' He stared down his nose at her and tried not to think of her freckles, of the taste of her and the softness of her skin beneath his hands. 'And you just said it wasn't about that.'

'No, I didn't. I—' She broke off and looked uneasy, then waved one hand in dismissal. 'What I said isn't the point. It would be wiser for me to go.' Her frustration showed in the low, impatient sound she made… 'But, as you clearly don't share that opinion, and you know you have me locked in, let me just say this.' Her eyes narrowed into warning slits. 'There will be no repeat performance of that kiss between us.'

She turned. Her body quivered with whatever feelings she fought to suppress and, oh, Zach wanted to unleash it all. To let it free and lose himself in her. Maybe he did have feelings…

But he couldn't let himself do that. He didn't acknowledge her statement directly. Instead, he turned away too. 'Now that this conversation's over, perhaps we can get some work done.'

For the rest of the morning, they worked hard and spoke only when necessary. Zach buried himself in paperwork and told himself he didn't have to want her. That his growing admiration for her didn't have to mean he was becoming emotionally involved, either.

When, ever, had it been other than choice for him to want any woman? There was no reason Lily should be any different. If she truly wasn't interested, he didn't have to be, either.

Just before lunch time, the phone rang. Zach happened to glance at Lily as she answered it. He wasn't addicted to the sight of her, nor had he stolen countless other glances since the start of the day. A man needed to keep an eye on his business, including what his secretary was doing with her time. That was all.

'Mark.'

She put such warmth into the name that the hair on the back of Zach's neck stood up. There was a short pause as she listened to the voice on the other end of the line.

Then a smile like sunshine crossed her expressive face. 'Oh, I'd love to. Now? That would be wonderful. I'll see you soon.'

Zach turned his back on her. He snatched up a file and carried it to his windows, although he did no more than flip it open and pretend to give the first page his attention.

When an older man walked into the office minutes later, Lily flew out of her chair and straight into the man's arms. In response, he pecked Lily's cheek in an avuncular manner, and stepped back to smile at her.

Their obvious close friendship brought a surge of unexpected jealousy to Zach. He tossed down the folder and joined them before he could examine that reaction. 'Hello. I'm Zachary Swift, Lily's boss.'

'Mark Uden. It's a pleasure to meet one of Lily's assignments.' The man shook hands and withdrew.

Zach found he didn't like being referred to as an 'assignment.' He didn't like the man's salt-and-pepper hair and air of mature sophistication, either, which was quite irrational of him.

Lily collected her bag from her desk and hurried to Uden's side. 'We should get going.'

Before Zach could do anything, she muttered a farewell in his general direction and swept out of the office, her arm entwined with Uden's.

Zach returned to his desk and ploughed his way through a stack of work, and a cheese and salad focaccia delivered from the building's twentieth-floor cafeteria. He swilled down orange juice and glared at the city stretched beyond his windows, his mood out of sorts for no good reason.

So Lily had flown to Uden as though the man were some sort of sanctuary. So what? Surely Zach didn't want to be the one she ran to, because that really would suggest a desire for emotional closeness, and he wasn't in a position to go there.

Who was Uden, anyway? What place did he have in Lily's life? Zach wanted to know, but he had no hold over

Lily. She didn't owe it to him to tell him about her friends. Telling himself to put Lily and everything to do with her out of his mind, Zach lobbed the crushed juice bottle into his waste-paper basket.

Just before Lily was due back from her break, Zach's phone rang. When he ended the call, he got up to prowl his office again.

Lily's soft footfalls as she returned to the office brought his pacing to an abrupt halt. He stepped into her office, and stopped just short of her desk. 'You omitted to give me a telephone message about a meeting scheduled for this afternoon straight after lunch.'

She gave a startled gasp, and swung to face him. The large, soft handbag she had been about to slip into the desk drawer dropped from her fingers and hit the carpet. 'Perhaps there's some misunderstanding? I don't remember anything about a meeting.'

As she spoke, she snatched up the phone message pad and began to search it frantically.

'You won't find anything there.' Zach drew closer, aware he was being unreasonable, but unable to stop himself. He *was* jealous of Uden, of the time Lily had spent in the older man's company, and he didn't much like himself for it. 'I've already checked.'

'I apologise for the oversight.' A haunted expression filled her eyes. 'If you'll tell me what needs to be done in preparation, I'll do my best to be organised in time for the meeting. And if you want to mark this against my record, against my company's record, I understand.'

The depth of Lily's remorse made him face where his jealousy had taken him. What was one small slip-up in the scheme of things? He wasn't angry at her over some stupid phone message about a meeting he already knew about, and had no need to prepare for. He hated the idea that she might trust and confide in anyone but him. His attitude shamed him.

'Lily.' He looked into her eyes. Saw the shadowed hurt reflected there, and knew he had caused it. His hands lifted towards her.

But a clerk hustled into the room, begging Lily's assistance with some information on one of their most urgent projects. She retrieved a large file from her desk, and they bent their heads over it.

Zach looked at his watch. The chance to apologise was lost; he needed to leave for his meeting. On a rare bout of uncertainty, the issue unresolved and sitting uncomfortably in his gut, he murmured a farewell and left.

An hour later, Zach's finance manager continued to drone on. Zach struggled to focus on the words, but all he could think about was Lily. He felt like a particularly ugly, beastly dog that had attacked a kitten for no good reason.

In the middle of the other man's speech about profit and loss, Zach tossed down the remaining sheets of paper and got to his feet. 'Just do whatever you feel is necessary with the rest, Steele. I have to go.'

He made his way back to his suite of offices in record time. 'Lily—'

'I'm glad you're back. I've just received a call from Gunterson and Greig.' She had a phone message clasped in her hand, an urgent expression on her face, and she kept the width of her desk between them.

She scanned the message before she continued. 'They say they're awaiting a formal expression of interest from you in relation to their Mulligan project, and will seek another buyer if they don't have your offer to table at their board meeting first thing tomorrow morning. I don't remember anything at all about this project.'

'The report was supposed to go out the week Rochelle was here.' Clearly it hadn't, and somehow Zach had overlooked following up on it as well. He had compiled the facts and figures and dictated the report. But it had never turned up typed on his desk.

This lapse of his was a much worse infraction than Lily forgetting that small, not particularly significant, phone message.

Lily seemed to sag with relief. 'I'll check for a paper file. If I can't find one, there may be something on computer.' She moved towards the filing cabinet. 'It's no use going through audio tapes, unless you've got any tucked away in your office that might still have a recording on them from weeks ago.'

Her lovely, straight back was presented to him as she began to riffle through the contents of the top drawer of the first filing cabinet.

Zach clenched his fists against the desire to reach for her. To run his fingers down the length of her spine, to cup her shoulders and turn her into his arms.

He had wanted a physical closeness with Lily from the day they'd met. Now he admitted he *did* want other things from her and with her. Things he couldn't have in his wildest dreams, yet somewhere deep inside he *did* dream of them. Lily was quirky and special, dedicated, intense.

And somehow, over all of that, she was hugely vulnerable. He didn't know why, but he saw glimpses of that vulnerability when her guard was down.

All these things attracted him, but Zach couldn't get involved in her life. Even so, he had to apologise. He directed low-spoken words at that very straight back. 'I acted like an ass, Lily, going off about one stupid message. I was out of line, and I hope you'll forgive me.'

She turned. Vulnerability shadowed her eyes. For long moments, she searched his face and seemed somehow torn. Finally, she nodded. 'Apology accepted. Now, we need to work out what to do about this Mulligan problem.' Her fingers continued their busy search of the files in the cabinet.

Zach watched those fingers move, and wanted them on his skin instead. He couldn't resist reaching for her, even though he knew it was dangerous to touch her when he didn't have his desire under control.

He touched her arm, gently turned her to face him. Said her name again. He wanted to ask her about Uden. Wanted to tell her again how sorry he was. Most of all, he just wanted to hold her close. 'Lily, my dear.'

'Please, Zach. Don't.' She turned tortured eyes to his face. 'If you hold me, I'll be lost, and I—I'm not for you. Besides, you made it clear you don't want to get involved, even if I don't really understand why.'

'After my relationship with Lara fell apart I made up my mind I wouldn't put myself or another woman in that position again.' Zach didn't know if explaining it would help or just make things harder. 'I'm a career man, with the responsibility of a widowed mother and a young brother to contend with. Those things fill my life and always will. Unfortunately, knowing that doesn't seem to be making any difference to the fact that I desire you.'

'I see. And, for me, just wanting someone is nowhere near enough. I guess that makes it pretty clear we have no common meeting ground with each other.' She turned away again, searched through the cabinet almost desperately, her agitation revealed in the swiftly moving fingers. In the death grip she had on the edge of the cabinet with her other hand.

Finally, her fingers stopped moving. She stared at him while he fought with himself, fought his need. And she seemed to be fighting hers.

'Hello.' His mother entered the room, breaking the taut silence. 'I'm glad I've found you together.'

A newspaper clutched in her hand, she glanced from his face to Lily's tense frame. 'Have I interrupted?'

It was Lily who stepped forward, and forced a smile to her face. 'Hello, Anne. How lovely to see you again. You haven't interrupted. You've found us with a work problem to sort out, that's all.'

As she spoke, she retreated behind her desk and sank into the chair. She tugged her notebook forward and held it tightly. 'We've just discovered a deadline that needs to be met, and there's not much time.'

'Oh.' Anne looked at Zach with a hint of puzzlement. 'You won't be able to come to the school, then, to watch the hockey match.'

CHAPTER SEVEN

'DAMN. I don't know how I can be there, and take care of this problem too.' Zach *never* ignored a commitment to his brother. He had never forgotten one before, either, but this had slipped his mind as all his attention centred on Lily. His computer diary would have beeped him a reminder, but even so...

'Well, I'll just explain, dear. Daniel will understand.' His mother forced a bright smile, and pushed the paper into his hands. 'I must be off so I don't miss the start of the game myself, but you'll want to see this. There's a lovely little article about your birthday in the society column on page eight, with some photos.'

Zach took the paper automatically and spoke quickly, before his mother could get out the door. 'Tell Daniel I'll be there.' He would figure out a way. His computer beeped that reminder as he spoke.

His mother left. Zach stuffed the Mulligan notes into his briefcase and cleared his desk, locking away anything that shouldn't be left for the nightly visit of the cleaners.

He could feel Lily's gaze on him, and glanced up. 'I can't believe my own stupidity. It makes me twice as angry at myself for the way I spoke to you earlier. About the phone message, and about—'

'It doesn't matter.' She cut him off quickly. 'Maybe it's a good thing that we cleared the air. We really do need to accept that there's no way forward for these…reactions we have to each other, and put them behind us. But, Zach, when did you say that offer has to be tabled?'

'First thing tomorrow.' He could put something together this evening, but it would take hours for him to type it into his computer, and it would still need to be tidied into a professional looking document before morning. 'Lily, it's not that easy to ignore a hunger that has both of us on edge the whole time we're together.'

'Yes, it is. It has to be.' But her eyes were wild and filled with the very hunger she so adamantly wanted to deny. She took a deep breath. 'Now, I'll come along to the school. I have a small computer note pad in my bag, although I don't use it often. You can dictate the offer while you watch the game. I can type it straight in. Then all I'll need to do is come in early tomorrow, upload it to the computer and format it properly, then print it out. You can sign it, and it can go by courier and be there when they open for the day.'

It was a good solution. It was the only one he could see would work, and he would be a fool to reject it. But did she really believe they could switch off what they felt for each other? Zach could disprove that theory in about three seconds flat. For now, he stuck to business, as Lily seemed determined to do. 'I don't like to ask you to put yourself out that way.'

She finished making a note in her diary, quickly tidied

her desk, and turned to face him. The heat in her eyes remained, but she had done her best to bank it. 'You didn't. I volunteered.'

During the drive in his car, Lily, notebook in one hand, phone in the other, worked her way through a number of text messages on her cell phone. He heard her mutter things like, 'Good work, Deb,' and, 'Good to know everything's going well,' as she made the occasional note. And Zach realised that he relished simply being near her, whatever she happened to be doing.

He parked the car near the school and got out, his gaze searching the grounds for his mother. Lily returned her cell phone and notebook to her bag and joined him.

'I appreciate this, Lily.' He took a step towards her.

'It's no trouble.' She cast one trembling glance in his direction, then hurried onto the school grounds and made a beeline for the huddle of parents already congregated in the observation stands at the edge of the oval.

The appreciation in Zach's tone touched a chord deep inside Lily. She needed to feel valued, and, despite being sharp with her earlier, Zach had made it clear he did appreciate her. He just apparently believed there was no escaping their attraction to each other, which was something that made Lily rather uneasy. 'Let's greet your mother and find some seats.'

Once they were seated on the painted wooden-slat benches that stretched across the sheltered stands, Lily decided she had better check her phone messages. She drew the phone out and caught Zach giving her an odd look.

There were no messages, and she quickly realised she must have already checked through them. Well, she would have written anything down if needed. 'I was just checking the time.'

'Looks like the game is about to start.' Zach drew her attention to the teams on the field. 'There's Daniel.' The pride in his voice was completely unconscious, and made something deep inside her tighten with longing. He clearly loved his family.

The two teams moved onto the field. Daniel looked up and seemed to immediately find his brother, and his mother, seated some rows away.

Lily forced her lips to smile. 'Is Daniel a good hockey player?'

'He's good enough.' Zach's grin suggested he thought his brother was a great player.

'Maybe we should look at the article your mother gave you.' Lily reached for the paper, and flicked through it until she found the article.

'Yes. Let's have a look.' Zach lowered his head to examine the article and photos.

Lily's interest in the article warred with more immediate ones. The knowledge of that head bent close to hers tingled through her. She could feel the heat of his body, could smell not only the scent of his cologne but also the pine-scented shampoo he used on his hair, and the fresh, clean scent of his skin that was uniquely Zach.

Her stomach pitched with a feeling of sharp awareness. His arm bumped hers as he moved closer to study the paper.

It wasn't easy to focus on the article when all she wanted to do was turn and look into Zach's eyes, and see if they reflected the awareness she felt. So much for fighting her reactions to him! 'It's a nice wrap-up of the party.'

One photo showed a group of people at the buffet. Another had her and Daniel grooving down, big grins on their faces. The last was of Zach and his mother, dancing beyond her and Daniel.

Lily doubted that a casual observer would have even guessed that the intent look on Zach's face had been directed right at her. She hadn't been aware of it herself, at the time. Or, rather, she hadn't been aware of that specifically. It had been more of an overall sense of unbreakable connection to him.

'I'm looking at you as though I want to swallow you whole.' As Zach moved to look more closely, his leg pressed against hers from thigh to knee. 'When it comes to you, I can't seem to control that hunger. I've tried.'

'W-well.' What could she say to such an honest statement? Particularly when it made her entire body sing with recognition. When she refused to look at him, Zach's fingers closed around the delicate bones of her wrist, clasping while he waited for her response.

It could have been intended as a comforting gesture. Lily's sensory reaction made it impossible for her to tell. All she could feel was his gaze on her, his body against her. His touch on that super-soft skin at the inner side of her wrist.

With effort, she raised her gaze to his. 'Look. The game has started. You'd best watch, or your brother will be disappointed.'

With a frustrated murmur, Zach turned his attention to the field.

Lily watched the game too, and lost herself for a little while in the fierce efforts of the boys on both teams.

'Daniel's very determined. Look at the way he goes

after the ball.' She watched the boy jump nimbly into the air and whack the ball away from an opponent, and felt Zach's pride as they both clapped.

Play moved to the far end of the field again.

Zach glanced at the electronic note pad on her lap. 'Let's get this offer down.'

He dictated between play and, scared she might lose it all and not be able to remember any of it, Lily saved her work frequently.

Eventually the work was saved for the final time, the mini-computer tucked safely away in her bag.

'Thanks for your help.' He glanced at her briefly before turning his attention back to the game.

It got cold. Zach removed his suit coat and wrapped it around her shoulders, and she sank into the scent and warmth of him, and wondered what was happening to her.

She and Richard had enjoyed the typical intimacies to be expected of any committed couple, sporadically, and there hadn't been skyrockets. But surely that was the stuff of fantasies, anyway? So why did the simplest touch from Zach, or just the scent of him, affect her so strongly?

As the match progressed to tied scores, tension in the stands escalated. Lily's tension climbed too, but for a different reason.

When Daniel scored the winning goal with just seconds of play remaining, Zach gave a hoarse roar, and Lily's own shout startled her.

She told herself it was the pleasure of the moment that had them in each other's arms, laughing. But a moment later that embrace changed completely, and Zach let out a feral growl as he drew almost roughly away from her. 'Do you see now, Lily, that this can't be simply shut off? I think we'd better be on our way, now.'

He didn't give her time to think. Just made for his brother and congratulated him. 'Well done, Dan.'

'Thanks.' The boy's pride was subdued. 'It's good exercise. I suppose I don't mind it.'

'Your brother seems a little melancholy?' Lily brought it up during the drive to her house, but Zach shrugged the question off.

'Dan's just growing up. He was probably embarrassed about his win today. Boys get like that.' He stopped the car. 'You've gone above and beyond the call of duty today. I'll be here to collect you tomorrow at seven-thirty, so we have time to organise the report and get it couriered.'

'I can catch an early train.' Her bag banged against her hip when she got out of the car, and she thought of Zach's firm thigh pressed against her.

His mouth tightened. 'You could, but I'd rather make it easy for you to get to work without any difficulties.' He paused. 'You don't drive, do you?'

'Oh, I can drive. It's just that I sold—' She straightened and turned away, shocked that she had almost told him about selling her car to finance the start of her business.

He climbed out of the car after her, caught her wrist in the circle of his fingers. Her pulse beat rapidly. Could he feel it?

'What if we explored the attraction, Lily? It might be a good way to get it out of both our systems.' His fingers stroked her soft flesh.

'Do you think that would help?' Each time he touched her, she wanted him more. She suspected a conscious exploration of their interest would only escalate it.

His gaze held hers. 'All I can think about is this.'

He didn't rush her. His hands invited her forward, but it was her choice to move close to him. When the heat in his eyes and the tight awareness on his face made it clear he wanted to kiss her, she was the one who lifted up, who pressed her lips against his in that first, reckless acceptance.

'I think this is the only feeling that's been right in my world since I met you.' The harsh admission was whispered against her cheek before he lowered his head again.

'Zach.' Even though she knew it was foolhardy, Lily gave in to the instinct that encouraged her closer.

He tightened his hold, drew her up against him, so that every part of her was pressed close. She welcomed it all. Their kiss changed, mouths softened. She gave vent to a tiny whimper of need.

'I could look into your eyes and drown in you and never stop.' His admission shook a tremor from her. 'I've never wanted to make love with a woman so much. I want to take you to my bed.'

'No. No... I don't want...that from you.' It was too intimate for the kind of temporal involvement Zach would want. Her body might say yes, but she had to listen to the warning of her mind. Her defences belatedly kicked in again. She backed away from him.

But Zach had only stated the truth. That he wanted her. And it wasn't that statement of truth that scared her. It was her temptation, despite everything, to yield to him and take whatever he was willing to give.

CHAPTER EIGHT

ZACH dropped a tape and several Manila folders into the tray on Lily's desk. Lily was delivering documents to Steele on the finance floor. She'd been gone about five minutes, and already Zach missed seeing her here at her desk.

He had it bad. With a sigh, he picked up the sticky note pad on her blotter, jotted the time and date and stuck it to the tape, then grinned a little at himself. Sometimes it was a case of Lily training him to do things *her* way.

Without stopping to think about it, he dropped into her chair and did a full three-hundred-and-sixty-degree slow swivel on it. The scent of lily of the valley clung to the fabric back of the chair. Zach closed his eyes and inhaled.

In the days since his brother's school hockey competition, he had tried to leave her alone, to forget her. But he still desired her. Still noticed her every move, still tracked her through the days whether he chose to or not, and dreamed of her through the long nights.

Maybe he should capitulate about having one of her other workers in to replace her. Yet, even as he thought it, he knew he wasn't ready to let her out of his life.

'Hello. Is Lily not here at the moment?' The familiar voice sounded from in front of the desk.

Zach snapped his eyes open and stared into Mark Uden's calm face. 'Ah, Uden. Good afternoon. No. She's delivering something on another floor, then we'll be packing up for the day.'

'I thought I'd give Lily a lift to her volunteer session at the institute.' Uden paused, and added, 'I saw your photographs in the paper the other day. Let's see, page eight, the society column, wasn't it? Many happy returns for your birthday. I hope it was an enjoyable event.'

'It was. Thanks.' Zach rose from the chair, but remained standing behind the desk. 'You appear to have a good memory.' And what did Uden mean about a volunteer session? What institute?

'I have a natural gift for all types of recall. Faces, places, names, dates. I've never used a diary in my life.' Uden gave a self-effacing smile. 'I confess, some of my colleagues find my ability quite aggravating at times. I try to keep the knowledge of that skill from my patients, of course. No need to make them uncomfortable.'

'Lily wouldn't last long if she tried that, but she does a great job with her diaries and calendars and sticky notes.' Zach *liked* her zany, intense commitment to recording just about everything that happened in her day.

It wasn't that odd. He scowled, recalling her commitment to her work, and his fixation on everything *but* her work, his fixation on Lily.

'She's confided in you!' Uden's smile was blinding. 'I'm so pleased to know that. Lily is usually very secretive about her history, you know.'

Lily's history? What could Uden be implying about Lily? Did the man mean her past engagement?

'Lily told me about her past, yes.' He refused to pretend that he found any pleasure in the knowledge that Lily had cared for someone once and maybe still did. He raised an eyebrow. 'Whether she's over it or not is open to question.'

Uden rocked back on the heels of his shoes. 'It's not really a case of getting over it. Rather, it's about making adjustments. Because of the injury to her brain, she's had to completely rebuild her confidence. That will take a long time, a lot longer than the year that has passed so far since her accident.'

'What?' Zach's gaze narrowed. They were clearly at cross purposes. What was Uden talking about? 'What do you mean, an injury? An accident?'

'Ah, I beg your pardon.' Uden drew himself up. 'Did you not just state that Lily had confided in you?'

'Lily told me about her *ex-fiancé*. I thought that was the history you meant, when you suggested she had confided in me. She hasn't said a word about anything else.' Zach faced the older man, stunned, unable to absorb that one, shocking truth. Lily injured. Her brain damaged.

It couldn't be true. He knew her. Had worked with her, seen her skills, her ability. Yet, even as Zach thought this, he recalled so many incidents that had meant nothing at the time.

Lily having to leave a note on her door to make sure she didn't let her cat get run over. Her difficulty remembering barrages of names or instructions. The way she had tried to check her phone messages twice before Dan's hockey game.

Zach felt awe and deep heartache for all Lily must have endured. He wanted to hold her close and protect her from ever being harmed again. He wanted to tell her she was incredible. But if Lily ever knew that he had accidentally uncovered her secret…

'I must ask you not to speak of what you've just learned to anyone, especially not to Lily.' Uden's face had paled. 'I might wish she would trust people more easily with the truth of her condition, but this still should have been her story to tell, if and when she was ready.'

'It's not your fault. I won't say anything to her, there's no reason she need ever know.' But Zach wanted to ask Lily about it, to understand, to offer support and comfort and encouragement…

'Mark! What's going on? Why are you swearing Zach to secrecy? What have you told him about me?' Lily's strident words brought Zach's head around in abrupt attention.

She barely looked at him. Instead, her glance slewed to the man at Zach's side. 'Mark?'

Lily could have heard everything. Zach had been too absorbed in Uden's shocking revelation to notice anything around them. All he knew was the hurt on her face now, and the need to make this situation right. 'Lily.'

'My dear…' Mark's voice trembled through pinched lips.

She looked at the older man with betrayal in her eyes. 'You did tell him! How could you?'

Uden's expression confirmed it. 'It wasn't intentional, my dear. I called in to ask if you'd like to ride with me to the institute and grab a bite at our cafeteria before you do your volunteer session. Your employer and I misunderstood each other, and I'm afraid I told him something I shouldn't have.'

Lily held a large envelope in her hands. She lowered it

to the desk with excessive care, and turned to face Zach as though she thought she might fly apart at any second. Accusation made her words sharp. 'How dare you mislead Mark into blurting information about me?'

Her voice trembled at the end. Unshed tears pooled in eyes that seemed to have lost all their vivacity and had filled, instead, with deep hurt. 'You had no right to pry into my affairs, and now you'll *know*.'

She came to a choked stop.

Zach took an automatic step towards her. He wanted to comfort her, to make this right, but she was so upset. 'It was a mistake. I thought—' He reached out a hand, but sensed her withdrawal even before she stepped back to avoid his touch.

'You thought what—that you would find out just who Mark was and what he had to do with me? All because I went to lunch with him?'

Zach *had* been jealous of a relationship he now realised must have started as that of mentor and student, and progressed to friendship. Lily must have studied under Mark Uden in order to learn to function again after her accident. What exactly had happened?

Zach didn't try to defend himself. This wasn't about that, anyway. 'I meant you no harm, Lily. I can only repeat that, and hope you believe me.'

Uden cleared his throat, and Lily turned her head towards him. 'It's all right, Mark. Why don't you go? I'll be there for my session, but I don't feel like eating first.'

The older man hesitated, then after a moment nodded and left the office.

But it wasn't all right. Zach waited until Uden's footsteps receded before he spoke again. 'Lily, please believe I would never have pried deliberately, and I'm sure your mentor wouldn't have betrayed you, either. It was a very short conversation, stopped the moment we both realised what had happened.'

'The end result is the same, isn't it? You know my brain doesn't work like it should. That I'm flawed and always will be.' She drew in deep gulps of air. Harsh spots of colour dotted each cheek, alabaster whiteness behind them.

'I'd like to understand about your injury.' *So I can help you. So I don't blunder around and hurt you, as I must have done the day I got angry at you for forgetting to write down a stupid phone message.*

'I'm so sorry, Lily.' A great well of protectiveness rose up, and Zach realised that he did care about her. That he cared *for* her. Wanted her in ways he had never wanted another woman. It wasn't love. It couldn't be that. But it was something outside of his experience, it was strong, and he wondered if he could control it.

He should exorcise those feelings now, but how could he, when he only wanted to take her pain away?

Silently, Lily moved past him and retrieved her bag from the drawer of her desk. Anger, pride and a great woundedness surrounded her as she shut down her computer. 'I don't want to talk about this any more. I can't think about it. I—I have to go.'

Zach wanted to find some way to get through to her and ease her hurt. But her hands around the straps of her handbag were clenched to whiteness, her expression haunted, and he knew now wasn't the time. He stood back and let her leave.

* * *

'Naturally, now that you know my situation, you'll feel it's best if I remove myself from your office immediately.' Lily had thought long and hard about how to handle this interview with Zach. She had lain awake much of the night, plotting and planning, and crying into her pillow, while Jemima batted at her head with a kindly paw, as though to say, *what's wrong? How can I help?*

Dawn had found Lily dry-eyed and determined. She had phoned Zach at his home. Had asked him to meet her at a coffee shop near his work at eight a.m., and had disconnected before he could ask questions.

Now they sat here, their knees almost touching beneath the small square table. Men and women in business clothing bustled in, bustled out, coffee in paper cups clutched in their hands as they anticipated the first caffeine fix of the day.

Few sat, and she and Zach had found a table tucked into a corner away from the general bustle. The coffee shop was redolent with the scents of ground coffee-beans, vanilla, and sweet pastries. Lily nursed her mocha caramel latte and knew she shouldn't have chosen it.

The warm, sweet smells inside the shop might promise enticing, creamy delights, but her rebellious stomach had other ideas and was twisted quite firmly into resistant knots. Lily would have been hard pressed to choke down a regular coffee at the moment, let alone this sweet, cream-topped version.

'That's why you wanted to meet early here this morning? To say you want to leave?' Zach pushed aside his sensible, simple cappuccino and examined her with a deep, penetrating gaze that seemed to want to see right into the very heart of her.

It wasn't fair that over the top of all the other, stronger scents she could detect his aftershave lotion. *That* made her stomach tighten in quite a different way.

'Why?' He went on. 'Just because I know there's a reason you write yourself a few sticky notes to ensure you stay on track?'

'It's a lot more than a few reminder notes!' Oh, she had been right to want to replace herself. If he had agreed then, she would have been gone before he'd known anything about her past. Already she could see a difference in the way he looked at her.

Zach leaned forward. His gaze seemed to contain a great deal of understanding—the pitying kind!

'I won't pretend that what I learned yesterday doesn't change things.' The softened tone of his voice confirmed her fears. He did pity her.

When he spoke, it only made it worse. 'I'll treat you differently from now on.'

'You don't feel the same way about me.' How *could* he still want her, now that he knew of her condition? 'I understand, Zach. You don't have to explain.'

'Thank you. It's hard to articulate…' He watched her silently for a moment, before relief slowly bloomed across his face. 'You have my respect, Lily. I think you're amazing, coping the way you do. This is very mature of you. I just…I don't want either of us to feel uncomfortable.'

This was just what every girl didn't want to hear. Next thing, Zach would say he hoped they would stay friends.

She decided to head that one off before it happened. 'I'm glad we had this conversation. It's always good to take the chance to clear the air.'

Zach seemed to hesitate, and said quietly, 'Before we talk about work any further, would you explain your situation to me? I'd like to know exactly how extensive your...difficulties are.'

'But I'll be leaving. Surely you don't need to know all that?' Panic welled inside her at the thought of exposing the details of her condition.

'You'll be staying to the end of the agreed time.' Zach sounded very calm as he tossed this statement down. 'But, as your employer, I think I should know how your condition affects you.'

'And how it might impact on my work for you.' An angry, determined part of Lily rose up and pointed out that she could do very close to as good a job as anybody else, even if she did go about things differently. 'I volunteered to leave. That's why I asked for this meeting. To let you know Deborah could take over now.'

'You may have decided that.' His voice softened to a silken thread. 'But I don't recall being consulted, and, as it happens, I don't consider it to be in my best interests to have to undergo a further change in staffing right at the moment.'

'Why not? Deborah—'

'I'll explain my reasons.' His gaze again pierced her. 'After you outline your condition to me.'

'Fine. I'll explain.' She didn't see what difference it would make, and Zach clearly did have a changed view of her now. Maybe he was able to simply forget he had ever desired her, and was willing to put up with her idiosyncrasies to avoid that further change of staff he had mentioned?

She kept her chin up, and hoped he couldn't see how much all this was hurting her. 'I have damage to a large portion of the short-term memory area of my brain. The majority of things that would normally be retained there now get forgotten instead.'

Zach gave a tight nod. 'Go on.'

Lily drew a deep breath. 'I've learned some patterns of things I'll regularly forget, and worked out ways to counteract the problem with those things. I leave a "memory trail". A notebook beside my bed at night. Other reminders are posted all over my apartment, and I employ the same style of reminders at work.'

Lily hated having to talk about this, and old resentments flared up, too, against her parents and Richard. She pushed them down again, and went on. 'I write down as much as I can manage so it's there if I need it, but inevitably, no matter how hard I try, I slip up sometimes.'

'This is why you didn't want to work for me initially, and why you wanted me to accept Deborah in your place once you'd sorted things out for me a bit.' He stopped and raked a hand through his hair, and that awful, pitying glance was back on his face again. 'And it's why you're trying to push Deborah onto me again now.'

He continued. 'In terms of your work commitments to me, Lily, this changes nothing. I still need you as my secretary, in that chair every morning taking care of the workload. I need it now more than ever, as it happens.'

'Deborah will be a much better choice for you—'

He swore—a soft, sharp, eloquent word. 'Deborah

doesn't know her way around the office, isn't familiar with it, with me and with my expectations and way of working. You're familiar with those things, Lily. Those things are locked into your head just fine.'

As though he expected her to argue the point, he held up a hand. 'We're already busy, and another project came to a head last night. It's a major deal. I need to look into it personally, and I need you with me while I do it. You, Lily. Not some clueless stranger.'

A part of her reached for the reprieve from leaving him—oh, foolish part that it was. If he needed her, couldn't she gain satisfaction from continuing to help him?

Before she could stop herself, she asked, 'What project, exactly?' Her hands shook as she opened her notebook and poised the pencil over it. Her gaze roved features that had become indelibly familiar, and far too dear. 'I'm just asking about the project. It doesn't mean I'll stay on, or have anything to do with it.'

His jaw clamped, but after a moment he took a folder from the briefcase that rested at his side. 'The project relates to a cartel of factory owners. They're looking for a financial partner to assist with a major expansion into the worldwide market. I had a brief phone conference with several of the head people about the idea a few months ago. Now they're ready to move on it, and I know I have to act quickly if I want in.'

He flipped the folder open to reveal a number of faxed pages, some with pictures of buildings on them. 'These are organics producers and their associated factories and farms. They deal in flours, nuts and grains mostly. There's also a confectionery factory.'

'They contacted you at home last night?' She guessed it from the different grade of fax paper in the folder, and from the fact that he had said nothing of it to her until now.

Then she reminded herself she couldn't be sure of that, and reached for her notebook to check back through the pages.

'This is the first you've heard of it.' He made the statement with that gentle tone in his voice again, and pushed the folder across the desk. As though it was nothing out of the ordinary to help her decide whether her memory had betrayed her or not.

She didn't know how to respond to that, and finally settled on, 'Okay. Thank you.' To take her mind off that awkward feeling, she opened the folder and began to study the contents, only to feel compelled to look up again when she felt his gaze on her.

In his expression she caught a glimpse of some deep, banked emotion, before he blinked and looked away. Pity. It must have been pity.

Yet it hadn't looked quite like that. 'The factories are all really rural,' she observed. 'On farms and at the edges of small townships, by the looks of this.'

'Yes.' He leaned forward. 'What do you think are the chances of the project being viable?'

Perhaps it was the fact that his voice turned to one of challenge, as though he really wanted to hear her opinion. Or maybe she just wanted to prove herself, now that he knew her limitations.

She didn't know, but, despite herself, she said with conviction, 'I know you'd definitely be interested in this. From what's here, I think you could make money out of it.'

'That was my feeling, too.' He sat back in his chair. 'We

need to leave later this morning to start our tour of the group of small farms and factories. We won't get back to Sydney until the weekend.'

And this was crunch point. Did she agree, or not agree? On the one hand, she would have him to herself for days out in the countryside, away from the demands of the office. She could bank up some memories, the kind that wouldn't leave her, but they would be of a boss-and-secretary nature. He felt nothing else for her now.

'We go to five different places.' He named each place, and flipped out a map that revealed the spread of the properties across parts of Victoria and New South Wales.

When he pointed to the final destination, she gave an involuntary start. *Albury-Wodonga.*

Actually, he said the factory was situated forty kilometres from the twin towns, and that their rental accommodation was set on a rural property not far from the factory. So it wasn't as if there would be any likelihood of Lily meeting up with her parents or Richard.

Zach gave her a frowning glance. 'Is there a problem?'

'No. It was just a random thought.' She drew a deep breath. 'I'd like to help you, Zach…'

'But you won't?' Before she could point out that she had been about to say she would do the work, his voice sharpened and his gaze hardened. 'I acknowledge things have changed, that they can never be the same between us now. But I didn't think you'd desert the ship when you have an obligation to stay with it. I thought you were stronger than that.'

Shock widened her eyes. So many emotions fought for space inside her that she felt quite faint. She had been a lot of things in the face of the damage to her memory, but, until now, no one had suggested weak was one of them.

'You thought I was stronger?' Her spine straightened, her chin pushed forward. She would *show* him that she was the opposite of weak, damn him. 'And I thought you were more intuitive than you apparently are, because you've missed what I was about to say completely.

'I *am* strong, Zach. I'm stronger than you'll ever imagine or know.' She bared her teeth in the semblance of a smile. 'You want me to work with you on this project? I'll do it. In fact, I'll work out the entire contract without a single complaint, just as you've wanted from the start!'

He had just better not blame her when he started to regret that she was still in his employ. 'Now, when do we leave for this trip?'

CHAPTER NINE

A PART of Zach wanted to treat Lily like the most fragile glass. To wrap her in cotton wool and carry her gently, so nothing could threaten even the least harm to her.

At first, Lily had been prickly and defensive after their talk at the coffee shop. It had taken hard work to see her relax again in his company.

And, all the while, his desire for her continued to torment him. He had thought the change in his knowledge of her had somehow ended her interest in him. The last day and a half had disproved that. She still wanted him, but was fighting to hide it.

Zach was tired of fighting the forces that drew him to her. His physical interest had developed into something so much more. He admired Lily more and more. He wanted to *show* her, in the best and most truthful way he knew how, just how special she was, even if he couldn't follow through with a long-term commitment. Maybe it was madness. He only knew he ached for her.

Lily examined the mass of licorice mixture in a vat at the final factory on their tour agenda. Zach watched her slender hands move as she tested the weight of the vat, and wanted to feel them caressing his chest, touching his face.

'It's heavy, isn't it? And that's just one small batch.' The owner grinned as they moved away.

'Let's take a look around, shall we?' Zach addressed his request to the owner, and Lily drew notebook and pencil from her bag.

The factory thrived in a concrete building with a large, built-on, hewn-log restaurant with windows overlooking a nearby creek. They moved from the receiving room to view the section of the factory where the flour was milled.

'It's a fully organic process from the day the wheat is planted to the day it ends up as flour here. We supply our flour to health food stores all over Australia. We also use it in our licorice, and in the cakes and some of the other products sold in the restaurant.' The owner showed them a handful of the grains.

Zach nodded, and hoped he looked more intelligent than he felt. Most of his brain space was taken up with noticing every move Lily made. She stepped closer to examine the wheat, and their arms brushed. Zach didn't quite manage to suppress a soft groan. Her gaze whipped to his and clung and, for once, the full strength of her desire for him shone through.

'I hadn't realised that flour was a key ingredient in licorice.' Lily looked at him, and confusion and questions shone in her eyes. Questions about *them*, not about this factory.

They continued their tour, and examined the tumbling machines that applied the many coats of fine chocolate to the licorice, before moving on to view the large restaurant kitchen. Lily continued to ask questions and take notes, but

Zach caught the slight breathlessness in her voice and reacted, because he was under the same spell.

Later, as Zach examined a long conveyor belt used for cooling the confection items in the factory proper, he heard Lily's name called in a questioning tone.

'Lily Kellaway? It *is* you. I could have sworn your mother said you were out of the country.' A woman broke away from the group making their way past. 'Don't tell me you've moved back to Albury?'

'Hello, um, Michelle.' Lily took the woman's arm and drew her away, and the factory owner drew Zach's attention with a complicated rundown of the batch flow they managed on each of the different days in the confectionery part of the factory.

Zach tried to take in the facts and figures. He heard no more of Lily's conversation, but was aware of her every second until she joined him again.

When she did, he glanced at her strained face and, without thinking about it, wrapped his arm around her shoulders and hugged her against his side. 'Are you okay?'

She looked up as he bent down to ask the question. His words landed a breath away from her lips. His train of thought disintegrated. She seemed to lose track, too, her gaze fixed on his mouth. The owner had walked on ahead and they were momentarily alone.

Zach forced himself to release her, but stayed by her side, unable and unwilling to take even a few steps away from her. That single moment of vulnerability on her part, even though she hadn't explained it, added to so many others to unlock something inside Zach at last.

Feelings welled up in him that he couldn't explain, or

even define, except to know that he wanted her to believe in herself, to regain her shaken confidence. His previous determination to be cautious towards her fled in the face of these feelings.

At the end of the tour, Zach left Lily browsing the gift shop and drew the owner aside.

Even as he walked away from Lily, his connection to her remained. He fixed his gaze on the owner, so he could impart the good news of his decision. 'As the last on the list, and the cartel's chosen leader, I know you've been on ten-terhooks. I won't keep you waiting any longer. I'm happy with the figures provided by your accountant, and I'm more than impressed with all the factories, yours included. You'll receive my written offer within the next few days.'

The owner gave a whoop and pumped Zach's hand as he thanked him. Zach nodded, and excused himself so the man could go share his news. And, before he went back to Lily, he pondered. Why had she not mentioned that her family lived so close by? Surely she would want a chance to see them during her stay here? They rarely got together...

On impulse, he pulled out his cell phone. A call to the phone's information service, and another quick one, and he tucked the phone away and strode purposefully to join Lily as she laid claim to a bag bulging with goodies from the gift shop.

Outside, Zach handed Lily into the rental car in silence. It was that or snatch her close there and then and kiss her to oblivion.

'It was a good tour, the best factory of the bunch.' Her words were soft, and somehow hesitant, but also held that breathlessness that Zach felt inside himself.

'I told him I'll buy in.' One glance at her was nowhere near enough. He forced his gaze back to the road, but couldn't hold back any longer. 'I still want to make love to you, Lily. If you gave me the slightest sign that you were willing, I would follow through on that right now.'

Did Zach have any idea what he was saying? How it tempted Lily? She had wanted memories from this trip. Now Zach was letting her know that her condition *didn't* stop his desire for her. He wanted her even so. She must have been mistaken about his reaction at the coffee shop! Or perhaps he had just needed some time to adjust to the knowledge.

She gave way to the longing to be accepted just as she was. And she knew she would take this chance while she could. A chance to make love with him, just once, while they both wanted it, while they were here in the heart of the countryside. A time out of time. 'Then I'm giving you a sign, Zach. Please make love to me.'

'I will.' He pledged it, all other thoughts buried beneath this need.

Silence licked around them in tendrils of expectant heat as he drove them towards the secluded Manor House Restaurant Inn set on private acreage a few kilometres beyond the tiny town.

When they stopped in the parking lot beside the restored inn, with its gabled roof, sweeping verandas and high, mullioned windows, the blue of Lily's eyes had darkened almost to indigo. She fumbled with the catch of her door, but her words were steady and determined when she spoke. 'Let's go inside.'

He checked them in quickly. They climbed the carved-wood staircase in silence. His heart raced when she moved unerringly to the door allocated to her, opened it with a trembling hand and pushed it wide.

In a heartbeat, he had shoved their luggage inside, freed his hands, and backed her into the room. He closed and locked the door behind them.

'Lily. Beautiful, wonderful Lily.' He kissed the side of her face, the shell of her ear, and revelled in the shudder that coursed through her.

'You're a very special woman. I want to show you how much I mean that.' He kissed her so long and so deeply that he almost lost himself. When he finally drew back, they were both panting, trembling.

Her arms snaked upward to twine around his neck.

Zach drew a ragged breath. 'I want to hold you as close to me as I can. I want to touch you and explore you and learn you.'

She moaned and closed her eyes. Outside, an owl hooted. The country sound gave this moment a feeling of being something out of reality. Zach pushed the thought aside. How could this be any more real?

When her hands reached for the buttons of his shirt, he held her gaze and felt the blaze of heat as her fingers worked to bare his chest. He shrugged the shirt away and clenched his teeth as she touched him, then leaned forward to press her mouth against his hot skin.

'You're going to kill me.' It seemed perfectly natural to tell her so. And equally right to draw her knit shirt from the waistband of her jeans and tug it over her head.

The freckles didn't go beyond her shoulders. The skin below was creamy white, soft and fragrant. With a deep groan, he buried his face in her neck, then after a moment dipped his head to trace the cleft between her breasts with his lips.

'I need you.' He could barely manage to say even that much. His hands tightened on her shoulders, stroked upward and into her hair.

She moved her hands across his back. 'I need you, too.'

'Give me your mouth. Please.' A harsh command, a begging request. Then he simply swooped, his heart hammering, every thought focussed on having her, giving to her, bringing them together.

Her lips melded to his in a fit so lush, so perfect, his entire body thrummed. His heart beat fiercely, and a well of something deep and agonising rose up.

She's the only one who can answer this feeling. The only one...

'Come to bed with me.' Her soft words wrapped around him, warmed him with sensual promise as her gaze met his, her eyes shimmering with unspoken feelings. 'Let's not think. Let's just be together.'

Zach breathed her name as he joined her on the bed. His arms found their way naturally around her as though they, and his body, had been made for this, for holding her, for being with her.

Yet her words stayed with him—because he *wasn't* thinking, was instead reacting fully with his senses, and what if that wasn't the right thing to do? What if Lily somehow expected more from him than that?

The thoughts came then, reminders of Lily's unwillingness to be intimate without commitment. He had started this for good reasons, but those reasons would not be enough for her later.

She stroked her hands across his back and shoulders, and onto his chest. 'Hold me, Zach. Just…hold me.'

'Yes.' He told himself this was fine, but, try as he might, he couldn't ignore those internal warnings. He wanted to, but he couldn't. Because he couldn't share in the emotional commitment that should be part of it.

Lily deserved all that and nothing less.

His arms stiffened as he confronted what he was doing far too late, where it would lead them, and the hurt that would follow if he let this happen.

This would hurt her anyway, and he tried to soften his words as he forced his arms to let her go. 'I'm sorry. I shouldn't have started this. I wanted to ignore what I know of you, but it is part of you.' It wasn't wrong for her to want commitment in an intimate relationship. It was right. But Zach couldn't give her that. 'The way you are won't change, and unfortunately I can't, either…'

His words petered out, stilled by the look of deep hurt in her eyes. With her lips pressed together and her eyes forced wide, as though if she let them relax they would reveal far too much, she shifted away from him and climbed from the bed.

'We got carried away. It was just desire.' She moved into the sitting room, drew a wrap from her travel bag, and slipped her arms into it. 'I wish I hadn't let things get this far, either!'

He silently dressed too. 'I can't give you what you need, Lily.' How he wished it was different. 'The depth of commitment and time someone like you would have to have.' *A woman made for loving and being loved in return.*

She gave a shrug that cut right to his heart. 'Caring about me would be too high-maintenance for you. I get it.'

Her words held a tremble that made him want to kick himself all the way back to Sydney, and keep on kicking. Disappointment and hurt still lurked in her eyes.

All he could do was stay silent, because he *couldn't* maintain a relationship with her. His commitment to his family would tear it down, just as had happened once before. 'I wish things could be different.'

'Oh, I'm sure you do.' Mouth pinched, she lifted her chin and held her shoulders back. 'But things aren't different. I'd like you to leave now, please. I want to be alone.'

There was nothing he could do. Zach gathered his travel bag and let himself out the door.

CHAPTER TEN

'HAS Ms Kellaway left her room yet?' Zach stood in the reception foyer and asked the question of the cheery Manor House owner who stood behind the old-fashioned check-in counter. Zach wanted to dislike the guy, simply because he looked happy.

'I believe so, but allow me to try the room.' The man reached for the phone.

'Thanks.' Last night gnawed at Zach. The knowledge that he had hurt Lily concerned him most of all, but something else gnawed at him, too. He had made a phone call yesterday on the spur of the moment while Lily had browsed the gift shop at the confectionery factory. Snap decisions weren't his usual style, but he had made one and acted on it. Now he had to tell Lily about it.

Surely she would welcome a face-to-face meeting with her parents? So why did he feel so uneasy about it now?

Because you know you've hurt her. You should have left her alone.

Yes...

He sensed her presence a moment before the owner's

gaze moved beyond him, and the man returned the phone to its cradle.

Zach turned. There were shadows under Lily's eyes, and in them. His stomach tightened as he acknowledged he had caused those shadows. 'I tried your room before I came down, but there was no response.'

'I went for a walk along the creek. The kookaburras gave a morning chorus for me from the gum trees. I'd forgotten what that sounded like.' Strain rasped in her voice. The same strain he felt inside, but she was putting on a valiant effort at normality. 'I'm ready to leave any time you like.'

'You've eaten already?' He had to forget wanting and needing her. For both their sakes, he had to forget.

She folded her arms. 'I haven't eaten, but I don't mind waiting until we get to the airport.'

All her barriers were up again, only this time it was worse. 'I invited your parents to have breakfast with us this morning.' He could see no other way to tell her, and the older couple should be here any minute. 'I thought you might enjoy a chance to see them. I meant to tell you yesterday afternoon, but it slipped my mind.'

His thoughts had been wrapped up in her.

At his announcement, her face closed up. She drew a sharp breath. 'How do you even know?'

'That they live in Albury-Wodonga? I heard the woman from the tour group say so yesterday.' He had only half tuned in to the conversation, but had heard that much before they'd moved out of range. 'It prompted me to try to give you some time with your family.'

'I'm not useless and incapable of expressing the desire to

fit a visit with my parents into our schedule.' Her low words struck out at him. 'If I'd wanted to do it, I would have.'

'I've made a mistake, haven't I? I'm sorry. After last night—'

'Last night has no bearing on anything.' She kept her voice low, but each word rejected him. 'We both got carried away by desire when we should have controlled it. But you've made it clear you didn't really want even a one-night stand with me, and I hope I've made my opinion clear now, too. Anything we thought we had is finished.'

'I stopped to protect *you*, Lily.'

'Whatever you say.' She obviously didn't want to believe him. 'Well? Where's this breakfast taking place?' Her face tipped up and her mouth firmed. She stalked towards the dining room. 'We're meeting them here, I assume?'

'That's right.' He watched her move to a table for four, choose a chair and sit in it, her back ramrod-straight.

Zach cautiously took his own seat beside her. He had only just done so when a middle-aged couple entered the dining room and quickly scanned it. When they spotted Lily and Zach seated side by side, they hurried over.

'Mr Swift. How nice of you to invite us to join you.' Lily's mother, thin, well-kept and…hard-looking…allowed her husband to seat her to Zach's left at the table. 'You must call me Dorothea, and my husband is Carl.'

'And I'm Zach.' He forced a smile, disconcerted by that rigid edge in the older woman. Physical similarities to Lily were there. They shared the same slim build, the same straight nose. Both had blue eyes, but Lily's were usually warm. Dorothea's seemed curiously devoid of life.

Lily's father, round-framed glasses perched high on the

bridge of his nose, gave Zach a thoughtful examination. Her father wore his grey beard and hair cropped close, and was tall with slightly stooped shoulders. He shook Zach's hand. 'I've read about a number of your success stories. You've dealt with quite a few influential and important people.'

Zach returned their greetings, but his attention was fixed on Lily's silent presence beside him as the small but salient facts began to sink in.

Her parents had taken their seats without more than a glance in her direction. No hellos. No, *it's wonderful to see you.* No kisses, no hugs. They had greeted *him*, and ignored their daughter. Why?

'Hello, Dad. Mum.' Lily's carefully controlled voice revealed no feeling. 'You both look well.'

'Run ragged with the usual volunteer work, but we're keeping our heads above water.' Her mother dispensed the response, and turned to Zach again. 'We do our best to be community-minded, you know.'

'A trait your daughter appears to have inherited.' He said it without inflection while his mind grappled with the re-alisation that her parents appeared more interested in him, and in themselves, than in Lily.

His conversation with Lily about last night hung over him, too, unresolved and uncomfortable. He wished they could be alone to maybe try to discuss things further. But then, what good would that do? Nothing had changed. 'Lily, too, is an active volunteer.'

'Really?' Dorothea Kellaway seemed to flounder. 'Well, I'm sure that's very nice.'

After an awkward pause, Lily's mother turned to her.

'Where do you volunteer? Is it any place that would know of, er, that would know your family?'

'I volunteer at the brain institute that helped with my rehabilitation after I moved to Sydney.' Lily's gaze was guarded, but also challenging.

Zach saw the pain in the backs of her eyes, and the spark of rebellious anger before she spoke again. 'I also run my own temp secretary agency, which is why I'm working for Zach at the moment. None of this has ever been a secret.'

'Well, we're always so busy when we phone you.' Her mother toyed with the edge of the table cloth. 'If there'd been more time to talk, perhaps—'

'You mean when I phone you.' Lily corrected gently. 'It's funny how things can get confused. Like some of my old friends thinking I'd moved overseas.' She looked away, but not before Zach saw her swallow hard.

Her mother had told people she was out of the country? It didn't take a genius to add it up. Her father hadn't said much, but this woman who called herself Lily's mother was ashamed of her! Zach's fists clenched beneath the table as he fought to control his reaction, his fury.

Lily's father cast a suspicious glance in his wife's direction.

'Well, I'd thought you might like to travel.' Dorothea almost snapped the words at her daughter. 'You didn't want the sanatorium, but your father and I set up an allowance so you wouldn't have to expose yourself.'

'But I've looked after myself. I haven't needed your allowance, or to be locked away.' Lily's low words brought a tight look to her mother's face before the older woman shifted her gaze.

'Let's order.' Lily's father spoke hurriedly.

A mixture of emotions stormed through Zach. Regret. Anger. Pride and fury. This wretched meeting was at his instigation, and the knowledge sat hard with him. Could he make things *any* worse for Lily?

'How is your agency going, Lilybell?' Her father raised his menu and buried his nose in it, but looked at her over the top with what might have been regret.

Lily lifted her menu, too, and her face softened as she looked at her father. 'It's flourishing.'

'Hmm. Well, I'm glad.' He disappeared into his menu again, thus avoiding a glare from his wife.

Dorothea plucked the menu wordlessly and rudely from Lily's hands, and Zach's gaze narrowed once again.

The waitress appeared.

Lily's chest rose and fell in shallow breaths, and Zach thought he could just, quite possibly, be on the verge of committing a crime of violence. Wringing Dorothea Kellaway's neck held a certain appeal.

Zach leaned towards Lily on a well of fierce protectiveness and deep regret. He set his lips against her ear. 'Let me end this. We'll just go.'

'No.' Steel threaded the single word. 'I'm not a coward.'

Dorothea hustled out her order to the waitress. 'And you can bring toast and a glass of water for Lily.'

Lily smiled nicely for the waitress as she turned to her. 'Actually, I'd like a pot of tea, yoghurt and stewed fruit, and toast and marmalade. Do you have low-fat French vanilla yoghurt?'

'Yes, we have that.' The waitress returned the smile and made a note on her order pad.

After a disapproving hesitation, her mother subsided.

Lily's father made his order in a subdued voice. Zach barely noticed, because he was seething so deeply it was all he could do to breathe normally and not start breaking things. He hadn't realised he had gripped Lily's hand beneath the table until she made a soft gasping sound and pulled it away.

'Toast. Bacon and eggs. Coffee. Juice.' He bit the words out, and made sure he gave the waitress eye contact to let her see he wasn't angry with her. 'Thank you. As quickly as you can manage it would be helpful.'

'So, Mr and Mrs Kellaway. How do you pass your time in Albury-Wodonga?' He'd forget calling them by their first names. They'd done nothing to warrant familiarity—quite the opposite, as far as Zach was concerned! 'Aside from your charitable works, that is?'

His jaw clamped, but words emerged through his clenched teeth. 'It's clear you haven't followed Lily's progress at all, which astounds me, considering she's forged a brilliant new career for herself in Sydney.'

'*Zach.*' Lily stiffened her spine even more than she already had.

Her father cleared his throat. 'I hold a management position at Towers University. Lily studied psychology there before—'

'I support Carl, of course.' Lily's mother quickly jumped in. 'A good man needs a strong woman behind him. We have quite a position in the community, you understand.' A tinkling laugh followed this pronouncement. 'One has to work to achieve such respect, but we don't mind, do we, dear?'

The food arrived. Lily's mother watched her eat her fruit and yoghurt as though she expected one or both to explode out of her bowl at any second.

Zach pushed his food around his plate, and wanted to stop all pretence of civility. He wanted to confront these people openly and utterly, and make them account for their behaviour towards their daughter.

For Lily's sake, he stuck with stilted, tedious small talk while the guilt for making this happen ate at him.

The moment the meal ended, he got to his feet, and took Lily's elbow in a tender hold that he hoped expressed the regret he couldn't yet speak out loud.

As she rose in response to his guiding grip, he offered a stiff nod to the two who remained seated at the table. 'We need to go. Lily and I can see ourselves off, so please don't get up. Finish your meal.'

'Goodbye, Mum.' Lily's gaze searched her mother's face before she turned to look at her father. Her expression softened a little. 'Bye, Dad. It was good to see you.'

Zach respected and admired her all the more just then as she gave her parents such courtesy. He managed not to express the wish that their remaining breakfast choke them. Instead he nodded, and hustled Lily out of the room.

The accommodation was pre-paid. Their bags waited at the ready for them. Zach passed several large bills to the owner. 'For the restaurant costs, if you wouldn't mind settling it once our guests leave. Please keep the change.'

A bag in each hand, he led the way towards the hire car. With each step, the fury he had suppressed during the meal rose. Those people, who called themselves her parents, treated Lily like an embarrassment. Particularly her mother, but her father shouldn't hide in silence while it happened.

His Lily.

They had apparently done so from the day her brain had been damaged, and somehow Zach doubted they had *ever* been particularly effusive in showing their love to her.

'You're twice as smart, innovative and capable as most people I could name.' He gritted the words as he flung their luggage into the back of the car and rounded it to get into the driver's side. 'They should acknowledge that fact!'

Lily climbed inside the car, too. 'What right have you got to say anything?'

She was right, but her parents should be shouting her praise from the rooftops, and showing people how proud they were of her. If she were his to keep, to have and to hold—

His breath caught as he realised the significance of those thoughts, and the long-term commitment they suggested. Well, if he had Lily in that way, if that miracle somehow happened—which it never would—he would praise her and be proud of her, and so much more.

Because he didn't trust his emotions, he subsided into tense silence.

They were halfway to the airport before Zach calmed down enough to notice that Lily was still silent too. He immediately turned off the road onto a tree-shrouded laneway and stopped the car. An apology was nowhere near enough, but he had to express his regret.

'I'm completely at fault for what happened back there.' He wanted to take her hand in his, but knew if he tried she would probably reject him again. So he told her the truth, and hoped it would go some way towards healing the fresh wound of this morning's meeting. 'Aside from last night, I can't think of a time when I've disliked myself more.'

Every word felt inadequate, but he pushed on. 'I should have asked if you'd like to see them. If I'd thought about the fact that you didn't speak of them much, I might have realised...'

His words trailed off, and he sought her gaze with a searching glance. 'I don't expect you to forgive me for arranging that episode, but I am sorry.'

She turned her head away, fixed her gaze at a point beyond her window. Her voice was flat. 'It's not as if their attitude is anything unusual.' Her face closed into a determined mask, and she turned her head to look back the way they had come. 'We should get back on the road. It wouldn't do to be late to the airport.'

Zach turned the car back onto the road, but his thoughts were still on their conversation. On all that had happened, and on the growing realisation of how much Lily truly had been forced to come to terms with.

Her mother had tried to hide her away in a sanatorium. If Lily had complied, would she still be there today, while her mother swanned about the place pretending her daughter didn't exist?

Zach wanted to take Lily straight to *his* mother. To give her the same love from Anne that had sustained him through the grief of losing his father, and through his fears about being able to hold up in his dad's footsteps.

He wanted to give Lily *family*. The one thing that had torn his life apart when he'd tried to commit to a woman.

At the airport, they separated briefly while he signed off on the use of the hired car. When he joined her again, it was to queue for their boarding passes and to check their luggage in. Lily didn't speak, but tension radiated from her. He didn't feel any better.

Memories of last night came back full-force as he absorbed her closeness, and with those memories came regret so deep he couldn't fathom it.

Zach acknowledged his confusion. Despite everything, he didn't ever want Lily to leave his life. He couldn't see his days without her there, part of them. Her sticky notes on his computer. Her forwarded reminders popping up in his email inbox just in time for her to come and tell him the same information when she retrieved it from her diary.

He cared for her. Too much. Too intensely. In ways he didn't want to examine. And it was all utterly hopeless, because he didn't have enough to give her. A few left-over crumbs of his life, after he'd handed the rest to his family and his job.

CHAPTER ELEVEN

'I'LL get some coffee. Do you want any?' Lily made the excuse because she needed a moment away from Zach.

'Nothing for me, thanks.' He let her go without protest.

Yet, as she walked away, she felt his gaze on her. Perhaps he was still angry over her parents' behaviour.

Well, she was angry, too. At him, *and* at her parents. Lily had been angry with her mum and dad for a long time. She hadn't realised the whole truth of that until this morning. They *should* have been there for her. Not just after her accident, but right through her life.

But Zach had rejected her, too, and then gone on to act as though *he* had a right to do that but her parents didn't.

While she waited for her coffee, Lily pulled out her cell phone to call Deborah, hoping just to hear her friend's calm, rational voice. There was no answer. As she disconnected, their flight was called.

After taking two sips of the coffee, she abandoned the rest into a trash bin. She joined Zach, and they made their way to the boarding area. Zach had just stepped through when she thought she heard her name called, and hesitated.

Several people filed past her and she looked back, and instantly recognised the man hurrying towards her. *'Richard.'*

He stopped so close to her that she could have touched him. She hadn't heard from him for twelve months, and suddenly here he was. How had he even known to find her here? What did he want?

'Lily. I understand from your parents that you're here with Zachary Swift.' His glance searched around her, behind her. 'I'd like to meet him.'

This was the man she had once pledged to marry. The man who had insisted she go kayaking in white water that day, despite her lack of experience, despite her protests.

Resentment stirred, but her life was what it was. And Richard was just a selfish, self-gratifying man who would have made her miserable.

In truth, she was well out of the relationship, and relieved beyond measure to know that he no longer made her feel anything but a rather abstract pity for the shallowness that lurked behind his pseudo-charming exterior.

'Did my mother put you up to this?' The moment she asked the question, she knew it was true. But why?

She let her gaze rove him indifferently, and said in calm, almost disinterested tones, 'I'm very well, Richard. My work is prospering. I'm in good health, all things considered. Thank you for asking.'

'You sound almost normal.' This fact appeared to confuse him. 'Where's your employer?' He all but snapped his fingers. 'Get him back here before your flight leaves. I want a word with him. I—' He cut himself off. 'I mean, the *university* could do with some funding, particularly in my area. It's a golden opportunity...'

'Ah.' So Richard wanted to meet the *prestigious* Zachary Swift. The man with money and connections who might give him a donation that would aid his climb through the ranks of university staff.

Richard was as bad as her mother, viewing everyone through a lens coloured by his desire to get to the top.

'My boss deals in the business of buying companies, and buying into companies. If you have one on your hands and need a buyer or a partner, make an appointment like everyone else.' She felt her lip curl in derision. 'Otherwise, stay away from us.'

The final boarding call came over the intercom. She turned and saw Zach paused, waiting for her, his gaze watchful, the rest of his face a blank mask.

She turned back to her ex-fiancé's angry face, and wondered how she could have been so blind about him. But, sadly, she already knew the answer. She had wanted to please her parents, and had tried not to see Richard's selfishness and his other faults. They had come home to roost the day he'd realised she would never get her full brain function back. Clearly, he hadn't improved with the passage of time!

An airline official approached. 'Ma'am? Are you taking this flight, or staying behind?'

'I'm taking it.' She turned away from Richard and moved towards Zach.

The flight was short, and Lily and Zach ended up seated in separate parts of the plane because of some mix-up with the boarding passes. Lily didn't mind. She welcomed the time away from Zach to try to pull her thoughts and emotions together.

When they arrived at Sydney airport, it hummed with noise. The moment Zach turned his cell phone back on inside the terminal, it rang.

'I'll get a luggage trolley.' Lily left him to stand beside their bags and answer his call.

When she came back with a trolley, she heard him address the caller as 'Steele', and knew it was a call from his finance manager.

'Is it really necessary for me to handle this problem right now?' Zach tossed their luggage onto the trolley, and started pushing it one-handed as he scowled into the phone.

Lily moved along beside him. She had told Zach she would work out her contract to the end. But would he still want that now, after all that had happened? Pride wouldn't allow her to ask again to leave.

'Why are Gunterson and Greig so upset? We got the proposal to them on time, and they sounded quite positive about the deal.' Zach's hand clenched around the cell phone and his voice harshened. 'Surely, whatever problem it is, it can wait until Monday?'

Steele talked on for another minute. Then Zach ended the call and snapped the phone shut.

Lily turned to him. 'What's wrong?'

'It's the Mulligan project.' He grimaced, and shoved the trolley faster as they approached the building's exit doors. 'They're thinking of pulling out.'

'What do you need to do to fix the problem?'

He gave a flat laugh. 'Wine them, dine them. Convince them they're the most important project I have on my books.'

Even if they weren't, but in fact the Mulligan project was worth a lot of money.

They made their way into the taxi queue and began the slow shift forward. Stop, start, stop, start.

Zach handled their luggage without seeming to even think about it. 'In my absence, Gunterson and Greig have gone cold on our proposal. Despite Steele's efforts, they refuse to talk to him or explain the reason for their change of heart. The deal was all but sewn up, and now I'm going to have to try to get it back to that position.'

And suddenly Lily had a focus, *and* a way to prove herself. To show she could just go on, no matter what had happened between them. No matter that Zach hadn't been able to make love to her in the face of her disability. She seized the chance to direct her thoughts towards fixing this business problem.

'What about a long lunch meeting with drinks and lots of table talk? Right now—today? Given that it's the weekend, and they'll know you're sacrificing your time for them, something like that might be your best bet.'

'That's a good idea.' He hesitated for just a moment. 'The lunch would go a lot better if you were there.'

She cautioned herself to remember that his invitation meant nothing at all, personally. Even so, she wanted to believe he still valued her *somehow*, even if only as his temporary secretary. 'You really think my presence would be of some help?'

'Yes. I'll bet you could think of a great place for the lunch, too.' He reminded her about her galloping garçon efforts that first day at work. 'Something good like that would get them in the right mood.'

Although they spoke of business matters, Zach's gaze on her held awareness, regret, hunger. Would it ever end— this heart-deep longing she felt for him?

'How many people work for the Mulligan operation?' She tucked her bottom lip in while she considered his request.

'Five hundred workers with specialised skills they won't be able to use elsewhere.'

'That's a lot of people and jobs. Why don't we book a venue right now? In fact, why not that fabulous cliff-top restaurant overlooking Whale Beach?'

Zach nodded and flipped open his phone once again, and Lily assured herself she could do this, could maintain her self-control for one short afternoon, and not fall prey again to the need that had swept her up during their trip away.

'The afternoon went well, I think. There's something to be said for setting.' Lily made the comment as they emerged from the taxi outside her apartment in the late afternoon. Nerves pulled at her, and she struggled to ignore them.

'It was as successful as we could have hoped.' Zach drew out her travel bag and leaned in to ask the driver to wait, then turned back to her. His hair was wind-tousled. When he stepped close to her, she could smell sea air on his clothes and in his hair. 'In large part due to you choosing that venue.'

'I know it cost you a lot of dollars. I'm very easy with your money, aren't I?' She wasn't really worried about that. He would have vetoed it if he'd disliked the idea. But she *was* uneasy, now that the day was over. What would happen next? 'I'd heard how beautiful the views were by sea plane over Sydney Harbour, but that's the first time I'd seen them from that perspective.'

'Yes. Very lovely.' But Zach's gaze rested on her face, and a chord resonated within her at the intensity of that look.

This afternoon, at times when she'd caught his gaze on her, it had seemed like he desired her and more. Oh, she was so confused! They walked to her front door, and he put the bag down. When he looked at her, she simply wanted to melt into his arms again. Why was it so easy for her to lose sight of all that had happened between them?

'Palm Beach and Whale Beach are both so beautiful, too. The Norfolk Island pines and that blue, blue water. The long stretches of golden sand and palm trees.' She forced the words to a stop.

But the few hours, despite being primarily for business purposes, had held a forbidden magic for her.

The views from the cliff-top restaurant windows. The feeling of Zach at her side through the afternoon. His hand clasped around hers as he helped her alight from the sea plane. The lapping of the sea beneath their feet as they'd walked the wharf towards the waiting restaurant car.

And that long, silent walk on the beach while they'd given their guests some space and time to discuss their options in private. Tension had buzzed between them, but she had soaked up that time together and tried not to think ahead.

'You looked beautiful with the sea behind you, and nothing but endless sand beneath your feet.' His voice was deep and hungry.

He seemed to realise it at the same time she did.

'I hope Gunterson and Greig's delegates will push ahead with the deal, now.' The key eluded her as she dug around in her purse.

'Whether they do or not, I'm glad I had you with me today. I doubt things would have worked out half as well without you there.'

Just as she found the key, his hand closed over hers. He lifted her hand and kissed her fingertips. Only that, but she wanted to cry.

Their gazes caught and held, and his mouth brushed hers while her heart cried *yes*, even as *she* cried no.

'No, Zach.'

He made a harsh sound. Turned his head away. 'You'll stay with me to the end of the contract.' He made it a statement.

She tipped her chin in confirmation. 'Like I said, I'm not a coward. But please go now, Zach. It's been a draining few days, and this isn't helping.'

His fists tightened at his sides and a flare of something dark washed across his face. 'There are things I want, no, *need* to know about what happened to you. I feel as though you're blaming that somehow for what happened back at the inn.'

'I don't know what you mean.' Inside the house, Jemima must have become aware of Lily's presence and started to howl loudly, adding to the general feeling of cacophony resonating within her.

The luncheon aside, last night and this morning had been tough. She had to be tougher. 'I'll see you at work on Monday.'

She took up her travel bag and used it to encourage Jemima backward into the house when she opened the door. A moment later, the door was closed and locked behind her, and Zach's footsteps were receding down the path.

Zach left Lily because she'd made it clear she was at the end of her endurance, but questions remained unresolved in his head. He didn't think he would be able to rest until he had answers to those questions.

Just how bad had things been for her as a result of her injury? How exactly had it happened? *Was* she blaming her condition somehow for the fact that he had stopped their lovemaking? If so, she had misunderstood him.

She still seemed fragile when she arrived at work Monday morning, so Zach kept his distance, although he couldn't prevent his gaze from honing in on her often as she worked away at her desk.

Partway through the afternoon, she stepped into his office to leave a stack of typed letters for him to sign, and he looked up and caught her gaze on him. Wariness pooled in her eyes, and Zach knew he *had* to have those answers *now*, whether she felt ready or not. 'You never told me, you know. How did your accident happen? That was your ex-fiancé at the airport, wasn't it? I heard you say his name. Why did he leave you, Lily? Why didn't he stay by your side and help you through what had happened to you? Why did he come to the airport to see you?'

'My mother contacted Richard.' Lily said it in a flat tone that still somehow managed to convey a sense of hurt. 'He came to the airport in the hopes of meeting you.'

'Me? Why?' This wasn't the answer Zach had expected. 'What could he possibly want from me?'

'Money.' Lily shrugged her slender shoulders. She seemed almost embarrassed as she went on. 'A grant, I think, which would make him look good and help him climb the ranks at the university. My father used to support him financially. I thought he still did, but maybe he doesn't.'

Zach curled his hands into fists. 'What did you tell Richard when you spoke to him?' *Was that all he wanted from you?*

A small smile hovered around the edges of her mouth.

'I told him to stay away from you, from me, and from this business. I think he got the message.'

Zach's mouth lifted, too, before he sobered. 'You don't…still have feelings for him?'

'No…' She didn't sound entirely certain.

Zach stood and moved towards her. 'Surely you must know how you feel?'

'I don't care about him.' Her fingers trembled as she raised her hand to brush her hair back from her face. 'I guess I feel guilty.'

Zach leaned forward in a protective move he couldn't prevent. 'Why? I can't imagine you've done anything to harm him.'

'I feel guilty because I've blamed him for my accident, and everything that followed.' She dropped her gaze, long lashes covering her expressive eyes.

A warning rumble started in Zach's throat. If Richard had hurt Lily in any way… He kept his voice deliberately gentle. 'Was there a reason for you to blame him? Tell me what happened.'

Her gaze rose again. 'Richard organised a kayaking trip with some business associates he wanted to impress. They were all experienced, and he wanted his fiancée there to add to his status in their eyes. I told him I had no experience and didn't want to go, but he insisted.

'When we got into white water I realised I couldn't cope. I tried to paddle to the bank but I lost control, went under and hit my head on a submerged rock. The doctors at the hospital told me later that my brain had bounced inside my skull. I was unconscious when two of Richard's companions fished me out, during the rescue mission, and for some time after. If those people and the doctors hadn't acted so quickly and taken such care of me, I'd have died.'

Her eyes darkened with suppressed memories. 'Later, I blamed Richard. I've been blaming him for a long time, but I realise now that I can't blame him. He shouldn't have insisted I go, that's true, but it was my responsibility to say no and insist he make the trip without me.'

'I'll kill him with my bare hands.' Zach muttered an expletive beneath his breath. He stared at Lily, and wanted to hunt Richard down. 'It was at least partly his fault. The man was irresponsible—'

'Yes, I know.' She smiled as she cut him off. 'But ultimately I was in charge of myself. The accident happened because I made a poor choice.'

'Did you break up with him because you blamed him?' He could understand that, and he still wanted to pound on the guy. But he also wanted to comfort Lily, and he reached for her hands, holding them tight as he waited for her answer.

Lily shook her head. 'Richard didn't come to the hospital for almost a week. When he finally turned up, it was to tell me he couldn't remain engaged to someone who would never regain the full use of her brain. My parents rejected me as well. They wanted to hide me away somewhere so they didn't have to face what had happened to me. It hurt so much, Zach.'

Something inside his chest ripped apart. His voice was hoarse when he spoke. 'He didn't deserve you, Lily, and if that's the best your parents can do they don't deserve you, either.'

She tilted her head back to look into his eyes, her breath

catching as their gazes locked. 'I've had so much anger inside me. I don't want to be like that. I want to live my life—to embrace everything and not be afraid.'

'You've been incredible and strong and amazing, in the face of the kind of odds that would wipe some people out completely.' That was what Zach saw. He groaned. That tide of feeling that had begun to well inside him earlier rose up again. 'If there's any guilt, forgive yourself and put it behind you.'

He looked down into her eyes, and he could only want her. *This Lily. His* Lily.

'Why are you doing this to me, Zach?' Lily's question was fraught with pain. 'You act as thought you want me, hunger for me, and all I want is to yield to that like I did before. But my memory loss is repugnant to you. I was there when you rejected me at the Manor House Inn, remember? Please don't do that to me again.'

'No, it's not like that.' He hugged her against his chest, held her there as he tried to convey the wrongness of her words to her through his touch.

Slowly, carefully, he held her at arms' length. 'I don't give a single damn about the state of your memory, other than to hate that it causes you pain. When have I ever said otherwise, or even led you to believe it?'

'But you pushed me away.' Confusion clouded her eyes, but now there were other emotions to be seen in her gaze and expression as well. Soft, hesitant emotions that wrapped around his heart and squeezed.

'We intended to make love, and both of us knew it wouldn't turn into anything more than a night together in that rural setting so far away from all we know here. But you still stopped.' She drew a soft breath. 'It can only be because of my condition.'

'Maybe I shouldn't have stopped, because your condition had nothing to do with it, Lily. Nothing at all.' He growled the words, and then he went on. 'I stopped that night because I didn't want to hurt you by ending it after that. And all I did was make it worse, didn't I? At least, if we'd shared that, you'd have been sure of how much I desire you just as you are.

'I want to make love to you more than I've ever wanted anything in my life. I want to hold you and show you that you're wonderful. I care about you, Lily. More than I should. I wish I could give you the world.' He took a deep breath. 'I guess I didn't do a very good job of expressing empathy that day at the coffee shop. I hurt for you, and didn't know how to help you, and you were so prickly about it.'

She stared at him, and her breath caught on a sob of sound. 'Then make love to me now, Zach. Right now, so I *can* believe you desire me enough to do that.' She said it softly, and her eyes burned with both hunger and vulnerability. 'You can't give me the world. I know that. But give me this.'

The decision was made deep inside him before he could even consider standing against it. He tugged her into the outer office, snatched up her bag and pressed it into her hands. 'This time there'll be no going back for either of us. You understand that?'

'I understand.' She tipped that lovely chin again, looked into his eyes. Let him see the desire that fired her expression. 'Take me somewhere we can be alone.'

Take me… Emotion bubbled through Zach. Lily's revelations, the pain caused by her parents, her guilt over blaming Richard, all added up to make him *have* to prove to her that he found her utterly attractive, appealing on every level. 'There are things I want to show you—in my heart—I want, I need—'

'I want and need, too, so many things with you. I never expected to tell anybody how much it hurt me to lose my parents' support, and to wrestle with the guilt of blaming Richard for everything that happened.' She said it softly, and slipped her bag over her shoulder then headed for the door. 'Somehow, telling you those things has freed me, and I know now that I want this with you, just once. So *show* me, Zach.'

As on the night of his birthday party, he had her elbow in his grasp before she knew what was happening. He kissed her in the empty elevator. Pressed her against the cold, steel wall and ravaged her mouth, her face, her neck. And then his kisses softened, and he worshipped her slowly, tenderly, as his heart ached for her.

Lily wrapped her arms around him and held him as he counted the minutes until he had her in his bed.

His bed, because nothing else would do. Not for her. Not for him. Not for this.

The lift opened directly into the underground parking lot. They crossed to his car with a very circumspect distance of several feet between them. The area was deserted. He guided her to the car, and in the dim-lit silence he pulled her close again. Pressed against her. Kissed her again.

'Where are you taking me?' She asked it when they finally sat side by side on the leather seats. Her question underlined her acceptance that this would happen now, with the inevitability of the changing of the seasons or the ticking of a clock.

That powerful knowledge raced through him. He started the car and forced himself not to rush his movements. 'I'm taking you to my house, my bed.'

'Good. I want to be there.' She tossed her bag onto the floor of the car with an air of acceptance, and her hands came to rest, lightly clasped, against her thigh.

Zach covered those hands with one of his own, then reluctantly let go.

The drive to his home took time, and that time could have defused the heat and emotion that had brought them both to this point.

Instead, each silent moment, each breath she took, each breath he took, seemed to just make more of it.

Until he finally said, on the brink of madness as they arrived outside his house, 'If I don't have you, I'll die.'

'If I don't have you, I might very well die too.' Her laugh was half sob.

He turned the car into the driveway, pressed the button for the automatic garage door, and tucked them away safely inside.

CHAPTER TWELVE

As Zach strode through his house, pulling Lily along by the hand, his destination and intent clear, Lily blurted one breathless concern. 'Daniel. You said he drops by here a lot.'

'He's at school, and he never comes here during working hours.' He pushed a door open and drew her into a cool, quiet room.

His room.

He reached for her, but, instead of tugging her forward with the demand that raged through him, he held her gently. Drew her to him gently.

'Your brother is a wonderful boy.' Zach had a family in the truest sense of the word. Maybe today, as they shared these moments, Lily could pretend just briefly that she was a part of that, too. Oh, what was she saying—thinking?

'A brother who can get the sulks as well as the next person, and, if you think small talk is going to make me forget how much I want you, you're wrong.' He buried his face in her hair and took a long, unsteady breath.

He kissed the crown of her head and caressed her shoulders, and shifted his gaze to look deep into her eyes. 'I can't ever be other than who and what I am, Lily. Even knowing that, I don't think I can walk away from this. I want you and need you too much.'

'I'm not asking you to stop, or trying to distract you. I know this is only about right now for us, and it's what I want too.' She couldn't deny herself this chance to be in his arms, to make love with him utterly.

Opening up about her hurts to him had taken away her last reserve. She would have this, hold this, carry this away with her, and maybe there would be pain later, but Lily refused to think about that now.

'The only thing I need to know is that this isn't an act of pity because of what I said back there in your office...' She couldn't bear to think that even an ounce of that emotion drove Zach's desire for her. 'I won't be your goodwill project, Zach. Anything but that.'

His face tightened with possessive determination. 'What you said to me mattered, because you trusted me enough to say it. I respect you more now than I ever have, because I understand how what you've been through has hurt you. I want you. I want to take away some of that hurt if I can. It has nothing to do with pity. Now, come here and let me love you.'

The room with its bank of built-in closets, the windows with gold and green drapes drawn closed, and the bed so very close to them, all faded from her mind as he drew her into his arms and began to whisper kisses onto her lips.

She wrapped her arms around his neck as she had done in the elevator, but softly, softly, and sighed as he kissed the nape of her neck. Pressed a caress of her own against the hot skin near his ear. Drew his head down to hers, and offered so much more of herself than she had believed she would ever give. To Zach. To any man.

But, oh, how could she think of *any* man? There was only Zach, and what he made her feel, and what she wanted him to feel for her. How could she hold back? Richard had never made her feel this way.

Her hands caressed the strong arms that held her close, rose to his shoulders and flexed against the muscles there.

She had imagined him raised above her, his shoulders bared to her touch. Had held him almost naked in her arms, just once, before he'd let her go. Now she would know all of it, and it was almost—*almost*—too much.

He threw back the quilt. Drew her shoes from her feet and settled her on soft ivory sheets. Kicked off his shoes and joined her. 'I want to hold you. Let me just hold you…close to my heart.'

At those wrenching words her heart melted, and any hope of guarding her feelings disappeared. This was enough. It had to be enough.

'Let *me* hold *you*.' She touched his face, the starkness and heat and the rasp of his skin. Drew in her breath, taking the scent of him deep inside, to a place in her memory that would never forget. She didn't want to forget any of this. Not a moment of it. In her heart, she knew she wouldn't.

Was this love? Real love? The for ever, all-encompassing kind? This deep, abiding need for him that had grown and shaped itself into something that lived with her, breathed with her, as much a part of her as her own deepest thoughts or secrets?

She had never cared for Richard like this, even when she'd tried to blind herself to his true personality. Now he was a formless shadow, less than a tendril of mist in the recesses of her mind. Zach owned it all.

Zach drew her in so close that their bodies touched, melded to each other perfectly, and then he lifted up above her, and looked down into her face through hazel eyes that shone with sweet, tender desire. And he kissed her slowly, druggingly, and she melted. Melted completely away...

'Lily of the valley. Beautiful, delicate and sweet. Will you fortify my soul?' The words poured out of Zach from a deep, still place that ached for only her. That needed her in ways he was only beginning to know.

He looked deep into her eyes, and began the slow and sensual task of removing every barrier that separated them. Shaking fingers opened the buttons on her blouse. Caressed soft, butter-yellow lace and warm creamy skin beneath.

He swallowed hard, biting back words that welled up. Promises and hopes and dreams, and things that he had denied himself years ago. That he had given up willingly because honour demanded it, but now there was this. 'I don't deserve this. I don't deserve *you*.'

Torn, longing, hungry, he cupped her face in his hands, stroked the soft skin. Watched her eyes darken as she leaned into that touch. Lowered his mouth to kiss her again because he couldn't do anything else.

Long moments later, he drew back enough to say, 'You take my breath away. Tell me again that you want this. Tell me you want it as much as I do.'

'I want to make love with you more than you'll ever be able to imagine or dream.' With those simple words, she felled him.

Emotion welled, wrapped around his heart, and even

though his body ached for her something deep inside ached and longed so much more.

Her hands rose in tentative exploration. Colour stained her cheeks as she met his gaze. 'Since that night at the Manor House Inn, since long before it, I've dreamed of this. Of being able to touch your skin, to see you above me…'

'Then touch me. Look at the body that wants you so much.' He helped her with the buttons of his shirt. Then he shrugged it off. Let it drop to the floor.

Her hands ran lightly over him. Touching, caressing, knowing him, until he felt he had always been hers, and she his.

When the last piece of clothing fell away, he looked at her and words crowded up and poured out. 'Let me show you how beautiful you are.'

And he gave her all the need and hunger that had built inside him as each day had etched her deeper into his senses, his thoughts, his emotions. He may not have the words. May not be able to promise her for ever, but he would give her this, and his fulfilment would be in hers.

Lily opened her mind, her spirit and her body to Zach in the only way she could. Utterly. Totally. And when he had loved her absolutely, gaze locked to her gaze, hands and body reverencing her until they lay twined in each other's arms in shattered stillness at last, she finally admitted the truth.

She loved him. Right down to the depths of her heart and spirit and soul, in a way she had never loved before, and never would again. The realisation brought a gasping sob to her throat. She choked it back, but a small sound escaped.

'What is it?' Zach whispered the question, and brushed

his mouth across hers. Touched her hair with gentle fingers, and clasped his hand over hers where it rested on his chest.

Could he know what she had discovered? Had she revealed the truth as they made love? Had it shone from her eyes? Could he possibly share those feelings?

His heart beat steadily beneath her fingertips, and he tucked her closer still in an intimacy that gave comfort, even as she struggled to come to terms with her new-found knowledge.

Lily pushed the thoughts away. She wouldn't think about her discovery or ask questions. Not yet. Right now, she was too vulnerable. She would want to believe too easily that this had changed everything, when they both had agreed that it wouldn't.

'It's nothing.' Shadows danced against the curtained windows, and danced at the edges of her heart and mind. She closed her eyes to the shadows at his windows, and distanced herself from those lying in wait at the edges of her heart. 'It's nothing at all.'

Instead, she embraced the comfort of his closeness. Nestled to his side. As he stroked his fingers across her shoulders, against her neck, through her hair, a soft lassitude stole though her.

When Lily woke, the shadows had lengthened. There must have been a tree outside the window, for long, gnarled arms seemed to reach right into the room ready to snatch her into their dry, crackling hold.

Disturbed by the mental image, she eased away from Zach's slumbering form, and paused to look down into the face now relaxed in sleep. A band tightened around her heart. How she wanted to wake beside him every day! To reach for him, and be drawn into his arms and welcomed. Making love had changed everything for her, but Zach had made his attitude clear before they did this.

Why can't you love me and want me for ever, Zach? Why can't I be enough for you to overcome those choices you've made about your life?

Heart sore, she gathered her belongings and drew away to the other end of the house. She used her cell phone to order a taxi, then tidied herself in the guest bathroom and let herself out of the house.

He hadn't made promises. This had been their beginning, and now it was their end. No matter how much that knowledge hurt her, she had no choice but to accept it.

'Come on, Lily, answer for me. You're my last hope.' *I need you with me while I face this.*

The inner admission of that need came freely to Zach, but it was a revelation that couldn't be examined now. He stood in the middle of his mother's living room and gripped the cordless phone in tight fingers. His brother had been gone since eight this morning. Over nine long hours, and nobody had seen him.

His mother wrung her hands. 'I should have seen him onto the bus. No, I should have driven him to and from school every day myself.'

Zach shook his head. 'There's never been a hint of trouble. I've only just got around to vetting the people who walk onto my floor at work. Why us?' Theirs was a wealthy family, but certainly not the wealthiest, or the only one around.

'Hello?' Lily's voice, slightly hoarse, came at last.

She had left him after their lovemaking, after the most

wonderful and moving moments he had experienced in his life, and had slipped away while he slept. Before he'd had time to come to terms with the hurt of that, or wonder at her reasoning or his own feelings, his mother had phoned in distress because Daniel was missing.

'It's Zach. Daniel's been gone since early this morning. We can't—we haven't been able to track him down.'

'Oh, Zach. I'm coming. I'll get a taxi straight away.'

The band around his chest eased the tiniest bit. 'I'm at Mum's house.'

'Give me the address. I'm not sure if it's in my diary. I'll leave right now.' After he rattled off the address, she drew a hurried breath. 'Daniel will come back to you safe and sound, Zach. He has to, because you love him so much.'

Those words echoed through Zach's thoughts as he paced the floor. Between them, he and his mother had contacted every conceivable person who might have known where Daniel had gone, what had happened to him. And they had discovered he hadn't been seen since before school.

'What more can we do?' His mother seemed to read his mind. She sprang up from the sofa to pace the floor, then moved to the window to stare out. 'I can't even tell if any of his casual clothes are missing, so I don't know whether he *planned* to go somewhere other than school today, or something…worse happened.'

Her mouth tightened. 'I should know every stitch of clothing he owns. A younger mother would be able to remember.'

'Don't do that to yourself.' He gave her a brief hug. 'I couldn't tell you everything that's in my own wardrobe, let alone anyone else's.'

'Oh, Zach.' She leaned into him briefly before drawing away.

'If it's a kidnapping, and they plan to contact us with ransom conditions, we could put him in jeopardy by contacting the police.' He stared out the window onto the street. 'If we *don't* contact the police, our resources are limited and we may be wasting precious time that could be spent by the authorities in trying to locate him.'

'I'm going to look through his room again.' His mother was still there when Lily arrived.

Zach watched Lily alight from the taxi and pay the driver, then hurry towards the front of the house. He opened the door before she could ring the bell. She looked straight into his eyes. A moment later, her arms were around his waist, and he was gripping her hard, close.

'I got here as quickly as I could.' She released him and stepped back, and he noticed that her eyes were red-rimmed and puffy. She looked like she had been crying long before he'd called her, and there was only one likely reason for that.

A reason he had been trying to forget since he'd first held her naked in his arms. They couldn't go on, because nothing had changed for him, even though he wished that were different.

Not now, you can't think of it now.

Her gaze searched his face. 'Is there any news?'

'Nothing. Come in. Mum will be glad to see you.'

Lily followed Zach inside his mother's house. Would Anne Swift be happy to see her? Or would she resent the intrusion, and feel that as an outsider to her family Lily shouldn't be here?

One look at Anne's tight, distressed face as she emerged from a room set off the hallway, and Lily forgot everything but the need to comfort her and help her.

Anne reached out a tremulous hand.

Lily squeezed it, and led Anne to sit on the living-room sofa.

After she took her seat beside Anne, she turned her gaze to Zach once more. 'What do you know for certain about Daniel's disappearance so far?'

Zach stood at the window and outlined all they had done. He explained that an aunt and uncle were at his house even now, in case Daniel happened to turn up there. Or someone else tried to contact Zach there about the boy.

'Have you contacted the police?' Lily hardly dared to say it aloud.

'Not yet.' Zach's shoulders tensed. 'We'll have to do it soon, if nothing else happens.'

Lily wanted to hold Zach and never let go. She wanted to pour encouragement and hope into him, and tell him not to give up. 'How much longer will you wait?'

'We'll wait until six p.m. If there's nothing by then—'

'That gives us almost half an hour.' She drew her notebook and a pencil from her bag and beckoned Zach over. 'Draw the curtains wide. We'll all be able to see anyone approaching. We need to go over every conversation, every social outing, all Daniel's school projects, and friends' parties, anything that might give us a clue.'

For the next twenty minutes, Zach and his mother turned their minds inside out as they considered all that had been happening in Daniel's life. The picture that emerged to Lily was of a boy who had changed from gregarious and outgoing, to more serious and quiet. Yet he hadn't struck her as unhappy. 'What were you like as a ten and eleven-year-old, Zach? What did you want out of life then?'

'I played with school friends, loved to kick a footy around, didn't care too much about my studies.' He gave his mother a wry glance. 'Homework time was a bit of a trial, but I eventually pulled myself together and got serious.'

'Did you get serious at Daniel's current age? When you were facing the looming thought of high school?' Something whispered at the edges of Lily's mind, nagging at her. If she could just pin it down...

Zach's eyebrows rose. He looked at Lily, then at his mother. 'Yeah. I changed a lot around that age. I got really interested in maths and commerce, actually.'

Lily's heart began to thump, but what if she was wrong? It was the wildest thought, with so little to back it up. Nevertheless, she said it. 'What if Daniel's attitude has been changing, and you haven't noticed? What if he's gone from being a young sports nut, playing with his friends, to a serious boy considering his future?'

Anne leaped to her feet. 'Oh, he has become serious. He has changed a lot in the past few months, but how does this help us?'

'He wanted to go to a Melbourne boarding school to study mechatronics.' The words finally burst from Lily. Somehow, they were all on their feet, and she turned to Zach hopefully. 'You vetoed the idea, but do you think he accepted that? Did you find some local classes for him to attend? How did he respond to the offer of those?'

Zach's face tightened. 'I made a couple of enquiries, but

came up blank. I told him there were no classes available and forgot about it. I thought it was just a whim of his.'

Anne gasped, and her eyes widened. 'Daniel didn't say anything to me. Why would he want to go so far away from here? From his family?'

A silence stretched as mother and son looked at each other. Shared the concern and pain, and a dose of self-re-crimination.

Lily broke that silence, but not before accepting that the bond of commitment and love they shared was nothing she had known, or would ever know. 'Is it possible that Daniel might have tried to make his way to that Melbourne boarding school on his own? Might his desire to attend there next year have driven him to do that, if he believed the chance had been refused him?'

'We have to consider it.' Zach snapped it out.

His mother spoke at the same time. 'What if he's not still there, or didn't even go?'

'I'll find out. I'll hire a private plane. That'll be the fastest.' Zach lifted the phone, and then turned to his mother. 'Use your cell phone to alert the train and bus services and the airports again. Especially anything coming back from Melbourne. Their security people are to watch for him in case he's already on his way back.

'We have to follow this possibility. It makes more sense than anything else so far, and you'll be here in case the phone rings…or anything.'

A movement outside drew Lily's gaze. She stared, then gasped at the sight of a boy with a gangling build dressed in a tee-shirt and jacket and a pair of grey school trousers, moving up the pathway with his shoulders hunched, his backpack almost dragging on the ground as he lugged it along beside him. A taxi drove away behind him. 'Daniel…'

Anne's head snapped up. Her gaze flew to the window. Then, with an inarticulate cry, she ran for the door.

Zach made a wrenching sound that etched itself across Lily's heart, and hurried behind his mother.

'Daniel! Where have you been? Are you safe, son?' Anne snatched the boy into her arms, and pulled him into the haven of their home. She drew back to look deep into his eyes.

Then it was Zach's turn to pull the boy close, and if Daniel had believed he would soon be able to break free of his brother's hold, to overpower him in a struggle of strength, the grip of Zach's arms around him now would put that belief to rest for a very long time.

Lily watched them from just paces away, but in her heart the distance was deserts wide, oceans deep. Even if Zach decided he wanted more than his career and this family, Lily could never compete. She knew nothing of this kind of love.

Finally, Zach let go of Daniel, swallowed hard several times and seemed about to speak.

Daniel spoke first, addressing himself to his mother, although one hand held a fistful of the back of Zach's shirt, something Lily felt certain the boy didn't realise he was doing.

'I'm sorry, Mum. I wanted to go away to Sarrenden College, and when Zach said no I decided to go and see it for myself so I could convince him to let me.' Daniel swallowed hard.

His voice trembled as he went on. 'Then I realised I was wrong to try to do it that way, and I tried to come home. I wanted to be back before you started worrying, but I got mixed up with the trains and I lost my cell phone, and I was scared I'd run out of money if I wasn't careful.'

'Oh, Daniel.' Anne lost her fight at last, and tears tracked down her round cheeks.

Daniel broke away from his brother and put his arms around her. A sob escaped. 'Sorry, Mum. *I'm sorry.*'

Zach stepped forward, and patted both brother and mother with large, strong hands that Lily now saw had learned their gentleness here in the heart of the loving family that had shaped him.

When Daniel drew back, and Zach laid a hand on his brother's shoulder and squeezed, Lily's heart squeezed with it.

'I'm the one who needs to apologise, Dan.' A muscle spasmed in Zach's jaw. 'For not listening to you, for brushing off your attempts to talk properly about it all. The truth is, I didn't want you to leave, but I have to learn to let you go. I'm just glad you're safe now, because you're very precious to us.'

Anne wiped her eyes, took a deep breath, and added her words of assurance, and sterner ones for the way Daniel had put himself at risk. 'This family will be making some changes in terms of keeping *all* of us safe in future. We've been so busy just living a simple family life that we've forgotten we're also worth a lot of money, and could therefore end up prey to blackmailers or worse.'

Zach nodded.

Daniel stood with head bowed inside their small circle of love. Then he looked up with a new maturity in his eyes. 'You're right, Mum. I hadn't thought about that. I wouldn't want anything to happen to you or to Zach.'

At that moment, Lily finally broke free of the stillness that had held her in place since Daniel's return, and accepted the utter truth that this was no place for her. She couldn't even maintain a reasonable relationship with her parents, and never had been able to.

While the family were busy with each other, she slipped outside to take her second taxi ride away from the man who owned her heart.

CHAPTER THIRTEEN

LILY walked into work the next morning dressed in a severe black skirt and skin-tight green top, and wearing a set of carved wooden bangles on her right arm.

Zach watched her enter the outer office, her chin high, her shoulders stiff and her face closed against any show of emotion. 'Good morning, Lily.'

'Hello.' She rounded her desk to put her bag away. Her face softened slightly when she turned to look at him and asked after Daniel's health. 'How is your brother? Does he seem all right after his gruelling day yesterday?'

'He's okay. Mum's keeping him at home, and they're going to spend the day looking into his options for boarding school next year.' He hesitated before he took a step towards her. 'Lily, about what we shared—'

'There's no need to talk about it.' She reached for the first file he had placed on the desk. 'We had a wonderful experience together, but we both know there's no future in it. I'm here to work, now, until my contract is over. Let's focus on that.'

Zach didn't want to agree, but he sensed if he tried to argue right now she would ignore everything he said. And he didn't know fully what he *wanted* to say. Only that making love with her had left more things unresolved between them than ever before, and that he didn't want their closeness to end there.

He gave a tight nod, and walked into his own room.

'What are you both doing here?' Lily looked up from her computer screen and stared at her parents in blank question.

If it wasn't the welcome they had anticipated, she couldn't help that.

Zach must have heard her greet her parents, because he emerged from his office and came to stand at the side of her desk. The show of solidarity, even in the face of the tense relations between them, made her acknowledge the impossibility of pushing him out of her heart. How could she do that, when he was more firmly entrenched there now than ever?

'We were in Sydney, and thought we'd drop by.' Her mother made this unlikely pronouncement.

Lily unconsciously toyed with the bangles on her arm. Her mother's gaze followed the movement, and her jaw dropped before she looked away again with an expression of distaste. So, okay, the bangles were a bit garish. But Lily realised something just then.

Her mother would look away in the face of anything about her daughter that caused her discomfort. Lily knew and understood that about Dorothea now, in a way she never had before. The knowledge was almost releasing.

Until her mother turned to Zach and pasted an entirely different expression on her face. 'Actually, our stopping by the office today has a two-fold reason. Naturally, we wanted

to check on Lily and ensure she wasn't causing you any…
That she was comfortable here, and settled into her work.'

Lily's father cleared his throat and looked unhappy. He
took a step closer to the desk, then stopped as if uncertain
how to proceed. 'I'm sure you're showing the highest stan-
dards as always, my dear. You've always done so.'

Lily's heart cracked open a little.

'Well, enough of Lily's progress.' Her mother slapped
it shut again.

Why had Lily never seen that there was nothing beneath
her mother's surface except more of what was on top? Lily
had gravitated to her father's side, had aligned herself to
him by attending his university, by trying to please him
with her grades. He hadn't been as harsh, although he was
by no means openly affectionate.

'You said there were two reasons you stopped by, Mum.
What was the other thing?'

Dorothea stepped forward, and Lily noticed the elaborate hairstyle that must have taken hours with a hairdresser.

Her mother addressed her words to Zach. 'Carl and I are
invited to a most prestigious function.' Here she paused,
as though to strengthen the impact of her next words.
'We're to dine with the State Governor, and as the invita-
tions are for ourselves and a guest each we came here to
invite you, Zach, to attend with us.'

As though realising her faux pas, she turned quickly to
her daughter. 'You too, Lily.'

'Unfortunately, Lily and I will have to decline your invitation.' Zach ground the words through teeth that threatened to crack under the pressure of his clamped jaw.

Something did, indeed, crack inside him as he stared at

the woman who had produced such a stunning, kind, giving, amazing daughter.

'But I'd like to extend an invitation to both of you. To a special event of my own that happens to be on in…' he heard himself say '…a little under an hour from now. My family will be there, and I'd like you and Carl to meet them. What do you say?'

When Dorothea looked trapped and uncertain, he said, quite mildly he thought, 'Don't concern yourself about time frames. This will only take about an hour. You'll be gone and back to your hotel with plenty of time to prepare for your night out.'

'Well, that's very kind of you, but are you certain you can't see your way to attending the dinner with us?' Dorothea didn't quite manage to hide her disappointment.

'Quite certain,' he said, and wondered if he was completely insane. 'But that doesn't mean I have to forego the pleasure of your company altogether.'

A choked sound from Lily drew his gaze to her.

'Will you come with me?' He watched her toy with some papers on her desk, and willed her to look at him. 'You don't have to.'

Finally, she looked up and their gazes met.

She glanced once at her mother, then brought her gaze back to his face and nodded agreement. 'I'll come.' Her half-shrug was meant to indicate she didn't care one way or the other, but tension bracketed the sides of her mouth. 'It's still work time for another hour, anyway.'

'Get your bag, then. We'll lock up here, escort your parents downstairs and see them into a taxi, then meet them at my venue.' Where Lily and her parents would spend an hour with his mother and brother. Was that why he was doing it?

Probably. It was past time her parents saw a real family in action. It might give them a clue about how it should be done! And her father had seemed…different. As though he had really wanted to see her. Well, it was too late to take the invitation back.

Zach was out of control right now, acting rashly, and he knew it. Something was building up inside him. He didn't know what it was, but a physical outlet for all that growing tension couldn't hurt. He would take what relief he could get.

Outside the building, Lily shivered as he hailed a taxi, opened the door, and waited while her parents climbed inside. Zach gave the driver the directions and a generous fare, and sent the cab on its way before either parent managed a word.

As the taxi merged into the traffic, he turned to Lily. 'Let's get to my car. I've got a warm jacket I can lend you.'

She didn't budge from the footpath. 'I agreed to come, but that's because of my parents. Where are we going?'

'To my touch-footy practice at French's Park oval. You probably think I'm mad.'

'Yes, I do, actually.'

She didn't speak again. Just got into the car when they reached it, and when he handed her the jacket out of his kit she wrapped it around her shoulders.

Zach's tension spiked higher. He wanted to be that comforting blanket in Lily's life. He wanted to be all sorts of things to her.

When they arrived at the park, he pulled his kit bag out of the back seat and slung it over his shoulder.

Then he turned to look at Lily, and it just happened. One minute he was watching the wind play with her hair, and wanting that hair spread across his pillow as it had been so recently. The next, love for her slammed through him, almost knocking him to his knees.

He had been so stupid, so blind, and now that blindfold was off and he knew. Knew that he loved her, knew that every second in her arms when they made love had been about showing her, convincing her, giving all of that love to her, even though he hadn't realised it then himself.

He wanted to say things to her, life-altering things. *Have my baby. Be my lover for ever.* Zach wanted to say other things, too. Things like *marry me*.

How? How could he say those things? His ex-fiancée hadn't hesitated to tell him it was his commitment to his family that had ruined things for them, and Zach cared about Lily so much more than he had ever cared for Lara. Yet Lily was so different to Lara. And she loved his family.

'There are my parents, and your mother and Daniel.' Lily gestured towards a rustic shelter. Tin roof, upright support timbers. It had little else to recommend it.

Zach reluctantly followed Lily's gaze. 'They don't usually attend my practice sessions, but after yesterday I guess we all wanted to be close.'

Now he had thrown Lily's family into the middle of that closeness. Zach's thoughts churned.

When a team mate yelled for him to get togged up and get on the field, Zach turned to Lily and said harshly, because of the confusion reigning inside, 'I have to go. Mum will look after you.'

He wanted to stay at Lily's side and sort out his feelings right now. But again that team mate called, and he reluctantly ran onto the field.

Zach practised football like a madman. This was Lily's observation as she tore her gaze from the strong legs displayed to advantage in a pair of dark blue shorts as he ran all over the field. He treated the football like an enemy he wanted to dispatch.

And she loved him. Loved everything about him. Even his obsession with a game that appeared to involve nothing more than butting shoulders with his colleagues, and seeing if he could knock any of them to the ground, then trying to avoid being knocked flat himself.

She watched him run to the other end of the field in pursuit of someone she had thought was actually on his own side. 'I thought touch football was supposed to be non-aggressive.'

'It's appalling, is what it is, and, oh, look. Now it's started to rain!' Her mother's sharp words were the first she had uttered since before the game began.

After meeting Zach's family, she had stood in speechless silence, too taken aback apparently by the outcome of Zach's invitation to be able to say anything coherent.

'Uh-oh.' Daniel's grin still held some shadows. He stood close to his mother, and had one arm draped loosely around her shoulders. He nevertheless cast a reluctantly admiring glance in his brother's direction. 'Looks like we're in for some mud and swearing.'

The eyebrows Lily's mother plucked so finely hiked into her coiffed and lacquered hair. 'I beg your pardon?'

Daniel just grinned and turned his attention back to the

field, where Zach and his colleagues did indeed appear to have transformed into mud-worshipping, loud-mouthed heathens.

Lily bit back a gasp as Zach performed a rather spectacular slide on his tummy right through a big, muddy puddle to stop the ball getting over the end line. 'He's acting like a maniac. He'll hurt himself. He could break his ribs doing that.'

'Something certainly seems to have got into him today.' Anne gave Lily a searching glance.

'Ah, hmm.' Lily's father bent his head towards her, his face tight, eyes uncertain, and said so no one would hear, 'I looked into your agency business, visited your website. And I read your staff recruitment policy.'

'Did you?' She hadn't meant to sound shocked, but she was. 'Why?'

'So when I complimented you on your business acumen and success, you'd believe it when I said that I'm proud of you.' For a moment, his eyes shone with what might have been the hint of some deep emotion. 'I miss you at the university. It's not the same without you. We could be ourselves there without... As for that Pearce, well, your mother liked him but I don't. Never have, really, but I thought you cared for him.'

His voice dropped to a near whisper. 'I'm a weak man, Lily. I can't walk away, and I'm no match for—'

'It's all right.' Her hand closed on his wrist.

He gave a tense cough. 'I could visit, if you'd like. I've got several trips to Sydney planned in the course of this university year.'

'That would be nice.' She swallowed hard on the

emotion that had risen, squeezed his hand and let it go. Followed his regretful glance to her mother, and gave a slight shake of her head. 'We are what we are, Dad. Let's just try to look forward, not back any more.'

Her father nodded and looked away, back out to the field where the game had wound down and the rain had stopped, leaving a puddle in the middle of the field, and a bunch of very grubby businessmen to hobble off that field in various states of exhaustion and bruises.

After a moment of silence, her dad turned back to her. 'Do you love him, Lilybell?'

She reached up and dropped a shaky kiss on his whiskery cheek. 'It can't work out between us, Dad, but yes. I love him. I can't seem to help it.'

From a distance, Zach observed the exchange between Lily and her father. The bent heads, the way she reached up to kiss the older man's cheek.

Her mother looked disgruntled, but this fact didn't seem to be bothering anyone but Dorothea herself.

Mud dripped from Zach's elbow as he approached and nodded to Lily's parents. 'I hope you've enjoyed the time with Lily, and thank you for taking the opportunity to meet my family. I'd introduce you to my team mates, who happen to be business colleagues, except it appears they're all anxious to get home and rid themselves of their muddy clothes.'

The park had a changing room, but not showers.

Zach gave his mother an air hug.

She grasped his arm before he could move away, and asked, 'What are you doing, Zachary?'

'I'm starting to realise some things I should have understood long ago, Mum.' Purpose filled him as he turned to Lily. 'Are you ready to leave?'

She dipped her head in agreement, said quick farewells to her parents, then to his mother and Daniel.

Did Lily love him, as Zach loved her? His heart burned to know the answer at the same time he feared it. If she didn't…

After Zach changed clothes, they made their way to her home in silence. When they arrived, Lily got out of the car quickly and hurried to her door.

Zach followed. 'Don't say goodbye yet.' He clenched his fists as he fought the need to reach for her. They had to talk first. He had to tell her what he had realised out there on the football field, and hope she returned his feelings.

'Why not? The day is over. What's there to say that hasn't already been said?' She turned fully to face him. Her eyes held the shadows of all that had passed between them. Lily opened the apartment door.

Before she could try to stop him, Zach drew her inside and stepped in too. On the sofa in the small living room, Jemima the cat raised a furry head, gave an interested rumble, and subsided again.

Zach attempted a wry smile. 'We forgot to watch for her, despite your sign on the door.'

'Forgetting is what I do best.' Her words were flippant, but he heard the bitter edge, and wanted to tell her not to be so hard on herself.

In some part of his mind, Zach noticed the warmth and cosiness of Lily's home, and his heart ached to be part of that warmth. That comfort. Was it possible? Would she even consider it?

'Lily.' He held her gaze, despite the wariness in her eyes. 'I was wrong to believe what Lara said to me five years ago. I realise now that I didn't even love her.' Love? He hadn't even known the meaning of the word until Lily had stormed his life and heart with her notebook and her pencil at the ready in her hands.

Lily took a slow breath. 'What exactly did Lara say that you shouldn't have believed?'

'That I couldn't have my family and have her, too. That I gave them all my time and attention and there wasn't enough left for her.' There were sticky notes on Lily's refrigerator in date order, left to right, row after row, outlining things she had to remember and do. A wall chart covered the area over the sink.

Two Bendigo pottery mugs sat side by side on the counter. Zach wanted to drink coffee with her out of matching mugs in the mornings for the rest of their lives.

His hands clenched at his sides. 'I believed what Lara told me. I thought I didn't have enough to offer any woman, that loving someone and caring for my family were mutually exclusive because I couldn't abandon them to focus on the woman in my life. But Lara was wrong.'

Lily's lips parted on a soundless breath. 'After seeing you all together the day Daniel went missing, I understand how close you are. I'm certain Lara was *right*. How could anyone else fit into what you all share?'

'You already fit in. You helped organise my birthday party, watched Dan play hockey, and stood in the rain to watch me play at practice today. You were there when Dan went missing. You've already proved you can be a willing part of my family.' All along, Lily had been fitting into his life and Zach had been too stupid, too scared to realise the truth until now.

He took a deep breath and held her gaze, his body tense as he watched for her reaction. 'I love you, Lily. You have my heart and I want to marry you and keep you in my life as my wife, my lover, *and* as part of my family.'

Lily choked back a gasp. Zach spoke with such intensity. There were lines of strain on his face that hadn't been there before. She wanted to smooth those tense places with the tips of her fingers. Wanted to put her arms around him and hold onto him and never let go.

She wanted to say yes to him, but they couldn't be together, no matter what he said. 'I can't. I don't—'

'You don't love me?' His mouth tightened, and he took another step towards her. He seemed to reach right into the depths of himself, to struggle before he finally said, his voice deep and hungry and determined, 'I don't believe that. I know you, and I love you, and I believe you love me too. It was there in every touch, every moment, when I took you back to my house and we made love. Are you going to tell me I'm wrong about that?'

Lily couldn't deny it, but she had to make him see the reality. He might think he loved her now, but, when he realised how much her injury really impacted on her life, he would change his mind. He wouldn't be able to remain committed to her then.

She tugged her hands from his, flung one arm out to encompass her home, pointed at the fridge with its notes stuck all over it. 'How can you want to be with this? Take a good look, Zach, and see that it's so much more than you've thought about or realised.'

When he didn't seem to get her point, she grabbed him by the arm and dragged him across to the room beyond the tiny bathroom.

She flung that door open, and gestured at the floor-to-ceiling shelves that covered one wall. They were already half-filled with notebooks, each one labelled and dated.

'My notebooks have glossaries, Zach, and I refer to them.' She sent another wild gesture towards the shelves. 'Sometimes I have to come in here and go through that wall of books and try to figure out what I've done or said, or where I've been or where I'm supposed to be going.'

'Don't.' He choked it out. Reached for her. Pulled her into his arms and wrapped them around her, and gave a harsh, aching sob of sound into her hair. *'Don't*, Lily. *It doesn't matter.'*

She wrapped her arms around his waist. Oh, blissful homecoming. Pressed her head to his chest, and listened to a heartbeat that would be part of her own for ever.

But this still couldn't be, and she drew back in his arms. Forced her gaze up until it reached his eyes. Love shone there. 'It matters, Zach. How can it not?'

'Yes, okay, fine, it matters, but not in the way you're saying!' He dropped his arms. Turned away from her on an abrupt movement that took him to those shelves. He looked his fill, and then he looked at her. 'Don't you see? You've got my whole heart right now, and you'll always have it. You can come *into* the circle of my family and be with me there.'

'But…'

'You're the one who's really backing away.' He said it on a breath of revelation, and stared at her with dawning understanding. 'I've been so wrapped up in fighting my own fears that it didn't occur to me you'd set up your own roadblocks, but you have.'

'They're not just roadblocks, Zach.' She thought back over the struggles she had endured. The battles she had fought to get her life back after her accident. Some she had won. Others had defeated her and always would. 'They're impenetrable walls.'

He glared at her, and those hands were fisted again and he made no effort to hide his anger or his accusation. 'You're hiding behind your memory condition to avoid committing to me, to us.' He drew a hard breath. 'You've always done that. It's why you refuse to work anywhere for longer than a few weeks.

'It's not simply because you're scared they'll notice you're different and that might make things uncomfortable. You're not worried about making mistakes and getting things wrong. It's because you believe, when they realise your condition, they'll reject *you*.'

'All right. I admit it!' Goaded, she flung her words at him like arrows, only it was Cupid in reverse, because this could only end it. 'I admit, I won't stay at anything too long. I'm scared if I do the people around me will realise I'm not like others, and won't want me any longer. I'm scared about that because it's *true*. I'm *different*. Less. *Not good enough!*'

For a moment, Lily struggled to control her emotions. She would not cry in front of him. 'If I opened myself to you right now, if I agreed to stay and love you for ever, you'd give up on me. Just like Mum did. Just like Richard did.'

'Listen to me.' He pulled her to his chest. 'Listen.'

She struggled, but he refused to let her go, and she subsided against him with a cry that mingled pain and the pieces of a life she had put together by her own might and determination, but that was still, oh, so fragile.

'I'm not them.' Zach breathed the words against Lily's ear. Beneath her hand, they reverberated in his chest, too. His words were all around her, and she couldn't reject them. He seemed determined that she wouldn't.

Then he drew her closer still. With a shaking hand, he cupped the back of her neck, stroked his fingers through her hair. He closed his eyes, pressed his cheek to hers and swallowed hard. 'I love you. I need you. *You*, Lily, just as you are. You're not less. You're *more*. So much more.'

Zach drew back, his gaze searching hers. 'I told you I want to marry you. I mean that. Your memory loss only makes me love you more. It's part of you, Lily, part of all that I love about you.'

Oh, how her heart soared before she dragged it back down and forced herself to tell the truth, to make him see all of it. 'It will never change, Zach. Every day for the rest of my life, I'll get out of bed and find my notebook sitting there with a sticky note on top telling me to record everything that matters.'

Her breath caught, but she forced herself to go on. 'I'll wash my hair and then not be able to remember if I did it or not. Clothes will go missing because I take them to the dry-cleaners and don't remember they're there. Little things will keep falling through the cracks in my brain.'

'We'll get shower-proof sticky notes and a waterproof pen. You can write down when you wash your hair.' His gaze roved over her. Softly. Oh, so softly. 'I'll remind you about the dry-cleaners. Hell, Lily, I wouldn't care if we lost every stitch of clothing we owned. It doesn't matter if you forget things. I'll remind you of what I can, and for the rest we'll just get over it. *I want you. That's all that matters.*'

Finally, hope took hold. Found fertile soil and put down its roots. Blossomed as her hands lifted, reaching for the man who had taken her heart, and would have it always. 'I...I love you. If you're sure about this—'

'*Lily.*' He clasped her hands. Rained kisses over her face. His eyes filled with tears and he laughed, blinked them back, fell on her mouth and kissed her with passion and longing and hunger. 'My Lily of the valley, my tiger Lily and Lily of peace. I'm not letting you go. Not ever. Do you understand that?'

He touched beneath her lashes where tears had pooled and spilled over. Kissed those tears away. Looked into her eyes and gave her his promise. 'I'm going to learn all about your memory condition, but not because I pity you. I'll do it because I want your life to be happy and secure and comfortable, and I'm determined to help you make it that way.'

'What about your family? Will they really be able to accept me?' As his wife?

Zach dropped a kiss on her brow, and a smile broke out on his face. 'They already think you're great. I know they'll welcome you into all our lives.'

'Together.' Could she really be a part of a loving family? Have that, and the man at her side? 'Oh, Zach. Is this really happening? Is it really all true?'

He took her latest notebook from its resting place on her desk. Flipped it open, and scribbled for a long time inside it before he snapped it shut. 'It's true, and in case you ever forget I've just written down for you that you agree to be part of my family.

'Sunday dinners at Mum's place. Visits to Dan at his school next year. Entertaining him when he's home. We'll do it together, Lily. Say you'll marry me soon.'

'I love you so much. I want to marry you.' Her heart pounded hard in her chest as hope and happiness welled up. But there was one last thing. 'What about…children of our own? I don't know if I can be a good mother.'

He laughed. Wrapped his arms around her and hugged her up tight against him, and then his laughter faded and he looked deep into her eyes and let his love shine. 'I want babies with you. We'll muddle through. Together.'

They were the sweetest words Lily had ever heard. 'Then yes, Zach, I want to marry you.'

'Soon.' He growled the command and scooped her up and into his arms, then crossed to her bedroom and flung open the door. 'Marry me soon, but make love to me right now.'

And that is exactly what she did.

EPILOGUE

'I'D like to say a few words before we head for the beach, and the fun part of the day for the younger contingent.' Zach stood at the long, elegant restaurant table and felt Lily's hand slip into his where she sat beside him.

It was the beginning of summer. After a Las Vegas wedding—he'd refused to wait and Lily, bless her, had agreed—they'd now been married eight wonderful months. Every day he wondered how he had got to be so blessed.

Today, his heart was bursting. And breaking a little, too. The expression in Lily's eyes showed she understood it all. She squeezed his hand.

Today was primarily about Daniel, and they had worked hard to ensure it would be memorable for him. Daniel's small group of young mates fell silent now, and looked at Zach expectantly.

Zach glanced at the rest of the guests. At Lily's parents who, at her father's instigation, were seeing her more often, even if relations would probably never be picture-perfect. Her mother was learning to curb her tongue, particularly when her husband told her in a quavering voice to do exactly that!

Zach's mother was accompanied by Vince Goodman today. Zach wasn't sure what he thought of that man's recurring appearance in his mother's life.

Lily's work colleagues, five lovely women aged between twenty-something to Deborah's 'young' forty, ranged beside her at the table. And there was Maddie, back from her time off months ago, and running Zach's office once again. They were all here.

He cleared his throat. 'Daniel, we couldn't be more proud that you've been accepted into Sarrenden College, and we hope that the experience is everything you could want.' A smile tugged at his mouth as he looked at his young brother. 'We'd all like to get in early and request computerised robots for next Christmas, but we'd settle for your company in the school holidays.'

Laughter echoed around the table.

'Thanks, Zach. Thanks, Mum.' Daniel's grin was wide and happy, and full of his hopes and dreams. 'I can't wait to get there.' He glanced at his mates. 'But I'll be back often. Maybe we could form a recreational hockey team and meet up every holidays.'

This suggestion met with enthusiastic cheers that took a while to die down. The boys had been good, but they were starting to get twitchy now that the food was finished and they'd had their share of caffeinated fizzy drinks.

'We're going to head to Whale Beach now so we can enjoy some sun and surf.' Zach said it cheerfully, but suddenly his throat tightened. He hadn't realised it would be so hard to say this goodbye, even. though Daniel wouldn't be going for quite a few weeks yet, and it wasn't as if he was moving to the other side of the world.

Zach smiled down at Lily, and wondered when his hand had tightened on hers so fiercely, and how she had known he would need that.

And he let the joy in his heart flow around the bittersweet acceptance that his little brother was growing up and needed to spread his wings. 'Before we leave the restaurant, there's another announcement.'

Zach drew Lily to her feet. He smiled with pride and pleasure at this woman who had unlocked a part of his heart he had thought closed for ever. Who had helped him to grieve for his father in ways he hadn't realised he had suppressed over all those years.

And who had let him into *her* world, and had blossomed somehow, even in the face of his bumbling attempts to be her rock, and to stand back so she could be her own strength too.

'A few months ago, Lily reapplied to finish her psychology studies. She's had a bit of shift in focus since then, but I'm very proud to say she received her acceptance letter recently.'

He saw the pride that crossed her father's face, and also the knowledge of what was about to come. Carl was the only one who knew, besides Zach and Lily herself. Sharing that particular secret had bonded them together in a special way.

Lily smiled at Zach, and then at the group of faces at the table. Her face, too, shone with pride and pleasure. 'I'm thrilled to have received that acceptance letter. It's important to me because I've proved I can do it. As you all know, Deborah has already agreed to take over most of the running of the job agency to allow me to focus on my studies.'

'My daughter was a High Distinction student,' Zach heard Dorothea brag to Maddie.

Lily heard it too, and gave a wry shake of her head. 'Well, Deb, I'm still going to need you to run the agency, and I'll still be going to classes for a while, but not at university. These will be classes of an altogether different kind.'

After a moment of complete silence at the table, Daniel gave an excited whoop that reverberated right through the restaurant. 'I know what she's going to say! I know it, I know it.'

'Yes.' Lily turned a smiling face towards Zach, and love and happiness shone in her eyes. 'With my business to take care of and…other things on the way, I don't feel I can go back to university studies just now. Instead, the classes I'll be attending are Lamaze.' Her voice filled with excitement and pleasure. 'Zach and I are expecting a baby!'

'Oh, my!'

'This is so wonderful!'

'I'm going to be an uncle.' This came from Daniel, of course.

Lily's mother dropped her wine glass and splashed a hideously expensive white all over the skirt of her navy dress. She was so busy gaping, she didn't actually notice.

Lily's girls got up and did an impromptu boogie dance right there beside the table, complete with excited screams, and quite a bit of bottom wiggling.

Daniel's friends stared, open-mouthed, at the spectacle of five adult women acting crazy in a really expensive restaurant.

While Vince probably thought Zach wasn't taking notice, he kissed Zach's mother. Right on her mouth.

'Don't growl,' Lily admonished.

Zach cupped the back of her head with his hand, and let

his gaze linger on eyes that shone like stars. 'I love you so much. Did I growl?'

'You were about to. I love you, too.'

'Go party.' He nodded towards the line of women still boogying behind her.

Lily joined her friends and danced around the table. Zach laughed, grabbed Maddie, who happened to be closest, and danced her around too.

His mother cried into Vince's dinner shirt.

Half a dozen almost-teenage boys thunked their heads on the table in disgust.

The other diners gawked. Some smiled, some shook their heads. But, in the end, if a little pandemonium broke out in one of Sydney's most prestigious and elite eating venues that Sunday afternoon, so what? They all seemed to have had a good time!

* * * * *

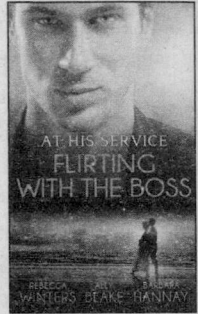